The Prophecy

The Prophecy

Lane Robson

THE PROPHECY

iUniverse books may be ordered through booksellers or by contacting:

iUniverse
1663 Liberty Drive
Bloomington, IN 47403
www.iuniverse.com
1-800-Authors (1-800-288-4677)

ISBN: 978-1-4917-3752-1 (sc)
ISBN: 978-1-4917-3754-5 (hc)
ISBN: 978-1-4917-3753-8 (e)

Library of Congress Control Number: 2014915451

Printed in the United States of America.

iUniverse rev. date: 12/08/2014

Chapter 1
Midnight Alchemy

Why me? Jens thought. *I'm just the boot boy, and any one of the kitchen staff could have been sneaking a midnight snack, or it could have been one of the royal guards for that matter—they're always in the kitchen. Why couldn't it have been one of them? They're brave and would have told. I didn't mean to spy on the princess. Why did she have to come down while I was there?*

Fresh berries were a seasonal treat, and the crates unpacked earlier in the day had offered a temptation Jens couldn't resist. He had waited several hours, until everyone in the castle was asleep, before he dared to sneak down to the kitchen. Barefoot, the boy had navigated the dark hallways and circular steps without making a sound.

The head cook personally checked all the fruit and vegetables and culled the choicest produce for the royal family. There was always a lot left over, and Jens was pleased to find the berries already separated and in bowls on the preparation table. There were several large soapstone bowls filled with berries that had not been chosen for the royal family. What was left was appreciably less than what had been delivered, and Jens was sure that the kitchen staff and senior royal attendants had already eaten their fill. As such, he started to feel less guilty about sampling "his" share. Now that the tasty berries were within reach, his pangs of guilt disappeared in favor of pangs of desire and hunger.

I'm just as important as any of the kitchen maids. Why shouldn't I enjoy a few berries that no one will miss? he rationalized as he scooped a handful into his mouth.

The berries were wonderful, but later, Jens would wish he had never eaten a single berry and feel sure that none would ever taste the same again.

When Jens first heard the footsteps, he presumed one of the maids was sneaking down for the same purpose, and he might not have hidden but for the realization that the person coming down the stairs was wearing shoes with metal toes, an affectation peculiar to the princess, and the soft but unmistakable clicks confirmed her identity as surely as if a royal herald had announced her name.

The pantry served as a convenient hiding place, but even with the door closed, Jens could still see most of the kitchen through the cracks. Of course he looked, but afterward, he would wish the door had been solid.

The princess was carrying a sack, which she placed on the table. There was something wriggling inside, and Jens wondered what creature was trapped and for what purpose.

After lighting candles in the wall fixtures and several on the table, the princess started a fire under a small black cauldron she had filled with water. The candlelight softened the princess's gaunt features and imparted a warm yellow tone to skin that normally looked pale and anemic.

She wore a long black tunic gathered at each shoulder with oval brooches, between which hung a string of carnelian beads that connected with a larger round brooch in the middle of her chest. The brooches were silver and had an intricate design of intertwined serpents with tiny rubies for eyes. Under the tunic she wore a gray silk chemise without sleeves that was buttoned at the top with a carnelian bead the size and shape of a small acorn. Her bare arms were thin and wiry and reached out to similarly shaped fingers capped with nails bitten to the quick. An amber clip secured thin, translucent, plaited hair that fell over her back and between her bony shoulder blades.

In this light she almost looks pretty, thought Jens, but then the princess's red eyes flashed in the firelight. A cold chill rippled down his spine, goose bumps erupted on the back of his neck, and Jens thought otherwise.

Once the water was boiling, the princess opened the sack and removed a toad the size of a kitten, which she dropped into the water before the poor creature could so much as croak a protest. The princess stoked the fire and again brought the cauldron to a boil and then went back to the table, where she rummaged in the sack and removed several items.

Jens watched while the princess placed the bloated body of a dried fish covered with tiny spines, the skull of a small animal, some brittle leaves, and the dried roots of several different plants in an alabaster mortar. She ground these items with a pestle and transferred the resultant dirty gray powder into a wooden bowl. The cauldron with the boiled toad simmered on the fire, and the princess skimmed a translucent oily scum from the surface with a wooden spoon and added the thick fluid to the powder in the bowl. As she mixed the contents, she chanted an incantation, most of which Jens could not hear. The only part that he thought he heard was "the living dead," and he heard this only because the princess repeated the phrase several times.

After the princess added the oily scum, the powder in the bowl turned from dirty gray to glistening white and crystallized into what looked like salt or sugar. Jens watched as the princess carefully transferred the white granules into a tiny vial, taking special care not to let even a grain come into contact with her skin.

The princess carefully cleaned the mortar and pestle and put the bowl, spoon, and sack into the fire. When the flames were high, she immolated the remains of the toad on the tiny funeral pyre. Once the toad had been consumed, the princess doused the fire with water from the cauldron. After a glance confirmed that all evidence of her nocturnal visit was gone, the princess placed the vial into an inside pocket of her cloak and left.

Jens did not come out of the pantry until the soft clicking had disappeared far up the stairwell. When he did emerge, the vapors from the toxic fire still lingered and made his eyes, nose, and throat burn. *Poison,* he realized, *but for whom?*

Jens considered whether he should inform the king, but like most of the castle staff, he was frightened of the red-eyed princess, and the fear hindered his otherwise good intentions. He spent an agonizing day trying to steel the courage necessary to do the right thing, but each time he started toward the royal chambers, he lost his nerve and returned to his cleaning duties.

Later that day, as he was cleaning boots in the stables, he learned that Queen Freyja had just collapsed and died, within seconds of eating some vegetables that she had salted. When Jens cried, everyone thought his grief was for the queen, but his tears flowed more for shame than for sadness.

Chapter 2
Hiking into a Prophecy

"Hardly anyone knows about this valley," Kate remarked as she hoisted herself up onto a shelf that looked north over a pristine spruce forest punctuated by alpine meadows. The last week of July found the area alive with Indian paintbrushes that waved in the warm southerly breeze that had followed them all morning.

"Apart from the native Indians who hunted this far north, few others have bothered with this rugged corner of the British Columbia wilderness," Kate said. "My great-grandfather might have been the first European to trek into this valley. He was a prospector at the turn of the nineteenth century. Since then, our family has returned many times. Now it's a tradition, a back-to-our-roots sort of adventure."

"Works for me," said Ian, "although being a week away by horse from the nearest highway, hundreds of miles from the nearest town, and out of cell phone range makes this more than your average adventure. When we left the horses this morning to hike along these tiny mountain goat trails, I wondered if we were a little crazy. What if the weather turns or we're attacked by a grizzly bear?"

Kate, who worked for Parks Canada as a wildlife-management specialist, smiled as she took his hand and helped him onto the shelf beside her. "This view alone is worth all the effort and the very acceptable risks. Besides, you and I need to know this country well. Someday we'll take our son or daughter on this trip so they can continue the tradition. And as for weather, do you seriously believe nature can throw anything at us that we aren't prepared for?" Both Kate and Ian were experienced, fit, and well-equipped backcountry hikers.

Kate's thick, shoulder-length blonde hair was tied in a ponytail with a green ribbon. She seemed taller than her five feet, until she stood next to Ian, who at six-foot-two, towered over her. Her smile was happy and her green eyes inquisitive.

Ian gently squeezed her hand, but the apprehension he'd begun feeling just after they left the horses had continued to grow, and he hoped that Kate didn't sense his concern. He conjured up a confident smile.

By nature, Ian was not prone to anxiety. At twenty-nine, he had recently finished four years' service attached to a Canadian Special Forces unit, a commitment that he had undertaken a decade earlier upon entering the Royal Officer Training Program in Kingston, Ontario. Courtesy of a master's in geological engineering at Queen's University, he had been commissioned as a lieutenant and quickly promoted to captain and had served in the Canadian Armed Forces in a variety of peacekeeping operations, first with NATO in the Balkans and more recently in Afghanistan. During the latter, his skills as an accomplished mountaineer had been important, and by the end of the tour, he was no stranger to the dangers of war or wilderness.

Ian's curly red hair spoke for his Scottish heritage. As a young lad he had been covered in freckles, but most had disappeared with puberty. He had a handsome symmetrical face with a ready smile and a countenance that made him look younger than his age.

For the last year Ian had worked as a PhD student for Kate's father, Mac, a professor of geology at the University of Calgary.

Ian had known Kate was the girl he was meant to marry from the moment he saw her reading in her father's study. Now, after a year of courtship, they were married and on their honeymoon, and until that day, the trip had been idyllic.

For Ian, the growing angst was as unusual as it was unsettling. He remembered to the moment when he had first felt uneasy; the sense of foreboding had started just after they had stabled the horses.

They had spent a pleasant morning riding up a canyon. They had followed a mountain creek, now only a stream courtesy of an exceptionally dry summer that had followed a winter without much snow. Based on the width of the canyon and the water stains on rocks at the sides, they could see that the creek had been a small river at one time, as wide as a football field in some sections and at least ten yards deep, but now spruce trees populated the outer reaches of the riverbed, and the higher ground in the center was covered in mountain dryads. The yellow flowers of the dryads had given way to silken seed plumes, some of which pointed in the direction of the prevailing wind and others of which had started to unfurl into tiny umbrellas. In due course, wind gusts would release the tiny seeds, and they would float away like tiny parachutes to a new alpine home.

The horses found the silt beside the pebbled riverbed easygoing. The Rocky Mountain sky was cloudless; leathery silverberry bushes glistened in the midday sun; shrubby cinquefoil, showy aster, common yarrow, and yellow columbine were blooming along animal trails beside the river; and the air was fresh and still.

The animals they encountered were tamer than any Ian had ever seen and looked at him and Kate with friendly curiosity. Chipmunks strolled rather than streaked across their path, and red ground squirrels chattered without the customary alarm. Rather than run, the squirrels paused to watch them. Ian felt as if he were an animal in a moving zoo, and all the squirrels were the patrons who watched him from the tree branches. Instead of candy and popcorn, the squirrels munched on conifer cones. They rotated the cones in tiny paws as they cut away the husks with precise alacrity. The detritus fell onto red-brown heaps and grew into middens at the bases of the trees. Boreal chickadees hung upside down from branches and watched with nosy interest as they rode by. Gray jays flew from tree to tree and kept pace with them until the novelty of following wore off.

The canyon ended at a tiny emerald-green mountain lake surrounded by glacial boulders speckled in faded orange lichen that marked an edge otherwise encroached by tangled stands of lodgepole pine and Engelmann spruce. A tiny waterfall at the north end emerged midway up a mountain. The top of the mountain was capped with a modest glacier that sparkled in the noonday sun.

Ian was the first to arrive at the lake, and his horse, having journeyed there before, perked up and without instruction led Ian a short distance through a stand of aspen that blended into an evergreen forest, and thence into a tiny grove encircled by a chest-high fence that served as a stable. A lean-to was nestled into the woods at the southern end. The shelter was constructed properly to protect the animals from the colder northerly winds that swept down the valley in all seasons.

The fence looked very old to Ian, but the lean-to had been constructed later, perhaps only a decade or so ago. The structures were sturdy, built from the spruce felled to make way for the stable. Ian reckoned the fence and lean-to must have taken more than one person at least several weeks to build. He wondered who the builders were.

Kate must have sensed what was on his mind. "My father and mother rebuilt the horse shelter when they were about our age," she said. "You can still see a few timbers from the one built by Grandpa. No wood is left from the original shelter made by my great-grandfather, but Dad found some turn-of-the-century nails and used them on the inside."

With a proud smile, Kate continued, "I could show you the nails if you like. Great-Grandpa used them during one of his trips. Just like us, he needed a place to stable his horses and pack mules before he continued his explorations into the valley behind the falls. The trails ahead are okay if you're a mountain goat or bighorn sheep, but horses don't do well. Mules can make the trip but are real slow. We only use them to pack in heavy supplies."

Kate looked up at the waterfall with a resigned expression. "Seems like every year the falls are smaller," she said with a sigh. "In Great-Grandpa's journal, he wrote that the falls were so wide and thick that the base of the mountain was shrouded in mist. Then, one summer he arrived at the lake to find that the waterfall was only a modest trickle by comparison to the prior years."

"Were the preceding winter and spring really dry?" asked Ian.

"No, and that made the change all the more remarkable. The preceding winter and spring had been unusually wet! Even in the wettest years since, the waterfall hasn't seemed to increase much in size. We keep expecting to arrive one year to find that the waterfall has stopped."

"That is curious. I don't think even a string of dry seasons could make such a sudden difference. Has the glacier above changed in size over the years?"

"No, the glacier is roughly the same size, which makes the reduced volume of water even more of a mystery."

"Wow. That is a puzzle. The water must have gone somewhere. It's almost as if the mountain swallowed the water," offered Ian. "Well, even if the waterfall is less than it was, the falling water still looks great to me. From my perspective, that waterfall is our Niagara. This is our honeymoon, and there's more than enough water for us." Ian gave Kate a tender hug, and she responded by raising her lips to his.

Ian looked over at the horses, and Kate anticipated his next thought. He liked that about her. They seemed to spend time in each other's mind.

"Don't worry—the horses have more than enough grass to graze, water to drink, and even a salt lick."

As she spoke, Ian saw that notwithstanding the drought, a creek flowed through a corner of the grove and within the boundaries of the stable.

"We've regularly left the animals alone for up to two weeks," said Kate. "Grandpa told me that his father once stabled the animals for most of the month of August, and he only lost two pack mules, a male and a female. It was a bit of a mystery. The animals disappeared, but the fence was intact. Great-Grandpa found some bear tracks outside the stable and wondered whether the bears had killed and dragged away the mules, but there was no blood or other evidence of a struggle. Anyway, we don't need to worry because at this time of the year, the bears have lots of berries to pick and trout to catch."

After a light lunch, they filled their water bottles in the stream, hung supplies for the return trip high in a tree, and brushed the horses. After she offered each horse a parting apple, Kate secured the rope latch on the stable.

As they shouldered their packs and started toward the falls, Ian saw an osprey land on an old snag of a dead tree trunk that reached out over the lake. *What a great spot to fish from,* he thought. The purple gloss on the dark-brown back of the osprey glistened in the midday sun and offered stark contrast to the white belly and head. The bird was close, and with the sun behind him, the pale blue cere at the base of the beak was clearly visible; it was the color of a hazy summer sky in the prairies. Bright, alert, gold-colored eyes penetrated from the brown eye patches and seemed to speak to Ian.

Suddenly, out of nowhere, a raven descended toward the raptor from a scraggly spruce. At first Ian thought it was a common crow, but the larger size, heavier-arched bill and large nostril, and shaggy throat feathers clearly identified the bird as a raven. The hoarse *curruk-curruk* call had an eerie malevolence.

At first the osprey seemed to ignore the raven, but its persistent croaking and intimidating swoops finally drove the great bird into the sky. After a few slow powerful wing-beats, the osprey glided in a circle and headed back toward Ian, who heard the melodious *chewk-chewk-chewk* before he saw the bird return.

Just before the raven had arrived, Ian had made eye contact with the osprey, and the searching gaze of the golden eyes had brought to mind his father, a career officer in the Canadian armed forces and an outdoorsman with a sixth sense about danger. Ian could hear his father's standard caution: "Careful, son. Don't rush; take time to read the signs."

Whereas the osprey fit well with the natural colors of the alpine forest, the raven seemed out of place. The brown and beige colors of the osprey conferred a woodsy charm and contrasted starkly to the raven's colors; the metallic purple luster and green glossy wings made the bird look slick, vain, and urban.

The osprey made several low passes over Ian, nonplussed by the continued pestering antics of the raven. Each time, the great bird dipped a wing just as he passed, as if to beckon Ian to follow, and then the osprey flew south and back along the riverbed. Ian wanted to stop, but Kate had already disappeared into the forest, and he could hear her bushwhacking around the lake toward the falls.

Just before he stepped under the forest canopy, Ian felt as if someone were watching, and he looked over his shoulder in time to renew eye contact with the osprey. This time, the great bird looked anxious. This caught Ian off guard, since he'd never considered that a bird might be able to show emotion.

"Ian!" Kate called out. "Are you there?"

Ian blinked and brought his mind back to the present, to the ledge and the beautiful valley vista.

"Yes," he replied, "I agree—this view is worth the effort." But he was thinking, *Yes, I remember now—this bad feeling started with the raven.*

"The view is great, Kate, but this side of the mountain is even steeper than the side we just climbed. Looks like we'll need our ropes and gear to descend."

"No," answered Kate, "there's an easier way, but first we must climb higher."

They scrambled up a scree slope to a notch in the crest and then traversed up the ridge for several hundred yards until they emerged into a tiny ravine with a gorge that descended through a series of gentle switchbacks to the valley floor. In places, the passage was barely enough for a person to squeeze through, but mostly the path was sufficient to walk comfortably single file.

"This is a great way to climb down," remarked Ian. "In some places the rocks almost look as if they were placed to make steps."

"That's true. My family has improved the trail over the years," Kate replied, "but watch your step—the sun doesn't reach the floor of this passage, and the year-round ice and snow can be slippery."

As if to confirm this advice, a drop of water fell from above and dripped down Ian's neck; he shivered. Ian looked around at the wet walls that reached up twice his height and saw icicles melting from some of the overhangs.

"Oh, and don't walk under any icicles. Sometimes they fall," warned Kate.

"Does water ever run in the gorge?" questioned Ian.

"Not much. As far as I know, the gorge is mostly dry, except for a few weeks during spring melt and with heavy rainstorms."

"Well, the walls of this gorge are deep and were carved out by rushing water, so at one time there must have been a lot of water."

"There was a lot more running water during my great-grandpa's time. The gorge became passable at the same time as the waterfall changed."

"The plot thickens," said Ian. "This is a real geological mystery. I wonder where the water went."

"I don't know. My dad poses that same question every time we come here. Why don't you solve the mystery and impress my dad?"

"Right," said Ian. "But if your dad can't figure it out, I doubt anyone can."

Several times the osprey flew over the gorge. Ian never saw the bird, but he could hear the *chewk-chewk-chewk* call. Once, when the osprey flew in front of the sun, Ian saw the shadow of the great bird on the gorge wall. The wall had been polished smooth by millennia of water flow, and for an instant the shadowed outline of the osprey was as distinct as a black and white photograph. Ian wondered whether the bird was following them.

"Kate, are osprey common in these mountains?"

"Yes, and there are also golden eagles and bald eagles. They come for the cutthroat trout and grayling in the mountain lakes. Did you see an osprey at the lake?"

"Yes, but a raven chased him away."

"That's common," said Kate. "When you hear ravens or crows making a fuss, a raptor is often close by. I've always wondered why raptors allow the crows and ravens to chase them away. Any thoughts?"

"Maybe ravens don't taste good," offered Ian. "Or perhaps a raven is a more formidable adversary than we imagine. One thing is sure—I don't like ravens, never have; they give me the creeps, but I can't tell you why. Isn't that silly?"

"No, I don't like spiders, and I can't tell you why either. But don't worry; I'll protect you from the evil ravens if you promise to protect me from the nasty spiders," Kate quipped, smiling.

"No problem," Ian said with a laugh, but inside he still felt anxious. He had sensed something decidedly unpleasant about the raven at the lake. As he thought back to the episode, he recalled that the raven hadn't followed the osprey to that perch; the raven had been waiting silently atop a tall lodgepole pine.

It was as if the raven was watching us, thought Ian, *and it was the osprey that interrupted the raven, not the other way around.*

"You know, Kate," said Ian a bit hesitantly, "the osprey at the lake seemed to be looking at me."

Kate's reply surprised him. "Yes, my grandma used to say that too. She believed ospreys brought good luck."

By the time they emerged at the foot of the mountain, the sun was falling fast, and they made camp by a tiny stream in a shallow swale, dense with willow, alder, and birch. The stream connected to a moss-flanked pool by the side of the mountain, and they had to search for a dry spot higher up in the trees to pitch their tent.

The valley stretched more west than north, which allowed greater afternoon daylight and also a lusher-than-usual alpine growth for the latitude and altitude, especially on the southeastern slope where they made camp. The glacial melt was well advanced, and the meadows were sprinkled with white globe flower, western anemone, and alpine buttercups. Alpine forget-me-nots provided a pretty floral cover between rocks by the pool. There was ample deadwood for a fire. After a long day of climbing, first up the southern face in the hot summer sun and then down through the chilly wet gorge, they enjoyed a warm meal, and afterward, they quickly fell into a deserved and comfortable sleep by the campfire.

Chapter 3
Nocturnal Visitors

Kate woke up when she heard something splash in the pool. A full moon imparted a silver hue to the forest, and although the light was welcome, there was an unnatural silence, and the still shadows were spooky.

From her sleeping bag, she saw nothing unusual outside the open tent flap. The surface of the pool was calm, and the rope to their packs that hung high in the trees was secure and still. The only noise was the occasional hoot of a great horned owl, but the call came from the wrong direction and was too far away to have made the noise. The pool didn't seem large enough for fish.

A boreal toad perhaps? she wondered.

The sky was cloudless and filled with stars that sparkled like diamonds. To the north, the sky was aflame with dancing colors, made magic by the aurora borealis. *Like my wedding ring,* thought Kate, as she slowly rotated her hand and watched the starlight play off the jewel she and Ian had chosen to symbolize their love. She looked lovingly over at Ian. *Wow,* she thought, *I'm married, and I'm here with my husband.*

The air was alpine crisp, and her breath made tiny white puffs in the moonlight. A contented smile suffused her face. *Husband.* She held the word close to her heart. *A starlit night and just the two of us—we're so lucky.* Kate smiled to herself when she thought of how they had zippered their sleeping bags together and cuddled upon going to bed. *Yes, we're very lucky.*

She was enjoying the special intimacy of the moment when a raven, as if somehow knowing and jealous, interrupted her reverie with a rude *curruk-curruk* that lingered in the still night air. The call was like a scornful laugh and brought a momentary frisson to the back of Kate's neck. She could see the raven at the top of an Engelmann spruce, silhouetted against the moon. Kate turned her flashlight on the bird and caught the reflection from unnaturally red eyes that looked mean and right through her.

Kate blinked, and the raven was gone. For a moment she wondered whether the bird had really existed. *No, the raven was real all right, and a nasty bird at that,* she thought as she closed the tent flap and snuggled in beside Ian. The chill night air no longer felt so good, and his warmth was welcome.

In the morning, the sun crept over the eastern ridge too slowly for Kate. She hadn't slept well after waking in the night, and she had been up since before dawn. The stars were still brilliant in the sky as she stoked up the fire that had dwindled overnight to only a few embers. She watched the sun break over the ridge while she enjoyed a cup of hot coffee.

Before Ian woke up, Kate had scouted around the camp to learn what had made the noise and had found a single paw print in some soft mud by the side of the pool. The print clearly showed four toes with claw marks and a triangular heal pad, a pattern common to the wolf, coyote, fox, and domestic dog. The large four-inch print suggested a wolf or an especially large coyote.

More likely a wolf, she thought. It looked like the animal might have stepped into the pool by mistake and then stopped and reversed. She looked farther and found more tracks that led along the stream and then disappeared into some rocks. Kate guessed there were two animals, maybe three. She also found some prints on a little rise that looked down over their campsite.

Odd, she thought. *The wolves seem to have been watching us. Pretty bold.*

Once Ian was up and had eaten, Kate showed him the signs. On the little knoll that overlooked the camp, Ian found a fluff of black down. "Raven?" he questioned. "Maybe the wolves and ravens have joined forces and are after us," he joked.

Kate became serious and told Ian about the raven with the red eyes and nasty caw. That made Ian's thoughts return to the raven that had attacked the osprey.

Kate had an unsettled feeling, which Ian could sense, and her uneasiness matched his own. Ian didn't want to dwell on anything negative, so he changed the subject of their conversation.

"Well, Kate, you're the trail boss. Where to now? I know we're headed north, but this is a big valley—must be ten miles long and four miles wide. Do we follow the stream? Does the stream extend the length of the valley? Are there any lakes on this side of the mountain?"

"Yes, no, and yes," replied Kate, who was used to a flurry of questions from Ian. His mind moved fast, and she liked that about him.

"Mostly we follow the stream, which ends in another small lake. But there are lots of animal trails, and I like to go in one way and out another. This is my fifth trip, and each time I've explored a different trail. Sometimes Dad chooses, sometimes Liz, and sometimes me, but we always try to vary the route. Why don't you choose the way? As long as we continue northwest, we'll eventually reach the small lodge my great-grandfather built."

"First, though, I suggest a warm bath."

"Pardon me?" said Ian.

Chapter 4
Nature's Hot Tub

"I'm not kidding," said Kate. "We can bathe in nature's own hot tub. A hot spring is only a mile or so away. What do you think? We haven't had a real bath in a week. The spring smells like sulfur and tastes awful, but the water is clean and clear." After a moment she added demurely, "Mind you, we didn't bring bathing suits. I guess we'd have to go skinny-dipping."

Ian didn't have to consider the idea for more than a second; his eager eyes and a playful smile replied in the affirmative. "Great idea!" he said with a wink, happy to put the wolves and ravens behind them. "Let's pack up and be on our way."

To reach the hot spring, they climbed back up the mountain through a mixed conifer forest that swept sparsely down the southeastern face. Lodgepole pine had become the dominant tree since a lightning storm had started a natural forest fire. Some of the old burnt-out trunks still littered the forest floor and provided homes for ants and other insects, deer mice, and chipmunks. Dead trunks that had not fallen, now weathered gray, provided good foraging sites for three-toed woodpeckers. On moist days the smell of burnt wood continued to linger in the air. Common fireweed was prevalent and provided a magenta cover to the forest floor.

The sun was slowly working down the opposite slope and was not yet high enough to have reached them. Their breath was visible in the chill morning air, and the frosty ground cover crunched as they walked. The showy asters were still closed and awaited the sun's arrival to unfurl their purple rays.

The forest ended abruptly as if there were some invisible line beyond which trees were forbidden, and the couple emerged on a mostly barren-looking scree slope from which the snow had only just retreated. Western spring beauty and white globeflower were sprouting in the lee of the receding snow and would bloom within days of emerging from the snow cover. The growing season in the mountains was short, and alpine plants lost no time to bear fruit. A fair amount of snow remained in the shadowed recesses of the rocky outcrops.

Ian spotted an oasis of low-lying green bushes, high above the tree line. "That must be it!" he remarked excitedly.

Kate was happy to see Ian so boisterous. *That's what this trip is all about,* she thought, *romance and excitement, an adventure of a lifetime.*

Ian quickened his pace and called back over his shoulder; "I can already smell the sulfur. Do you see the hot vapors condensing in the morning air? Do you think there might also be a fumarole or a geyser? Does the spring stay clear in winter?"

Each question was less distinct as he jogged ahead, and any answers were obviously less important than his impatience to reach the spring.

By the time Kate reached the tiny natural hot water vent from deep in the earth, Ian was already in the pool.

"This is great," exclaimed Ian. "Come on in. Maybe we should stay here all day. Wouldn't this be great for sore muscles at the end of a long day of hiking? Have you ever been here in the winter? Can we cross-country ski in the valley? How far down do you think the vent goes? The water feels about 110 degrees Fahrenheit."

Without pausing, Ian answered his own question. "Since the temperature usually rises about 30 degrees Fahrenheit for every mile below the surface, the reservoir must be at least a few miles down … Are there anymore like this in the valley?"

Kate smiled. Ian had the enthusiasm and curiosity of a six-year-old boy built into a six-foot man, all part of his charm.

"Could be," replied Kate to the last question, as she set down her pack and started to undress, "but we haven't found any others. Great-Grandpa found this hot spring during his first trip. As the story goes, he followed a grizzly up to the spot. One moment the bear was ambling along the mountainside in clear view, and the next second the animal was gone. Just before the bear vanished, the grizzly stood up on his two hind feet and seemed to point with his left paw. Great-Grandpa looked where the bear was pointing and saw the mist from the hot spring. When he looked back, the bear was gone. Real strange too, because there was no more cover then than now. It was like magic. Great-Grandpa looked for a cave or a hollow that the bear might have hidden in, but found nothing."

While telling the story, Kate had removed all her clothes except a long T-shirt that extended halfway down her backside. She sat with her feet in the spring and continued the story. "The main reason Great-Grandpa kept making trips to the valley was to look for the grizzlies. He visited the valley twelve times, and according to his journals, he spotted bears on the first eight trips. Then they seemed to disappear. He was obsessed with the grizzlies and made his family promise never to tell anyone about the valley or the bears. My dad promised Grandpa, and Liz and I in turn promised Dad."

Kate paused to collect her thoughts. "Ian, it was that promise that made it impossible for me to tell you about this valley until we were married. And I know this must seem like a strange honeymoon, but the valley is special. Promise you'll keep the tradition."

"No problem, Kate. This is a great honeymoon, and I'm honored to be part of a century-old family tradition. Don't worry; the secret is safe with me. I'd never do anything to disappoint you. You own my heart."

Kate beamed. The phrase "own my heart" was one that her father had often used to describe his love for her and Liz. "You know," she said, "we're the third generation to spend our honeymoon in this valley. You're such a sweetheart to go along. I just knew you'd understand." She pulled off her T-shirt, joined Ian in the water, and gave him a big hug and a passionate kiss.

"Say," replied Ian, a bit embarrassed by the gush of emotion, "what if those bears are watching? You know there are rules about this sort of thing in the national parks."

"We aren't in a national park, and if the bears want to watch, that's their concern, and besides, I want my way with you, husband." With that, she slipped again into his embrace.

Afterward, Kate sat relaxed on a natural ledge with her arms up on the moss that surrounded the spring.

"What a fabulous view," remarked Ian.

Kate wondered which view Ian was referring to. She glanced back at Ian, who blushed and then looked off down the valley.

"Which view, Ian?" she asked with a coy smile. "Give me another kiss. I don't think the bears have seen enough."

Ian blushed and laughed at the same time. "Well, the valley view is certainly more beautiful for your presence."

They enjoyed a long soak during which Ian relished a deepening sense of belonging to both Kate and the valley. "And no one else ever comes here?" he asked.

"Not that we know. Members of my family have hiked the valley dozens of times over the last century, and none of us have ever seen another person."

"Grandpa found some arrowheads, so we know Indians must have come here way back when. Did you know that the Blackfoot revere the grizzly as a healer? Dad has spent years studying native Indian mythology about bears."

"Has anyone but your great-grandfather seen the grizzlies?"

"Only Grandma and my mom, and even they saw bears on only one occasion each. Liz thinks I'll see a bear this trip because it's my honeymoon and thirty years since the last sighting."

"How does that work?" questioned Ian.

"Well, when Mom and Grandma saw the bears, they were on their honeymoons, and they married thirty years apart. Our honeymoon is thirty years to the month since my parents married. Not that I'm superstitious, but the coincidence is kind of amazing, don't you think? Liz will be disappointed if I see a bear because she thinks that if I do, then she won't."

"Well, Liz and your dad will join up with us in a few days, so maybe you'll see a bear together."

"I'd like that," replied Kate, "and you know that's exactly the reason Liz wanted to come along on this trip. It was all I could do to persuade her to give us a few days' head start. Good thing Dad is with her; otherwise, I'm sure she would have caught up to us by now. She's a fabulous rider. Dad decided to come because we have a rule that no one in the family ever comes to the valley alone. The only person who ever did was Great-Grandpa. It's kind of strange that neither Grandpa nor Dad ever saw a bear. Between the two of them, they've made dozens of trips. Dad believes the bears probably migrated farther south or toward the coast where the food might be more plentiful. He believes there might still be bears around, but he doesn't believe all the wild stories that Great-Grandpa wrote about them."

"What do you mean?"

"Well, Great-Grandpa believed that the bears were very intelligent, that they only walked on four legs when they knew people were watching, and that they talked a language that sounded like Icelandic."

"Icelandic?"

"I know that sounds strange, but my great-grandmother was Icelandic. She met Great-Grandpa in Gimli, Manitoba, where lots of people from Iceland settled during the last years of the nineteenth century. She spoke Icelandic around the home often enough that Great-Grandpa recognized a few of the words the bears were speaking."

"Bears speaking to one another!"

"Yes, several times he came across a group of bears talking about the cutworm moths."

"Moths?"

"Yes, army cutworm moths migrate to mountain regions, where they feed at night on the nectar of alpine and subalpine flowers. During the day they seek shelter under various rock formations. When the moths arrive in July, about 40 percent of their body weight is fat, and by August that increases to 70 percent, and these migratory insects become the richest food in the bear ecosystem. Bears can eat up to 2,500 moths an hour. In late summer, bear poop is mostly a mass of moth wings."

"Thanks for sharing," quipped Ian as he wrinkled his noise.

Kate spoke with the confidence that comes with a PhD in mammalian physiology. Like most members of her family, she was fascinated with bears. The title of her PhD thesis was *Urea Metabolism during Hibernation in Grizzly Bears.* Her research established that the yellow stains on the snow around the air holes of the winter dens was due to urea and that grizzly bears exhaled this waste product to compensate for the lack of excretion in the urine. During hibernation, bears did not make urine for up to six months.

"Okay, so what about the talking bears?" continued Ian, who though curious, wasn't as fascinated as Kate about the feeding and elimination habits of bears.

"Well, Great-Grandpa studied their habits, and when he found an area that the moths migrated to year after year, he built a blind upwind from the feeding area to study the bears. He was never close enough to be sure, but sometimes when the air was still, he was certain that the bears were not only talking but speaking Icelandic. He heard one conversation he was sure about. One of the bears said, 'The moths are better than last year,' and an old wizened grizzly replied, 'But each year there are less.' Great-Grandpa was also convinced that the bears knew he was watching from the blind but tolerated his presence."

"Talking bears does sound a bit out there, Kate. Did your great-grandfather speak any other languages? Maybe he thought the bear sounds were like Icelandic because that was the only foreign language he knew a bit about."

"That's my dad's theory, but Great-Grandpa was a learned man. He'd studied Latin and Greek in public school, and courtesy of his parents, he also knew some Gaelic. I don't know what to believe," said Kate.

She shifted how she was sitting. "This hot spring is fun, but the seats are a bit bumpy. And when they're not bumpy, they're slippery. The algae thrive on the heat and make the rocks slippery."

"Bumpy and slippery, but still fun," replied Ian. "Have you noticed the neat lichen on those rocks against the mountainside?" He motioned with his eyes. "Over there, just below the berry bushes. And what about that iridescent-looking moss around the edge? Even without the sun, the green seems to sparkle."

Kate moved to look more closely at the moss but slipped as she maneuvered. As she fell back, her gaze went up the mountain in one fast glance. She steadied herself and then looked back, blinked, and looked again.

Ian noticed a puzzled look on her face. "What's up, Kate?"

"For a moment, I thought I saw a wolf with a raven on his shoulder, but that's silly. Maybe these vapors are hallucinogenic," she joked.

"More likely the vapors created an optical illusion," responded Ian. "Then again," he laughed, "the hallucinogenic angle might explain your great-grandpa's story about talking bears."

"Or," replied Kate, "maybe the raven is playing a trick on us. The raven was considered a trickster in some of the legends of the coastal Indians."

Ian looked up the mountain and saw a mist creeping down the slope. "Say, Kate, doesn't the morning mist usually rise up from a valley? That mist seems to be rolling down the slope."

Kate looked up and shrugged. “Maybe some bad weather moving in. We better get out and dry off.”

“Okay by me,” responded Ian. “If I stay in the water any longer, I’ll look like a prune.”

He was out in a bound and offered his hand to steady Kate as she stepped out. Standing together by the hot spring, his inherent modesty caused him to blush again and then to self-consciously look around to make sure they were alone.

“Maybe the wolf and raven are voyeurs,” Ian quipped. “They just wanted us to jump out of the pool naked.”

“You’re silly,” she said with a smile.

They dried and dressed quickly, and moments later the mist enveloped them. It was a strange vapor that they could feel but no longer see. The sun shone through unobstructed, but the air felt colder, like when a cloud passes, and colder still when they took a breath into their lungs.

“All of a sudden I feel so tired,” said Kate, who had heavy eyelids and a dreamy, faraway look. “That hot spring really relaxed me. Do you think we could take a nap before we start off?”

“Sure,” said Ian, yawning. “A few winks in the morning sun will do us good.”

They propped their packs against some rocks in a mossy hollow, reclined against their sleeping bags, and within moments were fast asleep.

Chapter 5
Cold and Hot Trails

Ian woke with a headache, and he felt stiff, as if he hadn't moved for a long time, like he was getting up after sleeping overnight in an unnatural position in the seat of a plane or a car. Kate was not by his side, and as he looked around, he didn't see her anywhere. *Off somewhere exploring,* he thought as he yawned and stretched away the sleep.

Ian checked his watch and found the time to be only 9:30 a.m. The sun was still relatively low in the sky, which confirmed the early hour. *We didn't sleep too long,* he thought. *I wonder where Kate is.*

At first he presumed she was photographing wildflowers or picking berries, but after about ten minutes, when she didn't return, he called out, at first in his normal voice and then progressively louder. She didn't return his calls.

He scouted the area, checked the pool carefully, and climbed up the mountain to get a better view, but he still found no sign of Kate. *Where could she have gone?* he wondered. *It's not like her to play a practical joke. She must have had a good reason to wander off.*

He checked her pack but found nothing missing and everything in order. For the next half hour he searched the area in a series of widening circles, but he still didn't find any clue to her whereabouts.

Ian was worried and sat down to think. *However serious the situation might be,* he reasoned, *I have only two options. I can extend the search down one of the three trails that lead away from the hot springs, or I can remain here and wait for Kate to return. If I assume that she has just wandered off and has not come to any grief, and that she will therefore return, I should remain at the hot spring and wait for her to return … But what if she has come to harm?* he wondered.

Ian thought of the wolves, the nasty raven, and the stories of talking grizzlies. *How insane,* he thought. *A bear is a bear is a bear. Sure, they're dangerous, but they don't talk. The great-grandfather must have been a bit loony, and we haven't seen any sign of bears—no tracks, no diggings, no bark scratching, no scat, nothing.*

"But the wolves are real enough," he muttered aloud. "Yet, there are no new signs of wolves."

Ian continued working through his thoughts and finally reasoned that if Kate was in trouble, she must have wandered a distance, out of sight and sound, and if this were the case, then the sooner he broadened the search, the better. Having arrived at this conclusion, he felt anxious. *Rats! If she is in trouble, I've already lost precious time.*

Ian was no stranger to decision. He quickly stuffed a daypack with a change of warm clothes for Kate and the first aid kit, water bottle, and some nuts and dried fruit. He checked his survival knife and compass and slung the binoculars around his neck. *The lighter I travel, the faster I'll go,* he reminded himself. Finally, he picked up his stout hickory walking stick, which could also serve as a weapon if he came upon any wild animals.

Now, he thought, *which trail?* One trail led back to their morning camp and the valley floor, another moved along the southeast slope where they had intended to travel that day, and the last proceeded steeply up the eastern slope of the mountain they had descended the prior day.

Ian decided to backtrack to the morning camp where they had seen the wolf tracks. If there were no signs of Kate, he would return and scout forward on the southeast slope. The final trail up the mountain was in clear view, and since he hadn't seen any sign of Kate up there, he discounted the need to explore first in that direction.

But if after searching all three trails, I still don't find Kate, what then? he wondered. *Well, then I better return to the stable where Mac and Liz are scheduled to arrive tomorrow, because the valley is too big for me to search alone,* he decided.

As Ian stood up to go, a mountain bluebird fluttered onto the path from an alder grove and warbled a short, high-pitched call. The turquoise-blue back, paler blue throat, and white belly confirmed the summer plumage of an adult male. Ian expected the bird to dart away as quickly as it had landed, presumably with some insect treat as the reward for flying so close to him, but the bird remained in the middle of the path and chirped excitedly.

"Cheeky little bird," said Ian. "I've never seen one so tame." He stepped over the bluebird and proceeded down the trail to the morning camp.

A moment later, the bluebird buzzed past his head, again landed on the path in front of him, and this time started to drag his wing toward Ian.

Don't worry—I won't disturb your nest, thought Ian, who recognized the lame bird ruse as a defensive maneuver to protect eggs or a new brood. *Strange, though—by this late in the season, the nests should be empty. And how come it's the male bluebird? Isn't it usually the female that practices this ploy? And when they drag their wing, don't the mother birds typically walk or flutter away from you? This bird is limping toward me!*

Ian stepped around the bird again. The bird flew ahead of him and repeated the maneuver, but this time when Ian approached, the bluebird flew under his legs and onto the path up the mountain.

"What a very strange valley," Ian said. "In addition to 'talking' grizzlies and red-eyed ravens, there are crazy bluebirds." Moments later, Ian was otherwise absorbed looking for tracks or other clues to where Kate might be, and the bluebird was forgotten.

Back at the morning campsite, Ian found no evidence of Kate. Strangely, when he searched the pond and along the river, he found that the wolf tracks had disappeared. Even the ones on the little knoll were gone. *How could they just disappear?* he wondered. *There has been no rain, wind, or other weather to cause them to vanish.*

There was no obvious answer to the mystery, and more disappointingly, there was no evidence that Kate had come that way. Ian retraced his steps up to the hot springs, where he hoped to find Kate and her happy smile waiting for him. However, there was no sign of his bride there either.

He started at once down the trail along the southeastern slope but was again interrupted by the bluebird, who repeated the buzz-the-head, injured-wing, and fly-by routine.

Pesky bird, thought Ian. *Probably drunk on some fermented berries.* The bluebird's chirping seemed especially frantic as Ian headed into the woods.

He searched ahead for about an hour and then returned on the same trail. The forest was very still. *Much too quiet,* thought Ian, and he realized that he hadn't seen a single squirrel or chipmunk all day or, apart from the bluebird, any birds. *Very strange. And now that I think about it, I don't recollect seeing any animals since we left the stable, and until then, there had been lots.*

When he reached the hot springs, there was still no sign of Kate, and he sat down feeling forlorn and helpless, new sensations to Ian. Dejected at his failure to find Kate, Ian was trying to decide whether to spend the night at the hot springs or return to the stable to meet up with Mac and Liz. While he considered the merits of each option, the bluebird landed on Kate's pack, teased a silk handkerchief out of a side pouch, and flew onto a boulder beside the path up the mountain.

Ian was flabbergasted. "Hey!" he shouted. "I gave that to Kate for Valentine's Day." Ian jumped up and ran to the boulder, but the bird was too fast. By the time Ian reached the first rock, the bluebird was on another, and then another and another. "Cheeky little devil," Ian muttered. The bird continued to lead Ian on a merry chase up the trail. Ian remained always a step behind. "Pesky bluebird … I don't believe this."

Finally, the bluebird flew off the trail and made a dramatic display of dropping the handkerchief on a rocky ledge, after which the bird flew farther up the mountain and disappeared.

The ledge was not accessible from the trail. Ian reconnoitered and found that the best, but not so easy, way to reach the ledge was courtesy of a vertical crack in the mountain. The crack was about the width of two bodies, which allowed Ian to place his back onto one side and push his way up with the soles of his boots. When he reached the level of the ledge, he could see the green handkerchief in a natural recess that extended a few feet into the mountainside. Ian climbed a little higher and found some easy handholds that allowed a controlled swing onto the ledge.

As Ian picked up the handkerchief, he noticed prints scattered in some mud on the ledge. There were obvious human footprints and some bird tracks. Ian didn't know much about bird feet, but the tracks were large with three forward toes balanced by a single heel-toe, and he figured the size at least might fit with a raven. The human print was moccasin-clad and too large to be Kate's. Ian did not doubt the tracks were fresh. The ledge was exposed to the weather, and a mountain squall had passed over several days prior. These tracks had obviously been made since that time. As he looked around, Ian realized that the ledge offered an unobstructed but private view of the hot springs and the hollow that he and Kate had slept in.

Damn! thought Ian in a flash of understanding. *Someone followed us, watched us from this ledge, and while we were asleep, took Kate.*

Ian remembered the wolf and raven that Kate had seen from the hot spring.

But who was the human, and where have they gone? Oh no—how much of a head start have they got? Must be almost 3:00 p.m. He looked down at his watch. It was 2:36 p.m., which meant five or six hours had elapsed since he had last seen Kate. But then Ian noticed that the date on his watch read Sunday, July 28. *How could this be? It's only Saturday.*

When he and Kate had awoken at the campsite that morning, Ian had checked the time before putting on his wristwatch, and the date had correctly read Saturday, July 27. Somehow he had lost a day.

The mist, he suddenly remembered. *Of course. I was so stiff when I woke up because I'd slept around the clock.* Ian had a sinking feeling. *Kate has been gone for almost thirty hours! How will I ever find her?*

There were still at least five hours of sunlight, a half-hour of which Ian devoted to a thorough search of the trail up the mountain. Finding nothing, he decided to return to the ledge, the only place where he had so far found any clue to Kate's disappearance. *There must be some indication of where they went,* he thought, more out of desperation than any sense of certainty.

Above the ledge, the vertical crack continued higher and eventually emerged on an even larger shelf. Ian climbed up, and at this level, he found many of the same bird tracks and a black downy feather that further suggested the tracks might be raven. There were no trails possible from this higher point, and he climbed back down to the first ledge.

Below the ledge, the crack eventually opened up into a cave, down to which Ian climbed. The cave was really a hole that went straight down. It was four or five feet in diameter, and from the lip, Ian could detect the faint smell of sulfur wafting up from the blackness. He realized that the cave was a natural chimney and probably extended down to the same geothermal vent that supplied the hot spring, perhaps even to the hot spring itself.

Could that be how Kate was abducted? he wondered. *Was there a cave somewhere around the hot spring?*

Ian scrambled back down to the hot spring and scoured the area for any evidence of a trail or a cave into the mountain, but to no avail. Ian was disappointed. He had been certain there would be an entrance into the mountain. That was the only logical explanation that fit with Kate's disappearance from the mossy hollow by the hot spring as well as the prints on the ledge above and the absence of any tracks on the other trails.

Well, decided Ian, *if I can't find access from the bottom, perhaps I can from the top.* He climbed back up to where he'd found the chimney's opening. Ian had climbing and caving experience and knew the risks of solo descents, but this chimney did not seem troublesome, and he was too impatient to wait for Mac or Liz to arrive. The diameter was ideal for a controlled descent. He belayed himself to a massive boulder and secured the rope to a half-body harness he had in his pack. He reckoned the descent was less than one hundred feet to the level of the hot spring and probably more or less straight down, but even so, he chose an assortment of karabiners, chocks, and cams just in case the chimney changed direction or emerged on a cavern wall. He also packed his ascender to make any return climb easier.

After checking his equipment twice, Ian was reassured that everything was in order, and he dropped into the chimney.

At first the going was easy. For the first fifty feet, he only needed to slowly play out the rope though his figure-of-eight descending tool and otherwise control his descent with his feet against the walls. However, the descent became tricky as Ian closed in on the source of the heat. The walls started to bead with condensed water and became treacherously slippery. Ian was thankful he had a top rope.

The sulfur smell had seemed mild at the top, but every few minutes, he heard a popping sound that was followed by a rush of air so hot and thick, his eyes and throat burned. He quickly learned to close his eyes and hold his breath until the vapors passed. Even though the air cleared after these geothermic belches, the stench eventually became nauseating and the heat oppressive. His sweat started to sting his face, and he felt as if he were climbing down the spout of a boiling teakettle. He tied a handkerchief around his forehead to keep the salty sweat out of his eyes.

Finally, the sweltering heat, sickening smell, and slippery surfaces brought him to a prudent halt, and he secured the rope and dangled free to catch his breath and consider whether to proceed. He pulled up the rope below and counted only ten more feet of free line. The rope was a hundred feet, and the ledge had not looked to be more than that distance above the hot spring. *Surely the bottom must be close,* he reasoned.

Ian ripped off the lowest button from his shirt, and as he dropped this tiny depth gauge, he started to count. At three, he heard the button land, and presuming the bottom to be only a few feet below, he resumed the descent.

In the darkness, Ian missed the button, which had landed on a rock lip only a few inches below his feet. When he reached the end of the rope, he stretched as far as he could with his feet, but still found nothing solid. He looked up the chimney and then down into the darkness. What little sunlight still crept into the chimney from above was now only a faint dirty glimmer, and the vapors from below were so thick that he could barely see his dangling feet.

"That's it," muttered a disappointed Ian. "I'd better go back before it's too late. I won't be any help to Kate if I die of suffocation dangling at the end of this rope."

He braced himself with his back against the wall, stretched his feet out to the opposite side, and reached for the zipper to his fanny pack where he had stored the ascender. An ascender was the ideal tool for the situation. The device was designed to fit around the rope, had a comfortable handgrip, and could be locked in place with the flick of a switch. With the ascender, Ian wouldn't have to worry about his hands slipping on the rope as he climbed back up. The fanny pack was at his back and squished against the wall, which meant that Ian needed to shift his position a bit to pull the zipper open.

He was pulling gently and had almost opened the pack when a familiar but larger popping sound ushered in a massive geothermal burp. The gaseous fumes caught him by surprise and took his breath away. Ian instinctively brought his hands up to protect his eyes, but with this motion, his feet shifted slightly, and he slipped off the wall.

Reflexively, he grabbed for the rope, but he was too late. There were only a few feet of rope left and as he fell, the dangling tip of the rope slipped through the figure-of-eight tool and then slapped him in the face with a rude parting gesture. Ian grasped at empty air as the rope disappeared above him.

The fall lasted for only a few seconds but in such slow motion that it seemed like forever. The first sensation was pain as his body bounced once and then again along the rugged wet walls. Then the pain stopped, and Ian tumbled in a free fall through a completely dark space, and for a few seconds, he felt strangely good. Finally, he felt wetness, first on his calves and then enveloping him like a warm liquid cocoon. Instinctively, he put out his arms to slow the submersion.

Ian seemed to have all the time in the world to think through what was happening. He knew he'd fallen into a subterranean pool and wondered variously whether the water was shallow and he might end up with a spinal injury, or alternatively, whether he might be swept into scalding water or dashed against sharp-edged rocks.

Happily, none of these possibilities turned out to be the case. The pool was the same temperature as the hot springs, and although he submerged completely, the water was deep enough that he never touched bottom. Ian found himself treading water at the surface, happy not to be injured. However, his elation was brief. It was pitch-dark, and he couldn't see a thing in any direction.

Chapter 6
Valley Stories

"Hey, Liz, make sure the saddles are hanging well away from the trees; porcupines can climb, and they love leather. Do you remember how much they enjoyed my boots at Assiniboine?" Mac smiled as he recollected how excited Liz had been that summer morning when she saw her first porcupine. Her eyes had opened wide when Daddy pointed out the prickly animal on an aspen branch that extended over their cabin. But after Daddy had showed her his munched-on-boots, six-year-old Liz had showed off some precocious protective instincts and scolded the "naughty" porcupine. Mac could still see little Lizzy pointing her finger at the porcupine and telling the poor animal that chewing Daddy's boots was not nice. The episode had engendered much laughter and many stories ever since.

"Right, Dad," said Liz, laughing, "but do you know for sure that porcupines can't climb ropes? I'd hate to have to scold another poor porcupine just because they love the smell of your saddle."

They both laughed as Liz secured the saddles. Liz soon returned to her favorite recent topic. "Wasn't the wedding wonderful? Kate looked beautiful, and Ian is sooooo handsome. Kate's really lucky. Most men are only handsome, smart, or strong, but Kate found a beau with everything. He's even polite. Hope I luck out some day."

"I'm sure you will, Liz. Patience is a virtue. Kate didn't meet Ian until last year when she was twenty-seven, and you're more than two years younger. There's still a lot of time for you to meet the right man," reassured her dad.

Liz retrieved a note secured under a rock by the gate. "Look, Dad—Kate left a message. They arrived two days ago, on Friday, and will meet up with us at the lodge. We'll have the better part of a week together before we need to head back. Hope the weather holds."

"Well, you never know," Mac replied. "A summer storm could come over those mountains in the blink of an eye, and a few minutes later, we could be drenched and chilly. Snow falls twelve months a year in these mountains. Then again, the weather might stay hot and sunny for several weeks. I'm hoping on the latter scenario; the temperature has been stable, my portable barometer has not shown any change, and there is precious little wind. I suspect we'll be okay at least until late afternoon when the temperature starts to fall. But you never know."

"Dad, you are such a cynic."

"Me, the cynic?" her father replied with a fake incredulous look. He opened his eyes wide, left his mouth open a bit, and threw his hands into the air. "You're the one who just despaired about meeting the right guy. What happened to the optimism of youth? Don't forget, I'm the old guy, and cynicism is supposed to come with age and experience."

"Must be in the genes, Dad. Come on. Let's get a move on. The sooner we get going, the sooner we can meet up with Ian and Kate. Maybe we can catch up before they reach the cabin."

"Liz, much as I know you love your sister and how much she loves you, most couples don't plan family trips on their honeymoon. Kate and Ian probably want some time to themselves. And don't forget the secondary purpose of this trip. I'm trying to catalogue the wildflowers in the valley, and if we move too fast, I'll miss some of the less frequent varieties. Haste makes waste."

"Okay, Dad," conceded Liz with a resigned sigh. "But while we're walking, can you tell me some valley stories?"

Since they were toddlers, Liz and Kate had listened to valley stories, first at bedtime and later during car trips. Some of the stories had been passed along for three generations. Although they'd heard them all many times, they never tired of hearing them again and again.

"Sure, Liz. Any story in particular?"

"Tell me the story about Grandma and the bear."

"Okay, but first let's make sure we have everything we'll need, and then I'll tell the story while we hike up the mountain … You know, even with a leisurely pace, and stopping to photograph a few flowers, we could reach the valley in time for a hot tub. Might be nice to soak our tired muscles in the hot spring. We brought our bathing suits. What do you think? Can we do it?"

This suggestion brought an excited smile to Liz's face. "No problem, Dad. Kate and Ian will have cleared much of the new growth from the trail. We should be able to make great time."

Liz was a few inches taller than her sister but much thinner. She worked out almost every day. Her favorite exercise was running. She had competed on cross-country teams in high school and university. She also paid keen attention to her nutrition, and whatever extra calories she ate, she usually exercised off. Kate often kidded Liz that she was anorexic. Like Kate, Liz had long hair, although her locks were brown with reddish highlights and not as thick. She let her hair hang loose about her shoulders, where a natural curl developed. Courtesy of daily outdoor exercise, rain or shine, she always had great color in her face, and her complexion was flawless. She had her father's blue eyes.

As Liz secured the gate, she noticed the rope latch was almost gnawed through. "Hey, Dad, look at this. The rope has been eaten." As she twisted the rope around to examine the tooth marks, she went on. "Too high to be a porcupine, and the horses don't have incisors that could do this."

Liz's gaze went down to the ground. "And check out the tracks below the latch. They look like wolf prints to me. Four toes and a heel pad."

"How long are they?" asked Mac.

"The rear tracks are about four and a half inches from heel to toe; the front tracks are about five inches. And there are claw marks. The rear tracks are especially deep, almost as if the animal was standing on its hind legs while gnawing at the rope. Is that possible?"

"I don't know, but the description fits best with a wolf. I suppose an exceptionally large male coyote could make a similar print. What is the overall shape of the print?"

"It looks almost round."

"And are the middle toes parallel?"

"Yes."

"Almost certainly a wolf then," replied Mac. "Coyote prints are more oval and streamlined. Dog tracks can look a lot like wolf tracks, but the middle toes are not parallel, and the toes tend to splay out in a more haphazard than symmetrical fashion."

"Could the wolf have been standing on its hind feet?" asked Liz again.

"Well, now, let's see." Mac retrieved a magnifying glass from his pack, removed his glasses, and examined the rope. After a minute, he got down on his knees and studied the tracks. "Good call, Liz, but I've never heard of a wolf that smart. Besides, if a wolf wanted in the stable, why not just go over or under the beams? This doesn't make sense. If we believe the signs, the wolf wanted to free the horses … I don't think we can solve this mystery today, but we can secure the latch with some wire. I always carry wire when I hike."

"Dad, you always carry everything when you hike. Your pack is a walking hardware store," she kidded.

Liz had hiked with her father since before she could remember. When she was a baby, she had come along courtesy of a papoose sack Mac wore in front of his chest. Her first hiking memories were as a toddler, of riding on Daddy's shoulders along mountain trails and through forests. Whatever happened, her dad always had a solution somewhere in his pack. Whether they needed warm clothes, rain gear, cream or a dressing for a scrape or bite, a rope, or a book on how to identify trees, flowers, or tracks, the pack held the answer. Inside the pack were plastic bags of all sizes, different kinds of rope, electrical tape, a pulley, safety pins, wire, a thermometer, waterproof matches, candles, a portable one-burner stove, collapsible cups, a saw blade that rolled into a tiny container, and almost everything else they might happen to need. Mac took the Boy Scout motto, "be prepared," seriously. And there was always hard candy, nuts, and chocolate for quick energy or a treat when the going got tough. *Yes,* thought Liz, *Dad's pack is legendary.*

After securing the gate and doing a last check of their gear, they headed into the forest. Liz took the lead, hoping to set a fast pace. They weren't on the trail more than a few minutes when Liz spotted a tiny orchid nestled by some rocks in a bog by the trail.

"Hey, Dad, have you seen one of these?"

"Wow, Liz, a yellow lady's slipper. These are uncommon at this altitude. Usually, you only see them by streams or in other wet areas at lower altitudes. Mostly they're found in colonies. An animal paw or one of our feet might have transported the seed for this solitary flower a few years ago. At this elevation, the plant probably takes at least three or four years to reach the flowering stage. See how the lower petal forms a pouch that looks like a lip or a lady's slipper? We're lucky; this flower has just bloomed, and the lavender lines in the petals are especially vivid against the bright yellow background. The sun is just right for a photo."

Liz enjoyed flowers, and she was thrilled to see her dad so excited, and the more so because she had spotted the flower first, but the intricate botanical details did not interest her. The flowers she preferred came in a vase and were hand-delivered by a handsome beau.

Dad will likely spend five or ten minutes documenting this flower, thought Liz impatiently. She resigned herself to the wait and found a comfortable place to sit. "That's great, Dad," said Liz, trying to sound sincere as well as supportive.

She looked over at her dad and realized how lucky she was to have a father who was still fit enough to hike and enjoy nature. Mac was sixty years old but still basically trim. He had some extra weight around the middle, but his legs were thin and muscular, and his upper body was just as strong. Mac kept his silver hair cut short at the back and front but thick at the sides. His brown mustache and beard had lots of gray highlights and were neatly trimmed. His hair had been blonde when he was a boy, had turned brown during his teenage years, and then during middle age had changed from gray to silver. His blue eyes were vivid, and when Mac was excited about something, they seemed to shine.

Mac removed a digital camera from his pack and spent the next few minutes composing the shot. Mac always had the most up-to-date high-tech equipment, and this camera was no exception. The camera was a single-lens reflex model with a special macro lens attachment that allowed spectacular close-up photos.

"How does this look, Liz?"

"Great, Dad! How many photos can your camera take?"

"I have two cards, each of which holds up to 1,000 average-resolution photos. The motor drive in the base of the camera has eight AA batteries, and I have two dozen spare batteries in my pack. I could take up to 4,000 photos."

"Guess that's why your pack weighs so much," said Liz.

"Yes, but the batteries also power our flashlights, the GPS locator, and my Geiger counter."

"Geiger counter? Why on earth did you bring a Geiger counter?"

"Well, Grandpa was a hard-rock geologist, and he always thought the valley might contain uranium or other radioactive deposits—not that he wanted to mine it or anything; that would be too complicated. Grandpa had collected a lot of rock samples, but he never tested them with a Geiger counter, and I thought we might check out his theory. I have Grandpa's journal with the location of the outcrops he was suspicious about."

"Works for me," said Liz.

"You know, Liz, the uranium story sort of ties in with the story of Grandma and the bear."

"Grandpa found the uranium at the same time Grandma saw the bear?" questioned Liz.

"Kind of. Grandpa and Grandma were out collecting rock samples the day she saw the bear."

"But Grandpa never saw the bear, right?"

"Sad but true. He was pretty disappointed, especially considering all the stories that his dad had told him, but he was happy for Grandma."

"Where was she when she saw the bear?"

"Almost all the bear sightings have been around the hot spring. No one has seen a bear or even tracks around the cabin or beyond the lake in the northernmost section of the valley. Great-Grandpa occasionally saw signs of bear diggings on the southwest-facing slope. They like the tuberous roots of the yellow hedysarum that grows there in the spring."

"Grandma saw the bear eating berries, right?"

"That's the story. Grandpa was above the tree line on the southeastern slope. He was investigating the outcrop that he thought might contain uranium when he found some fossils, real neat ones too, nothing like anything he had ever seen before. Turns out they were similar to those later found in the Burgess Shale. Grandpa knew the fossils were worth reporting, but he didn't want to attract any attention to the area, so he never told anyone. Anyway, he was busy with the fossils, and Grandma wanted to collect some berries for lunch. The warmth of the hot spring makes it possible for a variety of plants to grow at an altitude where you would not otherwise find any vegetation, and Grandma had noticed some saskatoon berries and wild raspberries along the stream that trickles down the mountain from the hot spring. The stream flows all winter, and the persistent moisture, unique sulfur content of the soil, and extraordinary warmth allow a huge variety of flowering plants to flourish. Depending on the season, some of my best finds have been along that stream."

"Right, Dad, and you were saying about Grandma and the bear?"

"Yes, of course. So Grandma was hiking back up to the hot spring when she heard a snort, like someone blowing their nose, but a real deep nasal sound. She hadn't reached the edge of the woods, and she was below and upwind from the bear; otherwise, the grizzly likely would have been long gone. They have an incredible sense of smell. She paused and heard a sneeze and then a very loud wet sniff that was followed by another snort. She crept to the forest edge and was surprised to see a huge grizzly standing on two legs and working her way through a raspberry patch at the lower end of the stream, only a few yards away from the forest."

"How did she know the bear was female?"

"I asked her the same question, and all she said was that she just knew."

"What happened next?"

"Well, the bear seemed to be allergic to something, but the berries were obviously a choice enough meal for her to put up with the sneezing.

The bear would eat a handful of berries, sneeze, and then eat another handful and sneeze again. After every two or three sneezes, the bear would snort.

"Grandma felt sorry for the bear and muttered a very quiet 'bless you.' To her surprise, the bear nonchalantly said, 'Thank you,' and continued to pick berries."

"The bear spoke English?"

"No. The bear actually said thank-you in Icelandic. Grandma had spent enough time with Grandpa's mother that she knew some simple phrases in Icelandic."

"No kidding. I've never heard that part of the story before. What happened next?"

"Well, a few seconds later, the bear jumped as if startled and then looked toward Grandma. It was as if the bear had suddenly realized she wasn't alone. As soon as she saw Grandma, the bear dropped down on all fours. Grandma made eye contact with the bear and said in English, 'I'm sorry. I didn't mean to disturb you.' Then she started looking around for a good tree to climb. She looked back a second later, and the bear was running uphill real fast. The bear went over a rise and disappeared. Grandma decided not to follow and returned to where Grandpa was still collecting fossils. Together, they searched for the bear, but by then the grizzly was long gone."

"Now tell me the story about when Mom saw the bear."

"Now that is a great story. Your mom and I were on our honeymoon. It had been an exceptionally cold spring and summer, and there had been several very early and heavy snowfalls in the mountains, so even though it was still late July, we had to snowshoe in the higher passes. I'm glad your mom was an adventurous lady. Many women might not have found snowshoeing an attractive activity for a honeymoon. The wilderness after a snowfall has a special beauty. What with the snow sparkling in the trees, your mom figured I'd taken her to an ice-crystal paradise. The nights were pretty cold, but we had all the right gear. The mornings were crisp, and you needed a good fire to get your blood circulating. Afterward, we didn't usually dally around the campsite, and once the sun came over the ridge and the day warmed up, you could hike without a coat.

"I wasn't with your mom when she saw the bear. I was collecting firewood, and she was exploring on her own. We were camped by the stream. I'd told your mom about the hot spring, and she went off to look for it while I started the fire and made breakfast.

"Your mom spotted the hot spring right away. The mountainside is fairly bare-looking, even during the lush summer months, and a snowfall had left a white carpet that was broken only by the occasional solitary and scraggly spruce. The mist from the hot spring was pretty easy to spot.

"By the time she reached the tree line below the hot spring, the sun had crested the ridge. As the sun rose, the morning rays moved down the mountainside and had just about reached the level of the spring. Suddenly, your mom saw an explosion of snow from the mountainside close to the spring.

"Her first thought was an avalanche, and she instinctively sought cover behind a tiny stand of spruce. The prevailing wind down the mountain had blown the tops of the spruce over to form a tiny sheltered bower in the lee of the trees. By the looks of the tracks and scat, your mom realized she had not been the first animal to seek shelter in that spot.

"When she looked back up to the hot spring, the snow had settled, and she saw a huge grizzly mother sitting on the snow and basking in the sun, looking for all the world as contented as any sunbather on a tropical beach. The grizzly was sitting on her bottom like a person might; her hind legs were splayed out on the snow in front of her, and her long-clawed forepaws were folded in her lap. That she was a female grizzly was clear, courtesy of the three yearling cubs who were playing in the snow. She sat like that for a long while, occasionally barking a soft woofing sound when one of the cubs strayed out of sight. This admonishment always seemed enough for the adventurous cub to return.

"There was enough snow for the cubs to slide down a short stretch on their backs. They reminded your mom of the times you and Kate would toboggan down the hills by our home. She swears the cubs laughed and giggled just like they were human.

"Your mom watched for almost half an hour before I inadvertently scared the bear family away by calling out from lower in the valley. I had the fire and breakfast ready to go. By the time I reached your mom, the bears had disappeared back into what we presumed was a den. We never visited the hot spring that year for fear that we might disturb them. I was pretty disappointed not to enjoy the hot spring surrounded by snow, but it's not wise to disturb a mother grizzly with her cubs. We looked for the den the next summer but never found it."

"What great stories, Dad! Hope we see a bear this trip."

"I hope so too. I'd love to get some pictures."

"We've made great time, Dad. We're almost at the summit. In a few minutes we'll be on our way down the gorge, and in an hour or so, we could be at the hot spring. We have lots of time for an afternoon dip. Do you think Kate and Ian used the hot spring?"

"I'd be surprised if they didn't. My bet is they're having the time of their lives."

CHAPTER 7
LORD NULL

Kate woke up with a start, her body whipping back as the mule lurched forward. At first she thought she was dreaming since the last thing she remembered was falling asleep by the hot spring, and now she found herself riding a mule. At least it felt and smelled like a mule. There was so little light that even though sleep had accommodated her eyes to the dark, she could only just barely see the outline of the animal's head.

But this wasn't a dream. The disorientation created by waking in a dark unfamiliar place was quickly replaced by fear when she realized that although awake, she couldn't move her hands, which were tied to a saddle horn. For a moment, Kate felt panicky. She wanted to cry out for Ian, but somehow she knew he wasn't there, so she stifled the urge. Just as she knew Ian was not there, she also knew that she was not alone and that whoever had kidnapped her was somewhere close.

I won't give them the satisfaction of knowing I'm awake, she decided, and her fear lessened somewhat with this resolve. *Think this through, Kate. Pull it together. Start with assessing the situation. What do I know for sure?*

Well, my hands are sore under the ropes, I feel pretty stiff all over, and I have one of those irritable headaches that makes me cranky, but I'm alive, I can't feel any serious injury, and I seem to have all my wits about me. That's good, she concluded and felt better for her assessment. *Someone has kidnapped me, but why? I'm tied to a mule in some dark, warm, and humid place, which must be a cave. Why?*

Not being able to answer this question made Kate feel uneasy, and again she started to feel panicky. *I don't know where I am, what time it is, or even if it's night or day. For all I know, they've killed Ian and mean to rape or kill me.*

These thoughts enhanced her sense of panic, and suddenly, Kate felt an irresistible urge to scream. But even as she breathed deep to push the scream out, she found herself biting her lip to stifle the sound. *Screaming won't help. Keep it together, keep it together,* she repeated over and over again as a mantra to relax. *You are bright, strong and resourceful. You can figure this out. Just keep it together.*

Fear comes with loss of control. So I must take back some control. I need to figure out what's going on, preserve my strength, stay relaxed, and keep it together. As long as they believe I'm asleep, I have an advantage. Maybe an opportunity to escape will present itself. If I can loosen the ropes around my hands, I'll be in a stronger position.

Kate started to wriggle her hands and try to work the rope around her wrists loose. It was slow and uncomfortable work. *Even if I can't free my hands, it's important to try. I won't know if I don't try,* she thought. *And by trying, I'm taking back some control.*

While she quietly busied herself with this purposeful task, Kate retraced what she remembered, and she realized that the mist must have contained some sleeping drug. As crazy as that notion was, she also understood that somehow the raven with the red eyes and the wolves were involved.

Gosh, thought Kate, *none of this makes any sense. Why kidnap me?*

In the darkness her hearing seemed more acute. The hooves of the mule clattered a slow cadence that was answered by a soft echo, which Kate otherwise never would have heard. The subtle sound seemed surreal in the darkness.

Again and again, Kate wondered and hoped that this was only a cruel dream, or perhaps some delusional state brought on by the mist, like the effect of some hallucinogenic drug. With these thoughts, Kate drifted off into a fitful sleep, as if somehow just thinking of the mist were enough to induce slumber.

When she next awoke, her situation was unchanged, and Kate was upset that she'd dozed off when she should have been working on the ropes or thinking of ways to escape. Falling asleep seemed like giving up. She felt powerless again, and this sparked another anxiety attack.

Kate was starting to really lose it when an unfamiliar voice interrupted her panic attack. "Whoa," the voice asked the mule, and the animal came to a gentle halt. The voice was frightening and welcome at the same time—any sensory input was welcome at this point, even if the voice was that of her kidnapper. Kate instinctively closed her eyelids to all but a crack and looked in the direction of the voice, but she couldn't see a thing.

Suddenly, the passage was suffused with a green light that cast an unearthly glow and Kate gently closed her eyes.

"How long do you think she'll sleep?" asked the person with the unfamiliar voice.

Kate cracked open a cautious eyelid and saw a swarthy-looking fellow who fidgeted and cringed as he spoke. He had the deferential air and manner of someone who has been abused and is always ready to duck or run. The swarthy fellow maintained a respectful distance from a tall man.

"The longer the better," replied the tall man in a condescending tone. "She is much less trouble asleep. She is to be brought unharmed to the Green Cavern, and your life depends on it. The princess knows all, and if the woman arrives with so much as a scratch, you'll be flayed alive and fed to one of the serpents in the deep caverns."

"How does she know? The princess is thousands of miles away," the swarthy fellow responded with foolhardy cockiness.

"Fool, the princess has thousands of eyes in every corner of the underground kingdom. My eyes are her eyes. The raven's eyes are her eyes. The wolves' eyes are her eyes. If you had any brains, Lars, then your eyes would also be her eyes."

A picture of Argus, the mythical Greek fabled to have a hundred eyes, popped into Kate's mind, and she was amused that this thought should come to her in this surreal situation.

"I'll be rewarded, right?" asked Lars.

"Yes, you'll be rewarded," the tall man sneered. "Now, make sure her hands are still firmly tied to the saddle," he ordered.

Does he know? thought Kate, who found her right hand miraculously free, as if somehow she had continued to work on the ropes while she was asleep. The green light allowed Kate to see that they were in a passage and that the light came from a torch held by the man called Lars. *This is my chance,* she thought.

She spurred the mule and grabbed the torch with her right hand as the animal bumped past Lars. She heard Lars fall but never looked back as she raced down the tunnel. "Yes!" she cried out, but her elation was premature.

About twenty yards down the passage, the mule stopped short and started to shiver as if frightened. Kate kept spurring the mule with her heels, but the animal stubbornly refused to go any farther.

"That … was ill advised," she heard the tall man say with tiresome sarcasm.

The mule turned like a robot and slowly returned to where the man stood.

"You might have heard me say that you are not to be harmed. Let me assure you that I know ways to inflict pain that will leave no trace apart from a horrible memory." With that he grabbed a spot behind her knee and brought on an electrical jolt so excruciating that Kate passed out.

"She's unconscious again. You'll know better next time, won't you?" said the tall man to Lars, who looked more nervous than hurt. "Both of you will know better," he said with a laugh as he stared threateningly at Lars.

Lars threw himself on the ground in front of the tall man. "Forgive me, Lord Null. Please don't hurt me. I'll do better," whimpered Lars, shivering with fear.

"Yes, Lars, you will do better." Lord Null grasped the handle of his sword and started to massage the twin rubies that gleamed from the hilt. The sword hung suspended from a harness at his right side and was angled to allow easy access for his left hand. Lord Null's index finger slowly rubbed first one and then the other ruby.

The knuckles of his fingers were prominent, but not large. The joints seemed big only in contrast to his fingers, which were so thin that the skin seemed stretched over the bone. The skeletal-like finger moved in an unexpectedly gentle circular motion, like a caress, and drew Lars's eyes to the hilt.

As Lord Null continued the slow circular motion, Lars stood up and began to stare at the rubies, which now consumed his attention. The rubies looked like two blood-red eyes. A few seconds later, Lars's knees bent forward, his arms fell loose by his side, and his body went limp, like a puppet suspended by some unseen force. He remained in this position, mesmerized, his eyes transfixed on the hilt of the sword, until Lord Null covered both rubies with his hand, whereupon Lars collapsed with a thud to the floor.

"Yes, Lars," said Lord Null, "I'm sure you will try to do better."

Kate awoke a few hours later during an apparent rest stop, but she did not open her eyes, preferring to feign sleep so that she might eavesdrop.

Perhaps I'll learn enough to figure out a way to escape, thought Kate, but while enjoying this encouraging idea, she felt a sharp poke in her side, which made her jump and cry out.

"Ah, I thought as much. You're awake. And how long have you listened to our conversation?"

"See, Lars, didn't I tell you she was a tricky one? Best not say anything in her presence, or the words might come back to haunt you. You can't be too careful. Malicious doesn't tolerate the indiscreet. She has been known to boil court gossips alive. In the lava tubes at her fortress, the water is heated in cauldrons to temperatures that dissolve flesh."

"Yes, Lars, best not to say anything you might regret being repeated," said Lord Null, and the derisive tone of his laughter brought shivers not only to Lars's spine but also to Kate's.

Chapter 8

Alfred Brings the Wrong News

After flying for most of a day, Alfred was tired. True, being Malicious's favorite messenger raven had its rewards, but the long flights were not as easy as they had been when he was a young bird. Today he had flown many thousands of miles from the hot spring in the north toward Malicious's volcanic fortress.

The sun would set in an hour or so, and the sky below was cloudy, but it was impossible for Alfred to get lost or to arrive late. His wings were hardly necessary except to turn. Once he reached sufficient altitude, he brought his wings and feet together, and the dark energy of the princess drew him like a magnet at supernatural speed.

Alfred was glad the sky above was clear. From the tip of his bill to the end of his tail, his jet-black body soaked in the comfortable heat of the sun and compensated for the chilly air at his cruising altitude. Alfred knew that the violet gloss of his back and the blue-green sheen on his wings glistened and sparkled, and he wished that he had a mirror to admire himself. He considered himself a handsome bird and was proud of his sleek profile and the luster of his feathers.

Alfred had a variety of fantasies. One delusion was that he was descended from the creator raven revered by the Haida, one of the aboriginal peoples of the Pacific Northwest. Another was that he was descended from the ravens who sat on Odin's shoulder during Ragnarök, the last great battle of Norse mythology. Odin had two ravens, Huginn and Muninn, who represented thought and memory, respectively, and who served Odin in his capacity as a god of wisdom. Alfred had an exceptional memory, and Malicious often referred to him as "my Muninn."

By the time the sun had set, the glow from the volcanic cone was just visible and drew him like a nocturnal homing beacon. A toxic cloud often shrouded the summit of the volcano, and orange-red sparks and yellow flames periodically emerged. Notwithstanding these signs of activity, the volcano had not suffered a major eruption in more than a thousand years.

Alfred flew high above the volcano and then circled slowly until a break in the cloud cover allowed him to safely descend into the crater of the volcano. The castle was at the southwestern edge of the crater, and unless one knew where to look, it was difficult to identify. The nondescript gray blocks of lava that had been used to construct the castle blended into the volcanic landscape and were often obscured by the dirty smoke that puffed from cracks and holes on the surface.

Alfred was wary of the smoke and mists that swirled within the cone. Every day, new vents opened, and old ones closed. More than once, he had barely escaped either a choking death when a noxious gas had suddenly spurted from a new vent or a fiery demise when a lava plume had spit up from an active crack.

The three-story castle was square and oriented according to the cardinal directions. A solitary turret enclosed the private third-floor chambers of Princess Malicious. The east face of the turret had a large window and on cloudless mornings, the dawn sun streamed into her chambers.

As Alfred closed in on the eastern window, his thoughts were not about the completion of his important mission or about a well-earned rest. Rather, he was thinking about the tasty treat that might be his reward. Alfred knew that the capture of the woman was important and that this news might be rewarded with a fresh piece of meat, perhaps even man flesh, maybe even the eyes—his favorite. *Yes,* he thought, *this was what made the long journey and the risks worthwhile.*

He landed on the window ledge and then hopped onto a table ominously scattered with black feathers. Malicious was preparing something, and several small animals chained to the wall looked deservedly frightened.

She looked up when she heard Alfred land. "Alfred, my pet, come to mother. You must be tired. How many thousands of miles did you fly today? What a good bird you are to bring me news. You must be exhausted and hungry."

Alfred perked up at the mention of food. He saw that one of the chained animals was a small man who was cringing at the wall.

For me? he wondered. *Even a finger would do, or an ear.* But he steeled himself for disappointment. *I must not hope for the eyes; that would be too generous.*

Malicious allowed Alfred to relish his thoughts for a few moments before she put her arm out and called softly, "Come, Alfred. Come to mother."

Alfred fluttered over to her forearm and preened while Malicious stroked his head and back.

"Handsome bird, now pay attention to me and stop looking at the tasty-looking little man. Relax and look into my eyes, Alfred; yes, look deep into my eyes."

Alfred opened his eyes wide and allowed Malicious into his mind, giving her access to his every memory.

"Yes, my Muninn, I see. You found them where I told you to look. Good bird. And you took care of that pesky osprey. Well done … Now who is this? A young man, I see, a very handsome man, so fit. Hmm, perhaps I should send Lord Null back for him. All work and no play makes Malicious a cranky woman, but no bother with the boy. What about the woman? You didn't get a good look at her while they were at the stable then. Okay, well, what about that night? … Ah, she woke up as we planned, and of course you were in the perfect position to attract her attention. Naughty woman, she shone that awful light into your eyes, I see. And it must have hurt, but then you made good eye contact. Oh, very good. Perfect, my pet. Wonderful, wonderful."

Suddenly, Malicious's smug smile changed to a grimace. "No, no, no, this can't be—she's not the one!" screamed Malicious as she grabbed and pulled her stringy colorless hair. "Noooooo!"

Alfred knew from past experience to be on the lookout for bad news, and he flew out of reach and onto the window ledge with the first shriek.

Malicious settled down as quickly as she had exploded. "Alfred dear, do come back. It's not your fault. You could not have known, and you did exactly as you were told. The woman appeared at the hot spring during the month I predicted, the northern lights were dancing in the sky, and she was blonde and related to that Icelandic man who heard the bears. No, you could not have known. But I know, and she is not the one. There must be another woman, a sister perhaps. Did you see another woman?"

Alfred shook his beak.

"Well, nothing for it but to go back and look again." She opened a box that contained some mice. "Alfred, you deserve a treat. You like the white ones, don't you? I have a real plump one here … Shall I kill it for you?" she teased. "Ah, no. That's right. You like to peck their eyes out while they're alive, don't you? Well, have as many as you like, but then you must fly back to the Green Cavern with this message, and I don't need to tell you that speed is very important."

Malicious wrote a note and tied the paper to Alfred's leg. "If you return with good news, perhaps your next treat will be better." As she spoke, Malicious looked over at the little man, who squirmed at her glance.

Chapter 9
Groping in the Dark

Great, thought Ian, *pitch-dark, and I'm treading water in a subterranean pool.*

"Better get the lay of the land, or I guess I should say lake," he joked to himself.

His daypack and climbing gear suddenly felt very heavy, as did his boots, but Ian discounted taking them off. He knew he might still need the equipment, so he decided not to discard anything until he absolutely had to.

Ian started to swim in a random direction and soon hit a slimy, algae-coated wall, which he followed to the right for a few minutes. When the wall continued without change, he turned and followed the wall a similar distance in the opposite direction, but his investigations yielded only more wall and water.

Ian knew that his descent in the chimney had been almost vertical and that the ledge was only about fifty horizontal yards from the hot spring. *If I choose the correct direction, and if there is a connection with the hot spring, then I shouldn't need to swim for more than a few minutes to find the way out,* he reasoned.

He swam back and forth along the wall for at least twice as long in each direction but still found nothing. The wall he was exploring seemed more or less straight without any corners, but in the darkness he couldn't be sure. *What if the other side is only a few feet away?* he thought. *Maybe the first direction I chose after falling was wrong.*

Based on this premise, Ian swam away from the wall but found nothing but water, and a few minutes later, he turned back. However, now he couldn't even find the wall. *Guess my sense of direction isn't so good in the dark,* he admitted silently. *From now on, I'll never take sunshine or lights for granted. This must be how it is for a blind person.*

Ian relaxed and floated in the warm waters while he meditated on his options. Sadly, he realized he had few to choose from. Waiting for help made no sense. He had to continue exploring. He tried to reassure himself that because he had landed uninjured and because of his physical fitness, he would eventually find his way out, but even so, he was starting to feel a bit helpless. *Am I doomed to float aimlessly until I finally tire and drown?* he wondered. *Surely, I can find a way out. At least there is lots of air to breathe, even if it does stink.* At that moment, a smile crept over his face. Inspiration had struck.

Ian shook the water off his right hand and then lifted this arm above his head and waved his hand back and forth until the skin dried out completely. Then, after immersing only the back part of his hand in the water, he again lifted the arm high in the air. Ever so slowly, he turned the back of his wet hand through an entire 360 degrees. After several complete circuits, he discovered a slight breeze that consistently came from one direction.

The air flow must be coming from the surface, he deduced, now pleased and feeling confident, *and the way out will be in that direction.* Ian swam toward the source of the breeze, stopping periodically to test the direction against the back of his hand. Each time he checked, the breeze felt a bit fresher, and the air smelled progressively clearer. Finally, on one of the occasions when he stopped swimming to check the breeze, his feet touched a pebbled bottom. The breeze was fairly strong on his wet face as he waded across slippery boulders toward the fresher, cooler air. A few minutes later, he was on a dry surface, still in complete darkness, but at least on firm footing.

He was glad his first steps were cautious because the chamber was filled with hard, blunt, and sometimes sharp stalactites, any one of which could have caused a nasty gash on his forehead, and stalagmites that easily could have skewered him if he tripped on the pebbled floor. As he groped around, he found that some of the rock formations were razor sharp.

Time for knife work, he decided. Holding his survival knife at the end of his outstretched arm, he waved the blade through each quadrant before taking a step. Whenever he hit a rocky obstruction, he changed his direction modestly and continued to use the knife to feel his way forward. Soon he established a methodical and safe, albeit slow, routine and was making good progress through the maze of stalactites and stalagmites. The going was steadily uphill.

I must have fallen into an underground pool deep inside the mountain and below the level of the hot spring, he reasoned. *That explains why my rope ran out. Either that, or with all this climbing, I'll emerge at a cave entrance higher up on the mountain and looking down on the hot spring.* Ian didn't really care so long as the cave had an exit to the surface. He was confident he could climb down if need be.

Whenever the blade touched rock, the sound echoed for a second. Several times when he stopped to rest his arms, he thought he heard following footsteps. At first Ian presumed the sounds were an echo, but then he realized the timing was close but not perfect. He purposely stopped abruptly several times and listened carefully. Clearly the noise was not an echo.

Once, when he felt as if the steps were especially close behind, Ian changed the grip on his knife to a combat position, feigned forward motion, and then turned around suddenly, swiping the knife in a z-like motion, first across at chest level, then diagonally down, and finally back across at knee level, but his knife sliced only the warm humid air of the cave.

"The darkness and the echo are making me paranoid," he said quietly to himself. Still, the worry about someone following him grew, and periodically Ian also had the strange sense that he was being watched, although how this could happen in complete darkness, he did not know.

Once, when the blade hit a rock surface, some sparks flew, and for a moment the cavern lit up. The stalactites and stalagmites made fleeting long shadows everywhere, but just behind Ian and at the extreme periphery of his vision, one of the shadows, a massive shape, at least one and a half times as tall as Ian and three or four times as wide, seemed to move for a millisecond and then froze just before the light dissipated.

I best not get excited, thought Ian. *It's probably my imagination. Even if someone or something is tracking me, they can obviously see in the dark and could have attacked long ago. Whoever or whatever it is, must not want to harm me.*

The going was tedious, but he was rewarded with ever-clearer air and, since the cavern was also narrowing, a greater velocity of breeze.

Finally, he emerged into a chamber with a glimmer of light at the end of what seemed to be a long downhill passage. The stalactites and stalagmites thinned out and then disappeared, and a few steps later, Ian could see well enough to resheathe his knife. He looked around carefully but didn't see any evidence of whoever or whatever might have been following him. He reckoned that he had been underground for at least an hour and was thankful that the sun had not yet set.

As he came closer to the light, he heard voices and immediately pressed himself against the wall of the cavern. *The kidnappers,* he thought. *They might still have Kate.* He crept toward the light until he was positioned just a few feet from the muffled voices, behind some dense bushes that effectively concealed the cave entrance.

Knife at the ready, he impatiently broke through the bushes, expecting to take the villains by surprise, but the shock was all his—he landed in the hot spring a few feet from Mac and Liz, who were relaxing in their bathing suits.

"That's a good trick, Ian, but the knife is a bit much," said Liz. "Where's Kate?" Then her expression grew more serious as she saw the look on Ian's face.

"Thank God you're here," exclaimed Ian. "Kate's been kidnapped!"

Chapter 10

En Route to the Green Cavern

Lars whipped the mule mercilessly to hasten the animal along. The mule was accustomed to a slower pace and stopped at every tiny creek to drink and rest. No matter how much Lars beat the poor beast, the mule stubbornly refused to go faster or to leave any natural rest spot before he was ready.

"You mangy excuse for a beast of burden. Can't you smell the bears? I've seen too many fresh signs for us to rest up now. Unless we get a move on, a patrol might intercept us, and then you'll wish you'd moved faster. Bear claws will sink just as deep into your flesh as they will into mine."

So, thought Kate, *the bear stories must be true.* Kate had awoken some time back and was feeling a kinship with the poor mule. She had listened without letting on she was awake, hoping to learn more about the brutes who had abducted her, but all she had learned was that Lord Null was no longer with them, that Lars hated and feared Lord Null, and that Lars, who muttered continuously, was a simple fellow.

"Without that sword and those rubies, you're just a skinny old man," mumbled Lars, "and I could easily break your neck. Just give me the chance, and I'd break every bone in your scrawny body. What gives you the right to order me around?" Lars kicked the ground, whipped the mule, and complained almost continuously. Kate thought him pretty pathetic, but wretched and simple as he was, he was in control.

She had no idea of the time, or the day for that matter. Her watch was gone, as were the Swiss Army knife and compass she usually carried on her belt. The tunnels were hot and humid, and but for the torch carried by Lars, there was no light. Kate had never seen such a great torch. About a foot long and several inches wide, it had a handle carved to comfortably fit a hand, seemed fairly light, didn't give off an obnoxious odor, and was sturdy enough to withstand falling on the rocky ground. The light intensity could be varied from bright to a faint glow by adjusting an aperture device on one face of the torch, much like the lens of a camera. *I wonder what the energy source is,* she thought.

She was rather hungry and thirsty and realized that she had no idea how much time had passed since she'd last eaten. *Sooner or later, he'll stop to feed me,* she told herself, *and perhaps that will present an opportunity for escape.* She hoped Ian was safe. If he was, she knew he would try to find her. *And when he does, Lars will find out that more than bear claws can sink deep into his flesh.* Kate imagined Ian subduing Lars and felt good and bad at the same time for this violent thought.

Kate knew Ian had seen combat in Afghanistan. He never talked about it, but the medals he wore at military functions were much remarked upon and admired by the other officers. Kate had no doubt about Ian's courage. *If he's alive, he'll find me,* she comforted herself.

A crystal clear subterranean pool afforded a good opportunity for water, and Lars shook Kate's leg as if to wake her; once she responded, he untied her from the saddle horn and allowed her to dismount. He checked the ropes around her wrist and confirmed they were still tight.

As soon as she was on the ground, Kate verbally lambasted Lars in her most indignant voice. "Who are you, and why have you kidnapped me?" she demanded. With Lord Null gone, she hoped Lars might be convinced to let her go.

"You'll find out soon enough," responded Lars, "but I'm not supposed to tell. All you need to know is that trying to escape is not a good idea. Even if you were to get away, these tunnels are treacherous. Without a torch or experience, you wouldn't last more than a few hours. If you didn't die in a fall, a cave-cat would get you. They'd enjoy a well-fed sun-worshiper like you."

He paused and then with a callous chuckle went on. "Cave-cats like to play with their food." Then after clearing his throat, he added, "while they're alive, I mean. Not a very pretty way to die. I once heard a man scream for an hour while a cave-cat slowly ate away at his insides. Neat animals, though—never leave a trace of their kill. They wouldn't even leave a lock of your hair for that boyfriend of yours to find."

Kate was trying not to listen but perked up when she heard Lars mention Ian. "He's my husband, not my boyfriend. Did you capture him too?"

"No, we left him," said Lars glibly.

Almost at once, Lars realized his indiscretion and snarled a fainthearted rejoinder. "I mean, we left him for the wolves." But he bowed his head and hid his eyes as he spoke, and Kate felt elated. She knew Lars was lying. Ian was alive and very likely hot on their trail.

"You'd better hope the wolves got him. My husband is a great warrior, and if he catches up with us, you'll wish you had set me free. I'll bet he's close to us even now. Why don't you set me free? My husband and I will protect you from Lord Null."

"No, you won't. Lord Null has powers over all the animals and men. Only the princess is more powerful. Besides, Lord Null has promised to reward me for taking you safely to the Green Cavern. You'd better eat something because we need to leave soon," grumbled Lars, obviously uneasy with the direction the conversation was going.

Lars offered her some corn bread and a kind of paste that tasted like chicken. Kate was too hungry to be choosy and decided not to ask about the paste. The water from the pool was cool and delicious even though the air temperature was swelteringly hot.

"Why is the water so cool?" she asked.

"Comes from the ice on top of the mountains," said Lars.

Of course, thought Kate, *glacial fed. But the air is hot, so we must not be too far from the surface, or the water would have warmed up.*

Kate recollected that the path had risen and fallen much like hiking in the mountains, and at the peaks they sometimes passed side tunnels with a cool breeze that could only have come from a nearby outlet to the surface. *If we come close enough to another cold-air tunnel, I'll try to escape, cave-cats or no cave-cats,* she decided.

Lars allowed only a few minutes rest before he helped her back onto the mule, retied her bound hands to the saddle horn, and bullied the animal to continue. A few minutes later, he paused and pricked up his ears, which were slightly larger than the average human's and which moved like those of a deer toward the sound. "Hear that? A message wolf will be here soon, likely as not with orders from Lord Null or the princess."

A few minutes later, a lone wolf ran up beside him. "Is this the woman, the chosen one?" asked the wolf.

"Who are you to ask me?" retorted Lars.

"I am Geri Wolf and was sent by Princess Malicious to find Lord Null."

"We left Lord Null about a day ago," said Lars. "He was to have accompanied us to the Green Cavern, but a messenger raven arrived with new instructions for him. Do you have any news?"

"Hildolf, leader of the wolves, has slaughtered the people who live and work in the Green Cavern, and the road south to Popocatépetl is now patrolled by jaguars loyal to Princess Malicious. The armies of the southern warlords are marching north to the Green Cavern where the great battle for control of Asgard will be fought. We smell victory. Some wonder if King Bjorn will surrender rather than commit so many lives to be slaughtered by the hordes of soldiers that are now advancing on his positions."

"Were you with Hildolf when the wolves captured the Green Cavern?" asked Lars.

"Of course, all the wolves were there. We routed the king's forces. I personally killed at least a dozen men and women—and would have killed more but for a company of bears who intervened. Curse those bears. They saved many of the king's people that day. But for them, by now the entire kingdom would be in the hands of Princess Malicious. Even so, our time is nigh. All the dark subterranean forces have united under her banner. The flag of the red-eyed princess will soon fly over the Castle of Light and the entire Northern Realm."

Chapter 11
Liz Goes for Help

"Kidnapped—what do you mean, kidnapped?" said Liz. "You can't be serious, Ian. Who would kidnap Kate, especially here in the valley? You're delirious."

Ian did look out of sorts. He was soaked and mud-covered, his hair was disheveled, and the whites of his eyes were streaked bright red from the acidic sulfur fumes. His face and hands were covered in cuts and scrapes, his voice was unnaturally husky, and he was wheezing. Add his sudden appearance in ripped clothes and holding a knife, and he did look crazy.

"No, I'm serious. The wolves took Kate, and the raven helped. Except for the bluebird, I might never have found out, and I think the osprey is on our side."

Kate's father stepped protectively in front of Liz, and without taking his eyes off his new son-in-law, he motioned with his hand for her to get out of the pool. "It's okay, Ian; we're family. I'm sure there's a reasonable explanation. Perhaps you fell and hit your head, or maybe you ate some mood-altering mushrooms. Why don't you put down the knife and tell me what happened."

Ian realized how irrational everything looked and sounded. He sheathed his knife, climbed out of the pool, and went over to the packs, which were still propped up in the mossy hollow. He slumped down to rest, took out some water to drink, and then proceeded to tell the whole story with a calmness that rang sadly true as Liz and her dad listened with increasing alarm.

"All right," said their father, nodding. "Then we must go after them right away. But"—he paused and looked over at Liz—"one of us must return to the horses, ride out alone, and get help. We must notify the Royal Canadian Mounted Police. The RCMP has a detachment in the last town we passed on the way north. They have helicopters that can bring help in less than an hour."

"Not me, Dad. Send Ian. He's just barely family, and look at him; he's exhausted emotionally and physically. I'm the one who should stay."

"Liz, I know how you feel, and I respect your desire to give chase, but Ian is the only one trained for exactly this sort of problem, and I don't want to lose two daughters to whatever thugs have taken Kate. No, you're the best one to go for help. Besides, you are decidedly the best on a horse. You must ride as fast as safely possible and, once you reach the cars, get into cell phone range and call the RCMP. You must leave now and ride overnight. The moon will still be almost full, and the sky is clear. With luck you can be at the stables before midnight and on the trail again after a few hours' rest. You should be able to reach the cars in less than two days if you push hard. Take all the horses and rotate them so they don't tire out. You must, Liz."

"Okay, Dad," said Liz with a sigh, whose head agreed with the logic, but whose heart and soul didn't feel good about leaving without her sister. "What will you and Ian do?"

"Well, time's a wasting; Ian and I will pursue the kidnappers in the cave. We'll mark our trail so that you'll know where to follow when you return with help."

"Be careful, Dad; I love you," Liz said as she hugged her father. "Ian, give Kate a hug for me when you rescue her. I shouldn't have said you were barely family. You are family, and Dad's right—you should be the one to stay. It's just that, well, I love Kate and can't stand the idea that someone might hurt her. I know you'll find her." She gave him a hug, shouldered her pack, and then started down the trail.

Liz jogged toward the pool and made the journey in record time. Less than fifteen minutes later, she was kneeling at the side of the pool to fill her water bottle and rinse the perspiration from her face. The cool water felt great and helped her relax and settle down. She took a deep breath, let out a long sigh, pushed her hair back, and paused to look at her reflection as the ripples dissipated.

She expected to see only her wet face but was startled to see the reflections of wolves all around the pool. They were slavering and leering at her. After blinking several times in disbelief, Liz moved only her eyes and followed the edge around the pool and counted nine wolves. As Liz raised her body to a sitting position and started to look around, she was startled to hear one of the wolves speak.

"Best not to make any sudden moves; my brothers and sisters are a bit skittish. You see, they were punished when the first woman wasn't the right one, and they need a lot of reassurance, or they might decide to take their revenge out on you, and I might not be able to control them."

As if on cue, several of the wolves snarled, and Liz kept perfectly still.

"I am Freki Wolf, and if you do everything I ask, you will not be harmed. Now, while still on your knees, turn around, put your hands out in front of you, and hold them together at the wrist, so we can bind them."

Liz hesitated for only a moment while she looked around. She thought of crying out but knew her voice would not carry as far as her Dad and Ian. There were wolves everywhere, dozens of them, and a solitary raven with eerie red eyes that made her skin crawl. Escape was impossible, so she put her hands out and allowed them to be tied.

"Very sensible—and a big improvement, I might add, over the other woman. Is the blonde woman your sister?"

Liz was relieved when Freki used the present tense to refer to Kate, but she decided the less these villains knew, the better. "What woman?"

"Very, very good," complimented the wolf, with a sarcastic sneer. Freki looked around at the wolves. "This is a smart human, and we must not underestimate her. She has control of her emotions and doesn't show any fear. She is dangerous. Make sure she's tightly bound."

He turned back to Liz. "Whether you are a sister, a friend, or a complete stranger makes no difference to me. The princess knows, and that's all that counts. Our job is to bring you to the Green Cavern, and the sooner we leave, the sooner we'll arrive. You'll ride one of the other wolves. Never a good thing to make the princess wait."

Freki motioned to one of the pack, and a wolf took up a position by Kate. Half of the rest of the pack headed into some brush in front of the mountainside and disappeared. The wolf with Liz followed, and they entered a cave that was cleverly concealed behind the bushes. They slowed down as soon as they entered the cave, which was dimly lit with an eerie green light.

With the transition from sunlight to dimness, the wolf paused, and Liz was unable to see much for the few moments until her eyes accommodated. Nevertheless, as soon as she entered the cavern, she felt a presence. She felt as if someone was looking at her. Actually, she felt as if someone was looking inside her, if that were possible.

As her eyesight improved in the faint light, she scanned the chamber but could see only the wolves as they walked deeper into the mountain. The wolves walked in single file, and as they passed a dark recess in the wall, each animal paused momentarily to bow their head and bend one knee, before they carried on.

There's someone hidden in that recess, she realized. It was not lost on Liz that the wolves had genuflected in deference to the hidden person. *Whoever it is,* thought Liz, *the person must be very powerful to command that kind of respect.*

As if he had read her thoughts and knew that his presence had been discovered, the man stepped out of the recess. The closest wolves cowered with this movement. He stood still and stared at Liz, who felt as if everything about the man was measuring her. His eyes looked like black marbles set in hollow sockets. They didn't move, blink, or reflect the green light, but their gaze was penetrating, and Liz felt violated, as if her body was being burgled. The only motion on his face was a slow rhythmic flaring of his nostrils, which he lifted ever so slightly up, as if he were checking her scent. He never moved, but even so, Liz felt as if his skeletal hands were probing her body.

Freki halted in front of the man and bowed before he spoke. "We have the other woman, Lord Null, but she is not blonde. My wolves await your orders."

Chapter 12
Infrared Intelligence

"Are you okay to leave right away, Ian, or should we rest for an hour? What do you think? Kate could be over a day away, hidden in a subterranean cavern, but we'll make better time if we're well rested."

"True," admitted Ian, "but Kate might also be just around the corner somewhere, held captive in a spot close by, and every delay might give them an opportunity to harm her."

"You're right. Let's go. Should we take anything from Kate's pack?"

"Yes, some of her climbing gear. Otherwise, I suggest we lighten our loads so we can travel and maneuver easier."

With that, Ian removed all his extra clothes, several reading books, and his sleeping bag, tent, and cooking gear. It was so warm in the cavern that the tent and sleeping bag seemed unnecessary. The only food items he kept were those that would not require cooking. "The lighter we travel, the better," he reaffirmed with satisfaction as he looked at his almost empty pack. But then with astonishment, he looked over at Mac's pack, which still looked full.

"Did you thin out your pack?"

"Yes, I left behind all my extra clothes, my sleeping bag, and most of my books," advised Mac, who pointed to a pile behind him.

"I can't believe you removed all that, and the pack still looks full. Are you sure there isn't something else you could leave behind?"

"If the pack gets heavy, I can always lighten the load later. We don't want to leave something behind that might prove useful," admonished Mac, who was accustomed to comments that his idea of traveling light was unconventional.

"Okay, the gear is on your back, not mine."

Once inside, Mac pulled out an LED headlamp and strapped the gear over his head. He flicked a switch and the cavern lit up like a ball diamond.

"Wow," said Ian, "that's great. I wish I'd had that an hour ago."

"Well, you know what they say—the right tool for the right job. Mostly, I use the lamp to read at night, but it was designed for spelunking. I never thought that I'd ever use the gear for the job it was designed for." Mac started to walk forward but then paused and turned back to his son-in-law. "Ian, before this gets anymore complicated, I'd like to say something." Mac's voice started to break a bit as he spoke.

Ian turned toward him.

"Ian, my daughters are my life. They own my heart. I was the happiest dad in the world when Kate chose you. When you started to work in my lab and Kate took an interest in you, well, I just knew you were the right man. I know you love her deeply, and as such, we share something special. Now, more than ever, I know you were meant to be her husband. I also know that somehow we will prevail and that everything will work out. I feel it."

Ian didn't know what to say. His face flushed, and after mumbling a polite "thank you," he turned and proceeded to jog down the tunnel. Ian had not seen any soft side to Mac before, and he was surprised that Mac seemed so certain about the outcome. Mac was not prone to assumptions, and he certainly wasn't the touchy-feely emotional type either. Mac tended toward the serious and had always been straightforward, reasonable, and compulsively logical in Ian's presence.

The emotional outburst had surprised Mac as much as Ian. He didn't know where the words had come from. They had erupted suddenly and without any forethought, almost as if another person had spoken them. He was glad Ian had felt awkward enough to turn away. *At least he didn't see my face flush with embarrassment too.*

As Ian was thinking through this new twist to his father-in-law's personality, he realized he was maintaining a pace that Mac was unlikely to be able to keep up with, so he slowed to a fast walk. He purposely didn't turn to look at Mac but said over his shoulder, "You know, these tunnels aren't made for fast travel. I think we should slow down a bit."

"Okay by me," replied Mac, and the slightly breathless response confirmed that Ian had made the right choice.

"Haste makes waste," Mac continued, "and these caverns have fabulous geological formations. The shapes and colors are surreal. After we find Kate, I'd love to explore a bit."

Ian was amazed Mac could think past their immediate plight, but he could also appreciate the natural beauty of the caverns. Courtesy of Mac's head lamp, the stalactites and stalagmites now looked attractive rather than threatening. The light also revealed an obvious and well-traveled direction for them to proceed. Almost immediately, they found tracks, including signs of Kate.

Initially there were tracks of Kate, a mule, and two men. Kate's tracks were haphazard and always alongside the tracks of one of the men. Sometimes the tracks showed that she dragged her feet. Mac concluded that the man was helping Kate walk. Soon thereafter, Kate's tracks disappeared, and the tracks of the mule were deeper, presumably, they concluded, because Kate was riding the mule.

They followed the tracks in silence for several hours. Both Ian and Mac found ways to divert their worry. Mac trusted Ian to do the tracking, and with his geologist nature piqued, he was soon professionally distracted by the underground formations. He observed that the stalactites had been carefully, perhaps reverently, preserved in the caverns. Clearly some intelligent individuals had cut the paths in such a way as to avoid damage to the beautiful formations that had taken millennia to form.

In caves still wet, the stalactites were continuing to evolve, and Mac saw the formations in various stages. The diversity was amazing. Some stalactites were thin and fell like creamy white cords with periodic knot-like bumps. On sloping ceilings, stalactites were often side-by-side and had coalesced to form draperies that separated the upper portion of a chamber into compartments.

A labor of the ages, thought Mac. *The chemical reaction of carbon dioxide in the air with water to form carbonic acid is quick enough, but it must have taken millennia for the acid to dissolve the limestone bedrock and allow the calcium carbonate solution to drip down, dry out as calcite crystals, and form the stalactites.*

Sometimes there were streaks of different colors in the stalactites, courtesy of other chemicals that had leached into the calcite. Rust colors indicated the presence of iron.

They passed a number of tiny underground pools. Active stalactites often hung over these pools, and at the tips, Mac could see tiny drops of water, at the base of which grew the microscopic calcite crystals. The water in the pools was tinged blue, not because the calcite was that color, but courtesy of the presence of silica, which absorbed the red end of the color spectrum.

The stalagmites were equally remarkable. These structures formed when mineral-rich water dripped from the tip of a stalactite onto a surface that allowed the water to collect in a finite space. After the water evaporated, the minerals crystallized as a solid directly beneath the tip of the stalactite. Splashed water spread out the formation into a broad-based shelf that slowly grew up toward the stalactite. Given enough time, eventually the stalactite and stalagmite would merge. They came upon just such a situation during their tracking; in one exceptionally high cavern a stalagmite and stalactite were perfectly oriented and separated by only an inch. The cavern was quite dry and likely had been for many years. *But likely as not,* thought Mac, *something will change, like the climate or a shift in the crust of the earth. Water will again drip down the stalactite, calcite formation will renew, and eventually, the two tips will join and form a giant stone tree.*

Mostly, when a stalactite and a stalagmite came together, the formations were not perfectly aligned, and a shelf formed at the point of merger. When this happened, further drops cascaded over the side of the ledge and formed a secondary level of stalactites. This effect reminded Mac of a fancy wedding cake, with stalactite columns between the stalagmite layers, and he thought of the cake Kate had commissioned for her wedding.

In one massive cavern they passed by a giant oblique column, formed when a stalactite had met the ledge of a stalagmite. It looked as though the stalagmite had leaned over to reach the stalactite. The stalagmite was wide and layered with multiple levels of dripping secondary stalactites; the formation reminded Mac of the Leaning Tower of Pisa.

The diversity of crystal formation was tremendous. Mac identified dozens of different minerals, some with more than one crystal structure, and many stalactites showed evidence of multiple crystal formations. Some walls were covered in crystals that formed thick triangular plates. On other walls, the minerals crystallized as sharp, needlelike projections that emerged seemingly haphazardly. Some were as thin as sewing needles, and others the size of a sword blade. Others crystallized out as delicate cotton-like tufts or as flowerlike fronds.

During one of their infrequent rest stops, Mac looked down beside the rock he was sitting on and noticed what looked like a flower. *Surely no flower can grow in the darkness,* he thought. Closer inspection revealed that the delicate-looking "flower" was actually a collection of gypsum crystals.

On another occasion, Mac rested on the ground, and looking up with his hands behind his head, he marveled at a ceiling formed from rounded white mineral deposits that looked like fluffy clouds. *Who is to say that couldn't be a sky?* he thought. The geological diversity enthralled Mac, who had no caving experience and had only read about these spectacular formations.

During the first few hours, they had traveled about a mile or so deep into the mountain without finding any further clues apart from the tracks that were clear in the dust of the caverns. The tracks never seemed to change. The two men and the mule that carried Kate seemed to be moving at a leisurely pace.

"Why do you think Kate is on the mule?" asked Mac. This matter bothered him; he worried Kate might be injured and unable to walk.

"Likely because she was still drugged when they put her on the animal. I don't think she was injured. We would have seen some evidence of a struggle."

Ian's sensible interpretation reassured Mac.

"What do you make of the two people who have kidnapped her?" asked Ian.

"Based on their stride, one is quite a bit taller than the other, the shorter one is heavyset, and they are both wearing moccasins. Do you agree?"

"Yes, but I'm surprised that we haven't found any wolf prints, and there's no evidence of raven tracks. You might think me crazy, but the raven that chased the osprey was sinister-looking, and I'm certain that the wolves were watching us."

"Ian, it was men or women who kidnapped Kate. We know that for sure; we just don't know why. Your idea that the raven and wolves cooperated—well, that seems a bit far-fetched. Wolves and ravens are wild animals, smart in their own way, but rarely domesticated, and incapable of complicity in this kind of sophisticated operation. My assessment is that there are no wolf or raven prints because they didn't kidnap Kate. Dumb animals just don't kidnap people."

The indignant sound that followed surprised Mac.

"Pardon me, Ian?"

"I didn't say anything."

"I heard you harrumph. If you don't agree with my point of view, that's fine, but please don't mock me."

"I didn't say anything, but I did hear the harrumph, and I thought it was you."

Both Mac and Ian had the identical thought in the same instant. As they turned to face each other, Mac turned out the headlamp. In the moment before the light disappeared, their eyes met, and in that instant, their mutual expressions conveyed the same silent message: *we are not alone.*

In the darkness, they slowly crept back to the chamber from whence they had just emerged. They paused and listened quietly without speaking for several minutes.

Finally, Ian whispered, "I didn't mention it to you and Liz earlier, but when I was down here before, I had the uneasy feeling that someone was following me. I'll bet the same person is tracking us now. Could it be the kidnappers? Surely they would do more than just follow us."

"Whoever it is, we need to press on. I suggest we resume the journey with the lamp on, as if nothing happened. Keep a few feet apart, and stay alert."

They scoured the chamber for tracks but found none. Whoever was following was exceptional at concealing their tracks. In contrast, the mule prints were quite clear, and even where other tunnels merged, the trail was simple to follow. Early on, they had come across some of the tracks Ian had made during his lightless journey back to the surface. Otherwise, they saw no other evidence of human or animal presence. Even so, they were keenly aware that the myriad side tunnels provided ample places for the kidnappers or others to conceal themselves.

"Since we can still see the tracks of the kidnappers, I presume they never expected us to find the cave and follow," said Ian. "And that's good news for us. We have the element of surprise, and by the look of the tracks, we're moving faster than they are. The mule must be slowing them down."

"Does it follow that since we can't see the tracks of whoever is following us that these people are not the kidnappers?" asked Mac.

"I don't know," answered Ian. "They might be accomplices of the kidnappers who purposely stayed behind to watch our movements."

About an hour later, another tunnel merged, and this one also had evidence of recent travel. Mac examined the tracks. "No mule prints, the same moccasin prints, and lots of wolf tracks. Ian, I'm sorry for doubting you about the wolves."

"That's okay," said Ian. "Nothing makes much sense down here." Ian bent down to look at the moccasin prints. "These moccasin prints look the same, but they're both fresh. How could that be? Is there one man or two men with similar moccasins?"

Mac checked out the prints with his magnifying glass before he responded. "Looks like the same person made the prints. Look at the wear on the left heel pad and the stitching mark on the inside edge of the right foot."

Mac let Ian look at the prints more closely while he explored down the new tunnel.

"Look here, Ian. It's obvious that the man with the worn left heel pad turned down this new tunnel and returned some time later. We are definitely following the same man."

Ian added, "Looks like the tracks that we followed from the hot spring were made first, presumably yesterday, and the second set is more recent, maybe only an hour or so old. One of the wolves must be much heavier than the others because the tracks are much deeper."

"Yes, I noticed that," replied Mac, "but why did the man turn down this tunnel?"

"I wonder where the new tunnel leads to," Ian said. "Perhaps he left to meet up with the wolves."

"I don't know the answer to this riddle, but I do know that we don't have time to check out the new tunnel. Both sets of prints go in the same direction. We need to keep going."

The two sets of prints were impossible but fortunately unnecessary to separate; the direction continued to remain obvious, and by about midnight they decided to stop and sleep for a few hours.

They ate and drank a small amount of their modest provisions. Mac set out trip lines attached to two metal cups to serve as an alarm, and then they settled against their packs. The ground was rough but the temperature warm, and they quickly fell into an exhausted sleep.

Mac had set his watch alarm for five hours, but as usual, his internal clock woke him five minutes before the alarm. He opened his eyes and looked around the blackness. Ian's slow, deep breaths sounded distinct and loud in the silence of the blackness. Mac wondered whether the loudness was courtesy of the acoustics of the chamber or because in the absence of vision, his other senses were enhanced.

Mac lifted his arm to look at his wristwatch and confirm the time. He was surprised at how much light the luminescent dial shed in the cavern. As he switched off the alarm, he heard a noise and immediately froze into a still and heightened awareness.

The noise was a crunch, as if someone had stepped on and crushed a tiny stone. Then he heard someone say a distinct "shush." The noises had come from the other side of the chamber, about twenty yards away. Mac rolled over and purposely made noise, yawned, and then paused and pricked up his ears. He distinctly heard the patter of footsteps as several individuals crept out of the chamber. Mac gave them a few minutes to escape before he turned on his carbide headlamp. All the trip lines were intact, but it was obvious the intruders had come within the perimeter of his alarm system.

Clearly they can see well in the dark, thought Mac. A quick search of the chamber revealed no clues, not a single track. *Whoever they are, they can move quickly and quietly without leaving a single trace. Spooky!*

He woke up Ian and explained about the visitors.

"Well, clearly they could have hurt us if they wanted to. Wonder who they are," Ian said.

"You know, Ian, maybe we're dealing with native Indians. They lived and traveled in this country before we did; they wear moccasins; and they are revered for their ability to move quietly without leaving tracks. Maybe an ancient tribe survives in these subterranean tunnels."

"Sounds reasonable, but why would they kidnap Kate?"

"I've been thinking about that. Maybe they need women to expand the tribe. Lots of tribes stole women from neighboring communities and incorporated them into their society."

"That's the best theory yet, actually the only theory, and it does fit with what we know. But whoever they are, why didn't they harm me when they had the chance? And why haven't they tried to interfere with our pursuit? That way there would be no witnesses, no one to go for help. They probably don't know about Liz."

"I don't know why they didn't harm you, but Liz noticed that the rope latch on the stables was gnawed and found wolf tracks by the gate. They obviously did not know and never expected that two more people were following you and Kate. In the past we've all journeyed together. I bet the wolves were trying to free the horses. With the horses free, you wouldn't have been able to get out for weeks or might have died of exposure before you reached the highway. By then the kidnappers' trail would have been very cold. They never expected anyone to find the cave entrance and presumed we would eventually give up looking and assume that some wild animal had killed and eaten Kate. A good plan, and it would have worked except for your great detective work and caving skills."

"And a helpful bluebird," added Ian. "Come to think of it, that theory would explain why the wolf prints disappeared around the pool. The Indians might have swept them clean to conceal any trace of their presence. The animals in this valley are certainly more than they seem. I guess the stories your grandfather told about talking bears are probably also true."

"I don't know about that—domesticated wolves and a raven are one thing, but talking bears? Gee, I don't know. That still seems far-fetched to me. What we do know for sure is that whoever kidnapped Kate wants to keep these caverns just as secret as we wanted to keep the valley. Maybe they're testing us. I just don't know. One thing is sure: they have the upper hand, and I recommend we work from the assumption that they know everything about us. I'm hoping the fact they haven't hurt us means they don't intend to hurt Kate. Gosh, I don't know; this all seems so surreal."

Mac paused, and the look on his face told Ian that he was wrestling with a decision. When Mac spoke again, there was an angry resolve to his words, though he spoke them quietly.

"I'm tired of wondering who is following us, and I want to lay a trap for them. We might as well bring this cat-and-mouse stuff to an end. I suggest we pretend to go to sleep again, and I'll prepare a little surprise for these quiet stalkers."

He explained his plan to Ian, and they turned the lamp out and pretended to go back to sleep. They didn't have to wait long. Within fifteen minutes, Ian's young ears heard the intruders return, and he gently touched Mac's leg. Mac understood and quietly pointed his digital camera, set on infrared, toward the intruders. The click of the shutter echoed through the chamber.

A moment later, Ian spoke. "No need to be quiet now. They left as soon as you pressed the button and they heard the click. Hopefully they don't realize that we're onto them. Did you get a good shot?"

Mac turned on his carbide headlamp, quickly scanned the chamber to confirm they were alone, and then brought up the infrared image.

Both Ian and Mac were speechless for a few moments after they looked at the digital image. The camera had captured the distinct outlines of two inquisitive-looking grizzly bears standing by the entrance to the next chamber.

"Good gracious!" Mac exclaimed. "Great-Grandpa was right. They are intelligent. The question is, are they friend or foe?"

"My bet is friend," offered Ian, "or at least not foe. I never saw a bear print with any of the wolf, raven, or human prints."

Before they could discuss the possibilities any further, they realized they were no longer alone, and they were in fact surrounded by bears, and not the curious-looking two they'd captured digitally, but surly-looking nine-foot grizzlies with four-inch claws.

Ian stepped apart from Mac, picked up his walking stick, smiled at the bear he thought was the likely leader, and tried to otherwise look as if he were asking directions from a stranger on a busy street corner.

The only movement the bear made was to stare at the hickory walking stick, which Ian prudently set down again before he spoke.

"Hi, can you help us? We're following some men who kidnapped my wife."

"Her name is Kate," interrupted Mac. "I'm her father."

The bears did not reply, and although they were definitely grizzlies, the most intimidating animals in the Canadian wilderness, they didn't look immediately threatening. Their eyes were wary but intelligent. The bears looked calm and as if they had nothing to fear, which in fact was the case.

Ian turned to Mac. "Maybe they don't speak," he said.

A moment later, one of the two bears Mac had photographed entered the chamber. The other bears separated deferentially as the grizzly walked upright toward Mac and extended a huge paw.

The rusty brown fur on his back blended to a dark chocolate on his legs and belly. The fur over his back, especially along the spine, had silver highlights, which together with the gray hair around his mouth suggested his maturity, although this was contrasted by youthful-looking blonde hair around his snout and ears, and his movements were certainly spry. The bear's eyes were small, dark, and bright and looked friendly.

"I believe your custom is to shake paws when you greet someone. Is this true?"

"Yes," said Mac, "of course, how silly of me. Where are my manners?" he muttered as he extended a hand, which was gently but firmly shaken by a hairy paw, the copper-tipped claws politely extended to minimize contact with Mac's skin.

"My name is Ursus, and I'm sorry about your daughter. I hope we can help."

"You speak English," marveled Mac.

"Yes, all bears are taught the surface language as young cubs."

"My grandfather said you spoke Icelandic."

"We do."

"Then my grandfather's stories were true!"

"Yes, and in fact I once saw your grandfather when I was a cub. I was with my father and we were eating berries. Your grandfather came so often that eventually we abandoned the valley."

Ursus paused to let Mac catch up with the incredible realization that Ursus was over a hundred years old and then went on. "Please, may I look at what you are holding, the device that detected me?"

"Of course, please do," responded Mac, who showed Ursus the infrared digital image.

A much younger bear, the second of the two captured in the digital image, jumped forward from behind the ring of bears. "Grandpa, may I see too? May I?" he asked, just before he stumbled and fell, almost crushing Ian, who fell back into the furry arms of another bear, who gently helped him back to standing.

"I'm so sorry," the young bear apologized as the skin beneath his facial hair blushed crimson. "I didn't mean to bump you, but I tripped over something."

Everyone looked behind the young bear to determine what he had tripped over, but the ground was flat and unobstructed; it was in fact the only portion of the cave floor that was smooth. The other bears nodded their heads knowingly.

Ursus interjected, "Ah, may I introduce my grandson Connor; he means well, but he's sometimes a bit clumsy. Connor, come shake paws with our new friends, and don't forget to lift your claws; human paws are more delicate than ours."

Connor was a younger image of Ursus. His rusty brown hair shimmered with the sheen of youth, like freshly budded spring leaves that glisten in the morning sun and haven't been stuffed full of chlorophyll, and the deep chocolate fur on his flanks had a rich velvety look. The strawberry-blonde fur around the edges of his ears was almost translucent in the light of the carbide lamp. His eyes were a handsome chestnut brown and sparkled with enthusiasm. His claws were mostly black and about an inch shorter than those of Ursus, with only a hint of copper emerging on the tips.

After the introductions were complete and Ursus had showed his infrared image to the bears, Mac quickly brought the conversation back to their quest.

"Yes," acknowledged Ursus, "we are well aware of your problem. Indeed, your problem is also ours, but be assured that even as we speak, our forces are tracking the men who have kidnapped your daughters."

"*Daughters*?" cried Mac. "No, not Liz too! That's impossible. Liz went back to the horses—she must be safe; please tell me Liz is safe."

The silence in the chamber and Ursus's somber expression were more telling than any words their new grizzly friend might have offered.

Ian interjected, "The second set of prints from the other tunnel—Liz must have been on the wolf we thought was heavier."

Ursus nodded and then walked over to Mac. The great grizzly put a furry arm around Mac and led him to a natural rock ledge. "We have every reason to believe that both your daughters are unharmed and that they will remain so. It is even possible one of our patrols will recapture them, but I don't want to raise your expectations. They have a good head start and are traveling fast. Even if we don't rescue them in the next few days, they will likely stay unharmed for quite some time to come. But there is great danger ahead and much you need to learn. If you feel up to listening, I will explain as much as I can."

Chapter 13
Sisters Reunited

Liz awoke on a bed in a room lit with a greenish glow that seemed to emanate from the walls. She heard Kate before she saw her and turned to the familiar voice of her sister. Her joy was cut short when she noted a sickly green pallor to Kate's skin. She was up and hugging her sister in a flash.

"Kate, are you all right? You don't look well!" exclaimed Liz.

"I'm fine; it's just the lighting. The walls are made of an iridescent green crystal, really weird but easy on the eyes and more than adequate to see with. The torches they use in the caverns are made of the same crystal."

Liz looked around and studied the walls. "The rocks look like they might be a kind of malachite, or some other similar copper-based mineral."

"Liz, is Dad okay? Have you seen Ian?"

Liz related Ian's story and told about her capture at the pool. "They were both well when I left them, and they were determined to rescue you. Since I never escaped to bring help that means either we must escape, or they will have to rescue us. Dad is a pretty good tracker, and I expect that Ian knows his stuff."

Liz continued, "Did the wolves carry you here as well? I never knew how much wolves stink; their hair is so coarse and hard it almost cuts, and while running, the ride was anything but smooth." She rubbed her bottom to confirm how unpleasant the trip had been.

"No," replied Kate. "I rode a mule and was drugged for the first part. Apart from being frightened, the trip was okay."

"Kate, let's compare what we know … Do you know where we are and why we were kidnapped?"

"I really don't know much. We're at a place called the Green Cavern, and I've been here for almost a day longer than you, and you've been here for only a few hours. Lord Null, the tall creepy guy who kidnapped you, also abducted me, and he's in charge. There was another man with him. His name is Lars, but I haven't seen him since they put me in this room."

Kate paused reflectively as she thought of Lars. "Lars was frightened of Lord Null, and with good reason. Null is one nasty guy. He did something to my knee that hurt like hell but didn't leave a mark. Lars was pretty simple and expected to be rewarded for helping, but there was something about the way Lord Null treated him that made me think otherwise. Null bullied and belittled Lars at every opportunity, and he knew that Lars hated him. Lord Null doesn't strike me as someone who is willing to leave a potential enemy alive to create later problems. My bet is that Lars was killed soon after I arrived. I don't think we'll see him again."

Kate paused for a moment as the words she'd just spoken sank in. She felt a mixture of emotions that included anger, a curious sadness that Lars was likely dead, and anxiety that she and Liz might suffer a similar fate. Liz was similarly taken aback by Kate's chilly assessment of Lars's fate.

"Yes," agreed Liz, "Lord Null is certainly one vicious thug. He must work for the princess the wolves spoke about. Do you know anything about her?"

"Not much. She was the one who ordered our capture. Lord Null seems to be in charge of everything, but he definitely defers to her. The wolves and ravens are part of her army."

"Yes," Liz interjected, "I was surrounded by wolves at the pool. And there was also a weird raven with red eyes."

"Yes, I saw that raven too. The ravens take messages to Princess Malicious."

"Kind of a nasty name for a princess, don't you think?"

"If the shoe fits," replied Kate.

"So, why were we kidnapped?"

"I don't know. They've treated me fairly well. I overheard Lord Null say that I was not to be harmed. I presume that applies to you too. Until Lord Null brought you, I hadn't seen anyone else. Wolves bring food and water. Some of the wolves speak our language. I believe they can all understand what we are saying. The ravens too. I think the raven with the creepy eyes might be able to read minds. I don't have any evidence of this, and you might think I'm crazy, but when that raven looked at me on that moonlit night, somehow I felt as if the bird were in my head."

"I don't think you're crazy. If wolves can talk, I can well imagine that ravens can read minds."

"The good news is that Princess Malicious has enemies. There is a King Bjorn, and he has an army that includes bears, and the wolves are frightened of the bears."

"So, Great-Grandpa's stories are true," said Liz. "I always believed in the grizzlies. Wonder what Dad will think. I hope Dad and Ian have picked up our trail. I might want to believe in the grizzlies, but I don't want to rely on them to save us."

Chapter 14

Alfred Brings the Right News

Alfred presumed he was arriving with good news this time and could almost taste the fresh human flesh he considered his just reward.

Gritty ash in the air from the volcano had been blowing in his face for the last several miles, which meant that some part of the crater was more active than usual, so Alfred was extra careful and circled to make an upwind approach. Less experienced messenger ravens often suffocated in the sulfur or chlorine clouds that periodically popped up from active vents, and the crater floor was littered with the bleached bones of those less careful birds.

Bluish white clouds of steam and gas emerged from fissures in a jet-black tephra plain that was pockmarked with tiny holes from which lava had previously bubbled to the surface. Now these pits spouted only fumaroles as pale reminders of more glorious molten moments. Yellow splashes of sulfur and green splatter trails of manganese attested to the fiery energy of nature's smelters. Some of the lava was soapy and had the consistency of olive oil, which cooled to form a slippery surface. The crater could definitely be a dangerous place.

Malicious impatiently watched Alfred as he circled toward her turret, still high in the smoke-filled sky. She willed him to look at her, and when their eyes connected, the memory energy she sucked from Alfred sapped his strength, and he lost flight control. After careening off a jagged cliff, he went into an uncontrolled spin toward the ground. At the last moment he managed to pull up, but he landed with a jolt into a recently active crater.

Alfred shrieked and jumped out of the tiny crater with his feet smoking and drawn up close under him. He landed gently on a cooler but slippery surface, and when he stamped his smoking feet a few times, they slid out beneath him, which caused him to flip over onto his back and then slip down toward the active crater. His red eyes widened until they almost seemed to touch as the fiery pit loomed beneath his sliding toes. He just barely managed to dig in a claw on the rim of the crater, roll over, and flutter into flight. After arranging a few bent feathers, he cautiously flew up to the window ledge.

"Alfred dear, you really must be more careful," said Princess Malicious. "Those rocks are very unforgiving. What would I do if you had a bad accident? There isn't another raven in the world as handsome as you."

Whether this was true or not, Alfred believed every word and held his beak high in a haughty manner, preening himself while the princess continued.

"What a good bird. Rest yourself, and afterward, I have a special treat I know you'll enjoy, someone I've been saving especially for you." She cackled, and some chains rattled against the castle wall.

Alfred looked over to see the same frightened little man, still desperate but unsuccessful in his attempts to free himself.

Too bad, thought Alfred, *he looks thinner.*

"Oh, and thank you for the especially good news. I always enjoy watching you fly. You are such a strong bird. When our eyes connected, I learned everything. You found the right woman this time, and you deserve a rich reward." Malicious stood up and started to walk toward the door. "Sorry I can't celebrate with you, but I have plans to make. I'll leave you to your just deserts."

She opened the door but kept talking as she started down the stairs. "Do clean up afterward, Alfred; you know how I hate a mess." The sound of her voice and the clicking of her metal toes faded down the stairway.

Alfred turned toward the man, some anticipatory spittle dripping from his beak. *Such a special meal deserves planning,* he decided. *Let me see … for the appetizer I think the eyes would be best; then I'll tear a hole in the cheek and sample some tasty tongue.*

"Yes," cawed Alfred, "definitely the eyes first," as he flew toward his cringing meal.

Chapter 15
Ursus Explains

The story Ursus told was too fantastic for Mac or Ian to truly comprehend, and many times, Ursus was forced to request that for the time being, until they had spoken with the king, they trust his word.

"King Bjorn is wise and kind and will explain the matter in a way that you will understand. I am but a simple bear and not so wise in human ways, but our race has served the king's family for over five centuries, and I trust King Bjorn as a friend and brother."

Mac had learned enough to know that Ursus was anything but a "simple" bear. Ursus had a quick mind and was clearly respected by all the bears. Humility was not something Mac had much personal experience with, and he generally mistrusted this attribute in others. He had a standard rejoinder to comments about humility: "humility is an attribute of the intellectually impoverished," or conversely, "humility in an intellectual is usually feigned and a sign of inherent hypocrisy." Afterward, Mac often added with a touch of scorn, "I detest hypocrisy." As such, Mac's first thought was that Ursus's comment was meant to disarm. A proverb came to mind: "the subtlest act is to set another before you." Notwithstanding these baser thoughts, Mac smiled at Ursus, which displayed his own brand of subtle hypocrisy. Before Mac could offer any verbal reply to Ursus's reassurances, Ian interjected.

"That is all well and fine," said Ian as he stood up to speak to the entire company of bears, "but our concern is for Kate and Liz, and I want to pursue their kidnappers. You say they have been taken to the Green Cavern and that they are safe, but you also say that we all face great danger. Then let us proceed to this place and rescue them."

Ursus smiled and sighed at the same time and motioned for Ian to sit back down. "Please know that as we speak, everything possible is being done and that now is not the time to confront the dark forces of Malicious. Her forces in that region heavily outnumber ours, and any attack would only lead to unnecessary loss of life and would perhaps give the enemy the momentum to turn the tide in their favor. Many in the Middle and Southern Realms remain undecided and await the result of the first major battle to decide which side to support. Those forces faithful to King Bjorn have been gathering, and our position grows stronger by the day. We know that war is inevitable, but we dare not risk a major battle until we are either sure of victory or forced to respond to a preemptive attack by Malicious. For now, our best hope is that one of our patrols will overtake and rescue them."

Again, Ian jumped up. "Well then, let's send another patrol. How many bears will come with us?"

"Let me go, Grandfather. I know the way," said Connor.

Ursus smiled and motioned for both Ian and Connor to sit down. "Ian, I respect your desire to strike out immediately, but the enemy has too much of a head start, and even if you were to reach the Green Cavern with a company of bears, you would be hopelessly outmatched. We know the Green Cavern is filled with wolves and southern soldiers still drunk with the exhilaration of victory. There are too many. You would not stand a chance.

"However, we know that Malicious will want Kate and Liz to be taken to her volcanic fortress in Popocatépetl, a city in the Middle Realm. We also know that Malicious is not one prone to hasty action; although Kate and Liz are under close guard in the Green Cavern, she will likely wait until her forces have secured the route south to her fortress. Malicious has gone to considerable trouble to capture Kate and Liz. They are clearly important for her evil plans, and they will be well protected both from harm and from rescue. As such, we have some time to plan a proper rescue."

"Well, if we don't pursue them, what are we to do?" asked Ian.

"We must travel to the Castle of Light, the capital of Asgard, the kingdom of the Northern Realm, where you can meet with King Bjorn and learn more. Perhaps you will be allowed to participate in the Althing that has been called to discuss the war."

"Althing?" asked Ian.

"Asgard is an open society. Although there has always been a monarch, the king or queen rules by the grace of the people. Althing is a forum for all the people to discuss important topics and to make decisions in the best interest of the entire kingdom."

As Ursus spoke, Mac nodded his head as if he knew about Althing.

Ian looked at Mac, hoping he would disagree with traveling to meet King Bjorn, but saw with disappointment and surprise that his father-in-law was nodding in agreement with Ursus.

"I have read about Althing," said Mac. "My understanding is that Althing refers to the first Icelandic government and dates back to the tenth century AD, when the first assembly was held at Thingvellir, a spectacular plain about thirty miles outside of Reykjavík, the capital. Iceland can boast they have the oldest national assembly in Europe."

Ursus nodded.

"Okay," affirmed Mac, "which way to the castle, and how long until we arrive?"

"We must head back toward the hot spring and then take one of the side passages north. The journey will take us the better part of a week."

"Back! A week! You mean we must travel away from Kate and Liz? You can't be serious!" Ian exclaimed. "And surely, going overland would be quicker."

"Yes, overland would be quicker, but that is not safe for us, and without King Bjorn's approval, I cannot allow you to return to the surface."

"You mean we're prisoners," snapped Ian.

Mac put his hand over Ian's, which had grasped the hilt of his knife. "Ian, they could have harmed us at any time, and they have never showed any tendency to violence, only to reasoned discussion. I agree with Ursus, and I trust his judgment. We must make the best of a bad situation. It's time to learn more, not to rush off against an enemy we know nothing about and that has already outsmarted us twice."

Chapter 16

Trapped Like Wolves

The journey to the Castle of Light took longer than expected. A company of wolves snapped at their rearguard and significantly slowed their progress. The wolves rarely attacked boldly or in the open but rather chose to lunge at stragglers in groups from high ground or dark recesses, and some grizzlies were slightly wounded.

Ian took his turn in the rearguard and learned quickly to avoid the frantic snapping of wolf teeth and to parry attacks with his knife. During one especially bold assault, Ian fought his way through a dozen wolves to assist two bear scouts who were attacked while returning to report. Ian heard the din and rushed back along the passage until he came upon the two bears fighting back-to-back against a seemingly never-ending stream of wolves.

Ian's knife was everywhere at once, and his arrival seemed to turn the tide. Wolf bodies littered his path to the bears, and by the time the enemy retreated to lick their wounds, Ian had earned the respect of his grizzly comrades. The feeling was mutual, and Ian now realized they would not have stood a chance trying to rescue Kate and Liz, with or without the bears.

A direct consequence of this mutual respect was an invitation for Ian and Mac to participate in the first morning strategy discussions. The bears carried detailed maps of the underground caverns. The maps had been prepared by the royal engineers and were better than any surface topographical maps Ian had ever used. They incorporated precise information on depth as well as direction and distance. Ian studied the maps and noticed several subterranean pools along their chosen route. The following morning, he shared an idea with the bears.

"Most wolves don't prefer deep water," advised Ian. "They swim only reluctantly. Have you ever watched a wolf take a drink from a river or lakeside? They put their snout in the water, but they otherwise lean back and look as if someone were pulling on their tail. After a quick slurp, they move away and keep a healthy distance from deep water. Mostly they prefer to drink from puddles or to lick water off leaves."

The bears nodded; they had noticed this as well.

"I presume your observation has a strategic purpose," said Koda, the leader of the bear squad. Koda was larger than most of the grizzlies, and his brown fur was so dark as to be almost black, which made him look even more imposing. His fur had faint silver highlights, especially over the shoulders. He had a golden patch of fur that formed a half moon on his chest, and all four paws including the nails were the same color. He indulged Ian and asked him to continue.

"The wolves are really slowing our progress," Ian said, "and we should deal with them. Why don't we plan an ambush by one of the pools? The water will limit their movements but not ours."

Koda liked the idea and asked Ian to outline his plan.

Ian pointed out a pool that seemed ideal. A little-used side tunnel offered a route to backtrack and secure a position behind the wolves and block any escape. With grizzlies ahead and behind, the wolves could be trapped and either killed in paw-to-paw combat or forced into the pool to drown. The bears nodded their approval of the plan.

When they reached the pool, Koda sent half the squad back south along the side tunnel while the remaining bears positioned themselves by the northern exit from the chosen cavern.

Wolves prefer the dark, and the sudden appearance of torches and the sounds of bears behind them brought fear into their ranks. Yelping their dismay, they fled forward. The first few wolves who ran into the pool chamber howled a warning when they found themselves surrounded by grizzlies, but their short-lived yowls served little value. Within a few minutes all the wolves were in the chamber, and the bears had control of both exits.

Sköll Wolf, the pack commander, realized they had run into a clever trap and issued orders to form a half-circle against the wall opposite the pool.

The bears fought their way along the wall and through the pack until they joined forces and formed a line that pressed the wolves toward the pool.

Knowing retreat was impossible, the wolves fought with courage that had already discounted death, and the bears found more than one worthy adversary in the dwindling pack. Several times a small group of wolves almost managed to break through the bear ranks and escape into the caverns, but in the end the wolves were no serious match for the grizzlies.

Slowly but surely, the wolves were pushed back to the edge of the pool, and after a few drowned in waters now pink with wolf blood, Koda ordered a pause and asked the wolf commander to surrender. Koda offered mercy instead of murder and compassion instead of killing. Though reasonable, Koda understood the ways of the wolves and how bitter this offer tasted to their predatory natures, and he was not surprised when they refused to yield. None in the remaining pack could envision imprisonment or relocation to a remote part of the kingdom, and as for a prisoner exchange, well, that would only mean a delayed and more terrible death. The wolves intuitively knew that Princess Malicious would kill them for cowardice. Better to die fighting than horribly at her hand.

After the offer to surrender was rejected, the battle was rejoined, and although the wolves continued to fight bravely and gave their lives dearly, the cavern floor ran red with wolf blood.

Only once did a bear seem threatened with serious injury. A dozen wolves managed to separate Connor from the main group. One after another, they attacked—one jumped on his back and gnawed at the nape of his neck; another sank his incisors into Connor's flank; two wrestled with each leg; and the rest circled and looked for a chance at his soft and vulnerable throat or abdomen.

Connor roared and twisted his body to throw off the wolves; he flailed the wolves about, but their tightly locked jaws never loosened. Blood streamed and matted in his fur and gave him a wet and worn appearance.

When Ian looked up, having just dispatched a mangy wolf who had fought him face-to-face while standing on his hind legs, he spotted Connor and feared the worst for the young bear. But just when several more wolves seemed ready to lunge, Ian heard a sound resonate from Connor, a rumble like the growing sound of something powerful, primordial, and pent up, and that rumble resounded as an impatient roar. Ian could feel the menace in the sound, and so could the wolves, who paused to reconsider their quarry. Their fate, however, was already sealed.

Connor flung himself into the pool and sank deep beneath the surface. The water whirled and bubbled first in one place and then another. The course of the underwater battle was clearly marked by a pink froth that whipped back and forth across the surface. First one, then a second, then a third, and finally a fourth and fifth wolf floated to the surface. Then Connor emerged, with a sixth wolf limp in his giant jaws.

Connor dropped the lifeless body in the pool and then shook off the water, first from his head, then from his neck and shoulders, and finally from the rest of his body, in progressive massive shudders. The spray was like a fountain, and it dowsed Ian and Koda, who had arrived simultaneously to offer assistance.

"Wolves sure don't taste good," said Connor, who seemed totally nonplussed. "Salmon is much better."

The battle continued, and the bears continued to press forward until only Sköll Wolf, purposely spared, was left alive and snarling at the water's edge.

"You have fought honorably, wolf," said Koda. "Wolves were never meant to fight bears, and our wounds speak well for your dead comrades. There is no need for you to die. What shall I call you, leader of such brave wolves?"

"I am Sköll Wolf, descended from mighty Fenrir Wolf who ate the hand of Tyr. My ancestors served Odin and the other gods, and I will not humiliate their memories with surrender."

Sköll Wolf paced along the edge of the water, and his words came as snarls between barred teeth. "I will die honorably in battle, or I will escape to fight again. I do not fear either the red-eyed princess or any bear and certainly no man," growled Sköll Wolf as he looked directly at Ian. "No, I would rather die honorably in battle than surrender."

Koda was impressed with Sköll Wolf's speech and quietly instructed his bears to battle sufficiently to wound the wolf, but not fatally, and then allow him to escape with the illusion that he had done so on his own merit.

Whether Sköll Wolf believed that his escape was courtesy of his skill, blind luck, or Koda's mercy could not be determined, but when the way along the edge of the pool looked clear, he seized the opportunity and escaped in a flash.

About five minutes later, a howl was heard from within the tunnels where Sköll Wolf had escaped, and the baying continued unabated for several minutes. The sounds waxed and waned like a mournful melody, and everyone knew that the wolf commander was grieving for his lost pack. Several of the bears growled in response, but their growls were those of respect for a worthy warrior and not those of disdain for a conquered foe.

Koda thanked his bears for their valor and asked them to carry the wolf bodies to the nearest place on the surface and bury them in a common grave. "They died with honor and deserve our respect," remarked Koda. Koda also thanked Ian for his part in the fight. Ian had served in the thick of the battle.

Mac, who deplored violence of any kind, had observed the fighting from a raised shelf where he sat with Ursus, who though a fighter of some renown in his youth, believed like Mac that war was a plague.

Thereafter, the journey to the Castle of Light was trouble-free, and the bears hailed Ian not only as a mighty warrior but also as a sound military strategist.

Chapter 17
Prince Eirik

"Eirik, dear brother and future king, how are you today?" inquired Malicious in a sweetly solicitous tone.

"Wonderful, Malicious, but have you heard from Father? It seems like weeks since his last message. You know the Southern Realm has revolted, and some dark lord is gathering an army to attack our forces. Don't you think we should be in more regular contact with Father? Your volcanic fortress here at Popocatépetl is ideally situated to block the gathering enemy. Surely there are plans we should be making."

Ah, Eirik, my hopeless little brother, thought Malicious. *You've always been too nice and innocent by far. It was always "Isn't Eirik such a helpful and devoted son?" or "My, what a charming brother you have, Malicious." Well, now they'll pay attention to me. And imagine what they now think of you, Eirik. Some believe you've joined me. Poor little brother, you never understood how much I hated you. And now it's too late. Yes, Eirik, my fortress is ideally situated, but not to block the enemy, rather to facilitate my ascension to the throne, with or without you as a puppet figurehead.*

In the few moments during which these thoughts swirled in Malicious's mind, she never stopped smiling, and her deceitful reply was calculated to please Eirik's ear. "Yes, Eirik, you are absolutely correct, and even as we speak, our armies are converging to stop the rebel forces." She paused to smile at Eirik. When he remained silent, she continued. "You and Father are so close. You must have sensed that we received another royal communiqué. Just a few hours ago, a messenger eagle brought word from Father. In light of the growing threat, he has decided to move up the date of your coronation. He announced at the Althing that your marriage will take place on the day of the autumn solstice and that immediately afterward you will be crowned king and assume command of the Royal Forces. He is counting on you to lead our warriors to victory against the dark lord."

"Who is this dark lord?" asked Eirik. "I know you've told me many times, but I can never seem to remember his name. This sleeping sickness has confounded my senses. I am so forgetful. Please tell me again, Malicious—who is this person who would dare attack our kingdom?"

Yes, Eirik, thought Malicious, *you don't know the name, but that is not because you are forgetful, but rather because I have never told you. How could I? You never would have believed that the "dark lord" could be a woman, much less your sister.*

"Eirik, I am so concerned about you. You must rest. There will be more than enough time to answer all your questions once you have recovered."

"But will I recover?" asked Eirik. "This dratted sleeping sickness leaves me feeling so drained. Do you really think I am getting better?"

"Absolutely, Eirik! Why, you were awake for most of yesterday and spent the day teaching the young warriors swordsmanship. None could master your skill or match your energy. I would say that you are only days away from full recovery, a week at most."

"I cannot remember the swordplay, but more to the point, I cannot fathom how I could have wielded a sword. The illness has sapped my strength as well as my memory. Even so, I am happy to hear of swordplay, for this confirms that I must be on the mend."

"Yes, dear brother, but even so, your illness has been long and painful, and now it is time for you to rest. Don't worry about not remembering the swordplay. Forgetfulness can be a kindness. Aren't you glad that you don't remember the pain during the early part of your illness? It was quite awful. If you don't rest, you might experience a relapse. Don't forget, Father is counting on you. I've promised him that I would take special care of you, and I don't want to disappoint Father anymore than you do."

Malicious held out a parchment, as if the document were a message from their father. "This is the royal communiqué from Father. As usual, he has requested that you read and then destroy the message. There are spies everywhere."

Eirik took the parchment and began to unroll the document, but before he could start, Malicious interrupted him.

"Eirik, before you read the communiqué, let me have a quick look at you. I must check your palms, tongue, and eyes. As a royal healer, I must examine you at least once every day to follow the progress of your sleeping sickness."

"Of course, Malicious," replied Eirik.

Eirik extended his hands and turned his palms up. Malicious took each hand in turn and scrutinized the palms.

"Very good," she said. "The temperature and color are definitely improved. Swordplay must agree with you."

Eirik beamed at the good news.

"Now, let me see your tongue."

Eirik opened his mouth and stuck his tongue straight out.

"Umm," replied Malicious. "Your tongue is quite wet and a bit too furry. I will ask the cook to adjust your evening meal."

"Is that a sign of relapse?" inquired Eirik, as his eyes furrowed into worry.

"Oh no, I'm just paying attention to details. Perhaps you didn't finish your breakfast this morning."

"Well, I don't rightly remember whether I ate or not. In fact I can't remember the last time I ate. But I'm sure you could check with the royal attendants. They will know."

"What a good suggestion. I will do exactly that," replied Malicious. "Now, I always save the best part for last."

Eirik understood and focused his eyes on his sister's. The moment their eyes met, Eirik slumped back into the chair, and his still-open eyes became dull and vacant as if all thought had disappeared. His mouth gaped in imbecilic fashion. Even though his head fell back as he slumped, his eyes drifted down and continued to be drawn inexorably to hers. Malicious paced neurotically in front of Eirik as she spoke, but she never broke eye contact. Wherever she moved, Eirik's head moved robotically so that his eyes tracked hers.

"That's very good, Eirik. Each session is easier. There was a time when you resisted, when you had some power to oppose me, but that time is long gone. Now, you are no longer Prince Eirik, heir to the throne; now you are merely the younger brother of Princess Malicious, soon to be Queen of Asgard.

"Eirik, listen carefully. Your bride has been found. The prophecy has come true. A young surface woman appeared at a sacred hot spring during summer, when there was both a full moon and dancing lights in the northern sky. Her family is the Icelandic-speaking family who have visited the valley for the last century. Clearly, she is the one."

With a placid smile and dreamy eyes, Eirik asked, "Is her hair blonde?"

Malicious hesitated for a moment. "Yes, her hair is blonde, and her name is Katherine."

"Where is she? Can I see her now?"

"Soon, Eirik, but for now, you may see her only in your dreams. Look deep into my eyes, and I will show you how beautiful she is."

Eirik looked but could not see the image of Katherine, and his failure caused him to fidget.

"Sit still, Eirik," Malicious commanded in a loud and curt tone. "Concentrate. Look into my eyes."

Eirik obeyed, and after a few seconds he could see Kate. She appeared out of a red mist. Eirik could see both Kate and Liz. They were sitting together and talking. Although he could not hear what they said, their facial expressions suggested a troubling topic.

"Oh, she is pretty," offered Eirik with slowly slurred words, his eyes still glued to Malicious, "but so is the other woman with the brown hair—at least I think the color is brown; the mist makes it so hard to tell, especially in the green light. Are they sisters? They look like they might be. They don't seem happy. Who is the other woman with the brown hair? She is very beautiful and has an especially strong-willed and spirited manner."

Malicious broke eye contact, and Eirik's eyelids shut like curtains abruptly closed; his head slumped forward, and his chin thumped onto his chest.

"Yes, Eirik, your would-be bride is pretty, and so for that matter is her sister. They will arrive soon, but whether you live to marry will depend on whether my forces are victorious when they attack Father's warriors. If my forces are triumphant, there will be no need for sorcery, and the only realm where you might rule will be Valhalla."

Chapter 18

Differences in Faith

The bears had an uncanny ability to navigate the complicated passages, even in pitch-dark caverns, but unless stealth was important, they used torches, and the way was usually well lit.

At the outset of the journey, Mac had noted that each bear carried a torch to help light the way, but increasingly, fewer and fewer torches were necessary to sustain a comfortable amount of light, and he could not understand why.

Periodically, they passed through caverns brilliantly lit from overhead shafts. The well-lit caverns always included an underground reservoir and had obviously been developed into rest stops. There were stone benches carved into the walls and stalagmites transformed into tables. There were also natural ledges evident around some of the underground pools.

At one rest stop, Mac walked around a pool on a natural ledge that was several feet wide and at least a foot deep. The ledge extended right down to the surface of the water. At one time, thousands of years in the past, the water level had been as high as the top of the ledge. The ledge had formed when calcite crystals accreted on the surface and along the walls of the cavern. As the water level slowly fell, the ledge had become progressively wider and thicker.

Mac also came upon dry caverns with ledges created at a time when there had obviously been water. In these dry caverns, there were lines on the walls where the color had changed dramatically to a much darker shade. Mac recognized these color changes as watermarks that demarcated high-water levels in bygone times. The stalagmites in these caverns often had light beige tips, which changed to darker shades of brown below the past high-water marks, which meant that over time the caverns had cycled through water-filled and dry phases. These caverns usually had fine dirt floors, which were the remnants of silt and mud, and other telltale signs of the past presence of water. Now, however, many of the caverns were bone dry, and the only water was from the vapor in the breath of the travelers.

Mac asked Ursus whether the caverns had ever been filled with water during his lifetime.

"No, neither during my life nor that of my father," replied Ursus, "but centuries ago, some of these caverns were water-filled. The royal engineers found ways to divert the water and drain the caverns so they could become part of our underground road system. Every few years, during prolonged and heavy surface rainstorms, some of the caverns flood. None of the caverns with a history of flooding are inhabited."

Some of the caverns showed evidence of previous inhabitation, often by successive generations, and a few had primitive wall murals. In one such cavern, Mac examined the art of an ancient artist. The two-dimensional figure of a bear was clearly old, possibly the art of a native Indian and likely drawn several thousand years before King Bjorn's people arrived. The picture had been stippled into the rock face with a blunt object and depicted three men hunting a giant bear with bows and arrows. The long concave snout, small ears, and shoulder hump, and the traces of a brown color painted into the stippled areas suggested a grizzly. The men were unrealistically smaller than the size of the bear's foot, a disproportion that clearly underscored the artist's respect for the power of the animal. The feet were turned sidewise and showed five claws. Five animals with backswept horns were traveling in the opposite direction of the bear. Mac thought they looked like bighorn sheep. On the floor of the cavern, proximal to the cave art, was a tall stone covered in runes. The runes were carved about half an inch deep into the stone and ran together without any interruption around the periphery. Different colored pigments imbedded in the runes demarcated sentences.

Mac asked about the cave art and runic inscription. Ursus confirmed that the picture had been created long before King Bjorn's people had arrived and at a time when bears still lived on the surface with the native peoples. The runic inscription had been commissioned by one of King Bjorn's ancestors to commemorate the art. Ursus translated the runic inscription for Mac.

"Do all bears read and write the runes?"

"Yes. Ever since the time of Kodiak, every cub has been taught to write the runes."

"Doesn't it bother you that this inscription commemorates the hunting of a bear?"

"No, although these people hunted bears for our meat and fur, they had great respect for us."

"Yes," agreed Mac. "Respect for your culture is common in all the native cultures in the northern part of our world. Do you know the story of the stars we call the Big Dipper?" he asked Ursus.

"Not by that name at least," replied Ursus. "Please tell me."

"Well, the Big Dipper is also called Ursus Major, or the Great Bear. The bottom two stars in the vessel portion represent the front and back legs of the bear, and the top two stars are the head and the base of the tail. Depending on the myth, the handle depicts a stretched tail or pursuing hunters. During the daily journey of the constellation around the pole star, the bear shifts from a four-footed stance to a two-footed one and then back again. Each season, the position of the constellation in the midnight sky depicts the behavior of bears. In early spring, the constellation is head up, as with a bear emerging from the den; in midsummer, upright like a feeding bear; at the end of autumn, head down as if to enter the den; and through the winter, asleep on the back."

"Ah," replied Ursus, "yes, I am familiar with a variation of that story. Sadly, since we spend so little time on the surface and no longer commonly watch the stars, we no longer share these stories with our cubs … Have you ever considered how similar bears are to humans? Like you, we walk upright on two feet, with our front limbs hanging at the side. We also walk on the soles of our feet, rather than on the toes like many other animals, and our footprints show a distinct heel and arch and toes. We can rotate our forearm at the elbow, and we can pick up small objects with our paws."

"Yes," agreed Mac, "and like human families, bear families show great care and concern for their young. And also like us, bears are omnivores and eat varied and healthy foods according to their needs. In fact, I'd say that a bear diet puts most modern human diets to shame. The native Indians were fascinated by how similar their diet was to that of the bears. Both ate mostly vegetarian foods. The native Indians regularly found the grizzlies eating from the same berry bushes that they did and digging for the same tubers that they sought. Grizzlies hunted the same deer and elk, and during spawning season, the bears collected at the same rivers as the Indians to catch the salmon and trout. It's no wonder so many native Indian myths portray the bear as human."

"Yes," agreed Ursus, "and bears are exceptionally intelligent and wily in the ways of the woods. Many native Indians chose to hunt bears only early in the spring, before our ancestors had emerged from their dens. The Indians stalked our ancestors in the late fall to identify the dens and then returned in the spring and attacked while our forefathers were still hibernating—a cowardly tactic. Fortunately, the Indians managed to find the dens of only less careful bears; to avoid detection, our ancestors routinely laid false trails to typical den sites and then backtracked to occupy a more secure winter home. A standard strategy was to walk up to a false den site, go in, and then leave, stepping carefully in their own tracks for up to a hundred yards or more; then they would leap far to the side of the trail before continuing on to the true den."

Mac related some of the stories about his grandfather and the bears in the valley.

"Well then," replied Ursus, "finding us should not have been such a surprise."

"I guess not," responded Mac," but we have a saying, 'seeing is believing,' and until we met, I was never convinced that my grandfather's stories were true."

"Really!" replied Ursus. "I accepted everything that my father said as true, just as he did of his father. For a grizzly this acceptance is a matter of faith."

Mac wondered at this statement. As a young man he had been taught, and now as a scientist and professor he lectured, that no statement was exempt from the test of scientific scrutiny. At first he considered challenging Ursus's statement, but then he paused. Ursus had used the word *faith*. Mac had learned to be cautious around people who used this word. Science was not the final word for people with faith. He had few if any friends with faith and usually avoided conversations with these people. Mac didn't think he knew enough about Ursus to debate the point, and he decided not to follow up on the grizzly's statement.

By now, the main route had been cleared of dangerous stalactites and stalagmites, treacherous holes had been filled, and the paths had been made as level as the finest surface roads.

Courtesy of the natural light from the overhead shafts, the caverns offered a kaleidoscope of color Mac had never dreamed might exist so deep in the earth. Some of the walls had natural designs and colors that rivaled the art in museums. The most fantastic natural murals had been purposely highlighted with strategically placed overhead shafts of light. It was clear to Mac that these sections had been purposely left untouched, to preserve the natural beauty. The more he saw, the more he realized that the bears and King Bjorn's people were part of a cultured and sophisticated civilization.

Mac also noted that the tunnel walls had been polished to a high gloss, which reflected the natural light. *Perhaps that is why fewer torches are required,* he thought. "Who built the overhead shafts that permit sunlight to illuminate some of the caverns?" Mac asked Ursus.

"King Bjorn's people are wonderful engineers," replied Ursus. "Over the years they have brought the miracle of sunlight to the underground." Ursus spoke with obvious pride about Bjorn's ancestors and waited for an acknowledging look or comment from Mac. When none was forthcoming, Ursus elaborated. "For many centuries the royal engineers have carved out shafts to surface locations precisely chosen to admit the maximal amount of sunlight. The light is transmitted through a series of specially placed crystals that capture and focus the sunlight toward the cavern, where other crystals diffuse the light as it enters. Over the years, the royal engineers have learned to position the crystals such that even some of the smallest recesses are illuminated. The engineering in the major caverns was accomplished long before the time of King Bjorn. During his reign, the royal engineers have continued the work to bring light to the minor passages and caverns. Someday, torches will be necessary only at night."

"The overhead light doesn't feel warm," said Mac. "I would have thought that focused sunlight from the surface would be very hot, enough even to burn."

"Yes, quite true," replied Ursus. "Closer to the surface, some of the heat from the light is allowed to penetrate and warm up the tunnels, especially in the northern regions. However, at this depth, where the ambient temperature would otherwise be high, the engineers employ a special cooling rock that moderates the temperature."

With that comment, Ursus motioned to Mac to look at the wall. "Put your hand on one of those dull-looking stones," he suggested as he pointed a paw toward a triangular sheet of grayish stone set into the wall.

Mac felt the stone and then the cavern wall. "The stone is much cooler," he acknowledged. Mac removed his magnifying glass from his pack and inspected the surface. He found a wrinkled surface layer that reminded him of lichen. He tried to scratch off a sample.

"Please don't do that?" asked Ursus. "If you pick off the top layer, the stones won't be able to stay cool."

"That is very clever. It looks as if there is a kind of plant growing on the surface. What is the stone made of?"

"Made of?" replied Ursus, a little perplexed. "Why, the stone is made of what it is."

"Oh," said Mac. "That's right, but what I meant was what do you call the stone?"

"Oh," replied Ursus. "It's called coolstone."

"That makes sense," replied Mac. "I guess you call it that because the stone makes the room cooler. But why does it do that?"

Ursus did not reply to this statement and looked a little bewildered, as if the answer to Mac's question should have been self-evident.

Mac elaborated. "Do the royal engineers know why coolstone absorbs heat, or why the plant likes to grow on the stone, and do you have a classification system for minerals?"

"The plant grows on the surface of the stone because this was meant to be. The plant does not exist except upon the stone, and yet the plant appears as soon as the stone is exposed from the underlying rock. Without the plant, the stone is warm to the touch and has no power. Together, the stone and the plant are alive; separate, they are lifeless. Clearly the joining was meant to be. Together, they are coolstone. That is what they are. They are alive but different from you or me. They are not a bear or a man. They are coolstone. They are here by the grace of the God of All Creatures," responded Ursus, who looked pleased with his comment and smiled at Mac as he finished.

"That's ludicrous," said Mac, who responded abruptly and with an impolite glibness. "The plant is alive, I'll grant you that, but the stone is inanimate and serves only as a platform for the plant. This has nothing to do with any god. This is science, pure and simple."

"Ouch," responded Ursus, who saw that his comments had touched a sensitive point with his new friend. Ursus knew that strong words often concealed ignorance or fear. "I'm sorry, Mac. I didn't mean to upset you. Everyone is free to believe what he or she will. For my part I can only share my personal understanding of the world."

Mac felt bad that he had spoken so rashly, especially considering how considerately Ursus had responded. However, abruptness was a feature of the adversarial scientific world that Mac lived in. In the academic community few apologized for such outbursts. Thick skin was a prerequisite for academic advancement, and Mac's hide was thicker than most. He had achieved the rank of department head at the precocious age of forty. He was considered brilliant in his field and well read outside his areas of expertise. For the last decade few colleagues had dared disagree with him. When they did, they had suffered the lashings of Mac's intellectual tongue, and few made the same mistake twice. Mac's pride was well developed, and he rarely apologized. Even so, he felt as though he should apologize to Ursus, but he was too inexperienced to find the correct words. Instead, he changed the subject back to light.

"The overhead lighting projects explain the light in the well-lit caverns, but why are your bears using fewer torches today than yesterday?"

"You are observant," responded Ursus, who relaxed with the new question, "but I don't want to spoil your surprise. All I will say is that the number of torches is related to how far we are from King Bjorn's castle and to what extent the tunnel walls have been polished."

The several days' journey to the castle offered further opportunity for Mac and Ursus to talk. It was clear that both wanted to nurture the seeds of friendship, although initially there seemed precious little common soil for anything to take root.

Becoming good friends was an easier project for Connor and Ian. Initially, they were attracted to each other by the shared bravado of youth. Neither took himself too seriously or labored under the heavy thoughts of life. Fighting side-by-side and tasting the blood of a common enemy had forged a brotherly bond. They became fast friends, and their playful banter along the road was enjoyed by almost everyone.

There were many times, though, when Ian walked in sad silence. Connor understood and gave his new friend space and time to meditate. During these moments, Ian tried to sort through the incredible events of the prior week and to make some sense of why Kate and Liz had been kidnapped. Ursus had revealed much about the imminent war and the personalities on both sides of the conflict, but he had provided no information that helped Ian understand what Kate and Liz had to do with the whole affair. *Why Kate and Liz?* he kept asking himself.

During one of these brooding sessions, Connor interrupted Ian. "Hey, Ian, what do you call the big silver birds in the sky? We see them from time to time when we collect berries on the surface."

Ian laughed. "Planes, you mean. Planes are the modern equivalent of the mules you use to carry supplies, only they carry a lot more and move a lot faster." Ian thought back to the maps he had looked at during the morning strategy sessions. "They can fly from the Castle of Light to Malicious's castle in only six or so hours."

"Wow, that's about 3,000 miles and would take us at least a month," replied Connor. "Individually, the fastest bears can travel only about sixty miles a day along the underground trail system, and the best relay runners can achieve only 250 miles a day." Connor was silent for a moment and then continued incredulously. "Three thousand miles in a day. I don't think the golden eagles can fly that fast. We use eagles to fly important messages on the surface. Eagles are very smart, though not like bears, of course—nothing is smarter than a grizzly; no offense to humans, but everyone knows that bears are not only the most powerful but also the most intelligent animals."

"If that is the case," replied Ian, "then how come bears haven't built any planes?"

"That's simple," replied Connor. "Planes can't fly underground."

Ian laughed but had to admit the logic was sound.

While Connor paused and tried to fathom the idea that a plane flew so fast, Ian took the opportunity to ask the question that pressed most upon his troubled mind.

"Connor, why did they kidnap Kate and Liz?"

Connor responded without thinking. "One of the women is meant to be the wife of Prince Eirik." As soon as Connor spoke, his eyes opened wide, he pursed his lips, and he looked around with a guilty and worried expression. He seemed relieved that no one else had heard his glib remark.

"Oh no," said Connor. "I wasn't supposed to tell. Grandpa specifically asked me not to. You won't tell him I did, will you?"

Before Connor could continue, Ian exploded in disbelief. "Prince Eirik's wife! That's ridiculous. Kate is my wife, and Liz will choose her own husband. You don't know what you're talking about."

Connor blushed pink with embarrassment and apologized again for the untimely truth. "I know, I know, it isn't really right, but it has been foretold for centuries that a surface woman would be the bride of the prince in the millennium year. Grandpa says it helps keep the royal family healthy to choose outside the kingdom. I don't really understand that part; it's a human thing. Bears only choose from among their own, you see, and I don't really like the idea, but I'm not a man. And well, I am really sorry to be the one to tell you, but I don't really know why they have Liz, because she's not blonde and the tradition is that a blonde one will be chosen … so you see, Kate is supposed to be our new queen, and I like you and can understand, sort of, how awful it must be to give up your wife, but you see, that's the prophecy and—"

Ian didn't give Connor a chance to babble on further. "Prophecy be damned!" shouted Ian so loud that some of the other bears turned to look.

"Shush," said Connor, with a paw over his mouth. "We'll both get in trouble."

"Trouble?" yelled Ian. "You're absolutely right about that. You bet there'll be trouble. Big trouble. This is crazy."

"Please, Ian, don't listen to me. Wait and talk with King Bjorn; he is a wise man, and I know he will find a way to solve this problem. And my grandfather will help too. I know he feels just as bad as I do. You'll see; he'll help. But please don't tell anyone I told you."

"Okay," replied Ian, who settled from a shouting to a seething anger, "but only because there's nothing else I can do for now. I'll wait and find out what King Bjorn says, but if what you say is true, Eirik might just as well be dead—because he'll never marry Kate while I live, and I'll kill him and anyone else who tries to take her away from me."

The anger in Ian's eyes startled Connor, whose blush of embarrassment gave way to an ashen pallor; he feared for the lives of both his new friend Ian and his old pal Eirik.

Chapter 19
Castle of Light

Fossils were prevalent in the walls and rocks of many of the caverns, especially those that contained subterranean pools, and Mac saw evidence of both familiar and unknown prehistoric creatures. During a rest stop he noticed a wall filled with trilobites. Thousands of the tiny creatures must have died suddenly during some cataclysmic incident. A later geologic event had caused the horizontal deathbed to be conveniently thrown into vertical relief for travelers to witness. Mac excitedly pointed out the fossils to Ian, who shared his enthusiasm.

Connor, who was with Ian, remarked casually, "Grandpa Ursus says those are the carvings of animals that the God of All Creatures thought of making, but decided not to."

"But they did exist," replied Ian. Mac nodded.

For a second Connor looked perplexed by this dissenting opinion. His furry eyebrows furrowed. Then his eyes brightened, and he nodded his head as if he had accepted that it was possible for the two views to coexist. He smiled and shrugged, neither agreed nor disagreed, and amiably suggested they talk with Ursus if they wanted to pursue the subject.

When Ursus happened by, Mac asked him about the trilobites.

"Beautiful, aren't they?" responded Ursus. "I often wonder why the God of All Creatures never allowed them to live. They look a bit like beetles."

"But they did exist," replied Mac. "These are the fossilized remains of creatures that lived millions of years ago."

Ursus replied, "To me they look like carvings or models of what might have been, not what was. How can you know that these creatures were alive at that time?"

Mac explained that the mud around the living trilobites had been bombarded by cosmic rays that had created unstable isotopes of beryllium and aluminum. "These isotopes decay at a known rate and can be measured," Mac expounded. "The mud continued to accumulate unstable isotopes until buried by an earth movement. Thereafter, the cosmic bombardment was interrupted, but the isotopic delay continued. So in this manner we can determine to within a hundred thousand years or so when the trilobites lived and died." Mac seemed especially proud to impart this information and looked to Ursus for some sense of appreciation. For Mac the gift of knowledge was precious.

Ursus, for his part, had stopped hearing much after the phrase "isotopes of beryllium." Thereafter, he had courteously smiled and tried to offer the appearance at least of interest if not understanding. His response, however, certainly wasn't the blanket acceptance that Mac might have hoped for.

"Have you ever seen one of these creatures alive?" asked Ursus.

"No. Trilobites have been extinct for a hundred million years. No one has seen them alive."

"That is my point," said Ursus. The God of All Creatures thought about making them but decided not to after carving some preliminary models."

The comment astounded Mac. This was the second time that Ursus had proffered a naive interpretation of a scientific fact that was as obvious to Mac as the tip of his nose.

"Why, then, would your god make so many models?" replied Mac with more than a touch of smugness. "I've seen trilobites all over the world and in every mountain range."

"I would never presume to fathom the mysteries of the God of All Creatures," answered Ursus.

Mac bristled at the response.

Ursus could see that Mac was intent on pursuing this topic and that unless he agreed with Mac, a satisfactory resolution was unlikely. Fortunately, Koda happened by, and when he asked to speak with Ursus, the conversation was conveniently terminated.

Soon thereafter, the natural light in the tunnel was such that no torches were needed, and the level of excitement in the bear squad palpably increased.

"What's up?" asked Mac, who noticed the exuberant atmosphere.

"King Bjorn's castle is just over the next rise," replied Ursus.

"Ah yes," said Mac, "we've been climbing for miles, and I have noticed the intensifying glow ahead, almost as if the sun were coming up over the top of the next hill. That must be the city lights," he said. "The polished walls really transmit the available light. Asgard's capital must be an especially well-lit city, and together with the polished walls, that must be the reason the bears don't need as many torches."

"Yes," agreed Ursus, "the Castle of Light is an enlightened city in more ways than one."

Moments later, Mac and Ian were on a ridge high above the city, witness to a breathtaking view. The Castle of Light was really a city carved out of the center of a mountain that extended for several miles in every direction. For the first few moments the radiance from the city was almost blinding.

There was an extensive central plaza with many surrounding buildings. A castle was at one end of the plaza and looked across at an oval building, built in a style architecturally similar to the castle, but obviously of more recent construction.

Many small bridges linked roads and canals that crisscrossed the city, and even from a distance, Mac could appreciate that tens of thousands of busy bears and people lived and worked in this amazing underground city.

The city was lit with various kinds of light. The principle source of light was natural and emerged from overhead shafts similar to those Mac had seen in the smaller caverns. However, the roads and canals were independently lit and shone with a soft yellow hue. To Mac, it looked as if the roads and canals were paved with yellow iridescent rocks. A green light similar to that of the torches glowed from inside the buildings.

"What happens during the night?" asked Mac.

"The buildings, roads, and canals remain well lit with the green and yellow lights," answered Ursus, "but the city is otherwise only dimly illuminated from above by the available moon and starlight. The roads and canals were built with a light-emitting crystal mined at the base of an extinct volcano not too far from here.

"King Bjorn's father built a school dedicated to the exploration of the various light-emitting crystals in our world. Much progress has been made. Many different light-emitting minerals have been found.

Unfortunately, not all of them emit a safe light. Sometimes the light causes people and bears to throw up and develop unexplained bleeding."

"Oh no!" said Mac. "Those minerals were probably radioactive."

"Pardon me?" said Ursus.

Before Mac could answer, Ian asked a question. "Where does the water come from?"

Ursus pointed out a waterfall that emerged from the cavern wall below them. The waterfall supplied the river that ran around the city and through the canals within. Drawbridges allowed access through towered gates at multiple points. A lake at the foot of the waterfall was filled with sailing ships.

"That probably explains the reduced flow in the waterfall where we stabled the horses—and also the dry gorge we walked down," exclaimed Ian. "The surface water was diverted into the mountain, wasn't it?"

"Yes," agreed Ursus. "There are many surface waterfalls that have less water now. King Bjorn's people are truly remarkable engineers, aren't they?"

They climbed down stairs carved out of the cavern walls. Each step was broad, and the central portions were worn down and polished smooth from millions of steps over hundreds of years.

The steps took them back and forth across the wall of the cavern and crossed under the waterfall at several points before finally emerging beneath the cascading water, just before the torrent plunged into the lake.

The first time they passed under a waterfall, Koda called a halt, and Mac and Ian watched while all the bears retired to a side cave to empty their bladders. When Connor returned, Ian asked him about the communal voiding behavior.

"What was that all about? Some kind of end-of-journey ritual?"

"No," Connor said with a laugh. "It's just the way bears are. Every time we hear the sound of rushing water we feel the need to pee."

"That's weird," replied Ian.

"Not really. My grandfather says bears are more in tune with their bodies than humans. The bladder is an exceptionally emotional organ and very sensitive to suggestion. Also, most bears drink when they come upon running water, and it makes sense to empty the bladder to provide room for the new urine. My grandfather also says that if young boys paid more attention to their bladder, they wouldn't wet their beds as much."

"That's interesting. I never feel like peeing when I hear rushing water, and I used to wet my bed, until I was about twelve."

"So there it is," replied Connor as he lifted his paw in the air to acknowledge this confirmation of his explanation.

They continued to climb down to the Castle of Light, and each time they passed the waterfall, the sound was loud, but nothing compared to the deafening roar at the bottom, where the waterfall churned up the water and drove a mist high in the air.

"This is Franang's Falls, and the water at the base is called Hymir's Cauldron," said Ursus.

"Good name," replied Mac. "It does look like boiling water."

As they walked along the lake, Ian saw salmon jumping in the rapids leading up to the waterfall. A keen fisherman, Ian recognized the spawning shapes and colors of sockeye, chinook, and coho salmon. The sockeye with their distinctive brilliant red bodies and green heads were slightly smaller than the brownish-red, almost black coho and a lot smaller than the olive-brown chinook. The males with their humped backs and hooked jaws were easy to distinguish from the females with their bellies swollen with eggs. With each jump and twist, the round scales flashed like tiny rainbows in the spray and then disappeared back into the frothing water.

"Where do the salmon go?" asked Ian.

"Behind the waterfall is a subterranean river that continues up to the surface. Fortunately for the bear community, diverting the water from the surface didn't confuse the salmon. Each summer and autumn, they continue to migrate and to spawn in the surface streams and lakes where they were born."

Ian watched some young bears learning to catch salmon. They ran back and forth in the shallows, chasing the fish and finally pouncing. The young bears only rarely came up with a fish, while their mother-teachers were successful more often than not. The mother bears were very adept at pinning a salmon down with their forelegs and then grabbing the fish in their mouths.

Connor could see that Ian was interested. "It's all in the paw-eye coordination," said Connor. "All it takes is practice—hours and hours, mind you, but once you have the knack, it's not so difficult. I could teach you, if you like."

"No, thanks," said Ian, "but fresh salmon sounds great for dinner. I thought bears caught the fish in their teeth?"

"Sometimes, but for that technique to work, the salmon must be swarming up the falls in great numbers, and catching a fish in your mouth usually requires more luck and patience than skill. It is far more efficient to grab them under a paw."

Numerous bears were cleaning the salmon caught that day, and they were happy to share some of their catch with Connor. From the reception Connor had with the young cubs, it was clear that he was a popular grizzly.

While Connor was obtaining some fish for supper, Ian observed young cubs returning salmon skeletons to the river. When Connor returned, Ian asked why the cubs did this.

"The salmon is a very powerful animal," replied Connor. "Some salmon swim thousands of miles to spawn. We admire the wisdom of the salmon, their knowledge of how to find their home. They are an important food for us. Returning the bones of the salmon to the river is our way of paying respect to this great fish. By returning the skeletal spirit to the river, we hope the fish will return again. The extra work involved is also a reminder not to take more salmon than we need to survive."

Ian had also observed that bears on the shore separated the skin, brain, and eyes from the rest of the salmon. "Do they throw out everything but the meat?" he asked.

"No, we don't throw anything away, and if we did, it would be the meat," replied Connor.

"Really?" said Ian. "But the meat is the best part."

"Perhaps for a man, but for a grizzly, the skin, brain, and eyes are the best parts. We save the meat for King Bjorn's people. We would only eat the meat if we had nothing else. If men ate the brains and eyes of the salmon, they would be smarter."

"I don't understand," Ian said.

"By eating the brain, eyes, and skin, grizzlies transfer the power of the salmon into their bodies. Of all the forest animals, grizzlies are renowned for their ability to find their way home or to past feeding spots, which comes from eating the brain. We have excellent intuition, which comes from eating the eyes, and we can stay warm in the cold glacial water, which comes from eating the skin."

"Oh," said Ian, who was sympathetic but skeptical of his friend's theory. "I thought maybe you were going to tell me that it had something to do with the fatty acid content of neural tissue."

"Huh?" said Connor.

"Nothing," said Ian with a laugh, "just some science that Kate shared with me … Do bears only eat salmon?"

"Gosh no," replied Connor. "We mainly eat roots and berries. Young cubs are taught to recognize hundreds of different plant varieties and the best season to harvest them. Bears know a lot more than humans about the plants in the forest. We also eat insects."

"Yeah, I know," replied Ian. "Kate told me about the moths."

Connor motioned for Ian to look over at a mother bear with two cubs on a grassy river bar. Ian watched while the grizzly mother used a paw to turn over a boulder that four men could not have budged. Her twin cubs immediately pounced on the beetles and other insects that scurried away. One of the cubs chased a cricket into the river. The cub was soon over his head, and Ian worried he might drown. However, the mother was there in a flash and gently took the whole head of the cub in her mouth and carried him back to safety.

"Wow," remarked Ian, "she was powerful enough to move that huge rock and yet gentle enough to carry her cub in her tooth-filled mouth. Clearly there is a lot about bears I need to learn."

Connor laughed.

The lake was filled with the sailing ships Mac had seen from high above, and now he could appreciate the finer details of their construction. The hull of each boat was built with overlapping planks that followed a massive keel with separate bow and stern pieces, which curved up and were fashioned from single pieces of wood.

Some of the prows had figureheads shaped like a dragon. The ships had a partially enclosed deck with sets of oars. Brightly colored shields hung at the gunwales. Each boat sported a square, gaff-rigged sail that was also brightly colored.

"Those look like longships," remarked Mac, "the ancient ships used by the Vikings."

"Well, that makes sense," replied Ursus. "They are Viking ships, built by the descendants of Icelandic people who settled here almost a thousand years ago."

Mac could not decide which was more incredible—their first view of the Castle of Light or Ursus's statement.

The road beside the lake was well traveled with people and bears. They passed small communities where bears and people lived and worked side-by-side.

"Did you ever think that one day you might visit a community of bears?" asked Ursus.

"Until now, no," replied Mac.

"We never considered the possibility either until about five hundred years ago. Until then, bears mostly mistrusted men and refused to cooperate with them."

"Based on how I've seen men treat bears in my world, that was a prudent position to take," responded Mac.

This statement obviously pleased Ursus. "Yes, after all, it was mistreatment by men on the surface that originally led bears to settle the underground caverns. King Bjorn's ancestors were mostly respectful of bears, but it took five centuries for real trust to develop. Finally, thanks to the leadership of the great grizzly Kodiak, a peace was established, and our peoples have grown closer and more interdependent ever since."

Mac noticed an island in the center of the lake that was barren apart from some old tumbledown walls that looked as if they had once been the foundation of a large building.

"Doesn't anyone live on that island?" asked Mac.

"No," replied Ursus. "That is Lyngvi. In the old days, the island was a prison for men who broke the laws of the land, but for many years we have lived in peace and prosperity, and there has been no need for a jail. The walls were dismantled centuries ago, and the island remains uninhabited as a reminder of the loneliness that comes from intolerance, greed, and jealousy."

When they arrived at the main plaza within the walls of the castle, the bear squad disbanded, and Ursus and Connor led Mac and Ian to the parliament, which was located in the oval building that faced the castle across the plaza. Inside was a covered amphitheater, with seating for about a thousand people, which served as the public forum for the open society governed by King Bjorn.

Althing was convened in the amphitheater when they arrived. King Bjorn sat alone in one of two thrones at one end of the oval chamber. Two smaller and empty chairs were set back and to the side of the thrones. Mac saw Ursus look sadly at the empty throne and chairs and heard his barely perceptible sigh.

The thrones were simple but sturdy and showed the signs of both wear and care. The seats and armrests had thinned as a result of centuries of daily use. The majesty of the thrones was due mainly to those who sat in them rather than to any ornate aspect of their design. The thrones were neither inlaid with gems nor plated with any precious metal, but master craftsmen had carved designs and runes in the backs, and the wood had been rubbed and protected with natural oils such that in areas where there was no wear, the thrones still looked newly carved and polished.

The animal designs on the backs of the thrones were carved in Jelling art style, characteristic of Viking art at the time King's Bjorn's ancestors had settled Asgard. The animals depicted showed heads in profile with open jaws, a curious curlicue or fold to the upper lip, and a long pigtail. The bodies were S-shaped and ribbonlike, with a ladder pattern running along them.

The walls behind the thrones were adorned with large woven tapestries that depicted the history of Asgard. The borders of the tapestries had geometric motifs.

Ursus, Mac, Connor, and Ian sat and observed the proceedings. King Bjorn listened patiently to representatives from the seven clans of Asgard who had gathered to offer counsel. The king seemed drawn and tired as he responded to a tall woman with thick black hair pleated to her waist.

Helga was a revered leader, and her attendants and their banners displayed the salmon insignia of the Kwakiutl clan. She wore a supple leather blouse, which was over-sewn with thousands of overlapping squares of mother of pearl cut from the inside mantles of oyster shells. The squares were heavy to wear but exceptionally well suited to turn or resist the blade of an arrow or knife. At her side, she carried a broad sword with a solid black argillite-inlaid hilt that was carved to fit two interlocking hands, so that she could wield the sword two-handed. The guard of her hilt was carved in the shape of an orca on one side and an eagle on the other.

"Thank you, Helga," offered King Bjorn with great sincerity, "for your wise advice and courageous support, which will not be forgotten. With leaders such as you, I am confident that we will put these dark times behind us." But even as he finished these rousing words, a sigh escaped from his lips, and those closest knew the king was troubled.

Even though Mac and Ian sat on seats far above the king, every word was as clear as if King Bjorn were speaking next to them.

"I'm impressed with the acoustics," said Ian.

"It's the oval shape of the amphitheater," replied Mac. "The king is sitting at the focal point of a parabola."

"Pardon me?" said Ursus.

Mac explained the acoustic theory of a parabola while Ursus listened politely. Mac felt pleased as he finished his mini-lecture. He was aware that Ursus might not agree, and so he offered up his most pleasant smile as he concluded.

To Ursus the smile seemed conceited and the explanation presumptuous. He decided not to respond.

Mac, however, would not let the subject go. "Doesn't that make sense to you?" he asked Ursus.

Ian could see what was happening; he had seen his father-in-law in action before. Although he had never personally suffered the sting of Mac's intellectual vanity, he had seen many otherwise well-meaning individuals derided by his father-in-law's vitriol. He motioned to Connor, and they stepped out of earshot.

Ursus still didn't respond but pointed out other architectural aspects of the amphitheater.

Mac was not used to having someone ignore his questions. He persisted. "The parabolic theory was described by Appolonius several thousand years ago, well before the time of the Vikings. Have you not heard of this theory?"

"No," replied Ursus, who hoped the monosyllabic reply would dissuade Mac from further discussion on this topic.

This was not to be. Mac was like an obnoxious toddler who wouldn't stop pestering his sibling. "Then I expect that you have another theory to explain how well we can hear the king."

Ursus's response was accompanied by a tiny sigh. "In my view, we can hear the king because this parliament and the throne are sacred symbols of the independence enjoyed by our peoples. We believe in the freedom of speech. Words spoken in this room are so empowered and therefore travel freely such that all can hear. Statements within these halls, however much they might disagree with those of the king, are always welcome."

Mac believed in freedom of speech, but his innate arrogance more often than not stifled this liberty among those in his company. He was not practiced in polite discourse and felt a bit humbled by Ursus, who demonstrated a kindness and consideration that, although foreign, somehow seemed correct. This time Mac managed an apology of sorts.

"Of course. Forgive me. I have a tendency to push a subject along sometimes. I'm not always right, of course. Thank you for sharing your ideas."

Ursus smiled. The attempted apology, however vain, was not lost on him. *Perhaps there is hope,* he thought.

Mac's pride required a hasty retreat from this apology, and he changed the subject. "Are the empty throne and the chairs for other members of the royal family?"

"Yes," responded Ursus, obviously pleased with the new direction in their conversation. "Their absence is due to a double misfortune that has struck King Bjorn in the last year."

"Sadly, Queen Freyja died, some believe by poison meant for the king. Just afterward, Princess Malicious disappeared, and most believe it was she who poisoned her mother, although the official version is that the assassin was a disgruntled southern warlord. Eventually, we learned that Malicious had returned to her volcanic fortress in Popocatépetl, a city in the Middle Realm, and that the Southern Realm had declared war with King Bjorn. Most believe Malicious disappeared to nurture the seeds of war and to secure alliances between the various southern warlords. The Southern Realm has not enjoyed the same prosperity as the Northern Realm. Envy has simmered for centuries in the courts of some of the southern warlords.

"Malicious has made no secret of her ambition to succeed her father, but a thousand years of tradition are difficult to lay aside, and her self-serving claim to the throne was meaningless so long as Prince Eirik lived. The second family tragedy occurred a month ago when Prince Eirik disappeared.

"Those loyal to Malicious believe that the prince has joined his half-sister and that he intends to marry her, so that together they will rule as king and queen, but I for one do not believe this," said Ursus.

"Eirik and Connor grew up together. Eirik was like another grandson. He would never betray his father. I suspect he was kidnapped by Malicious and is either dead or under one of her evil spells.

"The Middle Realm where Malicious makes her home is a backward place. Those bears who have visited Popocatépetl report that the pervading scent is that of corruption. Many of the king's people call this place Niflheim, the world of the dead. Malicious has a castle in the caldera of the volcano that sits above Popocatépetl, and some believe this is also the residence of Hel, the hideous female monster who presides over the dead."

After a short pause and a silent prayer, Ursus went on. "These royal misfortunes have aged King Bjorn and brought great sadness to his life. According to tradition, Eirik was to marry and become king during this year."

"What's so special about this year?" asked Mac.

As Ursus answered, Ian and Connor rejoined them. "Well, this year is the conjunction of several special events. First and foremost, the year marks the 1,000th anniversary of the arrival of King Balder and his people to this land. Additionally, Prince Eirik turned thirty this year, the traditional age when the crown is passed to the firstborn son. Finally, this is the 500th anniversary of the alliance between King Bjorn's ancestors, the grizzlies, and the seven clans of the Northern Realm. Sadly, the peace that has reigned in the Northern Realm for five centuries will not survive another year."

"So," Ian said, "Eirik was meant to marry, become king, and then peacefully rule over the kingdom, and he would have, but for his jealous sister and a lot of envious warlords she managed to recruit."

Ian's tone was quite sarcastic and drew the surprised gaze of Mac and Ursus.

"Rough luck for Eirik," empathized Ian with false sincerity, "and who was to be his bride?"

"Ah," responded Ursus, "I think I understand." He purposely did not look at Ian, but in a sincere manner he said, "I think it best that King Bjorn explain that part of the story. Royal inheritance is a complicated matter."

Much to Ursus's relief, the Althing had just adjourned, and this allowed an opportunity to change the subject and introduce Mac and

Ian to King Bjorn. "Oh, look—perhaps we might speak with the king. Quick, let's hurry down."

As they approached the king, Ian was surprised by his height. Ian had always considered himself a tall man, but he was several inches shorter than King Bjorn. The king was many years older but looked very fit. He had reddish-blond hair and a full beard to match. His hair was long and gathered at the back with a woven braid of leather, and his beard was neatly trimmed. He wore a sleeveless shirt and trousers, both covered with a tunic. The shirt was died blue with woad, a plant pigment, and buttoned at the neck with a white quartz bead. Over the tunic he wore a cloak that covered one half of his body, but allowed his sword hand to be free. Both the tunic and cloak were edged with tablet-woven braids with interwoven silver thread. A large trefoil-shaped brooch, cast in silver with an intricate design of three gripping beasts, held the cape together at his shoulder. On his right arm he wore an arm ring that depicted two animals facing each other over the gap in the bracelet. The arm ring was fashioned from rods of silver that had been twisted together. When the king smiled, Ian noted a silver tooth.

King Bjorn was most gracious and invited Mac and Ian to dine with him. "Ursus, old friend, please join us. I always benefit from your wise counsel, and in these troubled times, somehow I see clearer just for your presence."

A meal awaited them in the dining hall, and the table was set for five. They enjoyed rye bread, oat porridge, cold herring-like fish, a dish of cabbages and onions, and a dish of berries and hazelnuts.

The hot porridge was served in soapstone bowls. Mac recognized the utility of soapstone for this purpose and turned to comment to King Bjorn. "I guess you use steatite for these bowls because this mineral retains the heat so well."

"Yes, although we call the rock *hotstone*," replied the king.

Mac thought of Ursus's comments on coolstone and suddenly became concerned that he had inadvertently raised a contentious issue, but apparently, he needn't have worried.

King Bjorn went on. "These bowls are precious because of that quality. My ancestors brought bowls made from hotstone found in Norway, but those bowls have long since broken. Deposits are uncommon in Asgard. The hotstone from which these bowls were fashioned was found along the fjords close to Haida."

They were offered a sweet drink that tasted like beer mixed with honey. For glasses they used cattle horns. Drinking from a horn was not as easy as it looked. It was necessary to drink the entire horn at once since the receptacle could not be put down like a glass. Mac found that the first trickle quickly turned into a tidal wave, and with his initial attempt, a few ounces overflowed through his beard and down his face onto his shirt. Ian laughed heartily until he tried to drink and similarly doused his clothing. Mac reciprocated with an equally robust laugh, and these antics effectively relaxed the evening into an informal affair.

King Bjorn smiled. "I apologize, I should have warned you. Drinking from a horn is an art that takes time to master. We should have offered you bowls or cups."

"No problem. Thank you for inviting us to your table. I will, however, accept your offer of a cup. What do you call this drink?" asked Mac.

"Mead," replied Bjorn. "Don't drink too much, or your head will feel heavy."

Thereafter Mac drank from a silver cup on which stylized images of animals were carved. The heads of the animals, in profile with open jaws, sported a long pigtail. The body of each animal was S-shaped and encircled the cup.

The cabbage and onions and the berries and hazelnuts were served in fluted silver bowls with similar stylized animals around the edges. Some of the bowls were engraved with a combat motif that depicted animals and snakes biting one another.

The dining hall was filled with statues of more than thirty past kings of Asgard. Each statue was carved from a different mineral, and all were polished to a luster that represented hundreds of hours of labor for the favored artisan of the time. Four bear statues were also present. Beside each human statue was a circular shield. Each shield was divided in quarters and was inscribed with poems and songs about the accomplishments of that king.

King Bjorn explained that the statues were arranged around the hall in chronological order and that the first statue was that of King Balder, the leader of the Icelandic expedition that had settled the kingdom.

"How was it that the Icelanders chose an underground settlement?" queried Mac. "Why didn't they choose a surface location?"

"Perhaps this might be a good time to tell the Saga of Balder," advised Ursus.

"Wonderful idea," replied King Bjorn. "I have not told the Saga of Balder for years, not since my children were young. Every cub and child hears and learns this story from his or her parents. It is our founding story."

Chapter 20
The Saga of Balder

And so King Bjorn began recounting the tale:

A thousand years ago, Balder, fourth son of Eirik the Red, set sail for a new world that had been discovered several decades before by Bjarni Herjolfsson. Bjarni had been blown off course while sailing from Iceland to Greenland and had sighted a land to the west that was flat and covered in woods. The new land was clearly not Greenland, where Bjarni's parents had settled with Eirik the Red. Although he did not land, he reported his discovery. It was Leif, Eirik's first son, who explored the new land. Leif and his two brothers, Thorstein and Thorvald, made numerous visits to the new world, and over the course of about a decade, they discovered and landed in Helluland (Rock Slab Land), Markland (Forest Land), and Vinland (Wine Land).

Balder planned to settle Vinland, a fertile land where his brother Leif had built a small outpost. Leif had built three longhouses on the northernmost tip of a large island that commanded the entrance to a huge gulf of water, which allowed passage deep into the new land. Leif gave permission for Balder to use these shelters until he found and settled his own land.

Vinland was a lush place compared to Iceland and Greenland. Leif reported dense forests of balsam fir, poplar, and larch. Leif also found grapes, butternuts, maples, wild rice, and grains. The temperature was so warm that the cattle could graze on green grass all winter. As such, Vinland was considered a potentially excellent place to settle. The only problem was the Skraelings, the native peoples. On one expedition, the Skraelings killed Thorvald, the second son of Eirik the Red, with an arrow with a quartzite tip.

As the fourth son of Eirik, Balder would inherit neither title nor land. Exploration and settlement of a new land was the only way for Balder to achieve the fame and fortune that his older brother Leif would inherit by birthright. Many natural resources were available in Vinland and Markland, which Balder hoped to sell or trade in Iceland. There were vast forests that could be cut to provide timber to build ships. The trees of Iceland had long since been cut, and good timber would fetch a good price in silver. Iron could be dug from the ground in Markland. The iron was close to the surface and of better quality than the bog iron available in Iceland and as such could also be sold for a handsome profit. Walrus ivory and caribou antlers were valuable and not obtainable in Iceland. Walrus hide could be made into strong ship rope. Animal fur and eiderdown were readily available and easy to transport and could also be sold or traded. The new land clearly promised significant commercial opportunity for Balder and his people.

Like his father, Balder did not accept Christianity, a new religion that had been made law in Iceland around the same time that Vinland had been discovered. Balder wanted to find a place where he could practice his birth religion. So Balder and his people set out for the new world to seek their fame and fortune and also to build a life where they could practice the religion of their ancestors. Although all were hardy and adventurous folk, none could possibly have foretold the results of their expedition.

They knew the hazards of the journey. A decade before, when Balder's father Eirik had set out to settle Greenland, twenty-five ships had embarked from Iceland, but only fourteen completed the journey. The North Atlantic was not a forgiving place.

Icelandic peoples are known for boundless curiosity, extreme bravery, clannish loyalty, generosity, and discipline, all exceptionally good attributes for those who would sail in uncovered ships, in largely unknown seas, to a foreign land.

After much preparation, 360 men, women, and children, together with all their worldly possessions, set sail on the day of the summer solstice, the longest day of the year. They chose this auspicious date not only because of the extended hours of sunlight but also to avoid icebergs, which were most frequent in the fall, winter, and spring months.

Five ships embarked from Iceland. Three were oceangoing cargo ships called knörrs, and two were longships similar to those you saw in Lake Asgard. The three knörrs were large, wide-bodied, sturdy ships, with a deep draft; a cargo hold amidships, with decking and oar ports only in the fore and aft parts; and a firmly seated mast that was designed to be unstepped only rarely. The cargo hold contained the livestock and supplies. Knörrs were well suited to ocean sailing; the wide, deep shape tended to minimize lateral movement in the wind. The ships were about fifty-five feet long by fourteen feet wide. The planks for the ships came from oak trees harvested in Norway; the nails were from bog iron smelted in Iceland; and the sails were made of wadmal, a wool cloth fashioned from the long hairs of Icelandic sheep. The wool was not washed, which preserved sufficient natural lanolin to ensure the sails were resistant to water. A beitiáss or tacking boom was used to hold the leading edge of the sail taut, which allowed the boat to sail as close to wind as otherwise possible.

The two langskip-warships were longer, sleeker vessels and carried a crew of about eighty men with their armament and some supplies. They had continuous full-length decking, a full outfit of oars, and an easily unstepped mast. When the men rowed, the mast was routinely unstepped to reduce wind resistance and improve stability. The warships were less suited to ocean sailing and required more rowing to stay on course. Each warship was divided laterally into thirty-two tiny compartments with oars for sixty-four men. These ships were about ninety-five feet long by about fifteen feet wide. The ships were steered by a single starboard-attached rudder that was balanced and could be raised quickly in shallow water by unlashing an upper fastening and moving the rudder about an external pivot. The prow and stern of each longship were adorned with the head and tail of a dragon, respectively. The dragonhead on the prow of Balder's ship was so well carved that the individual scales and teeth of the beast were visible for several ship lengths. The prow had previously adorned his father's warship and was considered especially lucky.

The royal shipwrights built the ships you saw in the lake around the castle to be identical to those sailed by Balder. The radially split planks for the sides were cut from sound and straight oak trees. About eleven oak trees, three feet in diameter and sixteen feet long, were required for each ship, as well as a sixty-foot pine tree for the mast.

The keels, selected from the hearts of perfectly straight oak trees, without any knots, and the T-shaped beams were carved with axes. The keels were built two-hands deeper amidships than the stern and prow, to provide stability. Angled pieces of the transverse frames were precisely cut from that portion of the oak where a major root joined the trunk. Long portions of the frames were cut from curved trunks and branches, as were the stem- and sternposts. Using single pieces of wood ensured remarkable sturdiness but did not limit the natural flexibility of a tree. Straked sides were fashioned from twelve sets of overlapping oak planks, which were secured by iron nails and which were narrow enough to allow graceful curves at the prow and stern. As necessary, the planks were scarfed from several pieces to make up the length of the hull. Planking was pared to the thickness of two fingers, which allowed for flexibility of the hulls in rough seas. The top line of the planking in the longships in Lake Asgard has the same distinctive shape as the ships of our ancestors; the sheerline, or top line of planking, is higher at the ends than amidships. The planks were caulked with tarred animal hair. Even so, the ships leaked considerably, and there was always a person assigned to bailing. The oars were made of varying lengths to match their station in the ship.

Like Balder's ships, those in Lake Asgard have a single square sail that can be set against the wind with a beitiáss. The standard rigging is a forestay, two shrouds, and a backstay. The sails on the ships in Lake Asgard serve only as a reminder of our seafaring past, because there is negligible wind underground.

Balder and his people set sail with favorable winds and sighted the coast of Greenland within the first week. Balder believed that the rapid and safe first stage of their journey augured well for the expedition.

They put ashore at Brattahild, his father's farm in Eiriksfjord, to visit with his family and to replenish water and food supplies. Eirik the Red was pleased to see his son and felt proud that he was embarking on such an important adventure.

Balder was following in some of his father's footsteps since Eirik had discovered and settled Greenland. Balder, however, had quite a different personality from his father. Eirik was renowned as an ill-tempered and aggressive fellow, and his nickname "the Red" derived as much from his fiery personality as from his curly red hair and beard. Eirik had been banned from his native Norway for an unjustified killing and, upon sailing to Iceland, had continued to solve problems with violence. After several killings over a commercial dispute, the Althing banned him from Iceland for three years. Eirik's adventurous spirit turned the punishment into opportunity. He sailed west and discovered Greenland, where he established two permanent settlements.

Brattahild was well chosen as a settlement for Eirik's family and followers. The settlement was at the end of Eiriksfjord and was sufficiently inland to escape the cold foggy weather and icy waters of the outer coast. During summer, the fjord was free of icebergs, which were a constant menace to the ships. The settlement was located on a lush plain through which a glacier-fed, freshwater river coursed to the fjord. The luxurious grasses and dense stands of dwarf willow and birch made the settlement a paradise compared to most of Greenland, which was otherwise barren and composed of rock and ice, with little potential for farming or grazing animals. The verdant lushness of the sheltered fjord was what justified Eirik's choice for the name of the new land he discovered.

Brattahild was also an excellent place for Balder and his crew to replenish their provisions. The sea was teeming with Arctic char, there were so many birds on the shores that Balder's people could hardly walk without stepping on nests, and caribou were plentiful in the mountain valleys.

They caught the Arctic char with nets and then salted and stored the fish in barrels. Great auks were common and easy to catch, and the meat was similarly salted. The fjord was home to dozens of different bird species. Puffins were abundant. They flew erratic flight paths and made belly-flop landings that looked comical. Their clown-like faces with brilliant orange triangular bills, together with their similarly colored feet, made them easy to spot, especially against the dark-colored rocks by the seashore. Although solitary at sea, they nested in colonies, and their eggs were easy to gather. In the alpine meadows, they killed and butchered several dozen caribou for the next stage of their journey. They kept the antlers to fashion into combs and cooking utensils. They also collected the feathers from hundreds of eider ducks to provide warm down for the quilts and clothing they would need during the coming winter.

The weather remained clement and the game plentiful, and they spent an enjoyable week socializing and replenishing supplies. The only unpleasant aspect of their stay at Brattahild was exposure to the ongoing argument about Christianity between Eirik and Thjodhild, his wife. Balder's mother had accepted Christianity and wanted Eirik to build a church in the settlement. Eirik was loath to do this. Although Balder disagreed with his mother, she had one argument that Eirik found difficult to refute.

"Our religion already has many gods. What is one more?" argued Thjodhild. "Let us add Christ as one of the gods we will pray to and build a church in His honor."

Balder could tell that his father would eventually give into his mother's wishes. Since Balder and his people did not believe in Christianity, they stayed out of the discussions and were glad when they left to continue their journey to a home where this argument would not arise.

Favorable winds continued, and after setting sail, they continued to make good progress until they passed beyond the sight of Greenland. As if this were the boundary of their good fortune, the wind disappeared, and they were becalmed. In this region the prevailing current and winds both flowed northwest along the coast of Greenland. As such, they struggled to row southeast in the direction of Vinland, but the following day a fog enveloped them, and since they were unable to take any bearings, they drifted for several days. A strong wind followed the fog, and they raised their sails, but a dense, overcast sky prevented them from determining the precise direction they were sailing. The wind was warm and wet, and in this region such winds usually came from the south, so they used their beitiáss, a wooden spar, to hold the leading edge of the sails taught, so that they might sail as close to the wind as possible. They sailed for six days and nights without any sight of the sun or stars. The sky was so dense with clouds that not even the sun-seeking feldspar that they brought from Iceland helped them to fix a sighting. Several times, they heard seabirds, which made them believe they were close to land, but the only solid objects they sighted were small blocks of ice, tiny icebergs, which they saw with increasing frequency, and which led Balder to believe they were sailing north rather than south.

Having not seen the sun or stars for a week, and therefore unable to take a bearing on their position, most of Balder's people considered themselves *hafvilla,* or lost at sea.

The presence of icebergs was an ominous sign; even a small iceberg could sink a ship. There were constant watches, and increasingly, the men had to row around tiny but threatening bergs, and Balder's people grew more inclined to give up their journey to Vinland.

On the morning of the seventh day, a new wind blew away the cloud and fog, and they were able to take a reckoning with the stars, which confirmed they had been blown far into the north. The fresh wind that brought the stars and sun was from the east, and Balder considered this a favorable sign.

They followed the wind for seven days, during which time they passed several barren islands larger than Iceland, but none that looked habitable. This land was thought to be Hellulund or Rock Slab Land, discovered by Thorvald, Balder's ill-fated older brother; it was considerably to the north of Markland or Forest Land, the land with tall spruce and iron ore deposits discovered by Thorstein, the third son of Eirik the Red.

The wind during the week was fickle and finally disappeared completely, and again they found themselves becalmed. Balder held a council of all the men and women on the five ships. Some wanted to row back toward Greenland and either return to Iceland or renew their journey toward Vinland. Others believed that the gods had purposely commanded the winds to blow them to their current position and that they were meant to continue west in search of habitable land.

None had seen anything but ice for a week, and all knew that the summer season in the land of snow and ice was preciously short. Balder was one of those who believed their destiny lay ahead, and he spoke strongly for the ships to continue, but he realized he was in the minority, and most of his people wanted to return. Thus, Balder was loath to put the decision to a quick vote.

The discussion lasted the better part of a day. As was the custom, a vote could not take place until every man and woman had been offered the chance to speak. Hrolf, Balder's cousin and second in command, was the most outspoken and influential of those who wanted to return. Over the course of the day, it was clear that more and more supported Hrolf than Balder. Finally, when every man and woman had spoken, and with nothing more to be said, Hrolf called the vote, and Balder resigned himself to returning.

But this was not to be, for just as Hrolf cast the first vote to return, the longship was attacked. A giant red eye the size of a shield appeared over the gunwale and was accompanied by a long tentacle that wrapped around Hrolf. The creature spat out a black inky substance that spattered over all those closest to Hrolf. A second later, the slimy creature disappeared beneath the icy waters with the unlucky Hrolf flailing unsuccessfully with his sword. It all happened so quickly that for several moments, the entire assembly sat stunned, silent and speechless.

ZM

Balder knew the creature to be a kraken, a monster reputed to live in the deepest, coldest water of the sea and to have eight snakelike arms, each as thick as a tree trunk and together able to crush a ship to splinters.

Balder was the first to speak. "Behold! The kraken hath awoken, and the monster has taken Hrolf. Who can doubt that this is a sign from our gods that we are meant to continue? I have long heard tales of this hellish monster, but having never seen the thing, I was reluctant to believe that the kraken really existed, and but for the black spittle from this denizen of the deep and the absence of Hrolf, perhaps some of us might still believe that this was more of a waking dream than the truth. But Hrolf is gone, and who can doubt that his death was not a sign?

"Do we still need a vote?" Balder continued. "Who would now risk the wrath of the gods and vote to return? Is there a man or woman who would join Hrolf?"

With such a clear sign of support from the gods, the matter was decided. Their spirits soared as they continued their exploration west.

The men rowed in a waterway between icy landmasses, some of which were as wide as Greenland. Although the passage was wide during summer, they had no doubt that ice connected the islands during winter, and therefore, in a few short months, return travel by sea would be impossible.

Finally, they emerged into a great northern sea. The skies were clear and sunny, and once out of sight of the icy passage, they came upon a fresh southwesterly breeze. After days of rowing, they were happy to restep the masts and hoist their sails. They sailed before the wind for several days, during which time the number of seabirds, seals, and walruses progressively increased, such that they knew land was close.

They came to a pebbled shore where hotstone was plentiful, which they considered a good omen. Sparse grass grew behind some scrub brush that lined the shore. They followed this shore west until they reached the mouth of a great freshwater river that flowed from the south. Thereafter, the coast stretched more to the north than to the west. To the northwest, they could see high snowcapped mountains that reached to the sea.

Balder and his peoples decided to lie to on the east bank of the river, where they took on water, hunted for fresh meat, and made minor repairs to their ships.

The land was bleak, with sparse vegetation and many insects. From the estuary, they could see sparsely forested mountains in the very distant west, but in the immediate vicinity there were only low-lying brush and a few scraggly willow trees. The lack of vegetation was compensated for by the plentitude of wild game. The river was filled with fish. There were numerous seals, walrus, and whales, which they hunted for their blubber and from which they made tar to recaulk their ships. They kept the walrus ivory to fashion into work implements and jewelry. Reindeer were plentiful, and there were thousands of birds, although nesting was largely over, and there were few eggs to be found.

Great auks were plentiful and too easy to catch, in contrast to the geese, gulls, ducks, and swans that flew or swam quickly away as soon as one of Balder's people drew near. Eider ducks were abundant, and the travelers gathered more feathers to fashion into winter wear.

Each morning, the river brought evidence of a more fertile land to the south. They found pine and spruce cones, tree branches, and berry sprigs washed upon the river shore.

After a week, Balder called another council to discuss whether they should remain for the winter at the mouth of the river, sail northwest along the coast, or row south down the river. Only a few considered farther exploration north to be wise. By then, the summer had peaked, and all could feel the approach of autumn; they knew that the nights would only get longer and colder. Some wanted to remain at the river mouth, where there was plentiful game they might depend on. These people did not want to sail farther north, where they would meet winter sooner, or to row south and battle the strong river current.

However, others wanted to leave and row south. These people believed warmer and lush climes would be found deeper in the new country and along the mighty river. It was also clear that native peoples had recently visited and hunted in the region, perhaps only weeks prior to their arrival. There was a concern that these people might be hostile Skraelings, like those who had killed Thorvald in Vinland.

That the native peoples were an advanced and worthy adversary was clear by the evidence they had left behind after hunting and fishing. They were obviously sophisticated and successful hunters. Balder's people had legitimate concerns that anyone who could kill so many whales and walruses could also kill them. They found broken harpoons and arrow points, some of which had been fashioned from iron. That the native peoples could smelt iron confirmed them to be an advanced culture and gave credence to the group's concerns.

Balder believed that the more fertile lands to the south were close enough to reach if they rowed hard from dawn to dusk. He argued that farther south, they would find stout pine trees to build longhouses and that the weather inland from the ocean would be milder. His persuasive comments won the day, and the next morning, freshly stocked with food, they rowed south.

Rowing against the current was difficult, even for the seasoned men, and the wind was fickle and didn't allow the sails to be set to their advantage. Often, no sooner had they stepped the mast and hoisted the sails than the wind would change. Mostly, the wind came from the south, and even with a tacking spar, they could not sail close enough to the wind to make any headway. Sometimes they spent more time adjusting the sails than the meager amount of wind justified.

But for the first week, the weather was fair and their spirits strong, and they made some progress. Balder estimated their speed each morning by determining how long his ship took to row a distance that he had measured along the shore before they embarked. His calculations showed only modest speed. Notwithstanding the efforts of his men, the current was just too strong. At the end of the first two weeks of rowing, Balder estimated that they had journeyed only several hundred miles. They could have walked farther in the same time.

Balder was concerned. His men were tiring, the land was just as barren, and they were not making good progress. Some of the men and women had started to complain, and as Balder remembered his stirring words that had led them south, he felt guilty for the optimism he had instilled.

Rains came and swelled the river but shrank their spirits, and on many days they lay anchored in storms that increasingly contained sleet and snow. For Balder and his people, the wrestling winds of winter arrived early and precipitously without much of an autumn. Old man winter showed a grim fist, full of frost, snow, and ice. Three weeks after leaving the mouth of the river and a little over two months after they had set sail from Iceland, Balder and his people found themselves in a waterway that was freezing over.

A council was called to decide whether to proceed or to pull the ships onto the shore for the winter. No one voted to go on. The reindeer and musk oxen were still plentiful, and the river teemed with grayling that hovered motionless in the ice waters—easy prey.

They hoped that their ships would somehow afford protection from the winter storms, but they could only pull the two lighter longships onto the shore before the ice locked in the cargo ships. They knew the ice would crush the hulls of the knörrs, so they transferred everything from the ships to the shore. They unstepped the masts and took the rigging ashore. They did their best to salvage as much wood from the knörrs as possible. To see the ships so dismantled was discouraging for Balder and his people; their groans matched those of the ice as it shifted and cracked upon the barren hulls.

They excavated an underground dugout as a temporary haven from the storms and then built a wood lodge over this shelter. They gathered and placed river stones as a base for the walls. Inside the stone foundation they built an inner frame consisting of two parallel rows of interior posts placed in pairs and connected by transverse and longitudinal beams. The foundation and posts were placed such that the planking from the knörrs bowed outward at the sides of the lodge. The outward bow, together with a curved ridge of the roof, gave the appearance of an upside-down longship. They covered the outside of the walls and the roof with grass sod. Between the posts and along the inside wall of the lodge, they built low benches. In the middle of the lodge, they constructed a long hearth from river stone to cook their food and heat the lodge.

The winter-like autumn winds were merciless, and during one especially powerful storm, the sod roof came off the lodge. Balder's people relocated to the underground dugout. The storm raged for several days and prevented any effective repair of the roof. The wind swirled within the lodge, and eventually the walls collapsed inward and left only a few posts, the stone base, and the foundation of the hearth standing. Building the underground dugout first proved to have been a good strategy, because, notwithstanding the severe weather and the cramped quarters, they remained warm and safe at least for the short term. The whales and seals they had killed provided not only food but also oil for their hotstone lamps and heat for their meals.

They felt good for surviving the storm, and they might have survived the winter in the dugout had provisions not become such a problem. They had stored a substantial amount of reindeer meat and fish while the game was plentiful, but they had expected to be able to continue to hunt and fish and thereby replenish their supply. However, the reindeer moved on, and the river froze, which made fishing difficult. Within a month, their provisions were all but exhausted, and everyone believed they were doomed to die of hunger.

Each day, men explored south along the frozen river, but they returned only with stories of more ice and snow and fierce white bears.

As the days passed without any better refuge or game discovered, Balder became more and more despondent, believing that he alone was the cause of their misfortune. Finally, Balder decided to set out alone. He vowed to find a haven for his people or to die in the search.

Balder walked for a week and subsisted on a diet so meager that he lost a quarter of his weight. His food choices were severely limited; many days, his only nourishment was the frozen remains of a bear kill, and even for this he had to compete with wolves.

Finally, when he had all but given up, Balder spotted smoke on a mountainside. At first he presumed that the smoke was from a Skraeling camp and that he might not be welcomed, but as he crept up to the site, Balder realized that the smoke was the mist from a hot spring. He had learned about hot springs in Iceland, where they were plentiful. When Balder reached the hot spring, he found a natural cave large enough to accommodate all his people. Given how many animals the hot spring would attract as well, Balder felt sure he had found a place where his people could survive the winter in warmth and safety.

Plants with dried berries surrounded the hot spring, and Balder enjoyed his first food in many days. While eating the berries, Balder heard a huffing sound and looked up to see a huge brown bear emerging from the cave.

Balder stood up suddenly and surprised the bear. The animal ran back a few steps onto a rise within the mouth of the cave and then turned to face Balder. The bear stood on four feet with his head low and his ears cocked. The hair above his hump stood on end. He chopped his jaws repeatedly, and his teeth made a sound like the ringing of an axe on metal.

Balder was concerned by the posture of the bear, and he expected the animal to attack at any second. Never once, though, did he take his eyes of the massive furry beast. Rather, Balder stood tall and showed a determined and confident manner; he spoke calmly to the bear as if he was talking to another person.

Every hair on the head and back of the bear seemed to have a life of its own; the fur moved and vibrated as if powered by each breath or heartbeat. The brown hump rippled as the bear moved from side to side. The grizzly lifted his head several times and revealed a patch of pale fur on the throat and upper chest. Suddenly, the bear lowered his head. He snorted, arched his neck, and took long, stiff-legged strides toward Balder. His large head swung violently from side to side as he approached Balder.

Scarcely a few feet away, the bear stood up on two legs and towered over Balder. For an anxious moment, Balder and the bear stood motionless, face-to-face, their eyes locked in mutual curiosity, neither knowing whether to attack or flee.

Balder knew of brown bears from Norway. As a young man, he had seen a few from a distance, but never one up close. He had heard enough tales of their ferociousness to realize that bears should be avoided, especially by a solitary man. In Norway the bears were hunted only by groups of experienced hunters, and even then, the killing of a bear was considered an awesome feat. Over the last few weeks he had seen several white bears, and he had managed to avoid them all. This bear, however, could not be avoided.

In his weakened condition, Balder knew he was no match for the bear, and now with the creature towering over him, he discounted making any overtly threatening gesture. He stood patiently for a few seconds that seemed like minutes and waited for the bear to make the first move, but the bear seemed similarly frozen.

Balder had some dried berries in his hand, and he nonchalantly started to eat some. The bear lowered his gaze to the berries, and Balder instinctively offered him some. As he stretched out his palm, he wondered if the bear would decide to devour his entire hand, as if the palm were a wafer of bread and the berries only a garnish.

Balder blinked when the bear sniffed and then ate the berries and was pleasantly surprised to feel only a rough wet tongue that gently lapped up the fruit. After finishing the berries, the bear walked past Balder and started to eat more of the berries directly from the tree. When the bear finished, the animal ambled back into the cave.

For the rest of the day, Balder scouted the area to look for wild game attracted to the warm oasis in an otherwise icy land. That day he trapped and killed several snowshoe hares. He started a fire by striking his knife against a piece of jasper, a flintlike stone, and cooked and ate one of the hares but left the other as fresh meat for the bear. The bear emerged to the smell of the cooking meat and accepted Balder's offer of the freshly killed hare.

That night, Balder and the bear both slept in the cave. When he awoke alive in the morning, Balder knew that he and the bear were somehow friends, perhaps only temporarily, but still friends.

Over several days, while he rested and recuperated, Balder continued to hunt game, which he shared with the bear. He spent seven days at the cave and regained some of his lost weight. On the final day, he killed two reindeer. He butchered one for his return journey and gave the other animal to the bear as a parting gift.

Balder had discovered the hot springs on the first day of autumn, the equinox when night and day are the same duration, three months to the day after they had set out from Iceland. During the week that Balder remained at the hot springs, the nighttime sky was clear, and the moon waned from full on his arrival to a half moon on his departure. Each night, the northern sky had displayed a miracle of colorful dancing lights. Balder came to believe that his life and the lives of his people were linked to the bear, the full moon, the dancing lights, and the life-giving hot spring. He was now certain that Njord, the god of the wind and the sea, had purposely led his people to this mystical place, that this was where they were meant to settle, and that all the hardships his people had endured were only a test to determine whether they were worthy.

Balder led his people back to the hot spring, and they named the colony Asgard because the location was a special place chosen by their gods.

The great bear, Balder's friend, was no longer at the cave when he returned with his people. However, Balder found several reindeer frozen in the snow and otherwise untouched, and he had no doubt that they were a gift from Ursavus, the name Balder had chosen for his friend.

That first night, the sky was exceptionally clear and the stars especially bright. Balder looked into the sky and saw stars that took the shape of a bear. He explained to his people that the stars were Ursavus, a bear giant who would always watch over them. A line drawn through the stars, to depict the foreleg and the head of the bear, pointed to the North Star, and to this day our cubs are taught that Ursavus points to the most northern and original settlement of our peoples, and from that day, Balder's people respected the bears.

Freyr, one of Balder's people, was a poet and knew the old stories. On that first night, when all Balder's people were warm and well fed in the underground cavern, Freyr told a creation story.

"Life began when the cold ice of the north met the hot fires of the south. The hot fires from the south melted the ice and freed Buri, the Grandfather of Odin. Clearly," interpreted Freyr, "Balder has discovered a sacred place of creation. The hot fires from the warm south have brought the hot springs and melted the snow and ice of the north. As always, we live courtesy of the grace of our gods."

All Balder's people rejoiced in their good fortune. By virtue of the warmth, ample water, and the animals attracted to the hot spring, Balder's people survived the winter in excellent shape. Their ships, however, did not. Ice storms destroyed the remnants of the two ships on the shore and removed any possibility of a spring sea journey to warmer, more southern climes. Balder believed this was another sign that they were meant to settle in Asgard.

Balder's people were able to salvage much of the wood from the ships. Some of the wood was used to create furniture that survives to this day, including the oak thrones and the seats in the Althing.

By nature, our people are an adventurous sort, and they soon explored the caverns and found an underground route to the more southern and warmer climes where we now live. The hot spring discovered by Balder is close to Inuit, the most northern city established by my ancestors. Hot springs are still a sacred place for our people. The hot spring you know is only one of many we have discovered.

Having given this background, King Bjorn walked over to the wall and showed Mac and Ian maps behind each statue that indicated the regions explored, communities established, and engineering projects completed by each king.

They walked along and studied the maps together. Mac was amazed at the precision. Even degrees of latitude were clearly displayed.

"Did your ancient forefathers have sextants?" asked Mac.

"Sextants?" repeated King Bjorn.

"Yes, instruments to tell map positions."

"They did not have any special instruments, but our peoples have always understood the stars and the sun; just as if we were on a strange ocean, we always know where we are and how far we are from our ancient homeland."

"So, that means that at each map position, you were able to take a sighting of the sun and stars?" inquired Mac.

"Exactly. Most of the sites are close to hot springs, cave entrances, or dormant volcanic vents that allow us access to the surface."

"Once you found an access to the surface in a warmer, more habitable land, why didn't your people relocate and establish colonies aboveground?" asked Mac.

"Our Icelandic ancestors came from a mostly barren land with hot springs and volcanoes. They understood how to live in their new world and settled in quite comfortably. Several surface colonies were attempted, but the Skraelings were warlike and outnumbered our people. After losing several battles, my ancestors decided that the safest and simplest course was to develop a subterranean world separate from the surface peoples.

"Our ancestors made a wonderful world, and so far, the secret of our existence has remained secure. During each generation, only a few surface people have ever discovered our world."

Ian wanted to ask how many surface people had been kidnapped, but he bit his tongue and continued to listen to the story.

But Mac could see that Ian was upset. "Ian, is something wrong?"

"Oh, no, I'm just worrying about Kate and Liz and wondering why they were kidnapped," he responded a bit sarcastically, while directing a searching look at King Bjorn.

King Bjorn met Ian's eyes and understood at once. He next looked at Ursus, whose countenance did not change, which was telling enough.

The king sighed. "So, you know."

"Know what?" asked Mac.

"About our royal traditions and the prophecy that a surface woman will be the bride of Prince Eirik," replied King Bjorn.

"Ah," Mac said, suddenly understanding, "a prophecy that I presume has something to do with my daughters. Yes, I see. I had wondered about that. But you are a just man, and surely now that you understand the situation, you realize that such a marriage is not possible."

Ian was bewildered that Mac seemed to understand what was going on. "How could you know?" he asked, looking at Mac. "Were you listening when …" But Ian stopped before revealing Connor's indiscretion. Connor looked sheepish, which was difficult for a grizzly.

"Pardon me," interjected Ursus. "Now I know what happened." He looked first at Ian and then to King Bjorn. "Connor probably revealed the prophecy to Ian. They became good friends during our journey, and while Connor is honest to a fault, he suffers the glibness of youth. Mac may not have been privy to Connor's indiscreet remark, but as I've come to realize, his intuition is usually very good. It seems he has deduced that his daughters were kidnapped, but not why, and his supposition about the reason is not entirely correct." Ursus turned to Mac. "It is true we would have kidnapped Kate, and that was the reason our bear patrols were in the area. However, Malicious outsmarted us and kidnapped the girls first."

Ian was still bewildered until Mac helped him understand. "They need new blood, Ian. Without intermarriage, their children would develop all manner of weird congenital problems and illnesses."

"Yes, that part is correct, Mac," interjected King Bjorn. "From the second century of our settlement, birth defects were evident, and our people realized that new blood was required, or our line would whither and die. After much debate, our ancestors decided to lure surface people to our world—native peoples at first, but for the last few centuries, your peoples as well. At the Althing, you might have noticed those with darker hair and skin. These clans have intermarried with the native peoples, and over the years, many of their ways have been adopted. We welcomed the diversity, and our kingdom is the stronger for it. I promise you that we never kept a surface person against their will. Most were happy to join our society, and those who were not were released after taking a memory-purging herb."

"But the royal family is still fair-haired and skinned, which means your direct ancestors have not intermarried with the native peoples," concluded Mac.

"That is not correct," responded King Bjorn. "Our family has regularly intermarried with native peoples, especially the daughters and the second-born and subsequent-born sons. Only the firstborn son, or girl if no sons are sired, the one who will grow up to become king or queen, is expected to marry a blonde-haired spouse. A bride or groom has usually been found within our own peoples, but this year is the millennial anniversary of King Balder's first colony, and on this date was foretold the arrival of a blonde surface woman of Icelandic heritage who would wed the current prince and usher in an age of untold prosperity. It was foretold that the blonde woman would appear during a full moon and when the lights were dancing in the northern sky. This event has sacred significance for our people."

King Bjorn looked at Ian, who was fidgeting and upset. King Bjorn moved closer and put his hand on Ian's shoulder. "Don't worry, Ian; we would never separate you from Kate. That is not our way. We respect the sanctity of your marriage just as we respect the bonds between our own peoples. Rest assured that I will do everything possible to rescue Kate and Liz and reunite your families. I must, not just for you and Mac, but also to stop Malicious from her evil plans." With that, the king turned away to hide his shame.

Ian felt sad and happy at the same time. He was relieved to be reassured by King Bjorn but felt guilty that he had presumed the worst of such a noble king.

King Bjorn turned to Ursus. "Ursus, how could this have happened? How could my daughter, my own flesh and blood, turn against me? What have I done to deserve this evil?"

"Nothing, my friend; you have done nothing to bring upon this misfortune. Rather, you have done everything to foster goodwill within your family and the kingdom generally. No, you are not to blame. Forgive my candor, but Malicious has been a conniving serpent of a girl since she was a toddler. You have been blinded by your love for your daughter and never saw Malicious for what she was. Her voice was always syrupy sweet for you, but a bitter breath for everyone else."

"Oh, I saw clearly enough," admitted King Bjorn. "I just refused to believe my own eyes; it is difficult for a father to accept a daughter's betrayal."

Ursus continued on behalf of King Bjorn. "Malicious has awesome powers. As a little girl, she begged her mother to teach her the seiđur ritual, a magical rite practiced only by women and used to influence people or prophesy the future. She learned the songs, chants, and incantations, and even before she showed her first signs of womanhood, it is said that she could summon spirits. She was considered by many to be a seeress. As a young woman she was seen sitting on graves at night, and some thought her a sorceress. She was often seen in the company of wolves and ravens, and some believed she was a *hamrammr,* or shape-shifter, and could turn into these animals at will.

"Malicious studied the plants that grow both on the surface and in our underground realm and has learned to concoct them into drugs that control the minds and bodies of people she could not otherwise bring under her power. She has befriended the slimy creatures of the deep and dark caverns where no light has ever penetrated. It is said that Jormungand, the ancient Midgard serpent, has been found and persuaded to her cause. There are reports that Malicious has studied the ancient human sacrifice rituals of the Aztec, Mayan, and Inca peoples and that she practices a form of these rituals in her volcanic fortress. She is well versed in astronomy and the ways of the planets and stars, and there are some who believe Malicious can not only read the future but also change the course of time. How much of this is truth and how much is myth is not known. What is known is that she is evil."

"Yes," said King Bjorn. "This is all too true. I remember the fated words of my beautiful wife Freyja, who once told me, 'Malicious seems to think she is one of the norns,' the minor goddesses who sit at the center of the world and spin the life thread of each individual and thereby determine their fate and fortune."

King Bjorn stood up and moved to a portrait of his bride, Queen Freyja. "My wife, my noble, generous Freyja, who died in my arms, her face twisted in agony, her body contorted in pain, her breaths short and gasping, and her color a sickly blue. She was the victim of some horrible poison. It is believed that Malicious was the assassin. While there is no proof, I have come to accept this bitter knowledge as the truth. Freyja and I shared a preference for salt. She often sampled portions of the meal before we ate and added salt to her taste. On that cursed night, the salt was poisoned, and she died for us both. By Thor, I wish that it had been I who sampled the poisoned food.

"My bride was the sweetest-spoken and most compassionate of persons, and she was loved by all who knew her. Freyja's presence brightened a room and brought smiles and laughter where there might not have been. Her smile was a splendor that radiated through the kingdom."

Ursus put his paw on King Bjorn's hand, in sympathy for his friend.

"Thank you, Ursus. You have been a true friend and have helped me more than you can imagine during these troubled times."

When the king went on, his face had changed from sadness to determination. "Now let us swear by Odin, by the memory of Queen Freyja, and by our ancestors that we will defeat this plague that was once my daughter. Swear with me now that we will give our all to preserve what a thousand years have accomplished and to purge the evil that has befallen us."

Ursus, Mac, and Ian pledged their support to defeat Malicious.

"By our law, I have the right of revenge for the murder of Freyja, and by your pledge, each of you is now empowered to kill Malicious on my behalf."

Chapter 21

Panther Express

Liz and Kate awoke to the terrified whelps of wolves in the next chamber, sounds that were snuffed as suddenly as they started.

A moment later, the door opened, and Lord Null walked in, flanked by two giant panthers. With their heads held proud and high, the sleek cats were almost as tall as a man even while walking on all fours. Their thick midnight-black fur shimmered like velvet as they slinked noiselessly around the room.

Liz purposely tried to make eye contact with the panthers. She wanted them to know that she wasn't afraid, but their piercing yellow eyes were everywhere but on the prisoners. Once they had scanned every square inch of the room, they took positions at either side of the door and sat on their massive haunches. Thereafter, they remained still, and but for the occasional movements of their whiskers, they might have been ebony statues.

Through the door, Kate could see the limp bodies of the wolf jailors scattered on the floor. "They're dead!" she exclaimed in a surprised gasp. From the unnatural way in which their heads slumped, she could tell that their necks had been broken.

Kate looked up at Lord Null. This was the first time either woman had seen him in a well-lit setting. Both recollected a tall, gaunt, and sinister-appearing man who seemed the more so for the darkness in the tunnels. Well-lit rooms usually limited fear, but in this case, his appearance seemed more terrifying for the light.

His eyes seemed sucked into his skull, like bottomless black pits on either side of a long, thin, bony nose with gaping nostrils that flared and contracted with a slow sinister rhythm. The green light intensified the naturally sallow color of his complexion. Looking at him, one would have expected every joint to creak, but his movements were lithe. There was no hair on his body, and he wore little clothes. He wore only a kilt and a short broadsword that hung from an over-the-shoulder harness on his right side and permitted easy access to his left hand. The harness was fashioned from a metal that had the suppleness of leather. The scabbard, which was also made of this metal, glistened with an oily sheen.

Lord Null didn't speak, but his busy eyes methodically searched Kate and Liz and left them feeling naked. Liz saw his right hand move slightly and watched while Lord Null rotated the hilt of his sword. Both rubies came into view, and Liz felt her eyes drawn to them. She resisted the sensation and instead focused on Lord Null's eyes. His eyelids closed a fraction, his eyes narrowed slightly, and his lips tightened into an almost imperceptible frown. She could see that her gaze bothered him, but she didn't know why. Lord Null shifted his gaze to Kate, and his facial muscles relaxed. Kate was staring intently at the red gems.

"Kate! Are you okay?" asked Liz, without taking her eyes off Lord Null.

Liz's words hung in the air. Kate didn't answer. Lord Null remained silent but returned his gaze to Liz. There was curiosity in his eyes. Liz continued to glare at him but broke eye contact when she heard a sob escape from Kate's lips. Kate stood frozen with her eyes opened wide and had an expression that suggested she was looking at something horrible. Liz stepped in front of her sister and took Kate's head between her hands, forcing her gaze away from Lord Null and the rubies.

"Kate! Look at me. Kate! Snap out of it!"

Lord Null turned to the panthers and away from the women. Liz glanced briefly back at him as he moved and then returned her visual attention to her sister. Kate finally blinked her eyes, but Liz could tell that she was still in a trance. Kate offered a smile that didn't fit with the situation and took a step toward Liz, stumbling slightly. Liz put her hand under Kate's arm to steady her. When she next looked back at Lord Null, he was on his way out of the room. As he passed the panthers, he paused to speak.

"You will take these surface women to the docks on the shores of Cauldron Lake, where the Nakota River and the River Fjorm converge. There you will receive further orders. The women must not escape, must not be harmed, and must arrive before the fifth day."

Several other men appeared and bound Kate and Liz into a sitting position on the backs of the panthers. They did not tie their hands, but the manner in which their legs were secured made escape impossible. A small pack of provisions was secured to the shoulders of each panther and was within easy reach of Liz and Kate's unsecured hands.

"Your journey should be uneventful," said Lord Null to the panthers. "The route has been cleared of enemy warriors. No bears have been seen.

You should encounter only jaguar squads, roving wolf packs, or soldiers who carry the red-eyed banner of Princess Malicious."

Lord Null looked straight into the eyes of the panthers and then down at the hilt of his sword. This action drew the panther's eyes to the rubies, and Liz saw the heads of the cats nod ever so slightly, so little as to be almost unnoticeable. In that moment, their eyes grew distant and changed from yellow to a fiery orange, almost red. After several moments, Lord Null covered the rubies with his hand, the eyes of the panthers resumed a yellow color, and the cats perked up into a state of hyperalertness.

Soon thereafter, the panthers, with Liz and Kate on their backs, left for Cauldron Lake. As they passed the lifeless wolf bodies, Kate asked the soldier who had bound them, "Why were they killed? Weren't the wolves on your side?"

Liz answered, "Secrecy, Kate. No one is meant to know of our journey." Then she looked straight at the two soldiers. "Hope you fellows don't mind dying for the cause. Somehow, you don't look anymore important than these wolves."

Almost before her words were out, the panthers took off at a full gallop. They emerged from the building where the sisters had been held into an open plaza that was filled with tall dark-haired men and women carrying spears and wolves who skulked about.

The soldiers and wolves parted deferentially for the panthers to race through. The few brief moments that Kate and Liz had to look around made them wish for better times and the opportunity to investigate the crystal chamber. Later, when they shared their thoughts about the Green Cavern, they both expressed a sense that the crystal had imparted something more than light. Somehow they had felt stronger, more vital, during the time they had spent in the cavern, and the brief period in the open and beneath the high vaulted ceiling of excavated cavern had been thrilling in a way neither woman could explain.

A few moments later, Kate and Liz plunged into darkness as they entered the caverns. How the massive black cats managed to see without any light in the passages was unfathomable to them. To Liz it seemed the panthers must have had some sort of radar. She could feel the brush of stalactites and stalagmites and sometimes the side of a wall as they raced around corners. Once when she looked back, she saw the faint gleaming eyes of the panther that carried Kate, luminescent yellow eyes that burned like a flame and that might have felt warm in a house cat, but that chilled her instead in these circumstances.

For hours and hours, they ran deeper and deeper into the earth while the temperature grew from hot to hotter. The panthers panted, but this was not enough to keep their body temperature down, and beads of sweat glistened on their fur. The cats stopped at every pool or stream to quench their thirst. However, the panthers never stopped to eat, which amazed Kate and Liz, who were tired and hungry even without having to sprint for hours on end. About twelve hours into the journey, they arrived at a rest stop, where two soldiers and two fresh panthers awaited them. The soldiers transferred Kate and Liz to the new set of panthers, and then the new pair of great cats left immediately to continue the journey to Cauldron Lake. This relay pattern continued such that Kate and Liz were on the move almost nonstop.

After they left the first relay stop, they had barely turned the corner when they heard the first set of panthers tearing into the soldiers.

"No wonder the cats didn't eat while they ran," said Kate. "They knew they had a meal waiting for them."

Four days, eight sets of panthers, and sixteen dead soldiers later, they had covered several thousands of miles. "Panthers are known to run seventy miles an hour, and even at half that speed, we must have traveled at least two thousand miles," calculated Kate.

"Where are we?" Liz wondered.

"I don't know," replied Kate, "but my provision pack had twelve separate meal packages, and we have eaten all but two. My bet is that we will arrive at Cauldron Lake before we finish the last two meals."

Much as they predicted, within a half-day of their last meal, they arrived in a huge underground cavern with a lake several miles wide.

At the north end of the cavern, the Nakota River, supplied by glacial snow from far above, emptied clear, cool water into the lake. The water in this northern portion of the lake was clear, and the bottom was plainly visible. At the shoreline in the middle of the lake were docks at which many ships were moored. There were a few Viking longships, but most were ugly barges with several hundred sets of oars, obviously meant for heavy transport and not for speed or maneuverability. Just south of the docks, a molten river of lava seeped from a volcanic vent and hissed into the lake, where it produced a steam cloud that hung low over the water. The far southern limit of the cavern was visible above the mist, but the entrance to the River Fjorm was obscured. The lava from the vent also streamed south beside the lake and continued to be visible as a misty ribbon of orange that entered the cavern wall alongside the River Fjorm and then followed a more or less parallel course toward Popocatépetl.

The docks had been built to the north of the entrance of the lava flow and where the visibility was good, but the wharfs were not so far away that the water was unchanged by the addition of the molten rock. The lake water was tepid to touch, had a disagreeable sulfur odor, and was turbid enough that the bottom was no longer visible. Toward the south, the lake became progressively murkier until finally it looked more like molten mud than water.

Liz noted that a company of men similar to those who had bound them at the Green Cavern was waiting by a longship that looked sleek beside the barges. There was no breeze to make a sail useful, and as such the ship had no mast. The thirty sets of oars suggested that the energy for the next portion of their journey south would be human muscle.

Kate and Liz were unbound and led onto the aft deck of the boat, where they saw, incredulously, that Lord Null awaited them.

"Right on time. Nothing like a panther for speed," he said with satisfaction. He then looked toward some men on the wharf who were waiting on his command. He only needed to narrow his eyes for them to understand. They cast off the lines.

Lord Null glanced below deck to another man who waited on his orders. Again a look was sufficient, and sixty oars moved in unison as the boat slipped away from the dock toward the center of the lake.

Kate turned to Liz as the boat got under way. "How could he have arrived here before us?"

"He probably traveled on the surface," replied Liz.

The boat passed into the mist, which made Kate think of the hypnotic haze by the hot spring, and she had a moment of apprehension. But although the mist was warm and humid and had a faintly disagreeable odor like that of rotten eggs, it did not make her feel tired. The mist had seemed thicker from the docks, but once surrounded by the water vapor, they found their vision limited but not obscured. Even so, in this shrouded setting, the rhythmic splashing of the oars in the water and the otherwise muted silence of the soldiers were unsettling. Lord Null did nothing to make them feel otherwise. He turned to Kate and Liz.

"Now, just so that you understand, while you are on this boat, an escape is impossible, and lest you think otherwise, please allow a demonstration."

Lord Null opened a basket and removed a small animal that looked vaguely like a weasel with enormous pale eyes and then dangled the terrified creature over the gunwale by its very long and naked tail.

The animal tried desperately to climb up its own tail and onto Lord Null's arm, but Lord Null kept flicking the creature back and forth, and his grip was surer than any purchase the animal could gain. Lord Null watched while the wretched creature wiggled helplessly.

"Stop!" cried Kate. "You're torturing that poor animal."

A smile crept across Lord Null's thin lips, and for a second his teeth even showed. He stopped flicking and allowed the animal to gain a grip on its tail and then to climb up. Just before the animal reached Lord Null's arm, the dastard let go, and the creature fell screeching toward the water.

"Hopefully, it can swim," whispered Kate, but well before the animal reached the water, a slender yellow tentacle whipped out of the water and snatched the animal in midair.

Both Kate and Liz gasped.

"There are many unpleasant life forms in Cauldron Lake. That one prefers live prey. Let me show you another." Lord Null removed a similar small but dead animal and dropped the carcass into the lake. Immediately, the water came to a boil as hundreds of tiny scaled creatures, more like snakes than fish, competed for a piece of the animal. After only a few seconds, the surface of the water became placid again.

"So," he concluded, "nowhere to run, and certainly nowhere to swim, so you might as well not bother with thoughts of escape. Under the circumstances, I won't bind you."

As Lord Null spoke, a yellow tentacle crept over the gunwale toward him.

Kate was the first to see the tentacle, and her first thought was benevolent. She opened her mouth as if to warn Lord Null. Then her thoughts turned spiteful. *Why should I warn him?* she thought. *He deserves to suffer the same fate as that tiny animal he victimized.* But benevolence was the stronger emotion, and before Kate could even form the words to warn Lord Null, her countenance betrayed her. With an alacrity that astonished her, Lord Null's sword flashed and severed the tentacle, which fell onto the deck and wiggled for several minutes before it became still.

The swiftness and accuracy of Lord Null's sword was not lost on Liz, but she also noted with interest that he drew the sword with his right hand. Back at the Green Cavern, Liz had noted that he carried the sword on his right and was left-handed.

The boat moved with amazing speed, not only because of the efforts of the sixty burly men who pulled in impressive synchrony but also because the current was strong and in their favor.

The lake became progressively murkier and finally turned black as they reached the River Fjorm. The molten river of lava that ran parallel to the river imparted a hellish glow that was sufficient for navigating the boat around the various hanging stalactites and lava boulders that obstructed sections of the River Fjorm. The air was almost unbearably hot. Periodically, the river and lava diverged, and darkness was a welcome trade for the cooler air. Kate was bemused that darkness could be inviting and said as much to Liz. Liz nodded in agreement but didn't share Kate's philosophical sense of things. She didn't like the dark, cool or otherwise. For Kate, this would not be the last time that she longed for the darkness.

The soldiers never stopped rowing for a week. They even ate while they manned the oars. Kate reckoned they had traveled several more thousand miles and despaired over how her father and Ian would ever find them.

Theirs was not the only boat on the river. Kate and Liz counted hundreds of barges that were headed in the opposite direction north, and each contained companies of jaguars, short swarthy soldiers like those who rowed their boat, or tall dark-haired men and women. At the stern of each boat was a black banner with two ruby red eyes.

The only time the boat stopped was at their final destination, a huge underground marina on the western shore of the River Fjorm. Behind the docks was an underground city built at the base of a mostly dormant volcano. A pinpoint of gray light high above allowed a glimpse of sunlight and a surface world that seemed a lifetime away to Kate and Liz. The cavern walls were honeycombed with mineshafts at various heights and stairways that had been carved to reach the mines.

While they were still on the boat, their hands were bound, and a squad of the soldiers escorted them to a staging area on the docks, where they waited amid a constant flow of soldiers and equipment.

Kate and Liz watched while soldiers disembarked from the barges arriving from the south. The soldiers were issued weapons and armor in a staging area, and immediately afterward, they were marched onto other barges that were rowed north.

During the hour or so that Kate and Liz waited in the staging area, they counted three hundred soldiers arriving from the south and, once armed, heading north.

"That's over seven thousand soldiers a day!" remarked Kate.

"I wonder how long this has been going on. I hope King Bjorn has a large army," replied Liz.

Some of the stairways had a pulley system that controlled elevators. Iron ore mined higher up in the volcano was transported down to smelters at dockside. Load after load of iron ingots from the smelters ascended back up to smithies where the metal was fashioned into weapons of death and destruction. One shipment after another of shields, swords, spears, and battle-axes descended to the soldiers waiting on the docks.

The soldiers all wore uniforms with a solitary red eye emblazoned on the chest. Their battle standards featured a set of red eyes that glared out from a shiny satin-like black cloth. The fabric of the standard was stretched between two horizontal wooden bars, much like the sail on a longship.

While Kate and Liz waited in the staging area, a raven circled above and then landed on the lower wooden bar of a battle standard held by one of the guards. They might not have noticed the raven but for the guard, who flinched when the bird landed. The hand that held the standard shook, and the look on the soldier's face confirmed that he was frightened by the bird.

The raven had red eyes, and for a split second as the bird walked along the bar and in front of the standard, the raven seemed to disappear into the black standard.

A squad of men arrived within moments of the raven, and they escorted Kate and Liz to a stairwell in the southwest corner of the city. They boarded an elevator, and Liz counted more than a hundred mineshafts before they stopped and entered a large corridor. Liz noticed there were several more mineshafts above.

Toward the end of the corridor was a room where Kate and Liz were taken and locked inside. The room contained two beds, a table, and two chairs. The table was set for a meal for two. The room was tidy but dirty. Compared to the ship and dockyard, the air smelled remarkably clean.

Chapter 22

Different Roads for Mac and Ian

The morning after their arrival at the Castle of Light, Mac and Ian attended Althing. King Bjorn introduced them, explained the circumstances of their presence, and requested that the assembly accept them as members.

Koda spoke to Ian's valor during the journey back to the Castle, and Ursus described Mac as a bright and inquisitive individual. Those present agreed unanimously to accept Ian and Mac as honorary members of the Althing.

It was the custom of King Bjorn to request reports from the various clan and grizzly leaders present and from any others who had news to share. He turned first to Koda. "Koda, tell us of your battle with the wolves."

Koda told the story of the battle, and the bears were congratulated on their victory. Connor's strength and courage were especially noted, and many of the men and bears present murmured that the clumsy cub had turned into a fine warrior.

Koda also reported on some stray wolves who had been captured by his scouts. "They knew only pack gossip," advised Koda, "but if true, what they related is of concern. All the northern wolves were summoned to the Green Cavern and are now under the orders of men from the Southern Realm, cruel men who have offered the wolves promise of human meat, but who are quick to punish disobedience."

Magnus, the commander of King Bjorn's armies, was the next to rise to speak. Magnus was almost bald, especially about his crown, and what remained of his once-blond hair was mixed with strands of gray and hung in disheveled curls to his shoulders, which gave him a wild look, tempered somewhat by a nicely trimmed and robust beard and walrus-like mustache. His facial hair still retained the blond color of his youth and showed only a few grizzled strands of gray. He wore a sleeveless shirt covered with a tunic, which left his legs bare below the knees. His arms and legs were covered with hair so thick that Magnus reminded Mac of a bear. His upper body was covered by a cloak, gathered at his right shoulder, and fastened by a penannular ring pin with terminals in the form of the head of a Viking warrior. Mac noted that the needlelike portion of the pin was much longer than that of the other warriors, a mark he suspected reflected the high status of Magnus. The pin was fashioned from carved silver, and the ring portion showed a stylized twisting dragon. A round silver brooch served to button his shirt in the middle at his neck. The brooch was intricately carved to show one-eyed Odin riding Sleipnir, his eight-legged horse. Mjollnir, the hammer of Thor, dangled from the brooch. A similar design adorned the rim of his iron helmet. The silver filigree was inlaid in a pattern that depicted Odin welcoming soldiers into Valhalla. There were scenes of Valkyries with horns of wine and beer, men fighting, and others feasting in a great hall. The helmet had eye and ear guards and a thin felt inner layer. He wore silver armbands above each elbow and thick hand-tooled leather bands about his wrists.

"Thousands of enemy soldiers occupy the Green Cavern," he said. "These men were recruited in the Southern Realm, crudely armed in Popocatépetl, and then marched or rowed to the Green Cavern. Scores more are en route to join them. Squads of jaguars are reported in the Middle Realm. They have been combing the countryside for conscripts or plunder. Our informants all speak of an upcoming attack where human and bear meat are promised as the spoils of victory."

The clan leaders murmured their discontent at this news. Some seemed ready to speak, but King Bjorn cleared his throat, and all grew silent. The king looked over at Magnus, who continued his report.

"All evidence points to a coordinated assault on the Castle of Light sometime in the next few months and all under the leadership of a pale, red-eyed woman with translucent hair. She can only be Malicious."

"So," responded the king, "war is imminent, after five hundred years of peace, and at the hands of my daughter." He sighed. "Well, if war it shall be, then let justice and freedom prevail, and if Malicious be the enemy leader, then let her die by my hand, or if I am killed, then by the hand of my heir and son, Prince Eirik." The king paused and then added hopefully, "Is there news of Eirik?"

All eyes were elsewhere when the king scanned the face of the clan leaders and their attendants. Their silence was sad. King Bjorn looked pleadingly over to Ursus, who could only shake his head.

King Bjorn lived in hope that Eirik was still alive and not totally under the spell of Malicious. He felt like crying, but rather than share his obvious grief, the king distracted himself by beckoning those present to accompany him to a massive quartz map, which was a centerpiece of the room.

The three-dimensional map had been carved out of rose quartz and was ingeniously lit from below to show all the known tunnels, caverns, and subterranean pools, as well as the hot springs, volcanoes, other geothermal vents, and nonthermal access points to the surface world. The compass directional scale was ten miles to an inch and the depth scale one mile to the inch, which allowed the ten-by-five-by-one-yard map to include 3,600 longitudinal miles from north to south; 1,800 miles from east to west; and sixty miles from the deepest known habitable region of the underground kingdom to the top of the highest mountain in North and Central America.

Magnus reviewed the basic underground geography for the benefit of Mac and Ian. "There are two main subterranean tunnel systems that connect the Northern and Middle Realms, or more to the point, that lead from Malicious's Volcanic Fortress to the Castle of Light. Currently, the coastal route is under our control, but several weeks ago, enemy forces occupied the inland route up to and including the Green Cavern." Magnus pointed to the Green Cavern.

"The coastal route is closer to the surface, and each of the six major centers along this route is still controlled by one of the seven loyal clans. The remaining clan, which controlled Nakota, the only major center north of the Green Cavern along the inland route, was attacked and overwhelmed several weeks ago. Thanks to the bravery of the Nakota warriors, their people escaped north. Since attacking Nakota, the enemy soldiers have regrouped in the Green Cavern, and our warriors have retaken Nakota. A garrison of bears is now stationed at Nakota."

King Bjorn asked Grettir, the leader of the Nakota clan, to relate the story of the attack. Grettir was a tall, shapely woman with long black pleated hair that fell over her shoulders to the middle of her back. The pleats were gathered in several places with bone clips on which runes had been carved. A tiny string of beads attached a single eagle feather to the highest bone clip, allowing the feather to hang beside her hair. She wore a supple leather shirt that was gathered at the neck with a rectangular beaded brooch. The collar of the shirt was similarly beaded in the fashion of the clan. Over the shirt she wore a leather tunic, and over this, she wore a protective breastplate of hundreds of wolf claws sewn into a thick leather doublet. She carried a seven-foot spear. The hickory shaft of the spear was an inch and a half thick and carried a tip of eighteen-inch solid quartzite, cut and polished to razor sharpness. A short sword and a knife were sheathed at her sides.

"In retrospect," related Grettir, "an unusually large number of Middle Realm merchants had visited Nakota during the preceding two weeks. We now realize these people were spies and saboteurs. On the day prior to the attack, roving packs of wolves were spotted in our communities, and on the day of the attack, the water supply from the dam suddenly stopped, which resulted in confusion and chaos.

"Without any other warning, thousands of Southern soldiers and packs of wolves converged on Nakota in the small hours of the morning. Fortunately, our sentries were able to raise the alarm, and our warriors delayed the enemy sufficiently for our people to escape north in an orderly fashion. We were lucky. We lost only a few dozen warriors. The outcome easily could have been much worse."

Magnus interjected. "Although our losses were small, the enemy paid a horrible price for their victory. A hundred wolves or men died for every Nakota warrior. Clearly, the enemy leaders had no regard for their own soldiers who where pressed into battle in such great numbers that their own men often trampled one another to death. They were successful more by force of numbers than by the skill of any of their soldiers."

"Yes," replied King Bjorn, "but they won nevertheless, and the outcome might have been different if not for the bravery of the Nakota warriors. They fought a determined rearguard action that allowed the people of Nakota to escape."

Magnus turned again to the quartz map. "After the capture of the Green Cavern, we established strategic points of strength here and here on the inland and coastal routes, respectively." Magnus pointed to these locations. "These positions are currently secure, and our warriors are moving to strengthen them.

"The coastal route is the longer of the two, and the major cities are still held by clans loyal to the king. But this is not so of the intervening tunnel systems. Malicious's forces did not attempt an assault on any coastal route city. Instead, they bypassed the urban areas and are wrecking havoc on travel in the intervening tunnel systems.

"Clearly, her plan is to draw us into a battle at the Green Cavern. By securing the intervening tunnel systems along the coastal route, she has prevented the southernmost clans from sending reinforcements for this battle. Without capturing a single coastal route city, she has effectively neutralized almost half our forces."

"Perhaps," responded King Bjorn, "but each day, messengers continue to arrive from the coastal route cities. The tunnels are not totally under enemy control. So long as we can delay the battle, I am confident that some of our forces might break free and reach the Green Cavern in time."

Magnus turned to the king, "The tunnel systems along the inland route and south of the Green Cavern are filled with enemy forces moving north. Our best estimate is that the bulk of the forces will have arrived at the Green Cavern sometime around the autumnal equinox and that Malicious plans to attack on or before that date."

"Is there something special about that date?" asked Mac.

"Yes, by tradition, the wedding of the heir to the throne takes place in his thirtieth year, at midday on the first day of autumn, when daylight and nighttime are equal, and six months before his coronation at dawn on the first day of spring."

"You mean that Eirik is planning to marry Kate in four weeks?" interrupted Ian, his voice filled with incredulity and his expression angry. "This can't be happening," he went on, as if talking to himself. "All this must be some kind of bad dream. Since the mist, nothing has made sense."

King Bjorn tried to comfort Ian. "Nothing will make sense until you are reunited with Kate, but rest assured that we will count no cost too high to rescue her and to thwart Malicious's evil plans."

"Then you have a plan?" asked Mac.

"Yes, we have decided on two offensive strategies, both to be implemented simultaneously," replied King Bjorn.

Magnus stepped forward to outline the strategy for battle at the Green Cavern. "Our forces are moving to positions north of the Green

Cavern in anticipation of a battle. We do not anticipate that Malicious will attack farther north until the bulk of her forces have massed at the Green Cavern. Based on our latest information, the bulk of her forces should have arrived by the equinox. By then we should have sufficient warriors and bears to resist her attack.

"The other plan involves a small party of warriors and bears who will attempt to capture or kill Malicious and rescue Eirik, Kate, and Liz. The rescue of Eirik will remove the false legitimacy that Malicious now claims to the throne and might rally some of the undecided clans from the Southern and Middle Realms to our side.

"So long as the impending battle at the Green Cavern is not won by Malicious, the lives of Eirik, Kate, and Liz are not in danger. While Eirik continues under her control, Malicious can claim legitimacy to the throne. However, should Malicious's army be victorious, then Eirik will likely be killed, and Malicious will present herself as queen by right."

"If Malicious only needs Eirik, why did she kidnap Kate?" asked Ian.

Ursus responded. "We believe that Malicious's original plan was to poison her father, which would have thrown the kingdom and the succession into confusion, and then to kidnap Eirik so that she could bend him to her evil purposes.

"Although she failed to kill her father, she did kidnap Eirik and immediately started to spread several false rumors. One rumor has it that Eirik will marry Malicious, and they will rule together. Although this might not seem acceptable to most of our people, the marriage of siblings is common among the royal families of the Southern Realm, where this rumor has gained in popularity. In the Northern Realm, Malicious has spread a different rumor, whereby Eirik will marry according to the prophecy and then abdicate in favor of his sister. According to this rumor, after a storybook romance and wedding, Eirik will renounce the throne to return with his bride to her home on the surface. Of course, the real end of this rumor would be the murder of Eirik and his bride."

"Well, that explains why Kate is necessary, but why Liz too?" asked Mac.

"We don't know," replied Ursus. "Kate clearly fulfills the prophecy. She is blonde and of Icelandic heritage, and she was at a sacred hot spring on a night with a full moon and when the lights were dancing in the northern sky.

"Why Malicious kidnapped Liz, who has brown hair, is a mystery and a worry. Malicious never does anything without a good, and usually sinister, reason. Some believe Malicious will use Liz in a human sacrifice ritual."

Mac had looked as if he might speak, but after Ursus's last comment, he went pale and still.

"Mac, are you okay?" asked Ursus. "Do you have something to say?"

Mac had been thinking about how inane it was to place so much significance on the color of a woman's hair. *Everyone sees through different eyes. Some men are color-blind. Looks can be deceiving,* he had been thinking, but he decided not to share his thoughts with the others. "No, but thanks for asking. I was just lost in my thoughts," replied Mac.

Much discussion ensued regarding how large the rescue squad should be and who should be included. All the bravest bears and warriors loyal to King Bjorn volunteered. Ian insisted that he be allowed to join the rescue squad, and King Bjorn agreed.

"Yes, Ian, you must be one of the chosen few. Your strength and courage were proven in the battle with the wolves, and your passion for Kate will drive you forward when others might falter. You have the pluck and resolve to see this through to the end."

Helga was chosen as leader of the rescue squad. She was acknowledged to be as fierce and fair in battle as she was compassionate and just during peace. "I will not disappoint you, King Bjorn," she said. "Thank you for this honor."

Helga offered her personal guard of three warriors, two men and one woman, each of unparalleled strength and courage, to accompany them, and this suggestion was accepted. The two men were Stefan and Thorfinn, and the woman was Gudrid. Gudrid and Thorfinn were twins.

Ursus suggested an equal number of bears, but King Bjorn turned down this suggestion. "Thank you, Ursus, but the smaller the number, the faster and more clandestine the rescue squad, and time and stealth are of the essence. However, I believe there is room for one mighty bear in this important group. Whom do you suggest?"

Ursus considered carefully the many valiant and seasoned grizzlies available but surprised King Bjorn with the suggestion of his sister Shabear, a grizzly of average size and no special battle talent, but learned and wise, especially in the healing ways of bears and men.

King Bjorn thought this suggestion excellent, and the group of six was unanimously decided upon.

Many men and bears were disappointed not to be included in this elite rescue squad, but none more so than Connor, whose youthful enthusiasm, boyhood friendship with Eirik, and new fondness for Ian had raised his hopes higher than his experience merited. Afterward, Connor pleaded with his grandfather to be included in the group.

"Is there a stronger bear or one whose heart is more firmly tied to King Bjorn?" demanded Connor. "Am I not the grandson of the king's closest friend and advisor? Did Prince Eirik and I not grow up together? Is Ian not my friend; have we not shared battle together? Did I not acquit myself bravely in the battle with the wolves?"

Ursus looked at Connor and realized how much he loved his grandson. Connor was the spitting image of Bär, Connor's father and a grizzly whose accomplishments were renowned.

"Adding one more bear won't slow the group down," continued Connor. "And besides, one bear is not enough. Everyone knows bears are worth at least five humans, and I'm stronger than most bears, and now I have battle experience too."

Connor paused to let Ursus speak, and his grandfather motioned for Connor to sit with him at a table. As Connor sat down, his massive grizzly thighs bounced the table up; to compensate, he leaned down on the top with his arms, a maneuver that might have worked with subtle pressure, but that instead caused the table to flip over.

Ursus had stood up and stepped back as soon as the table wobbled, as if he knew what was coming. He helped Connor set the table right and then with patient understanding looked over at his grandson. "Connor, your heart is always in the right place, but you might not be well suited for a mission where subtlety is more important than strength. Additionally, the king is counting on you to serve as commander of one of the bear battalions. War is a nasty business, and we will all be asked to serve in capacities we would not otherwise have chosen."

Connor was disappointed but polite. "Of course, I will do whatever King Bjorn decides. But I believe that I would best serve the king as a member of the rescue squad."

As Connor stepped away, he was obviously still unsettled that he had not been included as a member of the rescue squad.

Chapter 23
Connor's Vision Quest

Connor's disappointment was greater than he had ever experienced. His youthful passion struggled against a grizzly code that respected the authority of the elders. He went back once more to plead with his grandfather.

Connor found his grandfather in the library of their home. Ursus was sitting in his favorite chair, reading. Walls filled with books and portraits of their ancestors made the library a special place. Ursus had expected the visit from Connor and was surprised only that his grandson had taken so long to arrive.

"Connor, come sit with me," said Ursus, as he put down a book he was only pretending to read. "I was just thinking of you and hoping you would stop by for a chat."

Connor sought the comfort of a chair by the reading table that had served as his study desk for so many years. As he thought back, he realized that none of the lessons he had learned had prepared him for this disappointment. He had led a mostly carefree life, with all the privileges of position.

"Grandfather, I realize that a decision has been made, and I understand the reasons for that decision, but I just don't agree with them. I know this sounds presumptuous, but I know I can make a difference if the king allows me to go with the rescue squad. I feel it."

"I don't doubt your courage or sense of duty, and I know how disappointing this decision must be for you. Life takes us down many roads that we do not choose, and the greatest grizzlies have always found ways to make their journeys successful."

"You once told me that the greatest leaders often chose roads not considered by others and that these roads were sometimes the less traveled and more dangerous," said Connor.

"Yes, but that was when the decision was theirs to make. Grizzlies have always respected the decisions of our leaders, and our success is due in part not only to generations of wisdom but also to a steadfast loyalty peculiar to bears. Ours is an open and democratic society, and dissenting opinion is always welcomed and considered, but to change a decision requires more than a desire to do so. You must convince King Bjorn that you would be more valuable as a member of the rescue squad than as leader of a battalion of grizzlies."

"Then you won't speak to King Bjorn and ask him to change his mind?"

"I already did, and Bjorn told me that Magnus is counting on you to lead a bear battalion. You are young to be so favored." Ursus paused to add emphasis to this point before he continued. "Connor, my best advice is for you to embrace your new command. Look within yourself and find the discipline to accept the decision and carry out your command with eagerness and resolve. You have been offered a tremendous responsibility. Magnus has only three battalions of bears. Koda will lead one battalion, and Shasta, the mighty Kermode bear, another. To be named a battalion leader beside Koda and Shasta is high praise indeed. Look within yourself, Connor; reach back to our ancestors, and I am sure you will find the answer."

After talking with Ursus, Connor was still conflicted. He trusted the advice of his grandfather, but somehow the decision still felt wrong. After he left, Connor thought about his grandfather's suggestion to reach back to his ancestors. Connor couldn't physically contact his ancestors, but he thought of a way he might otherwise be able to follow this advice and seek the answer he was looking for.

As a young bear, Connor had been initiated into grizzly society according to ancient ritual. When he was of age, his family had held a celebration in his honor where he sang the songs and told the stories of their ancestors. For the prior year, Connor had memorized the songs and stories in preparation for the event. It was important that he be precise, since by tradition, only bears with a keen understanding of their family heritage could be initiated into grizzly society. Since the time of Kodiak, young bears had been taught to write, and all the songs and stories had been written down in the runic alphabet. Connor had studied hard for his initiation, and few bears had ever learned the stories as well as he did.

After the celebration, Connor had left to spend seven nights in a sacred place on the surface, a windswept mountaintop with a clear view of the rising sun, a location known only to his family. During that week, he took only water, and he otherwise fasted. He was expected to experience significant dreams that would guide him throughout life.

As soon as he awoke each morning, he wrote down his dreams and spent the day thinking about and memorizing the sleeping visions. Each night, he burned the written copy in preparation for the next dream.

When he returned to his family, he shared his dreams with a medicine bear. Shabear was the one chosen to help Connor interpret the significance of each dream. Each sleeping vision was considered important in some way. Most suggested some aspect of Connor's personality. Some underscored a major past experience in his life. Others foretold some significant life event to come. Sometimes a vision was so powerful that it was considered to be a "defining dream" for the young bear. Connor had experienced such a defining dream, and he realized now that his desire to be a member of the rescue squad was in no small measure linked to that dream.

Later that day, when Connor advised Ursus that he was preparing for a vision quest, Ursus understood and agreed with his grandson.

A successful vision quest required meticulous preparation. Connor visited and advised each member of his family that he was going on a seven-day journey. Everyone understood that "seven-day journey" was a metaphor for a vision quest, and without acknowledging that they knew, they wished Connor well.

On the morning of the first day, Connor had a sweat bath and then cleansed his body under the cascading water beneath Franang Falls. Only after all the dirt since his last vision quest had been symbolically washed away in this fashion would it be possible for a new defining dream to emerge.

He returned to the same sacred place where he had stayed during his initiation ritual and fasted for seven days. He brought only his medicine bundle, which was a collection of symbolic objects that he had collected during his initiation ritual. The dreams during his initiation ritual had suggested these objects, and Connor knew they would help link the two vision quests. Each morning he committed his dreams to memory.

For the first six nights Connor dreamed the same defining dream that he had dreamt as a young bear, with only minor changes each night. Finally, on the last night, the dream changed significantly, and Connor believed that he had dreamt another defining dream.

Excited, Connor hurried to confer with his grandfather, whom he hoped would interpret the dream as evidence that Connor should join the rescue squad. He found Ursus in the library, again pretending to read.

Ursus had expected Connor on the morning after the seventh night, not only because it was natural for Connor to share his vision quest with the senior member of his family but also and more so because of a dream Ursus had experienced the prior night. Ursus wondered if he had shared Connor's dream. If so, the predictive power of the dream was not in doubt. Shared dreams were rare and could not be ignored. Grizzlies believed that when bears dreamed, their spirit traveled and saw things otherwise invisible, mostly in the current time but sometimes in the future. The most significant dreams were those of the future, and the longer in the future, the more powerful the dream. Defining dreams were often of the future. Dream journeys were sacred to the bears, and defining dreams empowered the grizzly to great accomplishments.

"Grandfather, grandfather!" Connor shouted as he blustered into the library. "My vision quest was successful."

Connor had run without stop from the mountaintop and was trying to tell the dream in breathless segments.

"Wonderful, Connor," said Ursus, "but before you continue, sit down and catch your breath. I'm impressed that you still have the strength to run. You have lost weight with this fast, and many bears would have been hardly able to walk, much less run home. Have some berries while you compose your thoughts. I will return in a few minutes."

Ursus left Connor and sought out Magnus, with whom he had decided to share his dream. He found Magnus in the map room.

"When I return to the library," Ursus said to Magnus, "I will listen to Connor's vision, but I will not tell him that I have had a dream of my own. Afterward, I will ask Connor to share his vision with you. You will be in a position to determine whether we have shared a dream and to corroborate the event for King Bjorn."

After listening to Ursus's dream, Magnus was startled by the significance and agreed. "You are wise to ensure impartial verification of this possible shared dream," said Magnus. "These are dangerous times, and there are some who might otherwise consider your dream disloyal. I will listen to Connor's dream but will not reveal that I have heard yours. Should the dream be shared, it will be better if Connor looks surprised when King Bjorn is apprised of the vision. If Connor has shared the same dream, then he must follow his bear path and join the rescue squad."

By the time Ursus returned, Connor had eaten all the berries and was fidgeting through some books, trying to pass impatient time.

"I'm as excited to hear about your vision quest as you are to share it," said Ursus with a sincerity that was not lost on Connor, but that perplexed him. Connor had a vague inkling that his dream was prescient in more ways than one.

"I'm eager to hear," Ursus reiterated. "So tell me all. Did you follow the bear path and find wisdom?"

"The first six nights, I dreamed almost the same defining dream as I had dreamt on the last night of my initiation ritual. I was not surprised when this dream recurred on the first night, but I was disappointed when the dream kept coming back night after night. By the seventh day, I had decided that unless I experienced a new dream on the last night, I was not meant to be a member of the rescue squad, and I would devote all my energy to the command of a bear battalion. By then, I was hungry, but the fast had not eroded my strength nearly as much as when I was a young bear. I wondered if I had not been weakened enough to encourage a new dream. Father told me that significant dreams are more common when we are close to death."

"Yes, that is true," replied Ursus. "The initiation ritual is meant to emulate the cycle of life with renewal or rebirth as the sought-after goal. Just as bears on the surface go to their dens in the autumn, hibernate through the winter, and emerge in the spring, so the young grizzly is reborn as an adult after the fasting and isolation of the initiation ritual. The weakness is a symbolic death, and the vision represents the resurrection. Mortal danger and fear are common precipitating events for a defining dream. In the initiation ritual, the weakness due to fasting and the fears that come with the isolation are potent stimuli for visions. But even if you where neither weak nor frightened, a significant dream is still a significant dream."

Ursus listened patiently as Connor then described his dream. Connor was still excited and did not have a flare for storytelling, but even so, there was no doubt that Ursus had shared the same dream as his grandson. Ursus did his best not to look too excited or hopeful. The implications of the dream were too powerful to predict, and only King Bjorn could decide the proper course.

"Connor, I would like you to tell the story to Magnus before we visit with King Bjorn. Ordinarily, I would ask Shabear, but the rescue squad left yesterday, and in her absence, Magnus is an appropriate unbiased person with whom to share your dream."

"They've already left?" said Connor, obviously disappointed. "It's too late then. I must not have been meant to go."

"Perhaps, perhaps not," replied Ursus. "After you tell the story to Magnus, we will discuss the situation with King Bjorn. It is not too late for you to catch up with the rescue squad, but that will be the king's decision."

So Connor related the dream to Magnus, who, like Ursus, purposely maintained an unrevealing composure.

Ursus wondered what Magnus thought. Connor's story was very disjointed, and Ursus wondered whether Magnus had heard sufficient similarity to agree that the dreams were shared. As they walked to the royal palace, Ursus sought Magnus's eyes, and their look and a knowing nod confirmed that he had.

They found King Bjorn in the map room. For a man with as many concerns as he faced, the king was in exceptional humor. "Welcome, Ursus, Magnus, and Connor. Do you bring good tidings?"

"I believe so," said Ursus, "but you will be the best judge. Connor has just returned from a vision quest. On the last night he experienced a defining dream that requires a royal interpretation. I believe the dream is very important."

"I agree, King Bjorn," added Magnus. "Dreams are common on the eve of war, but I have never before heard of a vision so powerfully prescient."

"Indeed," responded King Bjorn. "All bears have dreams during their initiation ritual, but few have defining dreams. Connor, I recollect you had a defining dream during your initiation ritual. This speaks well of you and your lineage. Few bears ever undergo another vision quest, and fewer still experience a second defining dream. But then, defining dreams come naturally to the great grizzly leaders, don't they?" King

Bjorn put his hand on Connor's forearm in a fatherly gesture. "I hope the dream portends well for our world."

"I believe it does, King Bjorn," said Connor.

"Then relate your vision," responded the king.

"Relate the dream from your initiation ritual first," recommended Ursus. "The two dreams are linked, and this is one of the three reasons this vision quest is so powerful."

Connor nodded and began. "On the seventh and last night of my initiation ritual, I dreamt that I was walking on the surface in a valley. I was happy. The spring sun had passed overhead and was setting behind me, and I was following my shadow. I had just eaten some salmonberries and felt perfectly content with a full tummy. I ambled along in harmony with the valley. Suddenly my shadow disappeared. I looked up, and the sun was still bright in the sky, and there was not a cloud in sight, and yet, my shadow was nowhere to be seen. A soft breeze wafted the smell of a woman from the east, the same direction I had been walking. The smell was powerful, as with a woman who bleeds. I was aroused and started to run toward this smell. I ran for miles and miles while the smell slowly increased. The sun had set midway in the western sky when I heard the woman chanting. I continued to run for many more miles while the smell grew stronger and the chanting louder.

"Finally, when the sun had almost set, I came to a bluff and saw the woman by a river. She was dressed in the fashion of a person of high standing. There was a fire, and she was cooking something in a pot. Beside her I saw a raven feather, a snakeskin, the skull of a human, and the claws of a grizzly. She had her back to me, and I could not see her face. She had black hair. I heard but could not see a bear behind a huge boulder. The bear was chained to a great oak tree by the river and was huffing and struggling to free himself. The bear cried out to the forest animals to save him from the woman.

"The woman had a long spear with a shiny black, glass-like tip, which she dipped into the pot. She went behind the rock, and I heard the bear growl and then cry out. When she returned, the spear was bloodstained, and some fur and flesh were hanging from the tip. She mixed the blood, flesh, and fur into what she was cooking. The bear cried out again, and suddenly, I recognized the voice of my father.

"I ran down the hill toward the woman. I had never felt such anger. I was crazy with rage and wanted to tear her to pieces. Even so, I felt in complete control and stopped short of her. I stood up and told the woman to prepare to die. The woman turned toward me, but she had no face, and I could not identify her. I charged, and she threw her spear, which passed right through my chest without injuring me. Just before I reached her, she touched the feather, turned into a raven, and flew onto a tree branch overhead. I rushed behind the boulder and found my father, who was dying.

"'Beware the snake,' he said, and then he died. I looked behind me and saw the raven land on the snakeskin and turn into a huge snake, many times the length of a bear and as wide as the chest of a man. I wondered if the snake was Jormungand, the Midgard serpent of Norse legend. I charged the snake, and we wrestled until long after the sun had disappeared behind the mountains; neither of us gave or took any advantage. We continued to fight in the dark, neither able to injure the other. Finally, the moon rose behind me, and there was an eerie silver glow. I stood tall with my paws raised, and suddenly my shadow returned and blanketed the head of the serpent, which disappeared into the blackness. Then I woke up."

Viking rune stone that records excerpt from Connor's defining dream during his initiation ritual. "I charged the snake, and we wrestled until long after the sun had disappeared … We continued to fight in the dark, neither able to injure the other …

"I remember hearing of this dream," said King Bjorn. "There was much talk of the significance of your vision quest. Wasn't Shabear the medicine bear who interpreted your dream? What did Shabear say?"

Ursus answered, "Shabear believed that the dream foretold the premature death of Bär—my son, Shabear's nephew, and Connor's father—at the hand of a woman. The woman made a poison that killed Bär and transformed herself into a raven and then a snake. Therefore, she was a sorceress of great power. Her power was strong enough to steal Connor's shadow in the sunshine, but the shadow returned in the moonlight, which may mean that she has less power at night. As powerful as she was, she was not stronger than Connor, since her spear passed through him, but neither was Connor stronger than her. Their power was equal."

"Yes," said King Bjorn, nodding, "this was a defining dream of great significance, especially because several years later, Bär disappeared, and he has never been found." With these words, King Bjorn put his hand over Ursus's paw to help share the grief of his friend.

"And what of your new dream, Connor?" asked King Bjorn.

"For the first six nights the dream was almost the same as the defining dream on the last night of my initiation ritual. The only aspect that changed was the appearance of the woman. On the first night the dream was identical. The woman was faceless and had black hair. On the second night I could see the outline of her eyes, but they were empty without a black center or any color. Her hair was dark like the heart of a thistle, and her skin was the end-of-summer color of a person who lives in the sun. The next night I could see the black spot in the center of her eyes, but the spots were tiny, as if she were looking at a bright light. The eyes otherwise had no color, and they were piercing like those of a hawk. Her hair was the summer color of the female elk. On the fourth night red streaks appeared in the whites of her eyes, and the black center was a bit larger. The eyes looked sore and searching. Her hair was now a lighter color, like oak leaves in autumn. The colored portion of her eyes began to appear on the fifth night, with a pink blush like a rabbit, and her hair now had a rusty tint like dead pine or fir needles. Her skin was lighter, like the color of a woman who lives underground. On the sixth night her eyes were the color of the breast of a robin, and her hair was off-white, like the color of the bark of the birch."

Connor paused and looked at his grandfather, who nodded that he should go on. "The dream on the last night was the same as with my initiation ritual until I saw the woman from the bluff. I heard a cry from behind the boulder, but the voice was not that of my father. It was a man." Connor paused and looked at Ursus, who nodded again for him to go on.

Before Connor could resume, King Bjorn interjected. "Who was it? Did you recognize the voice?"

"Yes," said Connor, who paused and looked over at Ursus again for encouragement before continuing. "The man was you, your highness."

King Bjorn lost the color in his face and looked shaken. He asked Connor to continue.

"The woman dipped her spear in the pot, and I charged before she could stab you with the poisoned tip. She turned to face me. For the first time I recognized who she was. Her eyes were evil. Except for the black spot, they were the color of fresh blood, her skin was sickly translucent and laced with blue veins, and her hair was the color of faded straw. She laughed and called me 'Clumsy Cub,' the nickname she had always teased me with as a young bear."

"Malicious," said King Bjorn.

"Yes," said Connor.

"She hurled the spear at me. I stood still and watched, mesmerized as the shiny black blade approached in slow motion. I felt the tip enter my left chest and a burning pain as the blade went between my ribs and entered my heart. There was a sucking sound as my wind escaped, and I felt my heart stop. For a moment the world stood still, and I found myself floating. I saw myself standing on the ground as the spear went through my body. I watched as the shaft of the spear slowly shortened as it entered my chest and then lengthened again as the spear emerged between the ribs in my back. Once free of my body, the spear accelerated and then struck a pine tree, which instantly withered and died. Once the spear had passed through, I returned to my body and charged Malicious, who looked dumbfounded that I was still alive. The black centers of her eyes were now large and fixed, and the color darkened to that of coagulated blood. Her skin looked winter white. Just before I woke up, I had her head in my jaws, and she was shrieking in pain."

King Bjorn was visibly shaken. "What you have related is exactly what you dreamed?" he asked.

"Yes," replied Connor.

"Forgive me for asking," continued King Bjorn, "but did you embellish the dream in any way to enhance your chance to join the rescue squad?"

"No," replied Connor.

"I wish Shabear were here to help interpret the dream," said King Bjorn, "but even without her wisdom, I can see that you should be part of the rescue squad. During your initiation ritual, you dreamed that your father would be killed, and he has disappeared. During that dream the spear passed through you without any injury. During this dream my daughter Malicious was the woman, and I was the one threatened with death. Whether this represents the poison that killed Queen Freyja or some future threat is not clear. The spear injured you during the second dream but only momentarily. Your vital spirit left your body and thereby escaped injury. Clearly, you have the power to confront Malicious, but the outcome is not clear."

King Bjorn paused for several moments, deep in thought, before he continued. "Ursus, you mentioned that there were three reasons to consider this a defining dream. The first was the link to the initiation vision quest. The second must be the content of the dream. What is the third?"

"I had an almost identical dream last night. Connor and I shared the dream."

"What?" said Connor incredulously. "Grandfather, you never told me."

"No, I wanted you to tell the story to King Bjorn the same way you told it to Magnus and me. I told Magnus my dream before I heard yours. Magnus can therefore corroborate that our dreams were shared."

They all turned to Magnus, who said, "The dreams are too similar for any doubt. The dream was truly shared and must not be ignored."

"Then it's settled," said King Bjorn. "Connor, you must leave at once to join Helga and the rescue squad."

Chapter 24

Kate's Confusion

Princess Malicious beckoned Lord Null to accompany her into the room next to the one in which Kate and Liz were imprisoned. The room was empty and had curtains on two opposing walls. Lord Null drew one of the curtains to reveal a one-way crystal window that allowed them to see Kate and Liz in the adjoining room.

Lord Null self-consciously played with the rubies on the hilt of his sword and glanced at Princess Malicious to determine her mood and whether he should initiate a conversation or wait on her pleasure. He assessed that she was in an especially tolerant mood and decided to risk speaking first.

"The younger woman has a power, and she might be difficult to turn to our purposes, but she is largely unaware of her abilities and is no match for you. Still, she is a complication. Why did you kidnap her once you had the blonde woman?"

"Because the blonde woman does not have the power," snapped Malicious. "Curious, though, don't you think? The prophecy foretold the presence of a blonde woman of Icelandic descent, at a place sacred to my peoples, on the millennial anniversary of the founding of the settlement, and during a full moon when the lights danced in the northern sky. Yet the blonde woman does not feel her destiny. I have searched her mind, and it is cluttered with thoughts of a young man and her work, studying animals. She has no real power. And yet, the younger sister does have the power. She too arrived at the sacred place at the time foretold, but she is not blonde. Curious, don't you think?"

Lord Null could not fathom what was curious, but he deferentially agreed with Princess Malicious. "Your powers are great, your highness, and soon to be greater."

As they talked, some boars brought food for Kate and Liz. Lord Null and Princess Malicious watched keenly as the sisters ate.

"Can we trust this food?" asked Kate.

"Whether we can or can't, we need to eat," replied Liz, who selected something that looked like freeze-dried tomato. "Tastes okay to me." When the tomato stayed down, Liz went on to try a mixture of nuts and dried berries. "Now, this is great, almost as good as Dad's trail mix," she said approvingly.

Kate shook her head and wondered how Liz could enjoy anything under the circumstances, but she did experiment with some nuts and what looked like cornbread.

"So, the nuts are their favorite," said Malicious. "See to it the next batch is specially prepared," she said to Lord Null.

The following morning, the boars brought another meal that included the foods that each woman had eaten, and several new foods were also offered.

"Well," remarked Liz, "they don't want us to starve to death," and she started to eat a handful of nuts. "Best not to overeat though; we aren't exercising."

"Yes," Kate agreed, as she swallowed some nuts and a piece of a star-shaped fruit that tasted like an apple but had the fibrous consistency of a pear.

A minute later, Kate went over to her bed and lay down. "I feel so tired, and yet we just woke up. We definitely could use some fresh air and exercise," she said with a yawn.

"I feel tired too." Liz also lay down.

A few minutes later, as soon as both women were asleep, the boars came into the room and took Kate away.

When Liz woke up, Kate was sleeping beside her, and the plates with the food were still on the table. Liz noted that some of the food on her plate was missing and wondered if Kate had woken up before her and had a snack.

Kate woke up a few minutes later and also noted food missing. Clearly someone else had been eating the food.

"No big deal," advised Liz. "While we were asleep, the boars likely snuck in for a snack. They are pigs after all."

This pattern repeated itself each morning. The after-breakfast nap usually lasted about an hour, and there was always food missing, usually meat. Since no one but the boars had come into their room, they presumed the boars were the food thieves.

On the third morning, Liz was surprised when Kate mentioned that Malicious might not be the witch they presumed her to be.

"After all," remarked Kate, "no one has hurt us since we arrived, and we are certainly eating well."

"Kate," replied Liz, "are you crazy? We were kidnapped. We've been tied to mules, wolves, and panthers; intimidated by a horrible man; and witness to the murder of numerous people and animals. And we're imprisoned against our will. Get a grip, Kate; there's nothing nice about Malicious."

Kate persisted with the Malicious-might-not-be-so-bad theme the next day, and Liz started to wonder if her sister was suffering some sort of delusion brought on by their confinement. Sometimes Kate's eyes had a dreamy look about them, especially in the mornings, and Liz wondered if perhaps she had been drugged. That led her to think about the morning naps, and suddenly it clicked. *The food,* realized Liz. *There must be a sleeping potion in the food.*

The nuts were the only common food she had eaten each morning. Liz resolved to avoid the nuts the next morning and, if she didn't otherwise feel sleepy, to feign sleep.

The following morning, Liz pretended to eat some nuts, but instead she palmed them and then hid them in her clothes. Sure enough, Kate felt tired and was soon asleep, but Liz didn't feel sleepy at all. But Liz lay down anyway, closed her eyes, and waited to see what, if anything, would happen.

Liz was not surprised when the boars arrived. They took Kate, and Liz decided not to try to stop them. A few minutes later the boars returned and greedily gobbled some of the meat on the plates. About an hour later, Kate was brought back and placed on her bed.

Later, when Kate woke up, Liz decided not to mention what she had learned. Instead, she decided to plan a surprise for the boars. That night, while Kate was asleep, Liz crushed the nuts she had saved into a powder. The following morning she mixed the powder into the meat on her plate. She feigned sleep and allowed the boars to take Kate. When the boars returned, they ate the meat, and before they could leave the room, they were asleep.

"You guys should be on a diet," Liz groaned as she dragged the boars into the corridor. *And you sure stink,* she thought as she smelled her hands. Liz checked her watch. *I have about half an hour to find out what's going on.* Candles that gave off an unpleasant odor that reminded her of bacon grease dimly lit the corridor. *Ouch, when their living usefulness ends, I guess the boars end up as tallow for the candles.*

She opened the next door down the corridor and found a room that was empty apart from curtains on two opposite walls. When she looked behind the curtain and saw into the room where she and Kate had been imprisoned, she understood. *So, they've been studying us. No wonder we haven't met Malicious.*

On the other side of the room was another curtain. When she drew the curtain, she saw Kate speaking with a thin, especially fair-skinned woman with translucent hair elaborately knotted on her crown; she had red eyes like a rabbit and a flowing black robe that enhanced her pallor. The robe was gathered at the shoulders. A festoon of beads hung from silver brooches that fastened the fabric at each shoulder. The brooches were silver and elaborately carved. *Malicious,* thought Liz.

Kate seemed happy and relaxed, and her conversation with Malicious was animated and natural. Several times, Malicious touched Kate on the arm in a tender fashion and with a liberty that suggested that she and Kate were friendly. With each touch, the hair on the back of Liz's neck stood on end, and a cold shiver went down her spine. *You bitch,* Liz wanted to shout, *what have you done to my sister?*

Liz studied the conversation and noted how frequently Kate's gaze was drawn to Malicious's eyes. *Some form of hypnotic suggestion,* Liz concluded. Looking at her watch, Liz realized that the boars might soon wake up, so she hurried back to her bed. She had guessed at the correct number of nuts to put the boars to sleep and had lucked out with an amount sufficient to last just barely half an hour. She reached the bed just as the boars awoke. She feigned sleep and held her breath while she waited to see how they responded. They didn't seem to realize they had been asleep. *Thank goodness these pigs are so dumb,* thought Liz with relief.

That morning, Kate offered a new twist to the Malicious-is-okay theme. "Liz, did you know that we come from royal blood?"

"Pardon me, Kate?"

"Yes, our ancestors were kings and queens of Norway and chieftains in Iceland."

"And how do you know this?" asked Liz.

"Well, Princess Malicious told me. She really is quite nice. I've had tea with her each morning while you've slept. Her brother, Prince Eirik, has taken a fancy to me. Can you imagine me as Queen Kate?"

The extent of Malicious's hypnotic control was now clear to Liz. "Sis, remember Ian, your husband, the man you married about a month ago? The white dress, the church, the walk down the aisle on Dad's arm, with all your friends and family in attendance?"

"Of course I do, but still, Ian isn't a prince," remarked Kate, "and I, after all, am a princess."

Liz was aware that Malicious might well be watching and was careful not to explain anything to her sister. Rather, she chose to downplay her sister's madness. "Sis, you've had a nap every morning just like me. I think you've been in this room too long and are going a bit batty."

Kate ignored Liz and instead combed her hair with a dreamy look. "Do you like my new comb?" asked Kate. "Malicious gave it to me. She says the comb is a family heirloom. Would you like to borrow it? Your hair is really a mess."

Liz accepted the comb and started to untangle some of the accumulated knots in her hair. The comb was a light brown color and obviously very old. Some runes and the figure of a beast were carved into the comb. The stylized beast was chunky with a round face, huge eyes, and a neck tendril. The thin ribbonlike body had large muscular shoulders and hips. The legs ended in paws that gripped tightly to the edge of the comb.

"Malicious told me the comb was carved from an elk antler and belonged to one of the queens of Asgard."

Liz was happy to use the comb but sad to realize how much her sister was under the influence of Malicious.

The next morning, Liz drugged the boars again and this time explored farther down the tunnel, which ended at the stairway down to the city and dockyard. There were several more rooms along the corridor, but most were empty apart from scattered human bones, which attested to less well-fed and otherwise less fortunate visitors.

Liz kept a keen eye on her watch and had almost run out of time when she opened the last of the doors. Inside was a chamber fit for a king. An exceptionally good-looking young man was sleeping on a bed covered with a navy blue silk canopy.

Liz felt a tingling on her neck, quite different from the cold chill she'd felt upon seeing Malicious touch her sister.

The young man smiled with his eyes closed as if he were enjoying a special dream. "Katherine," he murmured, "such a sweet name."

Liz realized the young man must be Prince Eirik. Had Kate not married Ian, this fellow looked like he would have been a handsome match. However attractive though, he was the brother of Malicious and therefore the enemy. She quickly closed the door and ran back to her bed.

Several days later, Kate announced that she was betrothed to Prince Eirik and that the marriage was scheduled for September 21.

"I'm so happy, Liz. Imagine, I will be Queen Katherine, and you will be Lady Liz."

Liz resisted the urge to vomit and instead humored her sister, while stashing away more and more nuts and planning their escape. She had learned that the stairway at the end of the tunnel was never guarded during the morning hours that Kate was with Malicious. She had also learned about the elevator system that passed by the tunnel entrance about every fifteen minutes. The elevators carried a variety of cargos, including uniforms and weapons, on the way down and mostly smelted iron or food stores on the way up.

Although she had only a half hour each morning to explore the tunnel and plan their escape, Liz was always drawn to look in on the sleeping prince. *How could this man be Malicious's brother?* she wondered one morning as she shook her head. *He looks so wholesome and good, like a young knight, not like some thug. Could he be under the same spell as Kate?*

Liz checked her watch and saw she had about five minutes left, and in an impetuous moment, she went over and shook Eirik awake.

"Good morning," mumbled Prince Eirik, rubbing his eyes as he slowly awoke from what seemed more like a coma than sleep. Eirik sat up and looked straight at Liz, and his blue eyes sparkled a sincere and warm hello.

Chapter 25
Parting Gifts

On the evening prior to the rescue squad's departure, a steady stream of well-wishers visited Ian, and most brought a gift to help him in his quest. Koda brought battle gear in the fashion worn by the bears but modified for Ian's smaller size. The specially treated leather tunic was thin and supple but strong enough to deflect most arrows or blades, and it covered his body from neck to knee.

King Bjorn brought Ian the Sword of Olaf, the famous blade of the king who had brought peace to the Northern Realm. "Do not be deceived by the age of this weapon. Five hundred years is but a blink in the life of well-forged blade, and this sword has never seen defeat. Care for it well, and the weapon will care for you."

The sword had a runic inscription down both sides, and Ian asked King Bjorn to read the script.

"This sword was forged with iron obtained from a stone that fell from the sky during the reign of King Olaf the Great. It is said that whoever is courageous, compassionate, and honorable will never be defeated while he wields this sword."

The hilt of the sword was silver, and on one side was a depiction of Kodiak and King Olaf, sitting side by side on thrones, and on the other, an outline of the Castle of Light. A shallow channel, half an inch wide, ran down the middle of the blade. Ian asked the purpose of the channel.

"That is the blood groove," advised King Bjorn. "The channel allows the blood of your enemy to flow freely."

The sword came with an over-the-shoulder harness and a scabbard made of the same thin flexible leather as the battle gear. At the tip of the scabbard was a silver plate with the coat of arms of King Olaf.

"Go safely, Ian," said King Bjorn. "May your way be safe and may you return successful."

"Thank you, King Bjorn. My safety is better assured with the help of the Sword of Olaf. I hope to return the sword to its place of honor by the statue of your noble ancestor."

Helga offered Ian a net for fishing and a fishhook, small and lightweight items and symbolic of the Kwakiutl clan. "The warriors in our clan carry only a sword, battle-axe, knife, fishing net, and hook. With these tools we can satisfy our hunger and vanquish our enemies," she advised.

"Your warriors don't carry shields?" questioned Ian.

"Never," replied Helga. "A shield is a defensive weapon and is never carried by a true warrior. Warriors with shields might come to depend on them. It is too easy to hide behind a shield. We fight with a weapon in each hand and never take our eye off the enemy."

Ursus brought Ian some items wrapped in cream-colored leather. "During my initiation ritual, I dreamed that I captured and killed a white buffalo. In the dream it was obvious that the hide of this buffalo was meant to be the wrap for my medicine bundle."

"Medicine bundle?" questioned Ian.

"Medicine bundles contain objects considered personal and spiritually powerful to a bear. They are made after the initiation ritual and contain objects linked to the ritual and also honored items passed down through generations from father or mother to son or daughter. The bundles are sacred and especially important for those who aspire to be a medicine bear. In a sense, the initiation ritual is not truly over until the medicine bundle is complete.

"Within a month of my initiation ritual, I had collected all the objects to place in the bundle, but I was not able to locate a white buffalo. These great animals are so rare that none of the bears of my parents' generation had ever seen one. I inquired far and wide of the surface bears, and none of them had ever seen one either.

"After many months I despaired of ever finding a white buffalo and had almost given up hope of becoming a medicine bear. This was very disappointing not only for me but also for my parents, since as far back as the time of Kodiak, every generation of our family had included a medicine bear. At the time, I was the only cub in my family, and four centuries of tradition seemed threatened. Later, my sister Shabear was born, and she became a medicine bear and carried on this family tradition."

"Even so, you must eventually have found a white buffalo," said Ian as he accepted the medicine bundle. "This hide looks white to me."

"Yes, I did find the white buffalo of my vision, but only after I had stopped searching. Only after giving up the search and accepting that I would not be a medicine bear, was I able to find my true way, the bear path within me."

"How did you find the white buffalo?"

"The buffalo found me."

"You mean the buffalo came to Asgard?"

"No, the buffalo came to me in dream. By then my childhood friend King Bjorn had become king, and as his friend, I had accepted the responsibility to mediate treaties with the Middle and Southern Realm peoples. During a journey south, I stayed for some time in Siksika, one of our cities beneath the Great Plains on the surface. While there, I dreamed that the white buffalo was galloping over the prairie and calling to me. I saw myself on a high plateau looking down over plains that stretched forever to the east. The sun was behind me. I consulted Runolfur, the leader of the Siksika clan, and he recognized the place from my description and accompanied me to the top of a butte. I chose the last hour of the day to arrive at the butte, so that as with my dream, the sun would help guide my eyes."

"And the buffalo was there?"

"Yes, but far away, so far that he looked to be only a moving white speck on the horizon. Still, I was sure this was the buffalo of my visions. I ran all night in the direction of the buffalo, and the next morning I found him grazing by a river. But as soon as he saw me, he galloped away. Fresh from resting all night, the buffalo easily outdistanced me. Each night I closed the gap, but each day he widened it.

"I chased the buffalo without stop for four days and four nights until the great beast finally tired and turned to face me. I was frightened, not merely because all buffalo are powerful animals and equal in strength to a grizzly, but because white buffalo have a sacred strength that makes them invincible. I knew that more than brute force would be necessary to kill this awesome animal. I was fortunate, though; my father had instructed me well, and I knew what was necessary.

"First, I apologized for chasing such a mighty white buffalo and thanked him for stopping to talk with me. The buffalo was old, and I complimented him on his endurance to run so hard for four days and four nights. He thanked me for my courtesy and the compliment and responded that he had never before met a humble grizzly. 'Why do you want to talk with me?' he asked.

"I told him about my dream and asked his permission to kill him. I told him his hide would be sacred and would bring much power to my family. To my surprise, but as my father had predicted, the white buffalo agreed. He even explained the proper way to remove his hide so as to preserve the power. He asked that I share his meat with the native peoples of the Great Plains and told me where to find them. He told me that his horns also had great power and that I should save them to store medicine for my family. He asked that his skull be prepared and painted according to Siksika tradition and tied above the door of my home. I agreed to all his requests and killed the white buffalo with one blow to his head. I followed all his instructions. To this day, my family reveres the ways of the buffalo.

"Inside the medicine bundle you will find one of the horns. It contains a mixture of herbs and tobacco that you should smoke if you are confused about which direction to take. The smoke will clear your mind and show you the bear path."

Ian was embarrassed to receive such an important family treasure and tried not to accept the gift. "Surely this medicine bundle should be for Connor, your grandson and heir."

"No, Ian, the bundle was meant to go to you. I know this. The bundle would have passed down to Bär, my eldest son, and thence to Connor, but my son disappeared, and I believe he would agree that the bundle should be yours." Ursus paused after he spoke of his son, and a sad sigh emerged before he shared a memory with Ian.

"Bär had a majestic bearing, but he spoke with a common touch that endeared him to all bears. His loss was keenly felt throughout Asgard. His mother was a glacial bear, and Bär inherited her bluish-gray color. From a distance he looked like a black bear with graying fur on his back, but up close the royal blue fur with silver highlights was handsome, and he was admired by many. I loved him very much."

Ursus gently shook his head and blinked his eyes as if to help facilitate the passage back from this memory to the present. He went on to reassure Ian. "I discussed this gift with Connor, who has his father's medicine bundle as well as his own. My grandson agrees that you should have my medicine bundle."

Ian felt overwhelmed by such a sacred gift, and he thanked Ursus with a sincerity that pleased the grizzly. "I will respect your traditions, and one day I will pass this bundle along to my son or daughter."

"Thank you for respecting the bear way. It is precisely my hope that the bundle will help you rescue Kate and that the power will pass to your son or daughter. The hide has great power to protect," explained Ursus, "and is big enough for two bears. While wrapped in the hide, you will be warm during the worst cold, comfortable during the most severe heat, and dry during the worst thunderstorm."

Ian thanked Ursus again and carefully placed the hide and horn in his pack.

Other gifts bestowed on Ian included a lightweight torch specially carved to fit his hand and a rope woven with a fiber that was light and supple but almost impossible to break. From his original gear, he selected only his picture of Kate.

Chapter 26

Prince Eirik Learns the Truth

Eirik seemed a bit groggy, but his smile was warm, and Liz was drawn to remain and talk with him.

"I'm sorry, I don't think we've met. My name is Eirik. Are you a friend of my sister?"

"Yes," lied Liz. "But can you keep a secret? Although I'm a very good friend of Malicious, she doesn't know I'm here, and I'd like to surprise her, so don't tell her you met me. Okay?"

"No problem. I talk to her every day, but I'll keep your secret, especially if you stay and talk awhile. You see, I don't get many visitors. In fact, apart from my sister, I don't remember any visitors. I've been sick, and my sister is nursing me back to health."

Liz seemed startled at the revelation that Eirik was sick. To her he looked the picture of health.

Eirik noticed her reaction and wondered if the mention of his sickness might be a concern to Liz and if she might want to leave. "Don't worry, though; I don't have anything contagious. I have some kind of sleeping sickness. In fact, I'm surprised that you could wake me. I usually sleep all day until Malicious visits. Do you know what day this is? I seem to have lost track of time."

Liz sidestepped the question with another question. "How long has it been since you've seen your father, Eirik?"

"Well, I don't rightly know. Malicious brings me messages from him almost every day, so it seems as if it was only yesterday that Father and I were together at the Castle of Light, but now I am at my sister's volcanic fortress, which is weeks away from Father's castle, so it seems I have been here for a week or two at least. I guess I don't know for sure. I do know that if I recover by the autumnal equinox, according to the prophecy I will marry, and that I last saw Father on the first day of summer." Eirik wrinkled his brow and looked up as if he were trying to figure something out. "What day is today?" Eirik asked again.

"About four weeks before your wedding, which means you haven't seen your father for over two months. Does that make sense to you, Eirik?"

"Seems a bit long, doesn't it? But Malicious advises he is well and looking forward to my wedding."

"Eirik, do you know Lord Null?"

"You mean the creepy guy with the ruby-hilted sword?"

"Yes. Do you know that he kills animals for fun?"

"Well, I don't know anything about killing animals, but he isn't a pal of mine. He's a high-ranking security person who works for my sister. What about him?"

"How about wolves, panthers, and boars? Are they your friends, Eirik?"

"Not really. The wolves have always been a problem in the Northern Realm, and I hear that panthers and boars are a similar bother to our allies in the Middle Realm."

"But the bears are your friends, right?"

"Absolutely. Ursus is my father's most trusted advisor and friend, and my best friend is his grandson Connor. The bears have been our friends for five hundred years. Before that our people and the bears didn't always get along. Back in those days, we mostly tried to leave one another alone."

"So you love your father; the bears are your friends; wolves, panthers, and boars are a problem; and Lord Null is neither your friend nor a nice guy—is that right?"

"Yes, but what's this all about? Is something wrong with my father?"

Liz decided that truth was her ally and told Eirik what she knew.

Eirik was dumbfounded, and when he refused to believe Liz, she suggested a simple experiment to prove Eirik was being deceived by Malicious. "Eirik, is there something special you enjoy eating that is present in every meal you eat?"

"Yes, of course. I love nuts and eat them with every meal."

What a coincidence, thought Liz. "Eirik, don't eat anymore nuts. Instead, pretend to eat them and then fake falling asleep and see what happens."

Eirik looked skeptical.

"Promise you'll try. I must leave now, but I'll come back tomorrow. Please don't tell your sister you talked with me." With that, Liz was out the door, and a few minutes later, she was back in bed, simulating sleep and waiting for her sister.

The following morning, Liz did not need to wake Eirik. When she opened the door, he seemed asleep as usual, but an eyelid flickered, and when he realized the person entering was Liz, he sat up with a warm smile and another hearty hello. However, his countenance changed as he started to talk.

"You were right. I was drugged. I can hardly believe my sister has tricked me. My poor father—he must believe that I am dead. We must escape."

"Yes," agreed Liz, "but that might not be easy. Do you know much about the volcanic fortress and the tunnels that come here? Do you know a good way to escape?"

"There are only two ways to escape from the rooms off this mineshaft; either we go up to the top of the volcano and climb down the mountain, or we go down to the River Fjorm and escape down one of the tunnels or rivers. There are two tunnel routes to the north and one each to the south and east."

"Tell me about the top of the volcano," said Liz.

"My sister lives in a castle in the crater, where she studies the ancient myths and magic of the peoples in the Middle and Southern Realms. She is an expert on the medicinal uses of plants and animals."

"How convenient," interjected Liz. "Can we climb down from the top?"

"Theoretically, but I wouldn't want to try. The toxic gases that emerge from some parts of the crater can be fatal, the slope is exceptionally steep, and the summit of the volcano is often enveloped in a dense cloud that sometimes limits vision to less than a few feet. The only animals that seem to survive the crater are the messenger ravens. Malicious has taught them a precise aerial approach to her castle, and even at that, some die. I've walked on the crater, and the surface is covered in bird bones. I also saw human and other animal bones."

"Did you ever ask your sister about the human bones?"

"Yes, and she replied that over the years, a few of her staff have foolishly gotten lost."

More likely abandoned to their death, thought Liz.

"Even if we could climb down from the volcano, I don't know how to get to the castle from here."

"So escape from the top is not a great option. Okay. What about going down and taking one of the subterranean tunnels? Which would be the safest?"

"From what you've told me, I suspect the northern routes will be filled with my sister's soldiers traveling to the Green Cavern, especially the inland route that you came by. Perhaps the coastal route might be safer. We will not find any support going south, likely only peoples aligned with my sister. Traveling east will take us to caverns beneath ancient surface cities, long since abandoned, and now overgrown with jungle. The waters in these caverns are salty and lead to a warm ocean. The subterranean peoples in this region are fiercely independent, worship serpents, and believe in human sacrifice. We neither talk nor trade with them and only know of their existence because of periodic encounters with their people. These peoples were here before us. When we explored and settled parts of this region about eight hundred years ago, they had already established themselves in the Middle Realm, and they did not encourage trade or other contact."

Umm, thought Liz, *overgrown surface cities, a warm ocean, serpent worship, human sacrifice, and disappearance of the culture over a thousand years ago. That fits well with the Mayan peoples.* Liz shared her thoughts with Eirik. "I think I know the history of these peoples. My world has studied the ruins of some of the surface cities you speak about and have learned about their culture. They were called the Maya, and they disappeared about 1,100 years ago, and no one knows why."

"Yes, that is what they call themselves. We have little contact with the Maya. They are quite different from the Anasazi, another native people who, like the Maya, moved underground many years ago."

"You know the Anasazi?" exclaimed Liz.

"Sure, the Anasazi are one of the seven clans that make up the peoples of Asgard. The Anasazi used to live in caves built into surface mountains, but as with the Maya, drought forced them to seek underground water, and they eventually relocated their peoples to our world. They are a peaceful people who have always lived in harmony.

They live in one of the great cities along the coastal route. They are renowned for their exquisite art."

Wow, thought Liz, *the answers to two anthropological mysteries solved.*

"You know about these people?" asked Eirik.

"Yes, very much so. In my world I am a student of science. My main area of study is anthropology and archaeology, especially the ancient civilizations of the Americas. The disappearances of the Maya and the Anasazi have always been a real mystery. What about the Inca—do you know about them too?"

"Yes, they are a southern people, and like those you call the Maya, they practice human sacrifice. They are not friendly and have warred against our people since our first encounter. Likely, they are allied with Malicious. She has learned much about their history and myths."

"What about the Aztec peoples?" asked Liz.

"These peoples live in and around Popocatépetl. About five centuries ago, soldiers on the surface drove them underground. Only a few survived. My sister has studied the ancient ways of these people as well."

Liz looked at her watch and realized that she was several minutes late for a safe return to her room. "Listen, Eirik. I must get back. Be prepared to leave in the next few days. I trust you to choose the best route."

Before Eirik could answer, she was running down the tunnel. She arrived in her room just as the boars were waking. Fortunately, they were too dull and sleepy to notice.

Chapter 27

Kwakiutl

The coastal route would take the rescue squad through Kwakiutl, Siksika, Anasazi, and Toltec, the four southernmost cities in the Northern Realm, all allied with Asgard.

"We must travel three thousand miles in the next thirty days for us to arrive before the autumnal equinox," advised Helga. "Fortunately, there is a long underground river with a favorable current to speed us along for a good portion of our journey."

Helga, Stefan, Thorfinn, Gudrid, and Shabear could run all day without seeming the least bit out of breath. Ian had thought he was fit, but he soon realized the group was slower because of his presence. "I'm slowing you down," he acknowledged to Helga at one of the few rest stops.

"Yes, that's true," she admitted, "but you are young and strong, and each day you will run a little faster. We have taken your lack of fitness into consideration."

He was twenty-eight, recently discharged from the military, and supposedly at the peak of his physical prowess, so the realization that his "lack of fitness" had been taken into consideration was humbling. To his credit, this enhanced his determination.

Shabear overheard the conversation with Helga and offered encouragement. "I'm tired too, but our cause is worthy. Each of us has a reason to take this perilous journey. For you the reason is Kate. I am honored to represent the bears. The future of our culture might depend on the success of our mission. Malicious has long expressed her disdain for bears, and no one doubts that under her reign bears would be banished to the surface."

Shabear looked thoughtful and sad for a moment and sighed before she went on. "Our surface cousins are slowly disappearing. Many years ago, when I was a cub, there were several hundred thousand bears on the surface. Now, less than a few thousand grizzlies survive. Your people have been hard on bears. Those who survive do so mostly in the north and high in the mountains, in regions not populated by your people. If the bears living in Asgard were exiled to the surface, we would slowly disappear like our surface cousins."

Shabear paused, hung her head low for a moment, and said a silent prayer before she continued. "I am only a small bear, more used to mental than physical exercise, and but for you I would be the one slowing down Helga's men. We will both grow stronger over the next few days and weeks. Our passion will keep us strong. King Bjorn has chosen well. Each of us knows the enormity of our cause, and we will not be daunted by something as puny as tiredness."

By the time they reached the first city, Ian and Shabear were taking turns leading the group, and their endurance was no less than that of the others.

En route, they did not encounter any of the enemy, but they did see signs of their presence. Wolf tracks were common and in much larger numbers than usual.

"Clearly, packs of over a hundred wolves have passed by here in the last few days," noted Helga at a rest stop by an underground river.

They also came upon strange tracks, similar to those of a wolf, but much larger and without claws. "Cats have retractable claws that do not show in the ground, but these tracks are much larger than those of a cougar, lynx, or bobcat," advised Stefan. "The front feet are much larger than the hind feet and make a deeper impression, suggesting a lot of weight in the shoulders and chest. The walking stride is longer than that of any animal I have tracked. Whatever made these tracks is as long as a man is tall and as heavy in the chest as a young bear."

"That would be one big cat," offered Ian. "By comparison, a cougar would seem like a house cat."

The first city south through the coastal route was Kwakiutl, the home of Helga and her clan. Despite how fast they had traveled, messengers had reached the city before their arrival, and crowds of Helga's kin came out of the city to greet them.

"We made good time," concluded Helga. "We took only six days to travel four hundred miles, one day less than we estimated. We can afford to rest at Kwakiutl for the rest of the day, but tomorrow morning we must leave for Siksika, the home of the Blackfoot clan."

For Ian, the respite from running was reward enough, but the hospitality of the people of the Kwakiutl clan made the war and all their concerns almost disappear for an evening, which was even better.

Like the Castle of Light, Kwakiutl was built at the site of a natural and enormous cavern, which generations of labor had enlarged to accommodate a thriving community. All Asgard cities were built in caverns close enough to the surface to admit fresh cool air and sunlight and proximal to a subterranean river to provide fresh water. Finding caverns proximal to a subterranean river was never a problem since water flow was the natural force that had initially hollowed out the rock.

Ian understood the geology of the two basic cave types. The most common and longest developed when calcium carbonate, otherwise referred to as calcite, the principle mineral of limestone and the basic mineral of seashells from ancient seafloors, was dissolved by water, usually with the help of either carbonic or sulfuric acid. Carbonic acid formed when carbon dioxide in the air dissolved in water, and sulfuric acid formed when hydrogen sulfide from underground oil and natural gas deposits seeped up and combined with oxygen and water. The second type of natural cave formed after a volcanic eruption. In this situation, the flow of lava left a hollow tube within the molten igneous rock.

Although Ian understood the geology, he was amazed at how the Asgard engineers had helped nature along. The royal engineers had excavated connecting tunnels and expanded existing tunnels to create miles of continuous caverns. Clearly, they were talented and determined engineers. Until now, Ian had understood that the longest recorded cave in North America was only about 120 miles.

The Kwakiutl central plaza served as a commercial hub by day and a social spot by night. Storytelling was an important social activity, and there were storytellers with small groups of listeners in many sections of the plaza. They sat around totems carved by successive generations of Kwakiutl artisans. Ian wandered from group to group and listened and learned of the rich history of the Kwakiutl clan, a people forged from the intermarriage of the descendents of Balder with coastal tribes.

Shabear was one of the storytellers and had collected an especially large group of listeners. Most were children or cubs, but a number of young couples, presumably the parents, were also present. Shabear sat at the base of a totem that depicted a twelve-foot grizzly standing on two legs amid a river filled with spawning salmon. The grizzly figure held a human child in her paws. The bear was carved from a highly polished brown stone, and the child was fashioned from pieces of walrus ivory. The river was cut from a huge piece of blue lapis lazuli and was so expertly carved that changes in the light made the waves seem to move. The salmon were carved from amber and were meticulously overlaid with tiny copper scales such that the fish shimmered in the light and seemed to swim in the waves.

The bear in the totem drew Ian's attention. The artist had created an especially compelling facial expression that suggested great strength. Curiously, though, the power of the totem felt more emotional than physical. Neither teeth nor claws were visible in the carving, and the child was held tenderly in the massive paws. Clearly the artist and her people revered the grizzly, and Ian suspected that it was not by chance that Shabear had chosen this spot to tell her stories.

Ian listened while Shabear told a creation myth. "Many years ago, before the time of man, the forest animals lived in harmony with their world. The grizzly was the largest of the land animals but not the most talented, for a bear could not swim as fast as the salmon, run as fleetly as the deer, or fly like an eagle. Grizzlies understood that each animal had a unique gift, and they respected the other animals. They took care to preserve the rivers, forests, and mountains. As a reward for living in harmony, the God of All Creatures granted the grizzlies the gifts of speech and the ability to walk upright.

"The grizzlies were pleased with these gifts, but over time they yearned to share their thoughts with other animals. They prayed to the God of All Creatures for all the other animals to be given the gift of speech and the ability to communicate with one another. In answer to these prayers, the God of All Creatures created a man-child, another animal with the power of speech and the ability to walk upright."

With that, Shabear pointed to the child held by the grizzly in the totem. Some of the cubs and children nodded, having heard the story before; the younger ones, however, were obviously thrilled to learn the significance of the sculpture for the first time.

"When of age, the man-child married a female bear. Some of their children looked like grizzlies, and others looked like humans. That was the start of humankind. The first people respected bear tradition, but time passed, and the people and bears grew apart. They quarreled about so many things that finally the grizzlies decided to live apart from the people. Without the bears to help them, the people struggled to survive, but eventually they learned to hunt and fish on their own."

A young Kwakiutl asked Shabear if this was why their people prayed each winter for the return of the grizzly.

"Yes, winter is the time of hibernation for the surface bears. Tsetsehka, your winter ceremony, is a prayer for the return of the grizzly in spring, which is the time of spiritual and physical rebirth. According to this belief, so long as the grizzlies return, so will the salmon, which is the lifeblood of your people."

Shabear asked if there were anymore questions, and when there were none, she asked one herself. "You know," said Shabear as she looked directly at the children and cubs, "while we were talking, I thought I saw a person turn into a bear. Did any of you see the same thing?"

On that cue, a person wearing a carved bear mask stepped from behind the totem and came forward to sit beside Shabear. When the person separated the sides of the mask, the listeners were thrilled to see Helga, the leader of their clan.

"This is a bear transformation mask," said Helga. "The mask shows how closely we are related to our bear brothers."

The mask had the typical long disk-shaped snout, fierce canines, and small ears of a grizzly bear and was painted different shades of brown. Just below the eyes were holes from which emerged two sets of thin leather cords. One set was knotted inside the mask and coursed outside through the ears, down to the hands of the person who wore the mask. When these cords were pulled, the grizzly mask opened and transformed the bear to a human. The other set was knotted outside the mask and coursed inside through a hole in the forehead of the human mask, again down to the hands of the person who wore the mask. When these cords were pulled, the grizzly mask closed and transformed the person back to a bear.

Helga let all the cubs and children try on the mask. Afterward, she walked over to Ian.

"A very powerful story," remarked Ian. "Have the children not heard the story before?"

"Yes, most have heard the story many times but only rarely from someone as famous as Shabear," she replied. "Her power is great. She is a descendant of the first grizzlies who learned to live in the subterranean world. Ursus is her brother."

Ian acknowledged that Ursus had told him as much but that he found this strange since Shabear looked so much younger; he asked Helga how this could be so.

"You're right—Shabear is half the age of Ursus, but bears live more than a hundred of our years and continue to have children for many decades. Ursus is the oldest of the cubs in his family, the oldest grizzly of his generation, and the most revered of the grizzlies. Someday his statue will likely stand beside that of King Bjorn in the Royal Chamber."

"Shabear seems wise beyond her years," remarked Ian.

"Again you're correct. All bears are natural healers, but some, like Shabear, inherit the powers of the great medicine bears of ancient times. Shabear was well chosen to accompany us. Should any of us be wounded or fall ill from one of Malicious's many poisons, we will need her skill. Importantly, Shabear understands how to heal not only the body but also the mind."

"I've already learned that," replied Ian. "During the first few days, when I felt tired and depressed, her words gave me strength."

"Yes, I know, and I'm glad they did. And don't let her smaller size worry you; like all bears, she is strong and brave. In a mortal fight, I would be happy were Shabear at my back."

After much laughter, many good things to eat, and the enjoyable company of his new friends, Ian fell into a deep and peaceful sleep, the first such rest since Kate had been kidnapped.

Chapter 28
Escape

Liz was worried about Kate. Each morning, Kate spoke more and more about Malicious, seemingly her newest and best friend, and less and less about Ian. Each day, Liz saw less and less of her sister and more and more of this new person, molded into mindlessness, courtesy of Malicious's drugs and evil hypnotic powers.

Reassuringly, Malicious's hold on Kate gradually wore off somewhat during the afternoon and evening. The extent of her control was greatest immediately after each session, when for several hours each morning, Liz patiently listened while Kate spouted so much drivel about her future role as a princess and the wedding plans. During the afternoons, Kate usually complained of a headache and slept. It was only in the evenings that Kate seemed at all like her old self.

Liz decided an overnight escape made the most sense, and the next morning, she asked Eirik to be ready.

The boars always finished whatever food was left over, and Liz had saved enough of the sleep-inducing nuts to make sure the boars did not wake up all night.

The evening routine was always the same. The boars brought the meals and placed them on the table, and then they left and locked the door. An hour later they returned to pick up the plates. But they never ate the evening leftovers while still in the room. This happened only in the morning, when they presumed Kate and Liz were asleep. Liz had to hope that the boars on the evening shift were just as inclined to finish the plates and would be greedy enough to do so while still in the room if Kate and Liz seemed asleep. It would be easy enough for Liz to fake sleep, but she could not rely on Kate, who by dinner was still sufficiently under the control of Malicious that she might not cooperate. Liz decided to mix some nuts in Kate's evening meal so that her sister would be asleep when the boars came.

What dose should I use? wondered Liz. She knew that both she and Kate generally ate about ten nuts at breakfast. *The full dose made me sleep for about two hours, but Kate was awake when she was with Malicious, and that was within a half hour of eating the nuts.* Liz decided that Malicious must have given Kate an antidote for the sleeping potion. *I don't have an antidote, so I better use only a few nuts, or Kate might not be awake enough to escape.* Liz decided on four nuts and mixed these into Kate's meal. Liz did not eat and left a full plate, which she hoped might prove irresistible to a hungry and greedy boar.

The boars returned to find both Kate and Liz apparently asleep. Just as Liz had hoped, the boars found the food too attractive to resist. Liz had not dared to open her eyes and watch the boars, but even so, what she could hear was enough for her to picture what was going on. Soon after the boars entered the room, Liz heard some jostling as the boars squabbled over the full plate. Then she heard a few grunts followed by a muffled squeal as the alpha boar bit the other. This was followed immediately by a rude snort of sorts as the food was inhaled and then the clatter of the metal plates as they fell to the floor. The noise of the plates was followed by a huge thump that shook the floor. Liz cracked open an eye just in time to see the second boar wobble and then slump unconscious to the floor with another thump.

"Great," she said with a chuckle, "they went whole hog."

She tried to wake Kate, who seemed more comatose than asleep. Kate's breathing was very slow and shallow, and her body was limp.

Not good, thought Liz. *I guess I made a mistake with the dose.* Her first idea was to postpone the escape, but she realized that if the boars were still asleep when the morning shift arrived, there was no telling what would happen. At the very least, the security would get tighter, and another escape opportunity might never be possible. *We've got to go tonight,* she decided. Liz ran down the tunnel and thankfully found Eirik ready to go.

"Where's Kate?" he asked.

"We have a slight problem," she replied. "You need to carry Kate. She's asleep and might not wake up for a while. I had to drug her with some of the nuts so that she would be asleep when the boars came into our room. I tried to minimize the dose as best I could, but I must have given her too much."

"She likely always has some of the drug in her body. Probably Malicious only needs to administer a minute amount to sustain her control over Kate. Even the small amount you gave her was too much," replied Eirik.

Wow, thought Liz. *Why didn't I think of that? Eirik's not only handsome but smart too.*

Eirik continued, "Carrying Kate might be a problem. Our plan depends on our ability to blend in with the southern soldiers. We need to be inconspicuous. I don't think that will be easy to accomplish carrying your sister."

"I agree, but we can't leave her. She's my sister. We all go, or none of us go."

"Of course. We have no choice," agreed Eirik.

Kate was more awkward than heavy. The most efficient but least gracious way to carry her was slumped over Eirik's shoulder, head hanging down behind him, with one of his arms behind the crooks of her knees.

"Boy, I'll bet she'll be stiff when she wakes up. Does she have a temper?" asked Eirik.

"Sometimes, but under the circumstances, I'm sure we can cope."

The first elevator that stopped was unmanned but carried supplies, so they waited for one with uniforms, which they needed to help conceal their escape. The second elevator carried weapons but no uniforms. When the third also didn't have any uniforms, Eirik was ready to walk down the stairs and take their chances, but Liz wanted to stay.

"I've studied the elevators," she said. "I've never seen more than two go by without uniforms. Unless there is something different about the nights, one with uniforms should be along soon."

As she predicted, the next elevator contained a uniform shipment together with weapons. The uniforms were functional and unisex and came in only a few basic sizes. Leather helmets were sufficient to cover Kate and Liz's long hair. The cloth tunics were not protective in any battle sense but at least offered the freedom of mobility. A thick leather belt, with a loop for either a sword or a battle-axe, gathered the tunic at the waist.

Malicious's ruby-eyed symbol emblazoned the front of the tunic on the left side of the chest, just over the heart.

Eirik looked at his tunic and realized that the red symbol formed a perfect bull's-eye over his heart. "My sister might be bright in many ways, but I'm glad I'm not one of her soldiers facing the expert bowmen in our army."

Leather sandals completed their uniforms. Eirik chose a battle-axe and a sword from the weapons and fastened a sheathed knife at his waist. Liz chose only a knife, but Eirik suggested that she also carry a sword. "All the soldiers I've seen had either a battle-axe or a sword, and a few had both. None had neither."

"Good point," Liz responded. They outfitted Kate with a sword as well.

While carrying Kate to the elevator, Eirik had caught Liz watching him once or twice, and her look was flattering. Now as he changed into his tunic, he saw her give his physique a good once-over, again in a more than casual manner. As a gentleman, he didn't watch while she changed, but as a young man, he wished that he had.

Chapter 29

Dreams and Reality

Ian awoke with a start and looked around. He could hear Kate calling him from a great distance, and her voice, initially so loud and clear, trailed away and then finally disappeared.

This is a strange place, he thought. *I didn't go to sleep here. I'm on a mountain path on the surface.*

Ian heard the clang of swords and looked down onto a plateau where he saw two men fighting. One was very tall, bald, and skeletal and held a sword with two rubies on the hilt that gleamed like eyes. He was an expert swordsman and was slowly but surely maneuvering the other man into a precarious position at a cliff edge.

The other man looks familiar, Ian thought. *Poor fellow, he's only an average swordsman and doesn't have the advantage in height and arm length.*

As Ian watched, the man with the ruby-hilted sword flipped the other man's weapon into the air and caught the sword in his free hand.

"So this is the famous Sword of Olaf," sneered the tall man. "Too bad the bearer is not as good as the blade." With that, he pushed the defeated man over the edge with the tip of his sword.

The man looked up at Ian as he fell. Their eyes met, and Ian realized he was watching himself. The man's cries of dismay blended in with the shouts of Shabear.

"Ian, Ian, wake up! You're having a nightmare. Wake up!" shouted Shabear, who was applying cool cloths to his face.

Ian woke up in a puddle of sweat. His heart was pounding. "Where am I?" asked Ian. "Where is the man with the ruby-hilted sword?

He …" Ian stopped. He had been about to say, "He killed me," but then he reconsidered revealing this aspect of his dream.

"Relax, Ian; you're with friends. You had a bad dream, that's all, but it's over. Do you want to tell me about it? Some dreams are important. Sometimes they can even tell the future. I'm practiced at dream interpretation. You might want to share your dream with me."

"Seemed real to me," said Ian as he stood up and looked around. Thankfully, only Shabear was present to witness the nightmare. "Did I talk in my dream?"

"Yes," replied Shabear, "but most of what you said made little sense. There was something about a sword fight. Do you want to talk about your dream? Perhaps the dream is important for our mission. I might be able to help."

"I don't remember much now," Ian lied.

Shabear had a resigned look that suggested she did not believe Ian. "That's okay," replied Shabear. "I'm glad you're awake and feeling well. We're leaving shortly. If you do remember anything, we can always talk later."

Chapter 30

The Army of Asgard Marches

A thousand years of effort, five hundred years of peace, and a forever of hope marched with the brave warriors who stood proudly beneath the banner of King Bjorn and the flag of Asgard.

When King Bjorn addressed the warriors, he spoke from the heart and on behalf of all who wished for the prosperity of Asgard to continue for another millennium. There was hardly a dry eye in the audience. His people knew their cause was righteous, but they also knew that justice had a cost, and they hoped the warriors would return safely.

Afterward, Shasta spoke for the bears. The commander of the bears, Shasta was a white grizzly who was renowned for her fierceness and an innate ability to sense the next move of any enemy. She told stories of Kodiak, the great warrior bear who had forged a lasting peace with the ancestors of King Bjorn. Her words were stirring, and by the time the army left the Castle of Light, everyone felt inspired and hopeful of victory.

As the companies of men and women disappeared into the tunnels interspersed with columns of bears, Ursus visited with the many cubs and their mothers and fathers who had been assigned the important task of remaining behind. They had gathered beside the lake to wish their brethren bears Godspeed. Ursus knew these cubs were the future, and he had purposely stopped to share a prayer with them before he joined King Bjorn.

"Great God of All Creatures, thank you for showing us the bear path; thank you for teaching us to live in harmony with nature; thank you for instilling compassion in our hearts as a balance to the power in our paws.

"For five centuries we have lived in harmony with man and the other animals. Courtesy of your guidance, we found a common path to a kinder, more civilized world, and together we have prospered. Thank you for showing us the bear path.

"Today we march as warrior bears. I am ashamed that after five centuries of peace, we must take this unforgivable and uncivilized step. My heart bleeds for every animal, friend or foe, who will be killed or who will suffer in the upcoming battle. After five centuries of harmony, the twin evils of greed and envy have reared their ugly heads. Worse, we were witness to the birth of this malevolence and did nothing to prevent its growth. Rather than nip the blight in the bud, we allowed this horror to take root. We refused to believe that so much evil could be concentrated in one person or that evilness could be spread so quickly and to so many other animals. We naively believed that after five centuries of harmony, we were somehow insulated from the depravity of avarice and the baseness of jealousy. Today we march to pay the price of this naivety.

"Great God of All Creatures, we pray that you will allow harmony to be restored without the need for loss of any life. If not, we pray that success in battle will restore us to the bear path with as little loss of life as possible. We pray that you will spare the suffering of all creatures, even those who do not pray to you as the one God of All Creatures.

"Although I do not understand the why of war, my faith is strong. I know that whatever challenges lay before me, I am stronger for this faith and for my love of you."

When Ursus left the cubs, he felt better for having stopped to pray. He always did, and he hoped the cubs did too.

Smelters and smithies in the kingdom had worked overtime for months, and each warrior carried a forged weapon with a blade that would neither bend nor break. Most chose a long sword to carry at their side, a hilted dagger for their belt, and a lance. King Bjorn's men knew that their weapons were as true as their king and would never let them down.

The bears carried no extra weaponry. Why be encumbered with a metal blade when each bear was born with twenty deadly claws? They wore supple leather armor, since even bear hide was susceptible to blades and arrows.

The royal guards, who remained to defend the Castle of Light, along with those too young or old to be considered for the impending battle, gathered around the lake and at the bottom of Franang's Falls, where they cheered the warriors on their way. The assembled army took a full day to enter the tunnels. Hundreds of pack mules carried their supplies.

Mac asked Ursus about the mules. "Many years ago, a male and female mule disappeared from my grandfather's corral. Are these mules the descendants?"

"Yes, some of them are. I hope we did not inconvenience your grandfather too much."

That clears up another mystery, thought Mac.

King Bjorn joined the forces with Ursus and Mac at his side. Behind them followed Magnus, cousin to King Bjorn and commander of the men and women, and Shasta, commander of the bears.

"Is Shasta from the frozen northland?" asked Mac, who presumed she was a polar bear.

"No," replied Ursus, "but I know of the great white bears of which you speak. Balder and his people saw many when they first settled Inuit. Those bears live in the frozen north where they hunt seals and walrus. I have met a few in my day, but these bears still prefer to live on the surface. Men have not troubled them as much as they have the grizzly, and until they do, the great white bears will continue to live on the surface."

"So Shasta is a grizzly born with white fur," replied Mac.

"No. Shasta is a Kermode, a member of the black-bear family. That accounts for her smaller size compared to a grizzly. Her people live in the caverns below a coastal region west of the Castle of Light. Before her people relocated to the subterranean world, they lived on islands off the shore. The original peoples who fished and hunted in the forests above our Northern Realm revered the bears and especially the grizzlies as the natural rulers of the forest. The bears and their peoples lived in peace and harmony for many centuries. The original peoples who fished off the coastal islands believed that the Kermode were the spirits of ancient bears and that the islands were their final resting place. As such, the islands were considered sacred and treated with great respect. Only a shaman was considered powerful enough to walk on an island inhabited by the white bears. This changed when your peoples came in big ships to hunt the whales and catch the salmon. These men also hunted bears and especially the Kermode, and within a generation, almost all the white bears were killed. Those who survived found sanctuary in King Bjorn's kingdom. Today, about one in ten cubs born to bears from this region has white fur. Some even have white claws. Usually they are known more for their good counsel than for fighting, but some, like Shasta, are fierce warriors."

"King Olaf would be proud to see the descendants of both the bears and his people marching together in such a just cause," remarked Shasta.

"He would indeed," answered Ursus, "and so would Kodiak, the great grizzly who you invoked with your stirring speech to the army."

"Yes," interjected Magnus, "and the bears have been our brothers and sisters ever since. Within a year of the treaty that brought peace between our people and the bears, the Inca attacked Asgard. Kodiak and the bears answered our call and helped defeat the Inca at the Battle of Tegalupa. Since that battle, people and bears have stood shoulder-to-shoulder as a united culture, a symbiotic meld that serves as a model of harmony between animals."

"Let us hope our united culture will survive this challenge," said Ursus, "and that our example will serve as a model for other animal species. If only wars were about courage and justice, we would certainly be victorious. But sadly, this is a different war. The treachery and sorcery of Malicious is formidable."

"True," replied Magnus, "but the armies who support Malicious are motivated only by greed. They have the demeanor of feral dogs. We are motivated by a desire to preserve centuries of prosperity and enlightenment. Our cause is worthy, and our people and the bears understand this. We will vanquish the southern armies, the wolves, and any other sorry excuse for a soldier that Malicious has recruited."

"Well spoken, Magnus," said Shasta, and all those present nodded in agreement.

Chapter 31
The Moskoestrom

At dawn the next morning in Kwakiutl, Helga gathered the rescue squad at the edge of the river where a Haida war canoe was outfitted and awaited them.

"Our journey will be relatively easy for the next week while we paddle downstream in this canoe, specially built by Haida warriors skilled in the old ways. Groa, the leader of the Haida clan, expedited the construction to accommodate our needs. Courtesy of this sturdy craft, we should be able to travel more than two thousand miles over the next week, and this will shorten our journey considerably. The river ends several days north of Siksika."

The canoe was familiar to Helga, Gudrid, Stefan, and Thorfinn, who had traveled in similar boats all their lives, but the style was unfamiliar to Ian. He realized at once that the canoe had been carved from the trunk of a massive tree, and he marveled at the beautiful lines. A striking bear crest adorned the prow.

Ian asked Helga to explain how the canoe was built.

"The Haida hew this craft from the gigantic red cedar that grow on Haida Gwaii, an island off the coast. The red cedar has a perfect grain that confers the flexibility and strength to withstand mighty seas. The builders harvest the tree from a remote part of the island in the spring, and they work on the canoes through the summer and autumn on the surface. After the first large snowfall, the roughed-out canoes are sledded to the beach and then towed to the concealed entrance of a subterranean river. From there the canoes are towed to one of the underground communities below the island, where they are finished over the winter. In the spring the finished canoes cross treacherous

Hecate Strait to the mainland, and those boats that withstand the crossing without foundering are considered seaworthy and become part of the Haida fleet that navigates the subterranean rivers and carries trade goods throughout the Northern Realm."

The canoe built for the rescue squad was styled after a war canoe but was specially built to accommodate only six individuals instead of the usual two dozen and was modified from the roughly finished hull of a canoe originally intended as a fishing boat. As such, the length and beam were only twenty by four feet, instead of the typical fifty-six by six feet in a traditional war canoe.

The canoe was much wider amidships than the diameter of the trunk of the tree, and Ian could not fathom how this had been accomplished. "How did they make the canoe so wide?"

"After the cedar tree is selected and cut down, the side branches are removed, and the shape of the hull is roughed out with elbow adzes. To establish the thickness of the hull, small holes are drilled through the canoe, and premeasured yellow cedar pegs are inserted. The interior of the canoe is carved out with smaller adzes and curved knives until the ends of the pegs appear. The bottom of the hull is carved to a thickness of approximately three inches and the sides to two inches. Once the hull has the desired thickness, the canoe is prepared for steaming. A fire is built, and large rocks are heated until they are red hot. Prayers and songs are offered to the God of All Creatures for assistance with this critical stage. A protective layer of cold rocks is placed on the bottom of the canoe, and then the boat is filled with water. Hot rocks are placed on top of the other rocks to create steam, and these rocks are continually replaced to maintain the intense humidity until the sides of the hull begin to soften. When the sides are flexible enough, the hull is pulled out to the desired shape, and spreaders are placed between the gunwales. Thereafter, the hull is allowed to dry and harden into the final shape."

The graceful lines of the canoe were enhanced by upswept bow and stern pieces that were carved according to Haida tradition. The hull was charred black, but the carved bow and stern pieces were elaborately painted. The bear crest on the bow was chocolate brown with gray highlights around the snout and ears.

Shabear saw that Ian was interested in the bear crest. "The crest depicts Rhpisunt, the bear-mother-goddess of the Haida. The Haida believe that the carving will bring good fortune to those in the canoe."

Gudrid had the most skill with canoeing, so she took the rear position, and Thorfinn, who was the next most experienced, took the lead. After sufficient provisions were laid on, and with much fanfare from the Kwakiutl, the rescue squad pushed off to continue their mission.

The pace was relaxing. The current was brisk, and only Thorfinn at the bow and Gudrid at the stern had to expend any effort, and even this was minimal. Occasionally, Gudrid would ask the other paddlers to pull on one side or the other to help negotiate a turn or to avoid an obstruction, but generally the days passed without much effort. They beached the canoe to sleep at night but never encountered any sign of the enemy.

On the sixth morning, the last before the end of their canoe journey, they emerged from the river into a huge subterranean lake. The lake was so long that the southern limit could not be discerned, but it was narrow such that the sides were within easy eyesight.

"Is the lake deep?" asked Ian.

"Yes, but no one knows how deep," answered Helga. "No one has plumbed the depths in the center, but I know that even toward the shorelines, the lake is so deep that few have dived to the bottom. But that is not our worry. We plan to paddle over, not under, the lake, and we should be able to reach the southern shore after a day and a half of hard paddling."

"Just as well," said Stefan. "Apart from Gudrid and Thorfinn, the rest of us have grown soft and lazy over the last five days. The paddling will awaken our muscles and prepare us for the next part of our journey."

After traveling in the bubbling current of a rushing river, the lake seemed unnaturally still and quiet, but the motion of the canoe awoke the waters. The prow split the glassy calm and left a trailing wake, and each time a paddle plunged into the still water, the concentric circles eddied out. Even so, the wake and the waves dissipated quickly, and the lake resumed its sleepy silence.

Shabear and Ian were relatively inexperienced paddlers, and it took some time for the group to establish an efficient rhythm. Gudrid switched the positions of the paddlers several times during the morning to make the most of her crew. By midday she was very pleased with their progress. "We could race this canoe against the best the Haida clan have to offer, and I'm confident that we would fare well."

Their efforts afforded the rescue squad a speed they had not anticipated. During the early afternoon Helga was pleased to announce that at their current pace, they might manage the crossing in one day. Had they known what lay in store for them at the southern end of the lake, they might not have paddled with such vigor.

Helga's words were like a challenge that spurred each to extra effort, and by the time they reached the three-quarter point, their shoulder and arm muscles were tired and sore.

"Slow down," advised Gudrid. "Keep some strength in reserve. Who knows what enemy might lurk ahead."

No sooner had she spoken these prophetic words than there was a rumble from deep within the earth, and the glassy surface of the lake started to tremble. Soon the haphazard motion of the waves on the surface coalesced into a series of swells from the south. The first swells were small, but each successive wave mounted higher and higher.

"By Odin," muttered Stefan, "this is no time for an earthquake."

The air turned thick with dust, and they could no longer see the shoreline or for that matter the ceiling above. Although they couldn't see, they could hear rocks crumbling off the walls and tumbling into the lake. The surge of waves from the immense falling chunks of rock buffeted the canoe until none were certain in which direction the boat was pointed.

Just as suddenly as the rumble had started, the action ended, and for an eerie few minutes they waited and hoped that one shock would be the limit of the quake. Each sat perfectly still, as if any movement might somehow precipitate another tremor. Finally Gudrid whispered, "I can see the west shoreline. Those on the right, paddle until we are back on course, and then let's put some distance between us and this cursed spot."

They paddled hard, and when the lake had stayed silent for several minutes, they felt relieved and thought the best. But they shouldn't have because the first tremor, it turned out, had been only a tease. The next quake started ever so mildly, with a shimmer in the water followed by a slight quiver to the boat. The quiver turned into a shudder, which made the boat wobble in the water. They stopped paddling. The shudder turned into a shake, and the canoe started to roll about, and they were bounced back and forth from one gunwale to the other with such violence that they had to hold tight or risk being tossed into the water. The walls and the ceiling started to collapse, and they believed their final hour had arrived. Twice, they heard a massive crack followed by a boom, which ushered in a wave ten times the height of a man. Each time, Gudrid managed to point the canoe into the wall of water, and each time, they emerged miraculously on the other side of the wave. This quake lasted longer than the first and again abated with suddenness, but this time the stillness was not replaced with silence. Instead there was a sound like wind.

"What is that?" said Ian. "It sounds like wind. Has the quake broken an entrance to the surface?"

"No," replied Thorfinn. "Had it done so, we would see sunlight."

"We're moving," said Gudrid. "Is anyone paddling?"

No one was paddling. The canoe was moving slowly but surely on its own accord, and the group realized that somehow they had been caught in a current.

"Helga," asked Gudrid, "is there a current known in the southern part of this lake?"

"None that I know of."

"What's that?" said Stefan, who pointed to a wall of white water some thousand yards to the south.

"It looks like the spray or foam that you see kicked up by rocks on the shore," said Thorfinn.

"But we're miles from the southern shoreline, and there are no rocks that break the surface that I'm aware of," said Helga.

"Perhaps the quake has thrust up a new bottom for the lake," said Shabear.

The current seemed mild at first but steadily picked up as they approached the spray.

"It doesn't sound like wind to me," said Gudrid. "Or if it is the wind, it sounds as if the air is being sucked through some narrow space. I know this sound. I've heard it before, when I was a young girl, on the ocean." She lifted her head as if to perk her ears and strained to remember. All eyes were on Gudrid when suddenly she turned a ghastly pale. "Paddle! Everybody, paddle to the right! Paddle for your lives—it's a Moskoestrom!"

None but Thorfinn had ever heard the word, but they all understood the urgency and saw the fear in her eyes. They poured their hearts into their paddles and tried to veer to the right.

"What is it?" cried Helga.

"A giant whirlpool," responded Gudrid. "And if we don't break free, we'll be sucked into the abyss."

Try as they might, they could never reach the edge of the current. What started as a fairly wide band of flowing water grew narrower as they approached the vortex. They were speeding through a watery furrow that deepened with every stroke of their paddles. The current continued to accelerate, and the sound and the spray increased commensurate with their speed.

"Pull! Pull!" cried Gudrid in a cadence that they all responded to with every muscle and every sinew in their control. "Pull!"

The surface of the water turned oily as if some slippery substance had been added precisely for the purpose of greasing their journey into the vortex.

"Pull!" Gudrid shouted between grunts as she too gave her all to the waters that swirled about them. But as much as they pulled, the whirlpool pulled back, and slowly but surely they all came to realize that they could not break free of the current. Yet none gave into despair, and even as they approached the rushing circle, they continued to pull for their lives.

The edge of the whirl looked like a spinning fence of shiny spray surrounded by a greasy foam. As they neared the lip, they could see the funnel descend as a smooth ink-black wall of water that cascaded down at a forty-five-degree angle.

"Pull!" shouted Gudrid, and their muscles screamed in unison. "We can do this!" she screamed. "Pull for your lives—pull or we're lost!"

As they touched the lip of the funnel, the canoe spun violently around and tottered for a moment, as if undecided about whether to take the plunge. They all instinctively brought their paddles on board and braced themselves for their slide into oblivion.

The canoe jerked again, slipped into the funnel, and raced counterclockwise around the inner rim with dizzying speed. When they looked to the right, they saw a blurred wall of water hemming them into their watery misfortune, and to the left they stared down into a liquid void. The canoe surfed along the plane of the vortex, which caused the boat to tilt precariously, and although it looked as if they might fall out, the whirlpool pressed them into the canoe with such a force that they could barely move.

Inch by inch, and turn by turn, they descended slowly into the vortex. The gyrations of the canoe were mostly and surprisingly smooth, but every so often, they would suddenly fall several feet down to a deeper level, and with each abrupt descent, they were momentarily weightless and felt themselves rising out of the canoe. As they grabbed for the gunwales, their stomachs turned and their hearts palpated, and each time, they thought the end had come. But they stabilized at each new depth and lingered thus in their dying.

They screamed to communicate, but the roar of the whirlpool consumed the words, and all they could see of one another was open mouths contorted in horror. Only their eyes spoke, and they were never silent as the canoe continued to creep deeper into the vortex.

The canoe descended toward another lip from whence the water seemed to fall straight down and beyond which they realized they would meet their end. By some strange quirk the stern was leading and was the first to touch that fated boundary. When the stern tripped over that inevitable edge, the canoe wrenched this way and that and then back again and finally hovered on the brink, and in that moment, time seemed to pause, as if to allow each to say a sad farewell to life. In unison they lifted up their eyes for one last look through the swirling air. Suspended thus between life and death, they saw a ribbon of green crystal shining in the ceiling of the cavern where none had been before.

Suddenly, there was another great rumble, and the sucking sound grew shriller, as if the hole beneath might be closing. Hope sprang into their hearts. But even as their spirits lifted, the stern teetered down and dashed their hopes. Salvation was so close but yet so far.

Thorfinn turned his head and looked back toward his sister. Each sensed the unique precariousness and preciousness of the situation. In that final moment, the siblings connected in a way that only those who begin life together can do. Their eyes met with mutual purpose and understanding. No one else in the boat saw Gudrid slide over the stern and into the abyss as Thorfinn transferred his weight over the prow. But the change in the balance of forces was sufficient that the canoe tottered back and away from the edge. The rumbling and sucking sounds abated with an abruptness that felt final, and suddenly the canoe bobbed onto a calm lake as if nothing had gone before.

Helga, Ian, Shabear, and Stefan shook their heads and looked around in disbelief. It was several minutes before any could speak.

"Is this Valhalla?" asked Stefan. "Where are the Valkyries?"

"No! We aren't dead. We've been spared a sodden death. Clearly the gods meant only to test us," said Helga.

Ian wasn't certain whether the gods had spared them, but he knew that Gudrid's skill as a coxswain had made a difference. "But for the excellent skills of Gudrid, the outcome might have been different," Ian said. "Thank you, Gudrid," he said as he turned to the stern.

They turned to thank her, but her seat was empty. None but Thorfinn had witnessed her noble deed. They scanned the calm surface but saw no trace of their comrade. They looked to Thorfinn, who stood silent at the prow. The tiny tear on his cheek was testimony to her sacrifice.

Thorfinn took his sister's position at the rear of the canoe, and they paddled in silence until they reached the southern shore. Several hours passed before Thorfinn could share the story of his sister's selfless act.

Chapter 32

Jens's Guilt

Jens had continued to serve as a boot boy for the royal household and had never shared his shame with anyone. Not an hour went by without something reminding him of his cowardice. Jens put on a brave face while he worked, but most of the time, he indulged in guilt, a strong emotion for a person to contend with. Over time, Jens's sin of omission grew larger in his mind than the sin committed by the princess, and eventually, Jens came to believe that it was really he who had killed the queen rather than Malicious. Some days, he thought of leaving the royal household, but he couldn't bring himself to run away. He was driven to remain and to suffer the guilt as a way to atone for his sin. He wallowed in self-pity, which only further embarrassed him and enhanced his guilt. Other days, he considered killing himself, but he did not have the courage to commit suicide.

But the human psyche is remarkably resilient, and even relentless guilt can coincide with incredible day-to-day productivity. Although Jens had resigned himself to a tortured reality, he poured his physical energies into his work, and the effort was duly noted. He was promoted several times in rapid succession until eventually he was appointed royal message boy for King Bjorn. Ironically, the boy who had lacked the courage to inform the king about the diabolical plot that had killed the queen now served as the carrier of the king's most private messages.

When the army of Asgard marched to the Green Cavern, Jens was promoted again, and he accompanied the king as his personal attendant.

Chapter 33

Surviving the Iving

When Liz, Eirik, and Kate reached ground level, they found a stern-looking old soldier standing sentry at the stairwell. The soldier was surprised by their presence and questioned them briefly, but cursorily. He clearly did not expect spies or saboteurs.

"We were sent up to retrieve this sick soldier," advised Eirik, who gestured toward Kate, who was leaning limply against Liz.

"Sick, is he?" replied the soldier. "Well, if he's a friend, you'd better hope he recovers quickly. Lord Null doesn't suffer stragglers. The sick are taken to the lagoon, where they disappear. I don't like to think about what takes them, and if you know what's good for you, you'll make sure your friend recovers overnight. Maybe it's only strong drink. That way he'll be okay tomorrow; otherwise, at morning muster he'll be removed to the lagoon. Now get off with you."

Liz felt sorry for the old soldier. She anticipated that once the escape was discovered, this man and many others would likely lose their lives as a consequence of Malicious's wrath.

Eirik and Liz supported Kate between them and lurched down to the docks where the loading of troops and the unloading of raw material for the forges proceeded unabated even at night.

The shore of the River Fjorm was crowded with soldiers who were waiting to board the cargo ships from the south that had carried ore to be smelted into iron. As soon as a cargo was unloaded, the soldiers boarded, and the troop-laden ship embarked for the north.

The three escapees crossed over a bridge to the east side of the river and found a spot by the entrance to the tunnel that headed toward the kingdom of the Maya. They tried repeatedly to wake Kate, but to no avail.

A steady stream of soldiers marched north. Behind each company of men was a squad of jaguars that snarled and scratched at any stragglers and kept the army moving. One obviously exhausted soldier staggered and fell behind. Liz watched while a jaguar culled him out and with one quick swipe cut his throat. The big cats collected and devoured the man in a feeding frenzy that lasted barely a few minutes. Afterward, the jaguars resumed their rearguard positions.

"Well," observed Eirik, "guess they don't need to pack any food for the big cats, do they?"

"That's awful," remarked Liz, who looked over at Kate and realized that her sister could easily end up as a meal for a similar squad of jaguars, or as a snack for some hideous creature in the lagoon. "Eirik, if Kate doesn't wake up by morning, we should turn ourselves in to save her," she said impetuously.

"Well, that's one option, but I think the situation has changed. Soon, and certainly by tomorrow morning, my sister will know that I am no longer under her control and that you are a more worthy adversary than she suspected. She might decide to kill us. By the looks of this army, she might not need me to legitimize her right to the throne. I'd say we'd be doomed to die if we gave ourselves up."

"Another option," added Liz, "would be for Kate and me to give ourselves up, while you escape. That way, at least one of us might survive. You have the best chance of finding your way back to your father's forces." Liz hadn't even convinced herself, much less Eirik, but she continued, "You should leave; that's the most sensible course of action. Kate and I will remain behind."

Though Liz spoke with both a finality and a curious protective fondness that was not lost on Eirik, his response was adamant as well. "No way! I'll not save myself at your expense. Neither of you would even be here if it weren't for my sister, and I would not have escaped but for you. No, we'll just have to hope that Kate wakes up. If she doesn't, we'll find a way to buy some time until she does."

Liz looked relieved. She never would have given up. She only wanted to test Eirik; it was a foolish ploy, but under the stressful circumstances, she quickly forgave herself. *Yes,* thought Liz, *Eirik is the certainly the genuine article.*

Liz looked around at the hundreds upon hundreds of soldiers who were streaming north, mostly on the River Fjorm but also into the tunnels going north. Substantial numbers were marching into both the coastal and inland route tunnels. Liz realized their chances of escape north were slim to none. Similarly, a steady stream of soldiers poured forth from the south tunnels and made the opportunity to escape in this direction similarly hopeless.

"Eirik, what if we tried to escape to the east? This would give us more time for Kate to wake up. Perhaps later we might try to escape north."

"Makes good sense to me," he replied, "and I suggest we get moving. No sense tempting fate so close to my sister. The Iving River runs along the tunnels to the east, and if we need to leave the road, we can travel along the river."

They lifted Kate and carried her between them into the main tunnel to the east. After they had traveled far enough to leave the din of the dock behind, Eirik again lifted Kate onto his shoulders, and they made fairly good time. They had rested well the day prior to the escape, and courtesy of this rest and the natural adrenaline rush that comes with danger, their energy was great, and they were able to travel many miles before morning.

Kate was a little easier to arouse in the morning, but she still was not able to walk on her own. The traffic in the tunnel was steady, but fortunately there were few soldiers. Mostly they encountered merchants and local travelers, and they soon lapsed into a sense of security. They had traveled in silence for some time, each worrying in their own way. Eirik broke the silence with a statement of the obvious. "Malicious knows of our escape by now."

This had been on both their minds "Yes, but perhaps she'll just let us go," said Liz wishfully. "After all, she has a lot of other stuff to attend to right now."

"My sister doesn't like to lose," replied Eirik. "Likely she's sent patrols north, and when they don't turn up any sign of us, she'll send soldiers south and east."

Eirik could not have been more prophetic. Because of Kate, who could walk on her own now but in a foggy haze, they were traveling slowly, and merchants from the docks were soon passing them with stories about the escape and the search parties that Malicious had dispatched to find them. Soon thereafter, the same stories were also available from travelers coming toward them from the east.

"How can so many of them know?" Liz questioned.

"Malicious has spies everywhere, and her messenger ravens travel on the surface many times faster than we can."

Twice, they hid in a side tunnel as panthers ran by. One of the great cats paused and sniffed the tunnel they were in but carried on.

"They're looking for our scent," advised Eirik. "The next time the tunnel merges with the Iving River, we better cleanse ourselves, wash these uniforms, and find a way to change our smell."

At the next riverside, Eirik dug up the roots of a mossy-looking shrub and made a paste of the soft pulpy center. "Spread this on your face, hands, and legs, and then do the same for Kate." Kate's walking was more like sleepwalking; she was still not able to carry on a coherent conversation and was helpless to do anything for herself.

Liz and Eirik were washing the uniforms in the river when two soldiers turned up. Liz had removed her helmet, and her long brown hair flowed down over her shoulders. Fortunately, Kate was propped up and asleep behind some boulders and was not visible.

Eirik saw that the soldiers were suspicious and took the initiative. "We've been looking for the escaped prisoners, but no luck. How about you?"

One of the soldiers seemed to accept this comment and relaxed, but the other eyed Liz and Eirik carefully and never took his hand off the hilt of his sword, a posture not lost on Eirik.

"The panthers have already checked this area," added Eirik. "Have you guys ever seen such big cats?" He continued trying to make small talk, but the savvy soldier was having nothing of it.

"What company are you two with? Women aren't common in most of the units," replied the soldier as he looked at Liz.

Liz automatically separated herself from Eirik, who nonchalantly walked toward the soldiers. "You're right about that. We're a special team, just the two of us, sent by Lord Null."

The mention of Lord Null made both the soldiers flinch. "In that case, we'll leave you to your work," said the questioning soldier. Both men backed cautiously away from the river and into the tunnel.

"Good work, Eirik," said Liz.

"I don't think so," replied Eirik, who positioned himself by the tunnel. He motioned to Liz to draw her sword and stand at the other side.

Not a moment later, one of the soldiers rushed in and met the end of Eirik's sword. The second soldier followed quickly thereafter and met a similar deadly fate at the point of Eirik's knife.

"That's it," advised Eirik. "Soon more will come, and when they find these bodies, there will not be a safe square inch in these tunnels."

They submerged the bodies under rocks in the river and then started to walk upstream to further minimize their scent trail, but this soon became difficult. Kate could barely walk on land, much less over slippery boulders in water. Several times, they heard the now recognizable sniff of a panther in the bordering tunnel, and Liz was thankful Eirik had known to use the root smell to conceal their scent.

Eirik is certainly capable, she thought. *He was a few steps ahead of those two soldiers.*

Periodically, they tried to return to the tunnel, but soon, the area was swarming with soldiers, and they realized that however impractical, the river was their only hope.

Around midday, they paused to rest under a bridge where the tunnel crossed the river. Soldiers tramped over the bridge in both directions, and torches flashed along the banks as the search continued. Suddenly, Liz could hear panthers on the bridge above and then a chillingly familiar voice. A man was walking toward them and talking to the panthers. As he came nearer, Liz could hear the conversation.

"Found something, have you? The panther that finds them will be rewarded well," Lord Null said. "Under the bridge, are they? Soldiers, shine your torches under the bridge. Half of you get into the water on this side, the others on the opposite shore."

As soon as she heard the soldiers, Liz grabbed Kate's hand. "Kate, hold your breath," she whispered, and then she dived under the water. *We'll have to swim quite a distance before we're no longer visible,* she thought. *The water in this river is so clear, they'll probably be able to see us for fifty yards. But I can't stay under too long; I'm not sure how much of a breath Kate managed to take.*

But luckily, the dive stirred up fine clay silt from the bottom, and a moment later, the water was murky brown. Although this was excellent for concealment, navigation proved impossible. Trapped in the gloom of a silt-out, Liz became disoriented and could not tell which direction to swim. She even lost track of which direction was up. Believing they had swum far enough to catch a safe breath, she tried to surface, only to hit the bottom. Reversing herself, she emerged topside, only to find that she and Kate had actually swum only a few yards from the bridge, and they had to dive again to avoid a flurry of enemy arrows.

When they rose again and Eirik surfaced beside her, Liz looked over at him with a resigned look that as much as said, "Well, we gave it a good try," but he furrowed his brow with an expression that was anything but defeatist.

Kate started babbling some nonsense about dolphins and pointing in the water. Liz held Kate close and tried to comfort her.

"Liz!" Eirik called out. "The dolphins, they're here to help. Grab a fin."

Suddenly, the water was frothing with fins. Eirik helped Kate onto a dolphin and then jumped onto another just as a new volley of arrows splashed around them.

"Hold your breath," said Eirik, and a moment later, they were under the water and swimming upstream and past the soldiers.

When they surfaced a few minutes later, they could hear Lord Null shouting. "Good work! You caught one. Now find the other two."

Eirik and Liz looked at each other and realized the third dolphin was empty. "She must have fallen off," said Eirik.

A second later, the air was filled with arrows, and the dolphins dived again.

Chapter 34
Enemy Tracks

Within a few hours of landing the war canoes, Helga spotted fresh signs of the enemy and called a halt to discuss their strategy.

Stefan, who was an expert in tracking, studied the tracks. "The animal prints are definitely wolf. The prints are larger than a coyote, and the nails are evident, which means they are not those of a great cat. There are more than twenty sets of prints, which suggests a much larger pack than the customary half dozen."

"How about the other tracks?" asked Helga.

"Those are tracks of men, and by the stride I would estimate them to be taller than our people, well over six feet. I count at least a dozen different tracks of the tall men."

"Wolves are one thing," said Helga, "but these are the tracks of southern soldiers. Most likely we have crossed paths with a scouting party and a larger contingent is nearby. They could be waiting in any of the side tunnels."

"We have the advantage of speed and mobility," offered Ian. "We should press on."

"I agree," advised Thorfinn. "Time continues precious. We cannot wait for an opportunity to engage them at our advantage; we must press on, regardless of the risk."

"Yes," replied Helga, "but we need a strategy to pass every side tunnel, and some will be riskier than others."

"Yes, but we know these tunnels," Stefan said. We have traveled them since we were young. Let us avoid the riskier tunnels as best we can by taking the longer side routes. Farther south, we will lose this advantage."

"Good advice, Stefan, and when we must pass a side tunnel where fresh tracks are evident, we will proceed two at a time to minimize the risk," Helga confirmed.

Ian had been studying the map and spoke up. "If this scouting party knows of our mission and has set a trap, we should expect them where they can position men to surround us and cut off our escape. Between here and Siksika, there are two likely places." Ian pointed them out on the map, and everyone agreed with his assessment.

"We can avoid only the first of these with side tunnels," advised Stefan. "We will be most exposed at the second."

"We have several days until we reach this place, and we must be vigilant. We must presume the enemy to be around each corner and behind each rock," said Thorfinn.

"Ten yards between each of us," Helga advised as she took the lead and established the pace.

Chapter 35
Green Crystal

The pace set by King Bjorn's army was modest in comparison to that of the rescue squad, which was just as well for Mac, who needed time to think. Mac understood that the events of the last few weeks were out of his immediate control, but as yet, he hadn't come to grip with the concept that Kate and Liz might die. Every time this thought started to form, he distracted himself by studying the rock formations in the subterranean caverns. Mac understood that he was hiding from his emotions, but he had always done so; his was a practiced intellectual deceit. Like his own father, Mac had relegated the family responsibilities for emotional support initially to his mother, then to his wife, and lately to his daughters. Not only did he gladly relinquish this responsibility, but he additionally justified the act by convincing himself that he hardly ever needed any emotional support. Mac sometimes likened himself to a computer. Although this logical robotic façade might have convinced his colleagues and the world at large, his mother, his wife, and his daughters had all realized that he was the main beneficiary of the emotional support they offered. The possibility that Kate and Liz might die was therefore a serious emotional threat to Mac, whether he let himself think about it or not, and these feelings welled up with each uncertain day that passed.

Mac had rarely pondered the larger questions of life. He had solid scientific roots and was great at abstract reasoning, but he had no philosophical foundation, and he could not visualize anything that could not be rationalized to fact. Although he had just turned sixty, Mac had largely avoided the common middle-aged preoccupations with personal mortality. Had he pondered death, his thoughts might have led him to some sense of the meaning of life. Now, however, the possibility that Kate and Liz might die suddenly forced him to think at least about the meaning of their lives, and this led him to the uncomfortable consideration of his own mortality. He had told Ian that his daughters "owned his heart," and that outburst of emotion had been a personal surprise. For the first time Mac sensed that his daughters and the meaning of his life were intricately linked and that somehow their deaths might mean his as well. Although he felt this threat to be real, he could not explain why.

Life and death were heady topics for anyone and no less so for Mac. He'd lost his grandparents when he was still a young boy, and he had been very close to his paternal grandfather. He had cried when his grandfather died, but his father had discouraged this emotion. His parents had never discussed death with him—or life for that matter. Neither had his mother or father showed much emotion at the loss of their parents. Mac had learned this model, and when his wife suffered from and eventually succumbed to breast cancer, he shouldered his grief stoically without any outward show of emotion. He had wanted to cry, but he couldn't. Tears came hard for Mac. He'd been taught that crying for the dead was wasted emotional energy. What Mac didn't understand was that tears were usually for the living, and most commonly for the people who were crying. Mac considered that he was too logical, too scientific, and too strong to cry. Both Kate and Liz had wept after their mother died and still cried together about their loss. Mac had neither approved nor disapproved of their method of grieving. Now, as he considered the possibility that Kate and Liz might die, and as he began to consider how their death might relate to who he was and why he lived at all, for the first time since his grandfather had died, Mac actually felt close to crying. And cry he did, but only inside. He stifled the tears, and the drops never materialized on his cheeks.

They marched for at least sixteen hours each day. In the idle hours, Mac and Ursus shared stories of their respective worlds or played hnefatafl, a Viking game similar to chess. Like chess, the object of the game was to capture the opponent's king. However, the playing pieces were different, and the game was played on a square board with forty-nine spaces rather than the sixty-four found on a chessboard. The pieces were elaborately carved from walrus ivory.

As they marched toward their destination, there proved to be ample time to satisfy Mac's innate curiosity and to investigate the sophistication achieved by King Bjorn's people. Ursus was an enthusiastic teacher. Like every successful culture, King Bjorn's people had secured ample sources of food and water, arranged for good shelter, and developed solid systems for education, health, and justice.

Mac's inherent curiosity led to many questions that Ursus was happy to answer. Talking about how the ancestors of Ursus and King Bjorn had overcome the many obstacles to life underground was a pleasant diversion from the reality of battle that loomed closer with every step south. For Ursus, talking about the successes of their culture was also therapeutic. Ursus did not believe in violence, but his discussions with Mac helped him accept that war was necessary to preserve that which they had accomplished for future generations.

"Sadly," Ursus commented, "we have not outgrown the need for violence. War is necessary to protect our way of life, to ensure that all subterranean peoples can benefit equally from the advances in our communities, and to guarantee that every cub and child can grow up in a safe and secure world surrounded by caring and compassionate parents. Yes, war is necessary," he concluded with a sigh.

Mac had seen fresh fruit and vegetables in local markets but had not seen any underground crops. After biting into a juicy McIntosh apple, Mac asked Ursus where the orchards were.

"Most are still on the surface," replied Ursus. "Some crops were once grown in the valley discovered by your grandfather, but as soon as he started to visit regularly, those fields were abandoned. Fortunately there are still enough remote areas with good soil and an adequate growing season to provide ample food for our peoples. Sadly, though, each year we must abandon more and more cropland to the surface people, and we know that a day will come when all our food will need to come from underground sources. Our farmers have worked hard on this problem, and they are optimistic that by the time all our surface farms are abandoned, we will be self-sufficient."

"So you do grow crops underground?" asked Mac.

"Yes, crops will eventually be grown in the warm waters of every river and lake."

"Without soil?" queried Mac, who wondered if they had discovered hydroponics.

"Yes. Underground water is especially rich in natural plant food, and we add bat droppings to the water to enhance the growth. Some of our best water orchards are found in caverns where bats roost. Some of the caverns are home to hundreds of thousands of bats, and that makes for a lot of droppings. The warmth underground allows us to harvest multiple crops every year. The apple you just ate came from a huge orchard only a few miles from the Castle of Light."

"And does the light source for the crops come from the sun through shafts to the surface like I saw at the castle?" asked Mac.

"Sometimes, but mostly no. Our scientists have discovered another light that encourages plant growth equal to that of the sun. When we reach the Green Cavern, I will show you the source of this great power, for that is where it was first discovered."

"I presume the cavern is green. Is the color related to the plants?" asked Mac.

"Yes and no. There are wonderful plants that grow naturally in the cavern, and part of the greenness is related to this lushness, but the real source of the color is the power itself.

"The cavern was discovered about seven centuries ago and was immediately recognized as a special place because of the natural light and the lush plant growth without sunshine. Over the years, people reported that they felt stronger for spending time in the cavern. Eventually, the cavern became recognized as a healing place, and those with any illness or injury that could not be treated by the medicine bears or healers came there to seek a cure. Bathing in the waters from the cavern was especially beneficial."

"And where did the light come from?" asked Mac.

"From the Green Crystal in the cavern walls," responded Ursus. "King Bjorn's ancestors soon learned that they could mine this crystal and relocate the crystal to other parts of the kingdom. You have seen this crystal several times since we first met."

"Of course," responded Mac, "the torches."

"Yes, and every home in the kingdom has at least one room with this crystal, not so much for the light, but for the unique healing energy it provides. Usually, the crystal is placed in the sleeping rooms so that the bears and people are exposed to the energy for as long as possible during each day. Sadly, it is not the cure for all our woes, but it has improved the quality and the length of our lives. Bears and humans now live many times longer than they did before the Green Crystal was discovered!"

"So you must also use the crystal to supply the light for your underground crops."

"Yes," replied Ursus. "Our farmers cut thin panes of the crystal, which they fashion as walls and roofs around the crops. We call them greenhouses."

Mac laughed, the reason for which was lost on Ursus until Mac explained about the greenhouses in his world. "The color green is obviously important in Asgard," said Mac. "The flag behind King Bjorn's throne was green."

"Yes," replied Ursus. "The flag of Asgard is a green sun against a sea-blue background. The blue is for the sea that was like a home away from home to their ancient Viking forefathers, and the green sun represents the crystal. The flag of each clan also has a green background. Green is the color of luck for our people. Babies and newborn cubs are swaddled in green, and brides are married in this color. In some ways, the Green Crystal and the color have come to symbolize life itself." Ursus opened a little leather sac that hung from his belt and removed a tiny green sculpture, which he handed to Mac.

Mac marveled at the craftsmanship. The sculpture depicted a school of salmon intricately carved in such a way that as the figure was turned, the light from the crystal gave the illusion that the fish were swimming. "Amazing!"

"Is the sculpture for good luck?" asked Mac.

"Luck?" queried Ursus.

"Yes, you know, when something happens by chance—luck," replied Mac.

"But nothing happens by chance," replied Ursus.

"I mean when you can't explain why something happens," responded Mac.

"There is always an explanation," stated Ursus.

"Oh, you mean even though you might not understand why, there is a person who knows more, an expert in that field who knows why and can provide a logical explanation," stated Mac.

"No, I don't mean that. What I mean is that the God of All Creatures knows why," said Ursus.

This statement caused Mac to pause. He didn't believe in a god, the Christian God of his world, the pagan gods of King Bjorn's people, or the God of All Creatures revered by the bears and native peoples who lived in Asgard. He let this statement stand unopposed and changed his original question. "Okay. What I meant was, does the sculpture have some significance for you? Obviously it does."

"Yes, every bear has a medicine bag that contains, among other things, an amulet, and the amulet has a spiritual significance. Amulets are always crystal; some are natural shapes, and others are carved in the image of something sacred, such as a salmon. The amulet is a link to the God of All Creatures. Most amulets are now made of the Green Crystal. This sculpture was commissioned five centuries ago for Kodiak, the great grizzly who united the bears in peace with King Bjorn's ancestors, and was bestowed by King Olaf, who became Kodiak's best friend. My family are direct descendants of Kodiak, and as the oldest member, I am the keeper of this sacred sculpture."

Mac responded, "So someday Connor will inherit the amulet."

"Yes," replied Ursus, who suddenly looked sad. "Of course I had hoped Bär would inherit the amulet first. No bear wants to outlive his cubs. I should have given him the amulet while he was still alive. Perhaps the power of the Green Crystal might have saved him. Were it possible, I gladly would have died in his place."

"I'm sorry," said Mac. Listening to Ursus made him think of losing Kate and Liz, and Mac wondered whom he was sorry for, himself or his new bear friend. Mac felt uncomfortable with these thoughts and quickly changed the topic back to the Green Crystal. "Do you mind if I test the crystal with one of my instruments?" asked Mac. "The test will not hurt the amulet."

While Mac rummaged in his pack, Ursus asked, "What does it test?"

"For a special kind of energy," replied Mac as he pulled out his portable Geiger counter. "Watch while I test the rocks around us." Mac proceeded to scan the rocks without result. "Okay if I test your amulet?"

Ursus agreed, and Mac scanned the crystal. The Geiger counter immediately started to click, and a dial on the instrument swung into a range marked "active."

"I wondered," said Mac, nodding. "The crystal is radioactive, which means the energy is nuclear, and unlike most sources discovered on the surface, it is apparently safe. What a remarkable discovery!"

Mac was excited and tried to explain nuclear energy to Ursus, but as with all his discourses on science, Ursus listened with polite courtesy but no deep interest. This infuriated Mac, who considered that anything that piqued his interest must be of relevance to others.

Ursus understood how frustrated Mac felt and tried to offer an explanation that Mac might understand, but as much as Ursus wanted to help, he also realized that unless Mac opened his mind, any attempt was futile. "Your explanation might seem reasonable in your world, but it is unsatisfactory in mine. The Green Crystal is part of our spiritual heritage and does not require an explanation. It is sufficient that the crystal exists. The Green Crystal is the power."

Mac tried to compare the crystal to the sun.

"Yes," replied Ursus, "that is a good analogy. The Green Crystal is like the sun. Both the sun and the crystal are spiritual powers that deserve our faith and do not require any explanation. Trying to take apart the Green Crystal or the sun cheapens their power. The Green Crystal exists for our benefit just as the sun once did for our ancestors who lived on the surface. Peoples from many cultures have joined us in our subterranean world. Many of these cultures once worshipped the sun as a god. Now many of these same cultures revere the Green Crystal."

Mac hesitated after Ursus's mention of "faith" early in his response. "I apologize," said Mac, who only vaguely understood the concept of faith. For Mac, faith was a one-dimensional word. He could offer a dictionary definition, but he had never felt the true meaning. He did, however, realize that many people did feel the power of faith, and as much as he would have liked to discount their feelings, he had come across too many learned individuals who had faith for him to ignore the possibility that perhaps there was a kernel of truth at the center of this word. His response to those with faith usually depended on the social situation and his mood. Among the company of like-minded friends, within the privacy of his office, or secure in the bully pulpit of the classroom, he offered sharp testimony to the power of science and by implication the weakness of faith. However, in situations where he was unfamiliar with the background of the individuals with whom he found himself, he tempered his comments with a polite but insincere liberalism. When confronted with men or women of the cloth, he was always obsequiously silent. Mostly he avoided direct discussion of this topic. When Mac was honest with himself, he understood that fear and avoidance were the handmaidens of ignorance, but Mac rarely chose to dwell on uncomfortable topics.

An awkward silence ensued, during which Mac debated whether he should confront Ursus and try to explain again that the crystal was radioactive and that this fact superseded any religious significance. He genuinely liked Ursus and intuitively understood that he could learn from the grizzly, but his instincts were largely adversarial and geared more toward self-serving control of a situation rather than to humble acquiescence. Mac's egotism won out, and he decided that perhaps he had not presented his explanation properly and that another attempt was warranted. He wanted Ursus to realize that science could help his people to understand why the crystal had energy and how this energy could impart changes in cellular metabolic processes and thereby impart the beneficial effects on health.

"I really do apologize," said Mac, "and I would be the last person to disparage any person's religion or faith, but the crystal has an energy that I can measure with my Geiger counter, and that energy is called radioactivity. In my world we know of this energy. We use radioactivity to provide energy for our homes and businesses."

"All you showed me was a box with a tiny arrow that moved. You believe that the box measures the power of the Green Crystal. The Green Crystal is a gift of the God of All Creatures. I do not believe that anyone can measure the power of the God of All Creatures. Moreover, I believe that anyone who thinks that he can measure this power does not have any faith."

Ursus offered this comment humbly, without any personal rancor. He had no idea how much this simple statement would cut to the quick of Mac's vulnerable ego. And neither did Mac, who was rendered speechless; he felt emotionally naked. Ursus had disrobed Mac's intellectual conceit.

"Truth can never be told so as to be understood and not be believed," mumbled Mac, who recollected a proverb he had read somewhere.

"Pardon me?" asked Ursus.

"Oh, nothing. You're right. I don't have any faith. I don't believe in God. I think I should. I don't know why I think I should—because the concept of God doesn't make scientific sense to me. I've never much wanted to think about it. I think I'm afraid of God."

Mac's candor was refreshing to Ursus. Notwithstanding, Ursus worried about Mac's lack of faith. He considered pursuing the discussion but decided not to. He sensed correctly that Mac's confession was as much as he could handle at that moment.

Mac shared the view that any further discussion of his spiritual deficiency was too awkward for the moment. He actually blushed, and true to form, he quickly encouraged the conversation in a more comfortable direction. "Have you discovered the crystal anywhere else?" asked Mac, whose countenance now showed no remnant of the emotional consternation that had accompanied the baring of his soul.

"Alas, no," replied Ursus with a sad and serious look, "and the limited supply of the Green Crystal has much to do with Malicious's avaricious quest for power."

"How so?"

"It was no coincidence that Malicious's first military target was the Green Cavern. The Green Crystal is much desired, and any person who controls the availability of the crystal might also control the people who desire the crystal. King Bjorn and his ancestors have never limited access to the crystal; they believe the crystal exists for the benefit of everyone."

"Ah," said Mac. "I'm sure Malicious doesn't share that view. She'll use the crystal to gain influence and power, and since the Green Cavern is the only known source of the crystal, Malicious now controls access to the crystal," reasoned Mac.

"Yes and no," replied Ursus. "A few years ago, our mining engineers determined that the amount of Green Crystal left in the Green Cavern would supply the kingdom for only the next decade. When new sources of the crystal run out, we are worried that some people might hoard the existing crystal. We anticipate social problems. Those who do not have access to the crystal might demand access from those who do. You can imagine the problems that might develop."

"Right," agreed Mac. "The crystal represents power. Some people will covet that power. In our world an unfair distribution of money and material goods causes social problems very much as you anticipate.

Likely, some of your people will begin to trade access to the crystal for their own personal benefit. Productivity will fall in your economy."

Mac spoke these words with a detachment that seemed callous to Ursus. When Mac linked the Green Crystal to power and thence to money and material goods, Ursus shuddered. *Mac seems to understand, almost relate to, the base perspective of Malicious. What he doesn't seem to realize is that the Green Crystal is a spiritual power, and any attempt to pervert this power will only result in anarchy, and that for those who are swept up in this bedlam, their loss in faith is far more serious than any loss that can be measured in money or material goods.* But Ursus kept his thoughts to himself, and his silence encouraged Mac to continue.

"Have you developed any plans to prevent social unrest?"

"Yes, we are working on a fair way to ration the remaining crystal and methods to redistribute the crystal in our existing homes and communities. We hope to continue to guarantee access to all our peoples."

"Good," said Mac. "Even so, I can see that the dwindling supply of Green Crystal has a huge potential to create major social problems. In my world, the closest analogy might be the illegal drug trade. The drugs make people feel better. So long as people have access to the drugs, they feel good, and they become habituated to this good feeling. If the drug is taken away, the person usually experiences emotional and physical symptoms of withdrawal. In our world, dependency on drugs is a serious cause of crime. I can see how that might happen with the crystal."

"Yes, and Malicious will traffic in those withdrawal symptoms and pervert the affected people to serve her evil plans. Her seizure of the Green Cavern was an important first step, but her real intention is to control access to all the Green Crystal. To achieve that, she must seize control of not only the Green Cavern but also the entire Northern Realm, for the cities, especially the Castle of Light, contain the largest supply of existing crystal. Once she controls the cities, she will tax the people for ownership or access to the crystal and enslave them to her power."

Mac nodded. "Yes, of course she will. Any inherently cruel and evil person would."

Strange, thought Ursus, *Mac really does seem to understand Malicious's attitude. He must live in a very sad world.* Again Ursus kept his thoughts to himself. "Indeed," replied Ursus aloud. "By seizing the Green Cavern,

Malicious has struck at our symbolic and spiritual heart, and in a sense, she has taken the first step to capture our life force."

Ursus felt sorry for Mac, whose lack of faith and scientific detachment were clearly a source of spiritual discord. Ursus had seen this in other men and knew that Mac would never grow into a genuine person until he found his faith. That Mac had faith somewhere, Ursus was sure. Every creature did. *Perhaps I can help,* Ursus thought. *More concentrated exposure to the Green Crystal might benefit my new friend.* He decided that thereafter, every night after Mac fell asleep, he would position several torches to bathe Mac in the rays of the Green Crystal. Ursus hoped that like a plant that had struggled to survive in the darkness, his friend might thrive and grow toward the light.

He was encouraged the next morning, when after the first night, Mac awoke refreshed.

"Good morning, Ursus," saluted Mac. "I feel good this morning. We'll make great progress today. I just know it."

Ursus hoped that Mac was speaking more about personal progress than about the distance they might travel.

Chapter 36
Kate's Ordeal

When Kate finally woke up, she had a splitting headache, and every bone in her body ached. She found herself lying on a damp, rock-strewn dirt floor in a tiny room lit by a solitary candle on the wall. There was a door without a window, and apart from some chains affixed to one wall, there seemed to be nothing else in the room.

Kate tried to remember what had happened, but most everything seemed like a dream—or rather, a nightmare. She wished that it were only a dream and that she could wake up happy and safe, back home, cuddled in Ian's arms. *Oh Ian,* she thought mournfully, *please be safe, wherever you are.*

She remembered hiking to the valley with Ian and the strange raven and wolf. She also remembered the bald-headed man who had kidnapped her, a wild ride on a panther, and then a boat trip with Liz beside a lava river. But after that, everything was fuzzy. She had a vague recollection of Eirik. And though she didn't remember anyone else, she was haunted by the image of two red eyes.

The candle flickered, as if blown by a tiny puff of air, and the changing shadows on the wall caught Kate's attention. *Must be a breeze up there,* she thought, and she tried to stand, only to collapse in excruciating pain when she tried to put weight on her right leg.

Kate vomited, and after the wave of nausea passed, she felt her ankle, the source of the pain, and found it swollen to the size of softball and exquisitely painful to touch. She surveyed her body. Even in the dim light, she could see dark areas on her arms and legs. At first she thought, or rather hoped, that the discolorations might be shadows, but when she put her hand between her leg and the candlelight, the dark areas remained. Touching the dark areas was uncomfortable and confirmed they were bruises.

She lifted up her blouse and was relieved that no bruises were evident on her chest or abdomen. She felt her face and was reassured to find all her teeth and no cuts or bruises. *Who would do this?* she wondered.

The candle flickered again, and this time, the shadow of a torso appeared on the wall. Kate was perplexed as to what could have made the shadow. She rubbed her eyes, blinked several times, and squinted to see what was between the candle and the shadow, but she could see nothing. Unease crept into her beaten body; she sensed that the shadow was the cause of her injuries.

Kate pulled herself toward the door and away from the shadow, instinctively trying to escape. Her hands barely reached the latch, with which she fumbled, but she found the door locked. She whimpered a sigh and turned back toward the sinister specter.

Two red eyes gleamed from the dark shape, and these sparked submerged and brutal memories of the beating that had caused her broken ankle and all the bruises. She turned abruptly from the gaze and cringed in a corner, as if somehow she might be protected if she could not see the shape, but in the same instant she knew she was doomed, and she started to sob uncontrollably. "Leave me alone," she cried. "Please, please, leave me alone."

The red eyes swept over Kate and disappeared into the candle flame, which flickered out, and Kate felt an unnatural chill that made every bruise seem on fire. She screamed until she had no breath and then sobbed herself to sleep.

Chapter 37

Tree of Life

The dolphins carried Liz and Eirik many miles upstream to a sandy beach inside a limestone cavern. Liz flopped onto the hot sand and allowed the warm surf to lap around her legs. She rolled over and looked up at the ceiling of a stalactite-draped chamber and started to cry angry sobs. As exhausted as she was, she bristled with the pent-up energy of conflicting emotions. Although glad to be alive, she felt mad and guilty that they had abandoned Kate.

Liz had tried several times during the escape to swim back for her sister, but each time, the dolphins had herded her upstream. She knew intuitively that they had saved her life, but still, she thought, what right had the dolphins to decide for her?

And what about Eirik? she fumed. She had expected Eirik to intervene and do something to save Kate. Each time she tried to swim back toward her sister, she looked around and hoped to see Eirik similarly abandoning caution to the waves and striking out toward Kate, but each time, she saw that he merely clung to the dolphin. Several times he had even helped the dolphins shepherd Liz back upstream.

A mental picture of Eirik came to mind. He was astride a dolphin, and his eyes seemed to plead with Liz. In Liz's mind, Eirik's plea seemed like selfishness or even cowardice, and she used this image as a pretext to turn her guilt into anger and to direct this force at Eirik.

Eirik's eyes had indeed been pleading, but not to abandon Kate. Rather, his eyes had beseeched Liz to realize that her sister could not be saved and that it was her duty to survive. What Liz had twisted into selfishness was instead a protective and tender feeling. Each time they had surfaced during the escape, Eirik had tried to console Liz, but his well-meaning attempts had been consistently rebuffed. Liz had refused to speak to or even look at him.

Now on the beach, Liz could hear Eirik walking toward her. His footsteps in the surf sounded clumsy, and she purposely turned her back toward him. Eirik stopped a few feet behind her, and Liz heard him kneel in the sand. She could smell his wet hair as he leaned toward her. Eirik tried to brush some sand from Liz's hair, but his gentle caress was met with a sudden jerk away.

"Liz, I'm sorry about Kate, but they meant to kill us all. There was nothing we could do. Those arrows were coated with a poison that kills with even the slightest scratch, and through a prolonged and painful death."

Liz remained silent, with her back to Eirik.

"I know my sister," continued Eirik. "As a young girl she would stick needles through dragonflies, tie them to a string fixed to the ceiling, and watch as they flew in circles until they died. My parents scolded her, but this only made Malicious resent them. She was a very selfish girl and prone to petty jealousies. When we were little, my parents gave us a kitten. Malicious was impatient and teased the helpless little creature mercilessly. The kitten learned to scratch back, and this incensed my sister. One day I found the kitten dead. The poor thing had been burned alive. I always wondered if Malicious did it. I used to wake up dreaming of her torturing the kitten, and in every dream she was enjoying herself, as if killing was fun. No life is sacred to my sister. And every animal or person is only of value so long as they serve a purpose. Clearly we are no longer of value to Malicious. Those arrows were meant to kill."

After an unanswered pause, he added, "I feel awful about Kate, but we're alive, and because we are, we might still be able to help her."

Without looking at Eirik or even acknowledging that he had spoken, Liz got up and walked off in a huff.

Eirik decided not to follow. He lay down and looked up at the same stalactite-draped ceiling that had formed the visual backdrop for Liz's conflicting emotions. Although he shared her guilt, he could not share her anger. He sat up and put his hands over his face and whispered a prayer to Frigg, Odin's wife. "Mother Frigg, thou who knows the mysteries of life and love and who fathoms the minds of women, please help Liz to forgive herself for living and to forgive me for not sacrificing myself to attempt to save her sister."

Liz settled down after walking for a few minutes and was soon surveying the beach. There was a curious golden glow on the horizon in the distance. The glow grew brighter and had an energy that seemed to invigorate Liz. The closer she came, the lighter her steps became and the more carefree her thoughts. She felt keen to reach the glow and started to jog. The glow grew and drew her onward. The glow was so irresistible that she started to run. She felt giddy and breathless as she crossed into it. Once she was surrounded by the glow, Liz stopped running. This felt much better than sunlight, much better than anything she had ever felt. She stood still and savored the sensation.

The shoreline seemed to stretch ahead forever. Liz turned and expected to see the boundary where she had entered the glow, but the shoreline extended forever behind her as well. She could not see any evidence of her footprints in the sand. Neither could she see Eirik or the limestone cavern where the dolphins had brought them. There were no trees or rocks to break the two-dimensional plane of the water to the one side and the sand to the other, which similarly seemed to go on without end. Liz felt as if she were the only three-dimensional object in her surroundings. At first glance the glow had seemed like a golden firmament, but Liz didn't feel as if she were standing within the glow; rather, she felt as if it was somehow inside her body and emanated from her. The glow suffused her rather than surrounded her.

Liz felt the sensation of movement. Although her hair was not windblown, she felt as if it were. Even though she was standing still, she keenly appreciated a sense of movement and speed, and she couldn't decide whether she was flying or whether she was still and it was the ground beneath her that was moving in the opposite direction. She remembered experiencing a similar feeling when she was a little girl, traveling in a train over the prairies with her mother. She had loved to sit in the observation car; when she looked ahead, the flat prairie never seemed to change, but when she looked to the side, the landscape was a moving blur. She felt the same sense of speed and constant change now, but there were no objects in the golden glow to create a blur.

Liz was conscious of a vague sense of unease, a dread that perhaps the glow was not real. *Or maybe I'm not real,* she thought, but she discounted this foreboding. *Whatever,* she decided, *this glow is really wonderful, and like nothing I've ever experienced.*

Suddenly she was sitting in a meadow, surrounded by flowers. Now her hair was tussled by a wind, and the flowers waved in the same breeze. The setting was reminiscent of an alpine meadow she had shared with Kate. They had been young girls, perhaps six and eight years old, respectively, and on summer vacation at the lodge in the valley. They had spent the afternoon playing in the meadow where they had picked flowers to press and berries to eat. The warm sun, the cool valley breeze, and the happy bond that they shared as best friends as well as sisters had made for an especially wonderful and lasting memory.

Liz stood up and looked all around. She expected to see Kate, but there was only the glow. The meadow and the flowers were gone. In that moment it did not seem important that Liz couldn't see Kate and the valley or Eirik and the cavern, or anything else for that matter. The glow was enough.

She smiled and turned pirouettes in the glow and felt more free and relaxed than she had felt in all the years since that wonderful day with Kate in the meadow. Even when she closed her eyes, the glow that embodied this place persisted. The glow was everything and enough.

Again she felt the sensation of speed, and when she opened her eyes, she saw again the shoreline, the golden sand, the azure sea, and always the glow. *This feels so good,* she thought. *This must be what it's like to travel on a sunbeam. The glow is so light and soft, not like the heavy hot sun on the surface.*

Suddenly, Liz had a revelation. *This isn't real. This is too good to be real. What I feel is heavenly. This must be how they felt in the Garden of Eden. Nothing real could feel this good,* she decided. Even so, Liz recollected several times in her life when she had felt a similar, though less intense sensation. The first occasion was the time in the meadow with her sister. *Of course,* she thought, *the feelings were so similar that my brain immediately made the connection.* A rush of similar memories followed. She saw her mother smiling at her. *That was when I was about nine and sick with scarlet fever, and Mom was rubbing my back.* The touch of her mother's hands, that close, personal touch of love, had felt so glorious. Then she felt herself floating above an ocean and realized she was remembering the first time she had gone parasailing. She had been in the Bahamas. She remembered how she had laughed with joy for ten solid minutes as she glided above Nassau. *Wow,* she thought, *I'm glad I have such wonderful memories. I want to make more of these memories.*

Liz felt exhilarated. *This must be what life is all about. This feeling must be what we are all searching for.* But then she thought of Kate and her father and, curiously, also of Eirik, and Liz realized that there was more to life than the glow. *I need to share this feeling,* she realized.

Until now, Liz had been carried at the whim of the glow, but now she felt the need to choose her direction. She looked over the sea and wished that she were swimming, and in that moment she felt herself in the waves. *I'm swimming, and I have the power to choose,* she realized with satisfaction. Yet the swimming was effortless, the water was warm in a way that felt womb-like, and strangely, she did not feel wet.

Liz felt a curious and simultaneous sense of fear, anger, and joy well up inside her, and these conflicting feelings erupted as tears. She was frightened that the glow might be heaven and that she was dead. She was angry that Malicious had captured Kate. She wiped a tear that dripped down her cheek. "Thank goodness my tears are wet," she said, as if this confirmed she was alive. "What a weird but wonderful place!"

She thought again of Kate and then her father. These thoughts strengthened her, and when she next thought of Kate, she did not cry. Instead she felt a strange joy, as if somehow everything would turn out right, and she accepted this feeling without reservation.

When she next looked around, she found herself on an island in a pool in an underground cavern. Most of the island was consumed by a single huge stalagmite that reached up and joined a stalactite from the ceiling, forming a gigantic sedimentary tree. Pottery shards were scattered around the base of the tree, and on their surface, Liz recognized ancient Mayan symbols.

She walked to the water's edge and knelt down to take a drink. The surface was still, and the water was so crystal clear that every feature of the bottom was perfectly visible. As she watched, mesmerized by the clarity, a tiny dolphin appeared deep in the water and slowly grew in size as it swam to the surface.

Liz stood up as the head of the dolphin broke the glass-like surface. She watched as the concentric ripples spread out like a moving necklace around the head of the dolphin. She recognized the dolphin as the one who had saved her life.

"Thank you for saving my life—and thanks also to your friends for saving Eirik and trying to save Kate."

Liz was not surprised when the dolphin spoke in response.

"We are sorry we could not rescue your sister. As it was, we almost lost Prince Eirik too. The Evil One can exert her power at great distance, and especially in the presence of Lord Null. As soon as the panthers smelled your presence, the Evil One knew, and through Lord Null, she loosened Kate and Eirik's grip on the fins. Eirik had not taken any of her potions for several days, and he was strong enough to fight back, but Kate had no resistance." The dolphin paused before going on. "Had you remained, you would have died. In her anger the Evil One brought the river to a boil for many miles up and downstream. No living thing survived. We just barely escaped."

Liz thanked the dolphin again and then asked, "And this place, and the sunny beach?"

"You are in a healing place that is known by many names by different animals. If you like, I will take you back to Eirik, and together you can meet our queen."

"I'd like that," said Liz as she slipped into the water. "Yes, I'd like that."

A wonderful sense of knowing, a feeling of joy, an almost unbearable lightness suffused Liz as she waded out to the dolphin.

"Yes, I'd like that," she said again as she climbed on the dolphin's back. "Thank you."

Chapter 38
Ambush at the Crossroads

The journey toward Siksika had been largely uneventful. A few wolf packs had sniffed them out but quickly retreated when they realized they were dealing with more than trade merchants or locals.

Helga continued to see fresh tracks from sizable companies of southern soldiers, increasingly more the farther south they traveled, but they'd safely bypassed the first of the expected ambush points and had not otherwise encountered any of the enemy. Nevertheless, none of the squad felt complacent, and as they neared the second possible ambush point, the level of excitement was palpable, and all were mentally preparing for battle in their own ways.

Helga sent Stefan and Thorfinn ahead to scout the crossroads for any signs of an ambush. After several hours, they had not seen any fresh enemy tracks, but this did not reassure Stefan, who realized that the absence of tracks actually suggested a higher likelihood of an ambush. There were more than enough side tunnels to conceal the movements of enemy soldiers and still leave the main tunnel free of tracks.

Stefan and Thorfinn ran through the crossroads abreast. Each squinted down the side tunnels and searched for anything out of the ordinary, but neither saw any sign of the enemy.

"Strange, is it not, that there is absolutely no sign of the enemy?" remarked Stefan who was wily in the ways of ambush. "The tracks vanished about an hour ago. This cannot be a coincidence. Thorfinn, you go back, and I will remain at the crossroads until the rest arrive. I will call with my horn if I notice anything out of the ordinary."

Stefan carried a horn carved from the pectoral bone of a humpback whale that had washed into a coastal cave. With the marrow removed, the shoulder bone formed a good acoustical chamber, and when the instrument was fitted with a mouthpiece carved from the tip of a walrus tusk, the sound could be heard for many miles.

While Thorfinn ran back toward Helga and the rest of the squad, Stefan concealed himself behind some large boulders by a stream that flowed from the surface and formed a tiny pool. The water was exceptionally cool and clear, which made the crossroads a popular resting point.

The crossroads was actually a sizable cavern with multiple entrances and was exceptionally well lit, courtesy of not only a high ceiling with a natural shaft to the surface but also the exceptional engineering talents of King Bjorn's royal engineers.

Ever vigilant, Stefan studied the mud around the pool. Behind some small boulders and just at the edge of the pool, he noticed some knee prints where soldiers had bent over to drink the water. He also noticed fresh tracks that he had missed when they initially ran past. Further inspection revealed the ground had been otherwise meticulously swept clear of tracks. *An obvious subterfuge,* realized Stefan.

At just this moment, Stefan heard the muffled clatter of armed soldiers converging on the crossroads from both side tunnels. A moment later the first of the enemy soldiers entered the cavern and took up previously assigned concealed positions.

Flight was impossible. The enemy was between him and the tunnel leading to Helga and the squad. Stefan knew that Thorfinn had likely reached the squad and that without any warning they would walk into an ambush.

Southern soldiers took positions all around Stefan. He was surprised that none noticed his presence until he realized that his tunic was similar in color to theirs. He smiled with the thought that he had the element of surprise, and he decided to let the soldiers settle in before he made his move. He was in a good position to fight. His back was to a wall; he had sufficient room to maneuver his sword and axe; and given the right opportunity, he had an obvious escape route into the tunnel toward Helga and the rest of the squad.

Stefan reached for his horn and chuckled at the thought of how the sound would startle the soldiers around him. Given the acoustics in the chamber, he figured those nearest might even lose their hearing for a few minutes. Perhaps, he thought with a smile, a few might be so surprised they'd wet their tunics.

After the last of the soldiers had entered the cavern, Stefan took a last look around, blew one loud blast on his horn, and then hurled himself at the closest soldiers, his sword in one hand and battle-axe in the other. Just before he slew the first soldiers, Stefan shouted an invocation. "By the grace of Odin, the one-eyed Father of Battle, you may choose to die either by my sword or by my axe, but die you will!"

"A berserker!" cried the closest soldier, but those were the last words he uttered.

Stefan was ambidextrous and could simultaneously wield an axe in his left hand and a sword in his right. His moves were so fast that to the enemy soldiers Stefan seemed like two men with separate weapons. They barely knew he was in their midst before Stefan's axe swept a path through a score of the enemy. Most of the enemy fled without raising a weapon, but the officers turned them back with whips and humiliating insults.

"He is only one man, you dogs!" cried one officer.

"A chest of Green Crystal to the man who takes his ears!" cried another.

When the enemy soldiers did attack, they were on Stefan like flies, and although neither their weapons nor their skills were a match for his axe or his sword, their numbers slowly took their toll.

Helga and the others were about a mile away when Stefan's horn first resounded through the tunnels. They quickened their pace. They heard the din of battle before they saw the entrance to the cavern, and this heartened them, for the sound of fighting meant Stefan was still alive. Just before they reached the cavern, the sound of Stefan's horn echoed again through the tunnels. This time, however, the sound was not as strong; it had a plaintive ring and ended abruptly. An ominous silence followed. Although they redoubled their pace, they all knew that they had heard the last breath of Stefan.

The rescue squad suspected that the enemy would be upon them soon now. With surprise no longer their weapon, the enemy likely would be rushing toward them to wage battle in the narrow confines of the tunnel. Ian was at the vanguard when the first enemy soldiers met them. It was close work, but the Sword of Olaf never failed, and together with his comrades-in-arm, he worked his way forward, leaving one dead soldier after another in his wake.

The press of the enemy soldiers was endless, but they lacked skill. By the time Helga and the squad reached the cavern, each had stepped over countless bodies. Waiting for them were fresh and more experienced soldiers who sold their lives more dearly. But sell them they did until the floor of the cavern was slick with their blood.

Still, the battle raged, and Ian learned to fight back-to-back with his intrepid comrades in a rhythm that allowed each to wield their sword or axe in a most deadly manner.

Helga was everywhere at once, helping Ian now, Shabear later, then Thorfinn, then Ian again, and each time, she arrived out of nowhere, sometimes in what seemed the nick of time, and always to turn the tide. She personally sought out the enemy commander and dispatched him with a mighty two-handed sword blow that sent his head rolling down the tunnel. This last feat broke the enemy resolve, and despite the entreaties and threats of the remaining officers, the surviving men dropped their weapons and scurried every which way.

When the echo from the last clang of metal died away, there was an eerie silence. Not one of the squad was uncut, and most were injured in several places, but most of blood splattered across their bodies was that of the vanquished.

Helga looked around and saw that Thorfinn and Shabear were standing amid mounds of enemy bodies. Ian was nowhere to be seen. They searched the dead but did not find his body. They did find Stefan, who lay behind a heap of dead soldiers. Helga reckoned that Stefan had killed fourscore before a lance thrust had ended his life. Stefan's sword and battle-axe were still in his hands, and his horn still dangled around his neck.

"But for the warning blast of Stefan's horn and his valiant rearguard action, the outcome might not have been so good. To Stefan," saluted Helga, crossing her sword over her heart.

Their victory was great, but Ian's absence was a mystery. Was he dead or alive? Had he been captured?

Chapter 39

Good News, Bad News

An eagle uttered a *kee-kee-kee-kee-yep* and then fluttered onto King Bjorn's shoulder and dropped a scroll into his hand. The announcement call was necessary so that the king might brace his shoulder to receive the twelve-pound bird. King Bjorn loved his messenger eagles and had trained them to land gently on his right shoulder without digging in their talons. The bright yellow cere and feet, together with the golden nape feathers, confirmed the messenger as a golden eagle.

King Bjorn read the runes carefully, and as he finished and rerolled the scroll, a smile brightened his face.

"Good news then?" inquired Ursus, who had watched his friend carefully to judge the impact of the message. "If so, it's the first you've received in some while." Most messages in the preceding days had detailed the depressing reports of the massive enemy troop movements north.

"Yes," beamed King Bjorn. "Eirik and Liz have escaped from Popocatépetl."

"What about Kate?" asked Mac. "And how do you know?"

"We can trust this message because the runes bear the mark of Odontocetes, queen of the dolphins. That Eirik and Liz were safe when this message was written is unquestioned. The message also relates that Kate escaped from Popocatépetl with Eirik and Liz but that Kate is no longer with them and her status is unknown. We must presume she was recaptured."

"But Liz would never leave Kate unless she was …" Mac lost all the color in his face as his voice drifted off. His knees weakened, and he momentarily stumbled.

Ursus stepped forward to support him, but Mac put his hand out. “No, I’m okay. It’s just that …” Tears welled up in his eyes, and his words broke.

This time when Ursus came forward, Mac did not resist but instead fell into the soft fur of the bear’s chest and stifled several sobs. No one said anything, for short of news that Kate was safe, there was nothing anyone could say that would relieve her father’s pain.

For Mac, the few tears had been long in the coming. The trickle of stifled sobs was only a crack in a mighty dam that threatened to break, and Ursus understood that the venue for this release was too public for the moment and led Mac away to a place where he could cry in private.

Mac tried not to cry in front of Ursus. “I’m sorry to be so emotional. I usually have better self-control, but down here I feel so helpless.”

“I know something of your anguish. Since the day I lost my only son, I have never stopped crying. I know that my tears are about my loneliness, and I accept this, not as a weakness but rather as an affirmation of who I am and my relationship with my son. I loved Bär. I miss him. My tears celebrate my love for him, as do yours for Kate. Do not apologize for loving your daughter.”

This statement released the floodgates, and after sobbing uncontrollably for several minutes, Mac fell into an exhausted sleep. Ursus hoped that when he awoke, the emotional catharsis would prove liberating. He wasn’t sure, though, that this would be the case. He prayed to the God of All Creatures to help Mac, and he set the Green Crystal torches around him before he left.

Several hours later, when Mac did awake, he found Ursus by his side. “Thank you,” he said. “I feel as if a great weight has been lifted from me. You’ve been a better friend than I deserve. I haven’t ever been too honest with myself, much less with other people. I guess if you can cry in front of others, you can be honest about other things too. I’ve always thought my work was the most important part of my life. I thought my role as a husband and parent was to be a success and to pay the bills. My wife took care of our children, and then Kate and Liz grew up and started to take care of themselves. I thought I was taking care of my family, but actually, they were taking care of me. Now I have no one, and I’m afraid. Suddenly my life seems so meaningless. I guess somewhere along the way, I started to take my family and friends for granted, and that was wrong. You're very kind, Ursus, incredibly tolerant, and patient; you've helped me understand. Thank you for showing me the way."

Chapter 40
Queen Odontocetes

Liz had always enjoyed the water and was an expert swimmer, experienced scuba diver, and avid sailor, but none of her past aquatic experiences compared to the exhilaration of riding a dolphin through the warm crystal-clear waters of an underground river. *If this ride could last forever, it would be too short,* she mused.

When she arrived back at the sandy beach where she had started her walk, Liz saw Eirik still sitting in the same place, mumbling to himself. His eyes were closed, and his hands were clasped in front of him. He looked serious, and at first Liz wondered whether he might have been crying.

As she walked closer, she realized he was praying. She sat down beside him and waited for him to finish. When he opened his eyes, the serious look evaporated into a warm smile.

"I thought you were mad and figured you would be gone for a while. I'm glad you didn't leave."

Liz was puzzled by this comment, and what she did next was just as puzzling to Eirik. Liz reached over and gave Eirik a friendly hug.

"Eirik, you were right. Saving ourselves was the only way to save Kate. I'm sorry I was rude. Thank you for helping the dolphins prevent me from going back. I would have died."

"Gosh, thanks," he said, blushing.

"I thought you'd be gone for some time. What changed your mind?"

"I *was* gone for a long time," replied Liz, who looked curiously at Eirik.

Eirik looked perplexed, and Liz realized that what had seemed like hours to her had been only a few minutes or even seconds to Eirik.

Liz decided not to explain and instead said, "At least it seemed like a long time to me, but I guess it really wasn't."

Eirik was trying to sort out the mixed messages when a dolphin surfaced and called out to them with a high-pitched squeal.

"Come on, Eirik," said Liz. "We have to meet with Queen Odontocetes. These dolphins will take us to her."

"How do know that?"

"I just know. Come on. Time is of the essence." Liz paused to think about what she had just said. "Or then again, it might not be," she added, smiling quixotically.

"Pardon me?" said Eirik, now more confused than ever.

"Don't worry. I'm just goofy from holding my breath so long underwater. Might even be some nitrogen narcosis from the rapid ascent."

"Nitrogen what?" asked Eirik.

"Oh, right, I forgot you didn't go to the same schools as me. I'll explain some other time. Now, though, we need to get going."

Eirik seemed to accept this, and together they waded out to the same dolphins who had saved them. They held fast to the dorsal fins, and the dolphins swam toward Miocena, the underwater kingdom of Queen Odontocetes.

Although most of the journey was on the surface, there were portions that required submerging for variable periods, and during these times, they were treated to underwater scenery that to Liz seemed as strange as it was beautiful. The water was clear as crystal, the consequence of a natural purifying process. The layers of limestone above were porous and sponge-like. Any impurities in the surface water were absorbed as the water percolated down through the limestone.

Courtesy of luminescent crystals and phosphorescent algae, Liz was able to see well for tens and sometimes even hundreds of feet. There were ripples on some of the cistern floors that looked like those created when sand is continuously lapped by waves. This confused Liz since there was little or no current on the surface, and the pattern of the ripples was more characteristic of a strong current in shallow water, like a beach by an ocean. Once, when the dolphin was only a few inches from the bottom, Liz reached out her hand and was surprised to find immovable rock rather than shifting sand.

Liz realized that the rippled floor was indeed the result of wave motion on sand but that the pattern must have been formed at a time when the river was not as deep. Afterward, the river must have dried up, leaving the sand to solidify and thereby preserving the waveform architecture. Later, the cavern had again filled with water and left this geological story for Liz to unfold.

The dolphins took them through underwater forests of stalactites and stalagmites of all descriptions. Over centuries of geological history, the river depth had clearly fluctuated; sometimes the caverns had been completely filled with water, whereas during other times the caverns had been bone dry. In some caverns, the rock formations were polished smooth, which indicated centuries of water exposure, but in other channels the columns were still rough, which suggested more recent submersion. Liz wondered what had flooded the tunnels.

The dolphins soon discerned that Liz was curious about the underground geography, and they purposely swam by rock formations they considered might be of interest. The dolphins stopped at a small underground lake to show Liz some small perfectly round rocks just below the surface of the water. They looked like light-colored marbles, and Liz waded into the pool and tried to pick them up, but they were firmly embedded. Some were bone white, others beige, and some had a faint yellow or orange tint. Liz recognized them as cave pearls, spherical crystals of calcium carbonate that had formed around a grain of sand, in the same fashion as a pearl in an oyster.

Mostly, the water was crystal clear, but occasionally they swam through areas where the visibility was only a few inches. Usually this occurred where their underground river merged with another. The first time this happened, Liz could see ahead that the water was different. As they came closer, the water shimmered, and when they passed into this portion of the aquifer, Liz's eyes started to smart, and her vision blurred. She quickly realized they had swum through a halocline, a border where salt water from the ocean met fresh water from surface runoff. The border was very distinct, much like that between oil and water.

The next time they approached a halocline, Liz motioned for the dolphin to surface.

By now the dolphins were used to her insatiable curiosity, as was Eirik. "I want to swim up to the interface on my own," she advised, and she dived into the pool.

She stopped just short and studied the undisturbed halocline. The difference in the densities of the water was sufficient to provide a mirror effect, and Liz could see the shimmering outline of her face. As she passed through, the mirror broke up, and the image of her face dissolved into a shiny fog. When she turned to return, she realized Eirik had followed her. As they surfaced, he kidded Liz that she must be vain to need to use a halocline for a mirror. She blushed her disagreement, and they carried on.

As they continued, they passed through several schools of fish without eyes. In the dimmer depths, these fish negotiated the underground rivers with natural sonar. One portion of their route brought them to the surface. Liz found herself looking up at blue sky for the first time in a long while. The water level was about a hundred feet below the surface, and the vegetation around and hanging from the rim was lush. The sides of the pool were undercut from previous erosion, which made the sides slope up like a cone.

Looks like we're in a huge well, thought Liz, and then she realized they were in a cenote, a limestone sinkhole. Cenotes were created after a cataclysmic geological event, perhaps such as the one that occurred when the asteroid conjectured to have destroyed the dinosaurs struck the Caribbean Sea. Sinkholes were fundamental to the Mayan culture. Cites were built proximal to these natural wells, which served not only to provide water in times of drought but also as a vehicle to sacrifice objects, animals, and even people to their gods. The Mayans believed in both an underworld and an overworld. Their temples were usually built close to an underground cavern, often with an underground pool that might be linked to a nearby cenote, and the caverns, together with pyramids they constructed in the center of the cities, ensured access to the gods who resided both below and above.

The lushness in and around the cenote was impressive. The vegetation was even thick for a few feet below the surface of the water. Vines with red tube-shaped flowers hung down to the water's surface, and wedge-tailed sabrewing hummingbirds flirted with the flowers. The emerald green feathers blended well with the lushness and contrasted sharply with the birds' violet forehead, white belly, and black wedge-shaped tail. Liz watched while a hummingbird hovered in front of one of the tube-shaped flowers and repeatedly thrust its long, slightly curved bill in and out to drink from the natural nectar-filled vessel.

For a few moments Liz wondered if it might be better for her to climb to the surface. She knew she could find her way home through the jungle. *I could bring help,* she thought, but the lure of the surface reality was only fleeting, and she had no hesitation when the dolphins indicated they should carry on via the river.

Shortly thereafter, they passed through an underground cavern with quite a fresh breeze, which meant they were close to the surface again. At the bottom of the pool were the scattered bones of an ancient cave animal. *Perhaps ice age,* thought Liz. The skull looked feline, but she couldn't be sure at first. When she saw the huge elongate canines, she was able to confirm the animal had been a saber-toothed tiger.

A poem came to mind, which she refashioned to fit the situation and mumbled softly.

"Tiger, Tiger, dead and white,
In the darkness, lost to light,
What mortal hand or eye,

Fought you then, and made you die?"

"Pardon me?" asked Eirik.

"Oh, sorry for mumbling. Just an old nursery rhyme about a tiger," replied Liz.

The last submerged segment required Liz and Eirik to hold their breath for almost three minutes. Liz was used to holding her breath while snorkeling. For her the time went by in a breeze. Not so for Eirik, who had spent little time in the water, and even less diving. For the last minute he felt as if his lungs might burst, he reported breathlessly when they emerged.

They surfaced in an enormous underground lake surrounded by a cavern that sparkled with a golden glow. "I've heard of this place," panted Eirik, still trying to catch his breath, but obviously excited. "This must be Miocena. I never really knew whether it existed. Even my father, who once met the queen, has doubted the existence of this secret place."

The lake was immense and the home to many aquatic animals. Liz looked around and counted dozens of dolphin species, many of them with strange shapes she had never seen. Some had two tusks like a walrus and others a solitary tusk like a narwhal. She saw something that looked a lot like a duck-billed platypus, only with dorsal fins and tusks. The animal had a pouch and was clearly a marsupial.

"Those ones are as big as whales," offered Eirik.

"They *are* whales," confirmed Liz.

Some beaches were filled with sea lions and others with otters, and still more with walruses and penguins. There were furry animals like beavers, only much larger and with walrus-like tusks instead of buckteeth.

The dolphins dropped them off on an island filled with otters, who floated on their backs in the water, chased one another on the land, and otherwise looked like they were having a lot of fun.

"They're so cute," remarked Liz.

"Wait for an introduction," suggested Eirik, who watched an otter tear apart and eat a live crab. "They have sharp-looking claws and very sharp teeth."

The golden glow came from the walls of the cavern and from the sand, each grain of which was a tiny luminous golden crystal. Translucent stalactites emerged from the sand and served as prisms that made rainbows on the walls of the cavern. The lower walls were composed of a yellow crystal that over the millennia had been polished by lapping water to a mirrorlike finish. The sand and the stalagmites reflected the golden glow into every corner of the kingdom. Higher up, the cavern walls and ceiling were the same yellow crystal but with a rough surface that reflected rainbows from the moving waves and made the ceiling coruscate like multicolored stars.

"What a beautiful place," exclaimed Liz. "What a wonderful world."

"Thank you," replied a voice from the water, and Eirik and Liz turned to meet Queen Odontocetes. "Welcome to Miocena. You are the first land animals to ever visit our city, and but for the apocalyptic peril of this time and your importance to our world, you never would have been brought here." She looked directly at Liz as she spoke.

"Thank you, your highness," said Liz, bowing gracefully.

"Graciousness and courtesy are uncommon, and you wear these virtues like a princess, yet you are not of royal blood," the queen replied.

"No, your highness, but Prince Eirik is the son of King Bjorn and heir to the throne of Asgard."

For the first time, the queen looked at Eirik, who bowed.

"Your most royal highness," said Eirik, "I am honored to visit your kingdom. My father has always spoken most highly of his meeting with you when he was a young man."

"Your father is a good and honest man, a true friend who over the years has never intruded on our privacy. I sent word to him that you were safe and in my care."

"Thank you, your highness," said Eirik as he bowed again. "My father will be relieved to hear your news."

"You have traveled far today, and though we must talk, now is time for food and then sleep." The queen motioned to the otters, and within moments a meal was set before them. "Anon we will talk," she said and disappeared into the lake.

Chapter 41
Bear to the Rescue

Ian was fighting back-to-back with Shabear when he saw Thorfinn surrounded by a half-dozen enemy soldiers, his back to the wall; he was clearly in trouble. Ian leapt to Thorfinn's defense and succeeded in extricating him from the tight situation, but in the process Ian was separated from the main action in the cavern and found himself in one of the side tunnels facing a fresh group of soldiers.

His sword and knife flashed red through their tunics, but more and more soldiers joined the fray, and he was able to manage only a decent defense. Slowly but surely, he was progressively pushed back deeper into the side tunnel.

The enemy smelled blood, perhaps mostly their own, but with Ian backing up, their courage was enhanced, and over time, and notwithstanding his skill, Ian could feel that the tide had turned, and without some change in fortune, he feared they would soon overpower him.

Many times he surged forward and left several of the enemy writhing on the floor of the tunnel, but just as many times they pressed back. There seemed no end of them. Fortunately for Ian, the tunnel was just barely wide enough for several men, which meant that they could not easily flank him.

The enemy swords often broke under the Sword of Olaf, and Ian had learned to quickly use the knife in his other hand to dispatch a man so disarmed. Fighting against an axe required a different solution, and Ian learned to place his blows just below the blade, which severed either the shaft of the axe or the soldier's wrist. Both outcomes were satisfactory, and each time Ian's knife flashed to finish the job.

His main concern was the lance thrusts. He had been cut many times on his arms and legs, and each cut, no matter how small, burned and itched. The cuts felt like scratches from plant nettles. He was grateful for the leather tunic, which protected his chest and abdomen and had deflected countless thrusts already. Still, each scratch took its toll.

He had been pushed back far enough and around several corners such that he could neither see the entrance to the cavern nor hear the din of the major battle. Ian realized that as the distance from the cavern increased, his chances of rescue decreased, and although he had established a deadly rhythm and was certain the enemy were paying dearly, he wondered how much longer he could prevail.

A sharp pain pierced Ian's neck just above his left shoulder and caused him to drop his knife. He continued to parry the blades of the enemy with his sword, but his motions seemed increasingly clumsy, and he felt a growing and inexplicable tiredness. His eyes blurred, and he felt himself slowly slipping to the ground. An eerie feeling overcame him, as if his mind had somehow separated from his body. Then he saw himself lying on the ground surrounded by enemy soldiers who gloated over his prostate body. Just before he lost consciousness, he heard a throaty roar, and the air was filled with the swish and cut of claws that tore up a score of men in the space of a second.

"Thank you, Shabear," Ian mumbled, just before everything went black.

Chapter 42
Absence of Pain is Pleasure

Time had no meaning for Kate, who now lived only to survive from one encounter with the shadow to the next. *Total darkness is beautiful,* she thought, because shadows could not exist in the absence of light. Kate survived huddled against a wall, always with closed eyes, and always hoping, hoping beyond hope, that Ian would open the door and save her.

Kate awoke immediately whenever the candle flickered into flame. The light, however modest, burned through her closed eyelids, and each time, it felt as if hot red needles had been thrust into her eyeballs. This pain always ushered in a feeling of abject terror since the candlelight invariably meant a visit from the shadow with the blood red eyes. Kate trembled in fear with each passing second until the shadow finally arrived; with each visit the shadow varied the time of its coming, and with it Kate's angst. The waiting was the worst, and the shadow knew this. Although the waiting might last for up to an hour, the physically abusive session never lasted more than a few minutes. Oftentimes, the arrival of the shadow seemed almost a relief compared to the waiting.

The door never opened or closed; the shadow just appeared. The shape slithered around the walls, floor, or ceiling without any regard to the position of the candle. Kate wished she could suspend herself in the middle of the room, as if this location might somehow be safe from the two-dimensional terror. But there was no escape, and the kicks, slaps, and punches were decidedly three-dimensional.

Strangely, the physical pain eventually became tolerable; Kate understood that her bruises, scrapes, and broken bones could heal. What tormented her most was her helplessness, her loss of control. What she feared most was that she might give up and prefer death. Even more terrifying, she learned to hate the shadow. She often visualized herself inflicting the same brutality on the shadow. She grew to enjoy this pastime but hated herself for succumbing to such a base emotion and for wallowing in the depravity of violence. She knew that if she survived, the emotional scars would be the ones to linger.

After each session was over, and once the shadow had passed, Kate came to understand that in her reality, in her tortured existence, the absence of pain was pleasure. She always smiled at this twisted thought, and then she would lapse into a fitful sleep where even a nightmare somehow seemed safe.

Chapter 43
Siksika

Ian awoke to the smiling face of Connor, who was sitting beside his bed. "Connor! You big furry pal, am I glad to see you," said Ian, smiling back at his friend. He then looked around but did not recognize his surroundings. "I guess this means I'm back at the Castle of Light. I owe Shabear my life. She rescued me from certain death, and my wounds must have been bad enough to send me back."

Connor seemed at a loss for words, and rather than speak, he helped Ian to stand.

"How long have I slept? Is there any news of Kate and Liz? What news is there? Has the battle of the Green Cavern started? How is Mac? Did the others reach Siksika? Is Stefan okay? His horn warned us of the ambush. And how are you, my friend?" Ian gave Connor a healthy hug as he finished his barrage of questions.

"Do you always ask so many questions at once?" asked Connor. "I can't remember them all, much less the order, so instead, I'll just tell you what I know."

"You are not at the Castle of Light; rather, we are at Siksika. King Bjorn and my grandfather gave me permission to join you, and I have run hard for many days. You are recovering after a great victory that will live long in the songs of our people. A Siksika skald has already written a *flokkr* in your honor. Your blades vanquished an entire company of enemy soldiers.

"Helga, Shabear, and Thorfinn vanquished hundreds more of the enemy in the main cavern. Those who were not limp and lifeless on the battlefield fled for their lives into the tunnels, and many of those were captured by Siksika patrols.

"Only Stefan lost his life, but his life was well spent. Fourscore of the enemy lay at his feet, and the warning call from his great horn was enough to save the squad from certain disaster. It is good you have awoken, for today we will honor Gudrid and Stefan. They would have wanted you to be present. We have no news of Bjorn and his army, or of Kate, Liz, or Eirik.

"You have been asleep for three days while we have enjoyed the hospitality of Runolfur, the mighty chief of the Siksika clan. Come," said Connor, rising, "Runolfur asked that he be notified immediately on your awakening. He will be in the council chamber, where likely as not Helga, Shabear, and Thorfinn will also be found."

As Ian started to walk, he realized that his legs and arms were a mass of healing cuts that tingled as though these parts of his body were asleep. None of these wounds were either deep or painful. However, when he turned his head, he suffered an immediate and bone-chilling pain that brought beads of sweat to his forehead and made him feel sick to his stomach and weak in his knees. Ian instinctively tried to raise his left hand to investigate the wound in his neck but found that he could not raise his arm above his shoulder. When he explored the wound with this right hand, he discovered a scab-encrusted crater with a depression the depth and diameter of a walnut.

"My arm!" exclaimed Ian. "My left arm is weak. How will I be able to hold my knife?"

"Don't worry, my friend; Shabear believes that even that poisoned wound will heal. In time, your left arm will once again know the joy of a deadly knife thrust.

"But," Connor added, "you were very sick, and recovery was not always certain."

Ian looked up at Connor with eyes that beseeched him to explain.

"Shabear has hardly left your side, and it was her skill that brought you back from the gates of death. For two days and nights your life hung in an ugly balance while your sweat poured and fierce chills racked your body. You retched and poured fluid from every orifice. It was as if your body needed to purge itself of some terrible poison. Your words were crazy. You spoke of men on fire and horrid creatures that none of us could recognize. The medicine man of the Siksika clan believed you were possessed by some dark power. The wound in your shoulder turned red and then black and wept a brown liquid that Shabear forbade any to touch. Some seemed inclined to disregard her advice until Shabear put a small quantity of the liquid on a small willow tree, which withered while we watched. On the third day, your fever broke, and your body broke out in a faint pink rash. This morning, the skin of your fingers and toes peeled, and Shabear left your side confident you would wake today. I was instructed to wait by your side."

"Then Shabear saved my life twice," acknowledged Ian.

"Umm, yes," said Connor, who paused for a second. "Shabear did save your life. Come on; let's go to the council chamber."

The word spread quickly that Ian had recovered, and as they entered the upper level of the amphitheater, one after another of the council turned to look up at Ian as he descended the stairs. A rhythmic sound erupted when some of the warriors stamped their feet to honor Ian. The noise gained momentum as more and more stamped in unison until the chamber thundered with pedal applause.

The man Ian assumed must be Runolfur came forward and extended his right arm and grasped Ian's left elbow in a traditional greeting of friendship and introduced himself. His face, like that of his warriors, was stained blood red with iron containing earth pigments. Each warrior carried a bow and a quiver full of arrows, a knife in a leather sheath, and a battle-axe. They wore moccasins stained gray with ashes.

"Thank you," Ian said, embarrassed by this display of respect.

"No," replied Runolfur, as he lifted his head to speak loud enough for the council to hear, "it is we who must thank you. It is our honor to meet the warrior who single-handedly filled a tunnel with the bodies of a company of enemy soldiers. The bodies stretched back for almost half a mile from the cavern and were piled so deep that Connor had difficulty carrying you back to the cavern."

"Connor?" said Ian with surprise. "Then it wasn't Shabear who saved me?"

"Not then," replied Helga. "It seems we had a seventh member of our squad who was serving as an especially effective rearguard. Connor cleared the tunnel of the remaining enemy soldiers and then carried you back to the cavern. By then, a Siksika patrol had reached the cavern, and they accompanied us back to their city. We all had wounds, but ours were of the regular kind, and none were filled with the poison you experienced."

"Yes," explained Shabear, who stepped forward, "I am relieved to see you alive, for the poison was powerful."

Ian thanked Shabear for saving his life and then turned to look for Connor, who had disappeared.

"Oh," said Shabear. "You want to thank Connor. Well, he left a few minutes ago. He was too embarrassed to have you thank him in front of all of us. Connor is a very humble bear. But it is true that he saved your life and perhaps some of ours as well, for Connor also killed the soldier who sent the arrow into your neck, and this man had several more diabolical darts in his sheath. Who knows but that one of them might have found their mark in my hide, or in another of us?"

"Quite true," said Runolfur, nodding. "But the soldier who carried these poisoned arrows chose Ian as his first target, and that could not have been by chance. Why did this arrow not find Shabear, who has the gift of healing? Why not Helga, who is the leader? Why Ian?" asked Runolfur in a rhetorical manner.

"Malicious must fear him more than the rest of us," suggested Helga.

"Yes, indeed," replied Runolfur. "Clearly Malicious respects Ian's power. She must not want him to reach Popocatépetl. Perhaps she believes that Ian is destined to defeat her."

Shabear removed the dressing on Ian's neck so that all could see the scar, a hollow crater with a black center. "Yes," acknowledged Shabear, "Malicious has left her mark on Ian, and perhaps we should not be so quick to congratulate ourselves on his recovery. He still does not have the use of his left arm, although I am hopeful that with time, this too will heal."

Runolfur invited Ian and Connor to participate in the traditional sweat-lodge ceremony used to help heal a wounded warrior, and sent one of his warriors to retrieve Connor.

The lodge was made from buffalo hides stretched over a frame of fir trees that had been stripped and cut with an axe into planks and then slowly bent to the shape of a half circle. There was room inside for six to eight men, two bears, or two men and Connor. In the center of the lodge was a shelf with a pile of smooth stones that had been heated to scalding and carried into the lodge with a forked stick. Runolfur instructed Ian and Connor to remove their weapons and clothes and to sit as close to the stones as was possible comfortably.

Once the flap door was closed, Ian felt the heat at once and began to sweat profusely.

"Drink a lot of water," advised Runolfur. "The water is from the glaciers high above us and is clean and pure. The poison that is left in your body will leave in the form of sweat, and the glacial water will replace the lost fluids and cleanse your blood. You must drink constantly to keep up with your sweat. If you do not drink, you will become dizzy and sick."

Runolfur allowed them to acclimate before he began ladling water onto the hot stones. After each ladle of water, Runolfur rapped a drumstick made from the heart of a willow tree on the bucket of water. To the rhythm of the rapping, he sang a song that referred to the drumstick as the forepaws of the father of all bears and to the forked stick used to carry the stones as his shoulders.

After several ladles of water, the heat, which had been modest and fairly dry, intensified and turned humid, and the air, which had been clear, turned steamy. Ian could no longer feel the difference between the sweat that escaped from his skin and the water vapor that condensed on his body.

Runolfur placed some aromatic juniper boughs on the stones, and the sweat lodge filled with the smell of menthol. "Some of my people believe you are Star Boy," said Runolfur to Ian.

"Star Boy?"

"According to the legends of my people, there was once a time of great trouble, and the lives of all our peoples were in danger. Star Boy was a young man who was poisoned by the evil that caused the danger. For many days, Star Boy remained in the world between the living and the dead. His family and friends tried to help him, but a serpent prevented them. Many men tried, but none could make the snake go away until finally Moon Father intervened and sent enough rain to cause a great flood. The water drove away the snake, and Star Boy revived. This ushered in an era of prosperity for our people, and Star Boy joined Moon Father in the sky as the morning star."

"How does that make me Star Boy?" asked Ian.

"Our peoples are facing a great danger, and you have come to us after having been poisoned by the cause of this great danger. It's only natural for my people to think this."

"Just as long as they don't think I'm going to save them. Much as I want to help, my only goal is to save Kate and her sister and then get back to the surface and away from this crazy world."

The sweat lodge was awkwardly silent for some time after Ian's response. His honest but selfish reply had lacked a solidarity that Runolfur and Connor might have hoped for.

"Everyone will do their part to stop the evil of Malicious," said Connor. "Ian is a courageous warrior, and by rescuing Kate and Liz, he will help us all."

"We can only hope," said Runolfur with a sigh. "We can only hope."

CHAPTER 44

DOLPHINS ARE DYING

Liz had awoken refreshed and with an optimistic sense not justified by the past month's events. Even the gloomy information Queen Odontocetes was giving them did not daunt her growing sense that all would be well.

"It is well that you have such a positive attitude," said Queen Odontocetes. "Even though it was foretold that you would come, and though this augers well for our ability to prevail against this scourge, the outcome is not certain. Your strength and courage will be sorely tested in the days ahead. I will tell you our history," said the dolphin queen. "This will help you understand the gravity of our mission.

"Many years ago, before the time of men, the world was mostly water, and the aquatic animals lived in peace and harmony. We survived the times of the great upheavals when the floors of the oceans rose to create the land, and we adapted by sending some of our animals to live in the dry world, and we continued to live in harmony.

"When the great rocks came from the sky and brought darkness to the world, almost all the land animals died, but we survived. Again we sent some of our animals to live upon the dry land, and for many years we continued to live in contentment.

"The new generation of land animals thrived, and in a sad twist of fate, one of the new species that emerged became dominant and no longer sought to live in harmony with the other animals. This animal preyed upon all the others. No animal was safe, and over time this one presumptuous animal destroyed more species than all those who died during the great upheaval and the long darkness."

Queen Odontocetes paused. She looked irritated as if telling the story was painful. "These greedy animals eventually drove the other land animals high into the mountains or deep into the uninhabited forests and preserved the best land for their own. Even this wasn't enough. These avaricious beasts coveted even the oceans, lakes, and rivers. They learned to sail upon the waters, and soon no coast was safe for our people. We were driven into the deeper ocean where our peoples languished far from the warm shores."

Queen Odontocetes paused again. She looked upset. She took several deep breaths as if to steel herself to continue. "Finally, in desperation, some of our peoples sought refuge in these underground waters, and here we made our home, hoping to be free from the curse of that one creature that could only survive at the expense of others. We have lived in these underground lakes and rivers for thousands of years. Each year, more aquatic animals have learned of our haven and have joined us. Many have journeyed for over a year to reach us, and all have been welcomed.

"Sadly, even here, the accursed animal eventually came. Ironically, the first to come were driven underground by others of their own species. They had been oppressed and abused and were a tragic lot. Some of our kind wanted to kill these surface animals, but the majority took pity on these refugees and allowed them to coexist.

"Initially, we lived in harmony with these surface animals, but as the years passed, news of our underground world slowly seeped to the surface. Some of the land animals grew homesick for the sun, and when they returned to the surface, they told stories of incredible underground deposits of gems and minerals, and this attracted armies of the greedy surface animals ever deeper into our realm. As on the surface, these selfish animals sought to dominate, and especially from the south, we heard reports of death and destruction of all animals who resisted and enslavement of those who submitted to their will. With each passing year, more and more of our underground realm was usurped by this beast, the most selfish, arrogant, and destructive species that has ever lived—the human animal."

When she said "human," Queen Odontocetes looked first at Eirik and then at Liz. When their eyes met, Liz saw a look that changed from rapprochement to anger and finally to resigned sadness. Liz understood that nothing she could say could make up for the millennia of destructiveness that her species had wrought on the aquatic animals. Still, she felt obliged to apologize.

"I'm sorry my species has been so violent and inconsiderate of your peoples and indeed of all the animal and plant species of our world. Although I cannot hope to convince you that my peoples will change, I can tell you that more and more of us are working hard to protect our environment and to make the world a safe place for all the animals and plants."

"Thank you for accepting my rebuke of your species with such graciousness. If all humankind were like you, I believe we could all live in harmony," responded Queen Odontocetes.

"How can we help?" offered Liz. "Surely there is a way for us to defeat Malicious."

"Perhaps," replied the queen. "Your coming was foretold, and that alone gives us cause for hope."

"Foretold?" inquired Liz. "You've mentioned that twice. Please explain."

"Yes," replied Queen Odontocetes. "All the waters of the world were once pristine and pure and remained so even up to the time when we discovered our underground world, but several hundred years ago, we began to hear stories of surface waters going bad. The pattern was always the same. Wherever humans settled, they built cities that changed the natural colors. Once-blue skies turned ash gray, clear blue waters turned murky brown, and the lush greenness of the land turned into windblown sand. The sky became so cloudy that the brightest stars were no longer visible by day, and the waters so cloudy that our peoples lost their way. A plague descended on those aquatic animals who lived closest to man. Many of our brethren were discovered dead on beaches or bloated and floating in the surf. A few of those affected managed to struggle to our shores, but none survived, and all died horribly, choking on their own blood."

Two solitary tears appeared under the eyes of the queen and she paused to collect herself. "Our ancestors were frightened that this blight might eventually seep into our world, and they prayed to the God of All Creatures that this might not be so. They were all the more frightened because this plague had been foretold. Many years before, a dolphin respected for her wisdom had foretold the coming of murky waters and horrible deaths for our peoples on the surface. The same dolphin also foretold the coming of the murky waters to our underground world, and several months ago, this came to pass."

"No!" cried Liz. "I'm so sorry."

"Yes, at first we refused to believe the prophecy was coming true. When the first dolphins disappeared, we thought perhaps they had met with some natural misfortune, but when bloated dolphins were discovered on the banks of our underground rivers, we knew the worst had come to pass. My people are frightened and no longer venture into the river systems close to the underground cities.

"My scouts have brought back news of a toxic cloud in the water that emanates from the volcanic fortress of the Evil One. Fortunately, the water from our kingdom flows downstream to the fortress, and this has slowed the creep of the cloud, but each day, the misery defies the current and spreads a bit farther upstream.

"Our scouts also tell of strange aquatic creatures. Like humans, these creatures do not live in harmony with other animals. They seem to thrive in the toxic cloud. Some believe these creatures were born from the cloud."

Liz recollected the creature with the yellow tentacle that had grabbed the live animal dropped by Lord Null. She shared this news with Queen Odontocetes.

The queen sighed. "If the murkiness has already penetrated that far upstream to the north, it cannot be long until the toxic cloud reaches us."

"But there must be more to the prophecy," said Liz. "You said our coming was foretold."

"Yes, the wise dolphin who foretold the coming of the murkiness also foretold the arrival of a person with the power to cleanse the water. According to the prophecy, this person would be a surface woman of great courage but also a considerate woman who studied the old ways of her species and who was learned and sensitive to the ways of the aquatic world."

Chapter 45
Ian's Dreamscape Changes

Ian tossed and turned in his sleep, but it wasn't because of his many healing wounds or because the bed prepared by Runolfur's people was uncomfortable. No, what made his sleep fitful was his recurrent nightmare about fighting the bald-headed man.

Each night, he was awoken many times with the same dream. Until tonight the pattern had not changed.

After a physically demanding day, Ian would usually fall fast asleep. Several hours later, as his sleep rhythm changed from deep to light, he would start to toss and turn. His legs would move restlessly, and often he'd talk nonsense or cry out. Then, suddenly, out of a mumbo jumbo of random thoughts, Ian would hear Kate, her plaintive voice slowly fading, as if she were being carried farther away.

Then Ian would find himself fighting with the bald-headed man and inevitably falling off the cliff. The bald-headed man with the ruby-hilted sword would laugh at him from the rim of the cliff, and the laugh would linger until Ian awoke in a cold sweat.

Ian always awoke before his body reached the ground, but only just before, and each time, he woke up frightened. The fear was not about dying. He didn't believe that if you died in your dreams, you died in real life. What frightened Ian was his inability to control the dream and to change the outcome. Ian was no stranger to bad dreams, but over the years he had learned to control their strange power. As a young boy he had experienced recurring nightmares. Many nights he had awoken screaming or crying, and on some occasions his parents had spent the rest of the night consoling him.

His father, a psychiatrist with the Canadian Armed Forces, had taught Ian how to control these nightmares by separating himself from the dream. This required a lot of practice, but Ian had eventually learned how to step outside his dreams. From this mental vantage point, Ian learned how to objectively assess the dream events as they unfolded. In this manner he was able to study his nocturnal thoughts, and the knowledge he gained enabled him to change an evolving nightmare into an ordinary and even pleasant dream. Ian became so adept at dream management that he eventually learned how to create dream adventures at will. Mostly, though, Ian allowed his dreams to take their natural course. He knew that dreaming was important for his emotional health. He also knew that dreams could help him understand himself and his world. There were times, though, often when he was tired and frustrated about his work, that he exercised his imaginative license and created fantastic nocturnal adventures. He loved to fly in his dreams.

The recurring nightmare about the bald-headed man was a challenge for Ian to control because in this dream he was already outside of the scene and watching himself. Try as he might, Ian could not step further outside of this dream; he didn't know how. Failure to understand a situation enhanced his fear, and fear limited rational thinking, which engendered even more fear. Ian was trapped in a vicious circle; he felt as if he were in a vortex of terror and that his mind was spiraling down from the precipice in tandem with his body.

After years of successful dream management, Ian was proud of his ability to control nightmares, and his failure to control this dream was a blow to his ego. What Ian did not realize was that the dream was not his to control. The images were not a product of his past experience, and the dream was not originating from his own thoughts. Rather, the dream had been instilled by a power beyond his ken. Ian never realized—indeed he could not fathom—that there might be a power that could transcend his dreams. Had he understood that control was impossible, Ian might have learned to ignore the dream or at least to suppress the images. As it was, his inability to control the dream not only left him feeling weak and insecure but also brought back the uncomfortable memories of his childhood nightmares, many of which he relived during his tortured sleep.

Ian had now fought the bald-headed man innumerable times, often dozens of times a night. The dream had even pervaded his subconscious while he was in the deep coma and victim to the vile poison prepared by Malicious. During that time the dream had been particularly pernicious and vivid.

Tonight however, the dreamscape changed. Heretofore, the dream had always ended with Ian falling over the cliff. Now, Kate's forlorn voice seemed louder, and the bald-headed man merely laughed and mocked Ian's helplessness, but he made no move to fight.

"Stop laughing!" shouted Ian. "Draw your sword and fight me, you skeletal fiend."

The bald-headed man did draw his sword, but instead of attacking, he held the sword hilt up in front of his gaunt body and slowly walked toward Ian. The laugh continued, but the voice changed and became feminine; this new voice was infinitely crueler than that of the bald-headed man. The man changed from a warrior with a sword to a white-robed priest with a cross. With each step the robes looked darker and grayer until finally the priest disappeared into blackness, and only the rubies remained. The rubies were like pots of fire that grew larger and larger with red flames that licked the black void.

Ian wanted to look away, but he couldn't. His eyes were no longer his to control. The laughter grew into a deafening roar and then stopped long enough for Ian to hear Kate sobbing. Then Ian saw a woman lying beaten in a cell; her blonde hair was disheveled and matted with blood, her clothes were in tatters, and her breaths came in painful sobbing jerks. Her right ankle was swollen to the size of a softball.

"No, not Kate, no!" Ian cried, and as Kate disappeared, the laughter returned, and when he awoke, Ian was shivering with pent-up rage.

Chapter 46
Battle Plans

At the end of each day, Bjorn met with Ursus, Magnus, Shasta, and the leaders of the seven clans to review the news from their forward scouts and also to hear the messages that had arrived from more distant places courtesy of the golden eagles.

Mostly the reports were discouraging and told of the growing host of enemy soldiers that were pouring north toward the Green Cavern.

"Already, their forces outnumber ours by two to one," advised Magnus, "and with each week that passes, their numbers will triple. Our warriors are anxious to engage the enemy and would have us attack soon, before their numbers increase to unfavorable odds."

Bjorn turned to the leader of the Inuit clan. "What say you, Sigurd? Should we attack now?"

Sigurd was shorter and stockier than the other clan leaders. He wore leather guards plated with copper on his forearms, a sealskin shirt, and snowshoe-hare moccasins. A dozen narwhal spears protruded from a large sheath that was slung over his back. Each spear was naturally sharp and could pierce all but the thickest animal hide.

"My warriors are ready and will fight when called, but regardless of whether the enemy were to triple or quadruple in number, the tunnels limit the number of warriors who may stand shoulder-to-shoulder and do not favor a larger force. If we fight in the Green Cavern, their numbers might make a difference."

"How say you, Groa? What do the Haida advise?"

"The enemy is poorly trained in the art of combat, ill-equipped with brittle blades, and driven into battle out of fear. Each of my warriors is worth a score of their soldiers, and I fear attacking neither now nor later, even if their numbers were to multiply by ten."

"Well spoken, Groa," replied King Bjorn, and the other leaders cheered her brave words.

"And you, Rognvald, will you speak for Helga? As we speak, she is in harm's way and on a mission that might solve the riddle of this war without the need for the din of battle to be heard in the Green Cavern."

"Yes, King Bjorn, I will speak for the Kwakiutl. I favor waiting until all our forces are available and until we have further intelligence about the success of Helga's rescue mission. Helga is a mighty warrior. She has never failed in any task she has accepted. But if need be, the Kwakiutl are ready, willing, and able to do their duty. We will fight whenever called to battle."

Bjorn turned to the commander of the seven clans. "And what of the other clans, Magnus?"

Magnus explained that the bulk of the Inuit and Haida forces were still several days away from joining them and that the forces of the Kwakiutl, Siksika, Anasazi, and Toltec clans were required locally to protect their respective cities. "The Nakota clan has gathered just north of the Green Cavern, and we will join them there."

"What do the bears recommend?" inquired King Bjorn as he turned to Shasta.

Shasta was normally a happy bear who lifted the spirits of those around her. But today her eyes were especially dark and deep set and bored out like black holes from her beige-white fur. The darker golden-colored hair along her spine bristled as she spoke. She looked angry, and she spoke with passion.

"Regardless of whether we attack now or later, this war will not be won because of the number of warriors who face the enemy or because our blades or claws are keener, our strategy better, or our fear of dying less. No, the critical factor in this war is the envy of one person who has bred hatred and directed this vile energy at our peaceful ways, and whose greed has encouraged those who would rather take by force what others earn by right. To win this war we must defeat Malicious herself, and any success we achieve at the Green Cavern will not guarantee victory, but merely buy us time, until we defeat her forces in Popocatépetl. Our best hope to end this war, especially without terrible loss of life, depends on Shabear, Connor, Helga, Stefan, Gudrid, Thorfinn, and Ian. May the God of All Creatures protect them and us."

Chapter 47

Funeral for Two Heroes

On the same day that Ian awoke from his coma, the community honored Gudrid and Stefan with Viking funerals.

Siksika had been built in a cavern with a lake fed by an underground river. The cavern was long and narrow, and although the commercial part of the city was built around the lake, the homes of the Siksika clan extended for many miles upstream and downstream on either side of the river. Numerous bridges had been built across the river.

The ceremonies were held in the central plaza, where Helga honored Gudrid and Stefan. "The Valkyries will surely choose Gudrid and Stefan and escort them to the hall of the slain, where they will meet one-eyed Odin and join the Einherjar, the great warriors who fight each day and then feast and tell stories of their great victories all night. Tonight they will hear of Stefan, whose battle-axe and sword fought side by side and decimated the enemy ranks. Fourscore enemy soldiers lay dead at his gallant feet, and he might have slain more and still be alive today but for a spineless foe who was not brave enough to enter close combat, but who instead threw a cowardly and poisoned lance from a distance. The lance pierced his chest with a wound that would have stopped all but the most indefatigable, but before death claimed him, Stefan was able to blow one last call on his mighty horn, and this plaintive second blast carried through the dark tunnels and told the tale of his heroic death as surely as the first call had warned us of the ambush. To blow such breath with a lance in his chest is surely a feat worthy of comparison with Heimdall, the watchman of the gods whose Giallar-horn could be heard throughout the nine worlds."

Upon concluding, Helga asked Thorfinn to speak the eulogy for his sister, and he stepped forward. "Gudrid had the gift of life," Thorfinn began. "As a little girl she always took time to care for the less fortunate. When Gudrid was present, the sick and the helpless always knew where to turn for comfort. When she chose the path of a warrior, some were surprised, but I was not. Gudrid understood that strength of spirit might not be enough to protect those she loved. She realized that strength of body was also important. She was selfless in all her actions, and her sacrifice to save us was in perfect harmony with who she was. She was my twin and my best friend. I loved her and will miss her. Valhalla has gained a compassionate soul as well as a mighty warrior."

After the tributes from Helga and Thorfinn, those who knew Gudrid or Stefan each related a personal story of their fallen friend. These stories left no doubt of their worthiness as heroes of Asgard.

Helga had commissioned poems by a renowned Siksika poet skilled in skåldic verse. The poems were inscribed in runes on obelisks by the riverside. The poems told of their valor as Vikings and of the surety that they would join the other heroes in Valhalla.

After tributes from Runolfur, Stefan's body was placed on a faering, a four-oared boat styled like a longship, and his friends arranged his arms and personal belongings beside him. Thorfinn placed Gudrid's sword beside that of Stefan. Their ceremonial shields were placed over the gunwale. Two silver coins were placed in the boat to pay for their entry into Valhalla. Helga placed Stefan's whale horn beside his head so that he could sound their entrance to Valhalla, where no one doubted they would soon arrive.

The faering was towed upstream to the most northern part of the city, where the ship was set aflame and allowed to drift south down the river while the people of Siksika came to the waterside and honored their passing.

By the time the ship reached the central plaza, the fire had reached its peak, and Runolfur ordered all the lights of the city to be dimmed. The longship was completely surrounded by a bright orange blaze, above which danced blue flames with yellow tips that licked the sky like fiery tongues.

Ian saluted in the best tradition of the officer corps of the Canadian Armed Forces and thought about the funerals he'd attended of some of the comrades who had died in Afghanistan and Bosnia. Ian wondered whether these men might have gone to Valhalla. Turning to Runolfur, he asked, "Can a warrior who is not a Viking go to Valhalla?"

"This is possible," replied Runolfur. "The word *valr* means 'the slain.' Valhalla means the 'hall of those slain in battle.' So long as your friends died with honor on the field of battle, I see no reason why they would not go to Valhalla. If you are slain, I am sure you will be carried by the Valkyries to Valhalla. However, you could not be buried, as is the custom of the Christian peoples. The Christians take those they love and honor most and put them in the earth where the worms devour them. We burn our heroes in a fire so hot that in the blink of an eye they are liberated from their mortal body, and they go to Valhalla at that very moment."

Ian also wondered why Odin was always referred to as "one-eyed." "Shouldn't such a powerful god have two eyes?" he asked.

"Ah," replied Runolfur, "that is a good question. Odin gave up one of his eyes in return for wisdom. The trade was a worthy one, don't you agree?"

Many who attended spoke of seeing two Valkyries leap from the tips of the flames. They watched while the spirits flew onward and upward, carrying Gudrid and Stefan to Valhalla.

Chapter 48

Liz and Eirik Empowered

Liz admired Eirik's natural humility, something she had found lacking in most of her male friends back home. She also admired his strength and courage and was thankful that Eirik had escaped with her. They were becoming a good team, and teamwork would be important in the coming struggle.

Queen Odontocetes had suggested a plan that she hoped would allow them to rescue Kate, avert the war, and otherwise thwart Malicious's plans to defeat her father and become queen of Asgard. She also hoped this would stop the foul process that was polluting the underground water and killing the aquatic animals. "This is a mighty task," said Queen Odontocetes, "but Malicious is vulnerable so long as she thinks you are dead."

"Dead? But how can that be?" asked Eirik. "Lord Null saw us escape on the dolphins."

"Yes, but while you and Liz were lamenting Kate's capture, my dolphins took portions of your tunics and tore them in a fashion to mimic the feeding frenzy of some of the carnivorous fish that live in the river. The ripped tunics were allowed to float downstream where patrolling panthers smelled and retrieved them. Soon thereafter, all search operations along the road east stopped. Malicious must have presumed you dead. Malicious's attention is now focused north, where her armies are converging on the Green Cavern, and she will not expect any attack from the east. As such we have the element of surprise.

"Eirik, at some point you will come face-to-face with your sister. You must not look her in the eyes, lest her dulcet tones mesmerize you. Even without her sinister potions, she might be able to turn you to her will.

"Liz, I doubt you are susceptible to her control. If you were, she would have tried to turn you as she did Eirik and your sister. Even so, her powers are formidable. Even physically she is strong. I cannot advise you how to defeat her; I can only trust that as the chosen one, you will find a way.

"I have arranged for warriors to accompany you to Popocatépetl. They will attack the dock and fortress and provide a diversion so that you can gain entrance to the castle in the cone of the volcano. There you will find Malicious. Find a way to defeat her."

"Warriors?" asked Eirik. "Are there warriors loyal to my father in this area?"

"No, Eirik, the warriors represent a people you have hardly ever seen, individuals who have protected their existence almost as jealously as we have hidden ours. These people are the remnants of a once-great surface civilization, a race of scholars, teachers, and healers. They were driven underground by drought and the selfishness of other men. They call themselves the Maya."

Queen Odontocetes could tell by their reactions that both Liz and Eirik had heard of the Maya. Their familiarity with this secretive culture was a surprise, but not an unwelcome one. "Like us, they have found peace and harmony in this underground world, and also like us, their existence is threatened by Malicious. Some say they are wise in the ways of magic. If so, perhaps they might provide you with more than a diversion."

Two dolphins surfaced beside the queen. The queen gestured toward them and said, "My dolphins will take you to the land of the Maya, but before you leave, accept these gifts from the aquatic animals of our world."

Liz and Eirik were given hooded tunics woven from tiny fish scales. The fabric was so light, it felt as if they had no covering and so supple that no movement was constrained.

"Do not be misled by the lightness of the fabric," advised Queen Odontocetes. "These scales were formed from the crystallized tears of generations of aquatic animals who lost family in the surface world. The scales will change color to blend with your surroundings and help you escape detection. They will neither reflect nor transmit light."

Liz was also given a belt and pouch of the same material. Inside the pouch was a dolphin carved from the same golden crystal as the sand that lit the cavern.

“The dolphin is more than a memento,” the queen said. “When you look into the eyes of the dolphin, you will see further than you might otherwise. Be wary, though; you might not like what you see. Do not be intimidated by this glimpse beyond. If what you see disheartens you, focus instead on the heart of the dolphin. Above all, guard yourself and your soul carefully, lest you forget the things your eyes saw.”

The queen gave Eirik a glass vile carved from a deep blue crystal that precisely matched the color of his eyes. “The water in this crystal was taken from the river that bathes the roots of the Tree of Life. A single drop of this water on your tongue will give you insight.” Queen Odontocetes also gave Eirik a dolphin carved from amber. “Please give this gift to your father from the aquatic animals of Miocena.”

“Thank you, Queen Odontocetes. Amber is a precious stone in Asgard, and your gift of a dolphin sculpted from this stone is a special honor.”

“The amber is a precious stone in Miocena as well. The aquatic animals collect the amber from submerged pine forests that once graced the dry world. Sometimes the amber is washed ashore on our beaches.”

“Yes, I am sure my father will be pleased with this gift. I remember him telling me that our Viking ancestors combed the Baltic and North Sea beaches for this precious stone.”

As Queen Odontocetes accompanied Liz and Eirik toward the underground river where they would leave her pristine aquatic world, thousands of aquatic animals lined their route. They passed under a continuous canopy of jumping dolphins and beside the synchronized fountains of stationary whales. The cavern echoed with songs sung by choirs of seals who sat along the rocks by the entrance to the underground river.

Just before Liz and Eirik dived, all the dolphins and whales stood up on their tails and saluted, and Queen Odontocetes spoke for them all. “Be well, Liz and Eirik, and may we meet again in better times.”

Chapter 49
South to Anasazi

Connor was worried for his friend. Ian's wounds had healed, and, but for the one on his neck, all without a scar. And yet, Ian was no longer the same man. He could run as fast, his left arm had healed, and his knife thrusts were just as agile, but for all this evidence of vitality, there was a lifeless look that lingered.

Shabear shared Connor's concerns, and together they spoke with Helga and Thorfinn.

"Yes, I have seen these signs before," said Helga. "They are the mark of some heavy weight upon the soul, and whether we like this or not, none of us can help with his burden. Only Ian can shake this misery from his soul."

"Perhaps he should remain behind," suggested Thorfinn. "Depression can sap the strength of a warrior. Ian might be a danger not only to himself but also to the rest of our party. Can he be trusted in this melancholy mood?"

"Yes, I believe so," answered Helga. "We will offer him fellowship and be patient with his pain. Ian may continue with us as long as he is able. At the worst, he will die in an upcoming battle with the weight still upon his shoulders. At the best, he will accompany us to a place where he will live or die according to how his power compares to that of the monster that wearies him."

The evening before they left, the Siksika clan held a great feast in their honor, and for a few precious hours, Ian managed to forget about the dreams. Young children were everywhere and were seemingly oblivious to the talk of war. *What refreshing innocence!* thought Ian.

Ian watched while some young boys and girls acted out a play. Some were dressed like buffalo, others like deer, and one had on the mask of a grizzly. A girl and a boy hunted the animals as a team. The boy stalked the buffalo or deer until the animal ran toward the girl, who carried a wooden spear. Each time an animal was killed, the bear arrived, first to beg forgiveness from the soul of the dead animal and then to beseech the hunters to give thanks to the animal for dying so that they might live.

As Ian watched, Shabear came up and sat beside him. "Tell me about this game, Shabear," he said. "Did you, or some other bear, teach the children the game?"

Shabear smiled. "No. They are actually performing a ritual play that has been passed along from generation to generation for thousands of years. The ritual originated with the Siksika peoples, who settled the surface long before King Bjorn's people ever sailed from Iceland. Traditionally, this play is enacted during a sacred thanksgiving ceremony. The Siksika understand that their lives are intertwined with those of the other animals. During the autumn of each year, the hunters perform this play as a way to show their thanks for the animals they killed during the summer hunting season. According to their beliefs, unless the hunters show this respect to the animals, the hunting the next year will be poor."

Shabear and Ian watched while the children changed roles and played the game again. "The part of the bear seems to be the most popular role," observed Ian.

"Yes, that has always been the case," replied Shabear. "Bears have always understood the importance of balance in the world. We are often sought to mediate problems or to counsel those who are troubled."

Shabear paused, hoping that Ian might decide to talk about what was troubling him. When Ian broke eye contact, Shabear decided on a more forward approach. She looked genuinely concerned when she spoke. "Ian, I know that your concern for Kate must weigh heavily on you. I also know that something deeper troubles you."

Shabear paused again, still hoping that Ian might take the opportunity to talk about his worries, but Ian again broke eye contact.

"I can feel your pain and would be happy to listen should you feel the need to talk," she said. "We are still several weeks away from Popocatépetl, and I would be happy to help however I may." When Ian still didn't speak, she went on. "Ian, whenever you feel troubled, visualize these children who performed the play this evening. It is for children that we endure hardship, suffer pain, and risk our lives. Children are the reason why."

Ian thanked Shabear for her concern and then remained silent. He realized that his brooding had attracted the attention of the others, and although he did appreciate the concern, he was not prepared to talk about his dreams. Plus, although it was clear that Shabear considered children important, Ian could not understand how this might relate to his troubled thoughts. *This is about me and Kate,* he thought, *and we don't have any children.*

Ian continued to watch the children and was amused to see Shabear join them and participate in the play, quite appropriately, he thought, as the bear.

The following morning, Runolfur and his people gathered to wish Helga and the rescue squad well. Runolfur spoke for them all. "Our ancestors were no strangers to battle, and the clan leader always spoke to each group of warriors before they left to engage the enemy. Today I offer the traditional Siksika message to brave warriors: Run forward with eagerness to engage your enemy. Let them know by your war cry that you will relish the taste of their blood. Always look your adversary straight in the eye, and they will shrink from your conviction and courage. Never turn your back on the enemy."

With that, Runolfur raised his spear, and the entire Siksika clan joined him in a rousing battle cheer.

The rescue squad set out accompanied by a Siksika patrol, but the added protection was unnecessary, for no signs of the enemy were found at all that day, and they made excellent progress.

It wasn't until they had almost reached Anasazi that they caught up with trouble. The first suggestion that something was amiss was the increased numbers of cave rats, all heading north in the tunnels.

"This isn't the season for cave rat migration," observed Helga, "and these little animals are obviously frightened."

Voles, mice, and other smaller animals appeared in successive waves after the cave rats. Normally these animals were wary of men and bears, but the animals who scurried past did not hesitate even to run over Shabear's furry feet. Once, when Ian bent down to secure a thong on his moccasin, he was swarmed by hundreds of voles who literally scurried right over him.

"They seem in a panic, as if something has frightened them," agreed Shabear.

"Like rats deserting a sinking ship," suggested Ian.

Later they came upon the remains of an Anasazi patrol, their bodies stripped of their battle gear and mutilated. The ears were removed from each dead soldier.

"Why remove the ears?" asked Ian.

"There is a bounty on each warrior killed," answered Helga, "and two ears confirm a kill. After the war, Malicious has promised that each set of ears will be redeemed for a human slave."

Helga sent Thorfinn ahead while the others attended to the burial of the Anasazi men.

Chapter 50
Copán

The dolphins carried them south and east into an underground realm unknown to Eirik and his people.

"We must be close to a Mayan city," remarked Liz. "I've seen numerous stelae along the sides of the river."

"Stelae?" inquired Eirik.

"Yes, the stone pillars with the carved figures of people and animals."

"Right," remarked Eirik. "Now I understand. We call those rune stones. They are quite unique and show excellent craftsmanship. I've seen carvings of many animals, including some I do not recognize. The figures are understandable, but I can't read the writing."

"That's because the Maya used a syllabic script that incorporated logographs or word pictures, which is quite different from the alphabet-based writing of the Norse," responded Liz.

Soon thereafter they passed small villages that grew progressively larger until the river widened, and an enormous city came into view.

"Wow," exclaimed Liz. "This is like taking a trip back in time. The pyramids and buildings are just like those in Chichén Itzá, Palenque, Tikal, and Uxmal."

News of their impending arrival had preceded them, and huge crowds had gathered on the shores of the Mayan city, where an official-looking delegation was waiting to meet them. A short stocky man who wore a feather-trimmed loincloth, a jaguar pelt over his shoulder, and a headdress of green Quetzal feathers approached them with his arms wide and a smile to match. His teeth were embedded with jade and gold.

"Welcome to Copán. My name is Itzamna, K'ul Ahau of the Maya. Queen Odontocetes sent word of your arrival. You are our honored guests."

"Thank you, Itzamna. My name is Liz, and we are equally honored to visit with you." Liz stepped aside to introduce Eirik. "This is Prince Eirik, heir to the throne of Asgard. We come to seek your help to defeat Princess Malicious, an evil person who wishes to destroy your world and ours."

Itzamna nodded in understanding. "Our peoples have lived underground in peace and harmony for over six hundred cycles of the dawn star. Before that time, we lived for just as long on the surface, where our glorious civilization became the envy of peoples from the south and the north. Sadly, a prolonged drought devastated our peoples. A neighboring culture that had always been jealous of our achievements chose that time to attack us. These greedy people besieged our cities and ravaged our countryside. They tried to bully our forefathers into war. Rather than battle both the drought and the enemy, our ancestors decided to seek refuge underground, and we have lived here in peace and harmony ever since. Until now we have shunned contact, not only with the surface people but also with other underground peoples, because experience has taught us to be cautious of other cultures. Now, however, we face a common and terrible threat, and we can no longer afford to live in seclusion. It is our hope that together we can find a way to defeat the evil that threatens our collective ways of life."

Itzamna paused, looked up, and held his arms wide and high in the air, as if he meant to embrace someone or something. When he spoke, his words had conviction and passion. "Our gods have shown us the way. We will not be driven again from our homes. This time we will fight to protect our people, our temples, and our cities. My people have prayed, and the gods have told us that we must end our isolation and attack the hideous woman that pollutes our sacred rivers."

Liz and Eirik looked around and realized that all the Mayan peoples on the shore had emulated Itzamna and were looking up, with their arms wide and high in the air.

"Liz, look!" said Eirik. "Look toward the ceiling of the cavern."

Liz followed Eirik's eyes to a tiny point of light that twinkled in the west, the direction from whence they'd come. *Curious,* thought Liz, *the light isn't really on the ceiling. The pure white glow looks as if it is somehow suspended in the air. Just like a star,* she realized. *I wonder if the glow is meant to represent Venus, the morning or dawn star that Itzamna referred to.*

By the time Liz looked back at Itzamna, he had lowered his eyes and arms and was now looking at her. He had an especially serene and joyous expression. Clearly the glow in the sky had brought him much comfort. "We have much to plan, but first let me show you our city, after which we will eat, and then we can talk."

"The Mayan people are so well organized," remarked Eirik, who marveled at the clean lines and symmetry of the buildings and the straight streets that coursed exactly north and south or east and west.

They paused to watch a game played by groups of men and women in a huge court sufficient to hold many thousands of people. Itzamna explained that the object of the game was to direct a solid rubber ball through one of two vertical hoops situated at the sides of the court, about ten feet off the ground. The players wore protective padding and could not use their hands or feet, which meant that the ball had to be knocked through the hoop with an arm, leg, hip, shoulder, or head. Based on the size of the hoop and the ball, this achievement was rare, and the game was usually won based on other merit.

Liz was familiar with the game and asked if there was a prize for the winner or a penalty for the loser.

"The only prize is the pleasure of competition," answered Itzamna. Then he added, because he suspected Liz knew of the ancient customs of his people, "Many years ago, when my peoples still lived on the surface, the losers were sometimes sacrificed to the gods, but this was during the dark times when drought and the threat of attack made everyone crazy."

"So your people no longer practice human sacrifice?" asked Eirik.

Itzamna smiled. "No, although we do spread that rumor to help maintain our isolation."

After the game, they climbed a pyramid with exactly one hundred steps to a chamber that served as a shrine to Ix Chel, the Mayan goddess of healing and childbirth. The chamber was filled with translucent statues that served as prisms and that were carved from crystals like those that made the rainbows in Miocena. Light poured in from a source outside the pyramid and created shimmering rainbows on the walls.

"Ix Chel is the rainbow goddess," Itzamna explained, "and we must pray for her help in the coming battle. For those who will be wounded, she has great powers to heal, and for those who will die, she will arrange for the birth of a new child to replace their departed spirit."

The smell of burning incense suffused the chamber. Liz and Eirik bowed their heads respectfully while Itzamna prayed to Ix Chel. After the prayers, Itzamna took them to a great hall where a banquet had been prepared and where Liz and Eirik were offered traditional Mayan foods.

"The peppers are beautiful to look at, but the orange and red ones are too hot for my palate," Eirik remarked.

Liz agreed. "I never knew peppers and corn came in so many different colors." Liz especially enjoyed a chocolate drink.

"The drink comes from the cacao bean that we gather in hidden valleys on the surface," said Itzamna. "The beans are crushed and mixed with lime juice and the leaves of the coca plant, and then the mixture is boiled slowly for many days until all that remains is thick brown syrup. A small amount in a cup of water is enough to make the drink you are enjoying and will give you enough energy to walk all day."

After the banquet, Itzamna summoned his son, Xbalanque, the commander of the army that would attack the enemy forces at Popocatépetl and thereby create the diversion necessary to allow Liz and Eirik to gain access to Malicious's volcanic fortress.

Xbalanque strode confidently into the hall with the manner of a warrior and the demeanor of a prince. He was muscular but not tall and had litheness about him. His black hair was thick and full with a natural luster and fell straight to his shoulders. He wore a pleated skirt of a fine fabric interwoven with gold and silver threads that formed geometric designs. Over his chest he wore a breastplate fashioned from tiny plates of jade and obsidian. On his right arm he wore wide gold bands both above and below the elbow. He carried a carved wooden scepter in his right hand. Atop the scepter was a golden Quetzal embedded with emeralds for the green head, back, and plumed wing coverts; rubies for the red breast; and diamonds for the tail. Around his forehead he wore a red and white cloth headband, the traditional sign of Maya royalty. His posture was magnificent and his demeanor proud as he walked toward his father. The only time his step faltered was the moment his eyes spied Liz.

Itzamna introduced Liz first, and Xbalanque's eyes could not take in enough of her beauty. "Father, perhaps we have been remiss, secluding ourselves from the surface people. Such beauty as this would be worth the risk."

Liz blushed. Eirik smiled. Itzamna understood.

When Itzamna introduced Eirik, Xbalanque looked into the prince's eyes and offered only the polite greetings expected of one royal to another. As their eyes met, each saw a different relationship. Eirik saw a fellow prince, a comrade-in-arms, and a potential new friend. Xbalanque saw a rival suitor.

Together they studied maps of the underworld realms. The first map was a square drawn on the back of a giant turtle that floated in a vast sea. Each corner was a different color and represented one of the four directions of the compass.

"Is there significance to the different colors in the corners?" asked Eirik.

"Yes," replied Xbalanque. "North is white to represent the cold winds that bring snow to the high mountains; east is red to represent the sun at dawn; south is yellow to represent the sun that moves each day across the sky in this direction; and west is black to represent the disappearance of the sun at dusk."

At the center was a green circle that represented Copán, their underground city. Only the principle underground river and tunnel systems that connected Copán to the realm of King Bjorn were depicted on this map, and there was no attempt made to differentiate the various depths. Like the surrounding ocean, the rivers and lakes were all a blue color.

Eirik asked about deeper tunnel systems, and Xbalanque showed them a three-dimensional map carved from a block of a white crystal that had the luster and brilliance of diamond. The three-dimensional map showed not only the underground realm and the surface but also many heavenly levels. Liz admired the map and asked whether the crystal was diamond.

"I am not familiar with that word," responded Xbalanque, who was quick to follow up on Liz's interest. "This crystal is rare and very hard and will cut any other crystal known." He saw that Liz admired the crystal and added, "It would make a fitting gift for the bride of a Mayan prince."

Liz blushed. Eirik frowned.

Itzamna coughed and changed the subject. He explained that according to Mayan belief, there was an overworld and an underworld that surrounded the surface. "This map was drawn according to our creation story. Our peoples believe in the presence of thirteen overworld levels, a surface world, and nine underworld levels. We accept the existence of the overworld even though it is not possible for us to visit these levels during life. However, our peoples have always visited and worshiped in the underworld, and when the underground caverns proved to be a safe haven for our peoples, this confirmed the sacred significance of the underworld."

In the center of the three-dimensional crystal map, there was a tree. The roots of the tree were beige like the color of sandy soil and reached to the lowest underworld level. The trunk of the tree was chestnut-brown and extended through the surface level. The upper branches and leaves were a brilliant gold and reached up to the highest level in the overworld.

"What does the tree signify?" asked Liz.

"The tree is Ceiba, the Tree of Life," responded Xbalanque. "The Tree of Life links all the levels and symbolizes our spiritual journey during and after life."

"Like Yggdrasil, the tree at the center of our world," interjected Eirik, who was thankful for the opportunity to talk about his own culture. "Yggdrasil is the ash tree that holds together our nine worlds, including the overworld, where Odin and the other gods reside; Midgard, where we mortals live; and the underworld."

"Fascinating," said Xbalanque in a tone that to a subtle ear was mocking.

"Does Ceiba exist?" inquired Liz, whose curious and innocent interest in the Mayan version exalted Xbalanque at the expense of Eirik.

"Perhaps. The ancient stories tell of this tree," said Itzamna. "We hope the stories are more than legends. The stories tell of a giant underground tree in a sacred cavern in the underworld. The waters of this cavern were said to have powers that could slow aging, heal any wound, and perhaps even bring life to the dead. Our people believe that this tree was the root of the Tree of Life and that just as the waters in the sacred cavern nurtured the tree, so did the tree protect our peoples on the surface. In the beginning, the tree extended all the way to the highest level of the overworld. At that time our peoples lived in harmony with our gods, and they believed that the most sacred of the gods resided in the highest level of the overworld. As such, they studied the ways of the heavens and learned to predict the comings and goings of the stars and planets. They became wise enough to predict those times when the sun would disappear during the day. It is our belief that the gods became angry when our ancestors learned to predict these important celestial events, and they punished our peoples for their presumptuousness."

"How did they punish your peoples?" asked Liz.

"They took away the sun, and the Tree of Life withered and died," replied Xbalanque.

"Yes," offered Itzamna, "and to further punish the arrogance of our ancestors, the gods opened up the earth such that many of our cities were swallowed. In the aftermath of this great disruption, the mountaintops burned, and molten rocks flowed over those cities that had been spared."

"Many of our ancestors died," said Xbalanque. "The gods eventually sealed up the mountaintops and allowed the sun to return, but they never permitted the Tree of Life to grow again or allowed us to find the roots in the sacred cavern."

"Our peoples have searched in vain for the sacred cavern for many centuries," said Itzamna. "There are some who no longer believe the creation story or that the Tree of Life even exists."

"Do you believe the sacred cavern exists?" asked Eirik.

"Yes," replied Itzamna. "Although the legends date from before we settled the underground realm, they are clearly recorded in ancient codices, the books of our people."

"I too believe the legends," said Xbalanque. "I know the roots of the Tree of Life exist and that someday the gods will favor us, and we will rediscover the sacred cavern. It is said that the person who discovers the sacred cavern will know because time stands still in the presence of the Tree of Life. I would like to be the person to find this place for my people. It is said that when the sacred cavern is found, this will usher in an era of great prosperity."

"I hope this comes to pass, but I am worried the sacred cavern might never be found," said Itzamna.

Itzamna's voice suddenly faltered, and he stumbled forward. Xbalanque ran to his side and helped him sit down. It was a few minutes before Itzamna could continue, and when he did, a great sadness seemed to pervade his every word.

"Perhaps you will find the sacred cavern," suggested Liz, who felt so sorry for Itzamna. She wondered whether she should tell them about her experience with the glow and the stalactite-stalagmite tree in the underground cavern but decided that this would be inappropriate without seeking Queen Odontocetes's approval. So she said only, "Perhaps your prayers will be answered."

Xbalanque answered for Itzamna. "This is our hope as well—because my father and the other Mayan elders believe that Malicious cannot be defeated without the power of the Tree of Life."

Chapter 51
Pampered for a Purpose

Kate had lost all sense of time. She had no idea how long she had been in her tiny dungeon or how many times she had been beaten. At first her sleep had been fitful. She had awoken several times an hour, and her wakeful and dreaming thoughts had been preoccupied with the flickering candle and the red-eyed shadow. But the abject terror eventually gave way to resigned acceptance. Now Kate mostly slept, and her wakeful and dreaming thoughts blended together, and she never really knew when she was awake. Thoughts of the shadow faded and gave way to images of Ian, Liz, her father, and increasingly her mother. During her mother's last days, she too had mostly slept. Several times now, her mother had appeared in her dreams and had called to her, "Come to me, little one." Kate knew she was very weak and would die soon.

In this moment, Kate could feel herself being lifted, but she felt too tired to open her eyes, and she drifted back to sleep. There were voices, and she realized that she was among many women, and although she felt the strength to open her eyes, she was too frightened to do so. She felt the women lower her into a warm bath that felt so very good. Soft hands cleansed her wounds and rubbed life back into her bruised muscles and aching bones. They washed her hair and braided the blonde locks down her back.

This must be a dream, she thought, but even so, she was still too frightened to open her eyes lest the dream dissolve into the grim reality of the cell and the shadow.

When the women lifted her out of the water and set her body down, she cringed and braced herself, expecting the hard rock floor that had become her world, and was surprised when she sank into a soft feathery bed. The women dressed her in a white silk robe and adorned each wrist and ankle with delicate gold bracelets. They shaped, conditioned, and painted the nails of each hand and foot.

Kate smelled apricot and lavender and heard pleasant songs, and without ever opening her eyes, she drifted in and out of a glorious sleep.

When she awoke, she was still in the feather bed but was alone in the room. For many minutes she refused to open her eyes, still fearing the dream would dissolve. It was the smell of soup that finally led her to open her eyes. The smell reminded Kate of her mother. She saw a mental image of her mother in the kitchen, where she was surrounded by fresh vegetables and herbs, colorful pastas, and wholesome grains.

Kate opened her eyes a crack and saw the soft green light that she remembered from the Green Cavern. When nothing bad happened, she opened her eyes wide, looked around, and confirmed that she was alone and that the soup was real and on a nearby table waiting for her.

She was surprised how well she felt. Under the silk robe she could see the bruises. Most were yellow with age and no longer tender. Only a very few were purple-brown and more recent. None looked fresh, and Kate realized that she must not have been beaten for several days and that she must have slept continuously through this respite. Her face felt soft and untouched by any scar or mark, and her hair had a softness she had never felt before.

She felt famished, and a glance at her waistline and thighs confirmed she had lost a lot of weight. This might have been a welcome sight in other circumstances since Kate struggled to keep her weight down, but her thinness was alarming. She could not remember the last time she had eaten and realized it might have been days or even weeks.

She sat up in the bed and in so doing realized how weak she had become. She tottered and had to steady herself with a hand on the bed. *I better not try to stand too quickly,* she realized, *or I'll faint.* She lay back down and stared at the ceiling for a few minutes and then sat up again. She decided that she wouldn't even consider trying to stand until she no longer tottered with sitting.

But though her intentions were good, the soup was calling her, and she grew impatient. The table was only a few feet away. This time when she sat up, she tottered only a bit, and she managed to straighten up her back without the need to put her hand down on the bed. She took several slow deep breaths and then slipped one foot off the bed. "So far, so good."

She rolled over slowly until she was facing the bed before she put her feet down on the floor. She leaned over the bed as if she expected to collapse and to ensure that if she did, she would fall into the soft covers, but she didn't collapse. *I can do this,* she thought.

Kate pushed herself up to an upright position. Then, after steeling herself to the idea of turning, she pushed her thigh into the bed and slowly edged around until she was standing with her bottom supported against the side of the bed and was facing the table. Standing there, she paused to assess her strength. She felt good and wasn't dizzy, so she decided to try to walk the few feet between the bed and the table. The smell of the soup was irresistible and hastened her decision to take the first step.

Ordinarily, she would have needed only one step to reach the table, but today she needed many more. She shuffled more than stepped, and as she reached out and grabbed the back of the chair that accompanied the table, she felt woozy and realized that she was going to faint. As she collapsed onto the floor, she heard her mother call, "Kate, Liz, your lunch is ready! I've made your favorite soup. After lunch I'll drive you back to school."

In this wakeful vision, Kate was about nine years old and in fourth grade; Liz was two years younger and as many grades behind her. It was winter, and although the sun was shining, the air was chilly, and the ground was covered in snow. The school was only a few blocks away, but her mother was devoted and protective and drove to the school three times a day to chauffer her girls back and forth. The pleasure and the love were mutual.

When Kate next woke up, she was back in bed, and the table had been moved so that it was right beside the bed. Kate knew she must have been unconscious for quite awhile, but curiously, the soup was still hot and definitely just as inviting. This time when she sat up, she needed only to reach over and lift the bowl in front of her. The soup tasted better than anything she had every eaten. She savored every drop.

The soup was exactly like her mother's, and she wondered how the women who had been tending her knew. She wished she could thank them and wondered when they might return.

Why was I beaten so savagely and then pampered back to health? she wondered. She decided that she didn't care why. After she finished the soup, she felt exhausted. She sank back into the feathers and was soon asleep.

Chapter 52
Siege of Anasazi

Thorfinn returned with disquieting news: Anasazi was under attack by a huge army of soldiers, the enemy was patrolling the main tunnel to the city, and the neighboring communities had been pillaged by roving packs of wolves.

Helga looked at the map while she considered the situation. "We cannot backtrack and seek a tunnel that will bypass Anasazi; we do not have the luxury of time. For us to reach Popocatépetl in time, we must pass through Anasazi. This means we must fight our way in and then out again." Helga then questioned Thorfinn carefully about the manner in which the enemy was deployed.

Anasazi was built on a great underground plain through which coursed numerous rivers. The rivers carried runoff from the surface and deposited rich soil on the plain. Courtesy of an elaborate irrigation system, the rich alluvial deposits supported thousands of acres of corn, squash, and grain crops that were exported throughout Asgard.

The Anasazi clan built their homes on the sides of the cavern walls, according to their custom and so as to spare the fertile plain for the important crops they produced. Several centuries of peace had reigned when the Anasazi first settled the cavern, and the peoples did not build their city with a siege in mind. Nevertheless, the cliff homes provided the strategic advantage of height and were difficult to attack.

So when the enemy did attack, the clan had retreated to their cliff dwellings and abandoned the plain, which was now occupied by thousands of enemy troops, who where harvesting the crops to feed their own men.

Thorfinn painted a grim picture of the possibility of fighting their way across the plain. He had scouted the plain and the northernmost portion of the walls that supported the dwellings in the suspended city. "The plain extends for miles, and we would need to fight every step of the way," advised Thorfinn. "But," he continued, "if we gain entry to the city, we can travel safely through the city and leave by one of the southern tunnels. Hopefully, they are not all well guarded."

"That might work," said Helga, who had visited Anasazi before. "The cliff dwellings are connected by an elaborate maze of stairs and pathways that stretch the length of the cavern. There are numerous stairwells from the plain below, and we would be dangerously exposed to arrows and spears during climbing. However, upon reaching the cliff dwellings, we would be safe, and so long as the Anasazi clan continues to hold their positions, we would be able to bypass the plain without problem."

Helga turned to Thorfinn. "How many soldiers are positioned between the tunnel entrance closest to the cliff dwellings and the closest of the stairwells?"

"At least a company, but the distance is only about one hundred yards."

"We need a diversion," said Ian. "One hundred yards might be as many miles if the path is crowded with enemy soldiers. I suggest we start a fire in the cornfields, and when the enemy disperses, we can run to the stairwells under the cover of the smoke."

Their plan in the works, they carried on toward Anasazi and reached the tunnel entrance closest to the westernmost cliff dwellings without raising the alarm in the enemy camp.

"We were lucky not to run into an enemy patrol, and they didn't even bother to post any sentries at the tunnel entrance," remarked Helga. "Clearly they do not expect an attack."

"Even so, we must be vigilant," said Shabear. "Their patrols have pillaged the tunnels for some distance north, and they might well return through this tunnel. The absence of sentries might be misleading. I suggest we thank our good fortune and proceed expeditiously with our plan."

Ian crept into the cornfield to set the diversionary fires. The corn was high but not high enough for him to walk unseen. He crept through the ripening stalks, carefully weaving a pattern that kept him away from any soldiers, and eventually reached a place as close as possible to the stairway. He lit the first fire at this farthest point and then a new fire every ten or so yards back toward the tunnel. The smoke that billowed caused the soldiers in the immediate vicinity to scatter. A dozen or so tried to run into the tunnel where Helga and the squad were awaiting the right opportunity to make a run for the stairways. The soldiers were quickly dispatched.

Thorfinn, who had been sent back along the tunnel to act as a rear sentry, came running forward. Breathless, he related that an enemy patrol was only a few minutes behind. Even as he spoke, wolves appeared, but the animals stopped short when they saw Shabear and Connor. They yelped a hasty retreat. Men were possible prey, but bears meant certain death. They turned tail and disappeared back down the tunnel.

"We must go now, before the soldiers come upon us," said Helga, and she ran out of the tunnel into the cornfield.

The rest followed quickly, and thanks to the smoke, they reached the stairways without encountering more than a few enemy soldiers, and those they did come upon did not tarry to fight, but rather scattered into the fields. Ian caught up just as they reached the stairway. Shabear and Connor stood guard at the bottom while the others climbed up the stairs.

With the first sight of the smoke, the alarm had been raised in the cliff dwellings, and when the Anasazi realized the fire was a purposeful ruse, they provided a covering fire of arrows that rained down on the enemy soldiers who were converging on the stairwell. Shabear and Connor were the last up the stairway, and both suffered several minor arrow wounds.

The Anasazi warriors who had provided the cover fire congratulated them on their daring and escorted them through the passageways of their cliff-side city to a central plaza built on a great ledge that overlooked the plane. The architecture was amazing. Homes had been built into every recess and overlapped one another like honeycombs.

Sort of like modern apartment blocks, thought Ian.

When they reached the central plaza, they were introduced to Svein, leader of the Anasazi clan, who welcomed them. The plaza served as the market and was busy with merchants and traders from all over Asgard. Adults socialized, and children played.

"No one seems too worried about the siege," noted Helga.

"No, we are quite safe in our cliff-side city," replied Svein. "The enemy tried several times to breach our stairway security, but each time, they lost many soldiers, and they have not tried for many days."

"I expect they hope to starve you out while they feed their own troops on your corn and grain," replied Shabear.

"Their hope is in vain," replied Svein. "We have enough food stored in our granaries to last several years. In fact, we were just considering how best to burn our crops to prevent their use by the enemy when we saw the smoke from your fires. You must have read our minds." Svein laughed. But a serious expression returned as he asked, "What news have you of the war? Has King Bjorn returned the attack? Before the enemy occupied the plain, we received word that both armies had massed at the Green Cavern and that battle was expected any day."

Helga told them as much as she knew, which was mainly of their mission, and asked for their assistance to escape the siege into the tunnels leading south.

"That will not be a problem. The southern entrance is poorly guarded. Getting into the tunnels will be easy. The problem will be traveling south through the tunnels toward Toltec. We have not heard from Toltec for over a week, and I fear the city is lost. The enemy occupies the intervening tunnels in considerable force. Malicious's volcanic fortress at Popocatépetl is only a few days' journey beyond Toltec, and between these cities the tunnels are even more congested with her soldiers."

This was disappointing news, and they talked long into the night about various strategies to reach Popocatépetl. The few hours sleep they eventually received that night improved their spirits but not the available options, and the following morning, Shabear suggested they consult one of the spiritual leaders of the Anasazi.

"Is there a wise man or woman for us to speak with?" asked Shabear. "Someone who understands the ancient ways and can help us see the correct path?"

"Yes, there is such a person," replied Svein. "Her name is Zuni, and she is said to be older than any person in Asgard."

"Might we seek her counsel?" asked Shabear.

Svein sent a messenger to inquire into whether Zuni would talk with them, and the man soon returned with a quixotic invitation.

"Zuni advises that she will speak only with the two bears and the one whose heart is heaviest."

Everyone looked at Ian.

Chapter 53
Zuni

Svein led the chosen three toward Zuni's hogan, but he stopped well before they could see the entrance. There, he gave them directions for the final portion of the trip. "It would be impolite of me to proceed farther without an invitation," explained Svein.

"When you reach the plaza in front of her hogan, look to see if there is a light from within. The south side of the hogan faces the plaza, and there is a window in that wall. The door will be on the east side. If there is a light from within, stop in the middle of the plaza and call her name. If there is no light, sit quietly and wait for Zuni to call you. The more respect you show for her power, the more energy she can summon on your behalf."

When they reached the plaza, there was no light from the hogan, and they sat cross-legged on the carved stones and waited in silence.

For Ian and Shabear the time passed quickly. Ian was quickly lost in the same gloomy thoughts about Kate that now plagued his wakeful moments as well as his dreams.

While Ian fretted silently, Shabear meditated. Shabear was impressed that Connor could sit still and silent for so long. *He is gaining in maturity,* thought Shabear, who was proud of her nephew.

Connor had indeed found sitting still difficult and might not have managed had he not quickly dozed off. The stillness lasted about an hour. As Connor made the transition into deeper sleep, he started to snore, very softly at first, but as the depth of his sleep advanced, so did the loudness. Fully expressed, the snore of a grizzly sounds like the clap of rolling thunder.

A light appeared in the hogan, and Shabear quickly tried to nudge Connor awake. The light was followed by a voice.

"Tell me the name of the bear that snores in front of my hogan," a voice called out. "Any bear who can relax and sleep in front of the hogan of Zuni is either a witch or a great warrior. Which is it?"

Shabear had poked Connor in the ribs again as Zuni spoke, and her nephew finally woke up in time to hear the final question.

The three of them stood up, and Shabear stepped forward and spoke. "The bear is a warrior, a direct descendent of Kodiak, the great grizzly who befriended Balder, first king of Asgard."

Shabear paused, hoping Connor might decide to speak. When he didn't, Shabear went on. "The warrior bear's name is Connor, and he is also descended from Bear Old Man, who led the first peoples from the Lake of Emergence. His ancestors also include Great and Little Bear, healers of such power that the God of All Creatures placed them in the heavens, where they are worshipped."

"And who speaks for this great warrior?" asked the voice.

"My name is Shabear, aunt of Connor, sister of Ursus, and also a descendent of Bear Old Man and Great and Little Bear."

"Connor Bear, who snores in my presence, where is your tongue? Why have you come to my hogan?"

Connor did not respond right away, and Shabear worried that her nephew's inexperience had frozen his words.

But Connor had listened while Shabear spoke of their heritage, and when asked to speak, he did not wish to blurt out a glib reply. Instead, he thought carefully and then responded in a voice that sounded older and more mature than Shabear had heretofore heard from him.

"Wise Zuni, we have come for help in a time of great crisis. A sorceress with vile and ancient powers threatens our world. To defeat this witch requires the support of those who also wield the ancient powers. We have been told that you are such a person."

"Your answer pleases me, Connor Bear, and I welcome you and Shabear into my hogan. First, though, tell me about the man whose heart is so heavy that I have felt his presence grow in my thoughts for these last several days before your arrival."

Ian felt uncomfortable at the idea of Zuni sensing his innermost thoughts at all, much less from such a distance. He had always known that there were mysteries of life that he could not fathom, but it was not his nature to dwell on them. Ian was not philosophical or religious by nature. Ian had attended Sunday school as a preschool boy, but his mother had made it clear that the purpose of this exercise was to socialize and not necessarily to learn about the Bible. Like all elementary school children of his generation, he had spoken the Lord's Prayer at the start of each school day, but he had never paused to consider the words. His parents had not attended church, nor had they given him any reason to believe that doing so was worth his time. His parents said grace before a meal only when someone was visiting. In short, Ian had grown up believing that religion was a matter of convenience, a tool that might occasionally be useful to connect with other people, but nothing more.

During university, when confronted with students who seemed driven to discuss religion, Ian had mostly listened and rarely participated. Many of the students seemed more inclined to persuade others to accept their personal beliefs than to engage in any real meaningful discussion. During these debates, he usually witnessed more emotion than logic. His scientific courses were attractive because the knowledge was based on fact. He liked the idea of evolution and decided that creation theory was nonsense. By the time he graduated from military college, he was comfortable classifying himself as an agnostic. It suited him to believe that anything that he could not explain according to a mathematical or scientific theory was not true and, even more to the point, was not worth considering. To Ian, anything unknown was unknowable.

What remnants of faith that might have persisted had dissipated quickly when he was confronted with the death and destruction in Bosnia during his tour as an engineer with the Canadian Armed Forces. *God does not exist,* Ian had concluded. *No God would ever permit such pain and suffering.* While serving in Afghanistan, he had prayed with the men under his command before they went on any mission, but mostly as a duty for those who had faith, rather than because he felt any stirring of personal belief. He saw even more pain and suffering, and by the time he returned home, Ian was a confirmed atheist. Even so, Ian recognized that religion was a highly personal matter, and he chose not to share his lack of faith with his friends.

Soon after he met Kate, Ian realized that she did believe in God, and he recognized that this difference might come between them. Ian was a confirmed pragmatist, so when Kate eventually asked him whether he believed in God, he was ready, and Ian lied to please her. He felt a twinge of guilt, but he loved Kate, and he rationalized that their relationship was more important than a lie about something that for him did not exist. After this lie, it was easy for him to agree to a church wedding and to lie again to the minister who interviewed them before their marriage. As the lies and the hypocrisy added up, Ian felt that he had sullied his integrity somewhat, but he rationalized that the cause was worthy.

Over this last month, though, Ian had thought more about religion than ever before in his life. Despite his intellectual atheism, he felt an inexplicable emotional affinity for the concept of some higher authority to whom he might turn for help. In short, whether he acknowledged it or not, he felt the need to pray. At first he rationalized that this was merely another way of expressing hope. Later, when Ian learned that the world contained bears who not only were sentient but could even speak, he was humbled and understood that he had much to learn. The gift of Ursus's medicine bundle and the story of the white buffalo had moved Ian. For the first time in his life, he believed a story that involved a spirituality that he could not scientifically explain. His out-of-body experience just before Connor had saved him had also changed him. Again he was forced to accept something he could not explain with any logic other than faith. Now Ian felt himself in the presence of someone whose spirituality was overpowering and who, Ian was sure, would humble him further. It was with trepidation as well as gladness that he responded to Zuni.

"My name is Ian, and I am a surface man and new to the ways of the underground. Kate, whom I love, has been kidnapped by Malicious, and each day, she is cruelly tortured by this witch. I see her agony in my dreams and waking visions."

"Yes," replied Zuni, "I have seen these visions too. Come into my hogan, and together we will work the spells to cure sorcery and cast out witches."

A roughly hewn door opened and admitted the travelers to Zuni's hogan, which was an almost empty room with a dirt floor. Each wall precisely faced one of the cardinal directions. There was a small window in the center of each wall, except the one with the door. In the center of the hogan was a circular fire pit.

Along the walls were intricately woven baskets. Some of the baskets contained powdered minerals of a variety of colors, and others contained corn, bean, pumpkin, or squash seeds.

Zuni's expression, which was a mixture of grace, seriousness, and generosity, fit her tall thin and erect frame. She wore a woven beige cotton skirt tied with a red sash, and a dark-brown vest embroidered with tiny beads that formed stylized golden eagles. A headband that matched the sash encircled her head, and her thick black hair fell in a long braided ponytail halfway down her back. She wore moccasins that reached to her calves.

Zuni asked them to sit around the fire pit, with their backs toward the west wall of the hogan, and facing the door. They sat cross-legged, with Ian between Connor and Shabear.

After they had settled into comfortable positions, Zuni retrieved a bald eagle feather from a window ledge. She walked around the inside of the hogan and used the feather to sweep the floor from the center outward. After sweeping, she removed some pollen from a small leather sac that hung from her neck and sprinkled the powder, a symbol of harmony, she explained, on each of the windows and on the door.

She lit a fire in front of Shabear, Ian, and Connor. The burning wood smelled like sage. Then she retrieved a basket that contained a brown mineral that had been finely ground into a powder. She carefully placed the powder in a circle that enclosed Shabear, Ian, and Connor, as well as the fire. While she poured the powder, she always remained within the growing circle. She took care to ensure that the circle was continuous except for that portion where the arc would cross the door. Here, instead of completing the circle, she placed the powder in two parallel lines from the circle to the edges of the door. She continued to add powder until the mineral formed a wall almost an inch high. While so doing, Zuni sang a song in a language unknown to the others.

Having composed the setting, Zuni turned her attention to her own appearance. She rubbed her cheeks and forehead with a red powder; wrapped yucca around her wrist, chest, and the crown of her head; and tied an eagle feather in her hair. Then she sat cross-legged, stoked the fire, and remained silent for many minutes.

When Zuni spoke, she turned first to Shabear. "You are a healer, and so am I. We can be family."

Then she turned to Connor. "You are a warrior, and I am not. We can be friends."

Finally she turned to Ian. "You are a warrior and someday will be a healer, and I will help you on your journey."

Zuni brought out a pipe and asked them whether they had any tobacco.

"Yes," replied Shabear, "bears often smoke the berry of a low-lying shrub in our surface world." As she spoke, she removed some dried bearberries from her pouch.

"No," said Zuni, "this is not the tobacco we need." Zuni looked directly at Ian. "Do you not have any tobacco for us to use?"

Ian remembered the herb and tobacco mixture in the medicine bundle that Ursus had given him. He took this out and offered the mixture to Zuni.

"Thank you," said Zuni. "This is what we need."

Zuni set some of the herb and tobacco mixture aside and mixed the remainder with some dried yellow tobacco leaves that she retrieved from a basket. After carefully pressing the mixture into the bowl of the pipe, she sucked several times on the stem to ensure the airflow was adequate. With her thumb and forefinger, she picked up a burning ember from the edge of the fire and lit the pipe.

Ian was startled to see Zuni pick up the ember and even more startled that the fire did not seem to burn her.

Once the pipe was lit, Zuni held the pipe in front of her and allowed the smoke to curl from the bowl toward the ceiling of the hogan. "May the rising column of smoke connect us with the god that each of us chooses to believe in."

Zuni passed the pipe, and they smoked in silence. When the tobacco ran out, Zuni refilled the pipe and handed it to Shabear to light. Shabear picked up a burning ember and lit the pipe, and again they shared the smoke.

When the tobacco ran out, Zuni filled the pipe a third time and offered it to Connor, who too picked up an ember and lit the pipe. When the tobacco ran out again, Zuni filled the pipe a fourth time and handed the pipe to Ian.

Somehow Ian understood that this ritual was meant to cleanse his thoughts and open his heart. He held the pipe in front of his body with outstretched hands and then slowly raised the pipe level with his head while he looked down into the flame of the fire. Inside one of the embers, he saw the Siksika children acting the hunting play. Ian lowered the pipe to his mouth, and with his right hand, he picked up this ember and lit the pipe. He was not surprised when the ember felt cool. As he passed the pipe back to Zuni, there was a rush of wind through the door, and the fire blew out.

Zuni waited until the pipe was back in her hands before she spoke. "There is much power in my hogan tonight. I am humbled to be in the presence of descendants of Bear Old Man and honored to share a pipe with you." She pointed the pipe first at Shabear and then at Connor. "You will always be welcome in my hogan."

After a pause, Zuni continued. "It is well that we share our power tonight because the sorceress is attracted to this man with his heavy heart. The wind that blew out the flame was a cold and lifeless breath from an evil witch. We do not yet have the power to defeat the witch, but I believe we have the will to frighten her, and fear might cloud her mind and weaken her resolve."

Zuni stood up, and without stepping out of the circle, she retrieved a basket from against the wall. Inside the basket were smaller baskets, and each contained a different colored powder. Zuni took some of the brown mineral from the circle and made a smaller circle around the fire. Again she was careful not to complete the circle where the arc would cross the door, and instead she once more placed the brown mineral in two parallel lines that extended to the door.

With completion of the inner circle, Zuni chanted three times, "This circle is the sum of our powers, and our power is sufficient to frighten you."

Within the northern perimeter of the smaller circle around the fire, Zuni placed a tiny pile of white powder; to the east she placed a red powder, to the south a yellow powder, and to the west a black powder. Immediately to the east of these small piles, she placed a line of red powder above a line a blue powder. The lines were several inches long and half an inch thick. As Zuni completed each of these red and blue bars, she chanted four times, "These are the powers of light. These colors will never permit the darkness."

Zuni picked up a piece of charcoal from the fire, and within the smaller circle she traced the figure of a bear to one side of the fire, the figure of a man to the other side, and two bear paws leading into the circle. She outlined the bear in blue powder, the man in white, and the paws in yellow.

Zuni looked at the figures and colors in the circle and was pleased with what she saw. She lit the fire again, this time larger. From a pouch around her neck, Zuni removed what looked like a pale green disc that she crumbled into a powder in the palm of her hand. To this she mixed the remaining herb and tobacco mixture that she had set aside, as well as some very dry tobacco leaves that disintegrated into a green powder with rubbing. After cleaning the pipe, Zuni poured this mixture into the bowl and lit the pipe with an ember from the fire.

"Only take one breath," she cautioned, and then she passed the pipe to Ian.

Chapter 54
Return to Popocatépetl

"Our journey will be safe until we reach the River Fjorm and the tunnels that run parallel to the water. The river and tunnels are filled with soldiers from the south," advised Xbalanque. He thought for a moment and then added, "The word 'soldiers' does not properly describe the misfits, thieves, and other blackguards who have been recruited by the southern warlords. The loyalty of these men is based on the fear that Malicious and her henchmen engender. They have no skills in war and are issued ill-made weapons when they reach the docks of Popocatépetl. Still, they are capable of much individual cruelty, their numbers are formidable, and I do not underestimate the skill of their commanders."

"Men like Lord Null?" inquired Eirik.

"Yes, exactly."

"Who is Lord Null?" asked Liz.

"Some say he is the descendant of an ancient people from the Southern Realm. Sadly, some of the rabble that Malicious calls an army are the descendants of the once-proud Inca who ruled the southern surface world and who, in their time, built an empire as great as that of my people. Many believe that Lord Null is a descendant of the priest class of the Inca.

"But it is you who should tell me about Lord Null. You have been in his presence, have you not?"

"Four times," replied Liz, who marveled again at the ability of Lord Null to turn up everywhere as she thought back. "It was Lord Null who captured me on the surface world and arranged for my transport to the Green Cavern. He also arranged for the panthers to carry Kate and me to the River Fjorm. Strangely, he arrived before us and was present to command the longship that rowed us to Popocatépetl. I don't understand how he reached the boat before us. Lord Null had remained behind at the Green Cavern, and the panthers had carried us at breakneck speed for four days. Yet, he seemed to have been waiting at the dock for some time when we arrived."

"Perhaps other panthers carried him, and he passed you in the tunnels while you slept," offered Eirik.

"That is a curious story," said Xbalanque. "We too have heard stories of Lord Null's ability to travel far and fast, sometimes seeming to be in several places at once. Perhaps Malicious has endowed him with some special power. What does he look like? There are some who say he is tall like a giant."

"He is tall, but not that tall," replied Liz, "and he looks like an ordinary man. He is thin with a wiry strength about him. And either he is bald, or he shaves his head. He moves silently, like a cat, and I could usually feel his presence before I saw him. The first time, I felt a chill down my spine and goose bumps on my arms. On another occasion, his voice announced his presence. The sound of his voice seems to come from a great distance. His words are slow and measured. His most compelling feature is his eyes. They are dark and hollow, without expression, like pieces of black glass with a reflection that moves rather than the eyeball."

"Stories of his cruelty are common," said Xbalanque.

"And they are true," replied Liz. "Every animal or man who came within his presence was frightened, and with good reason. I heard him kill a squad of wolves that guarded Kate and me at the Green Cavern. And I watched helplessly while he tortured a poor little animal on the longship."

"It is said that no man or animal can walk in his shadow and live," added Xbalanque.

"I never saw his shadow," responded Liz. "But Lord Null looks like a loner, and I suspect that when a man or animal stops being useful, he kills them. That way, no one can get close to him, his shadow or otherwise."

"But he is only a man," interjected Eirik, "and his skin is no thicker than mine. Lord Null's hide cannot resist a blade forged by our blacksmiths, who combine the old Viking ways with the new and stronger metals we have discovered. I would like the chance to prove that his body bleeds like that of any mortal man."

“Be careful what you wish for,” said Liz, who looked at Eirik and felt threatened by his bravado, as well as protective of him.

“Bravo, Eirik,” said Xbalanque, whose thoughts were not nearly as protective. “It would indeed be a valiant deed to slay this demon. I hope you have your chance.”

Eirik turned to Liz. “Tell me of his sword, the sword with the rubies on the hilt.”

“The sword has a power I cannot explain,” Liz answered. “Each time I was in Lord Null’s presence, my eyes were drawn to the rubies, first out of curiosity and then as if willed to do so. I was able to resist this compulsion, but Kate was never able to look away. Kate spoke and saw little while in Lord Null’s presence, often, I think, because the glow of the rubies mesmerized her. The stones glow even in the dark. Whenever Lord Null wished to speak with Kate, he placed his hand over the hilt and obscured the rubies so that she would pay attention to him and not the rubies.”

“The armies of Malicious carry black banners with two red eyes,” said Xbalanque.

“The rubies on the sword and the red eyes on the banners are Malicious’ eyes and a symbol of her power,” said Liz.

“Her eyes are actually red?” asked Xbalanque.

“Yes, this is true; my sister’s eyes are red,” confirmed Eirik. “They have been since birth; she was born with a rare affliction. Her skin is translucent, and her hair has no color. Sunlight hurts her eyes and causes sores on her skin, so she has lived mostly in darkened rooms. As a child she was teased about her eyes and skin. My mother believed it was the teasing that brought out the meanness.”

Liz and Eirik continued traveling with Xbalanque and his personal escort of several hundred Mayan soldiers, and after several days’ journey, they reached the tunnel system on the east side of the River Fjorm and south of Popocatépetl. The passages were strangely deserted, and a strong hot wind blew from the north. They proceeded north for several miles without finding any travelers or enemy soldiers.

“The walls of the tunnel are bone dry,” remarked Eirik. “Usually these tunnels are humid and the walls damp. It is as if the wind has carried the moisture away.”

The breath of Hell, thought Liz.

Xbalanque studied the walls and agreed this was unusual. He sent a scout ahead. "Popocatépetl is only a few days' journey north. Even if the soldiers from the south had all passed by, we should at least have encountered traders in these passages."

The scout confirmed that the passages were empty as far as the immediate outskirts of Popocatépetl, but that the River Fjorm was still filled with soldiers surging north. A garrison of soldiers was stationed on the eastern shore of the River Fjorm, and sentries guarded each entrance from the south and east.

"So," Xbalanque deduced, "Malicious might believe you are dead, but she does not trust the Mayan people to stay neutral in this war. Perhaps the dry walls are due to a spell she has placed on these tunnels. We might not have the advantage of surprise."

Xbalanque led Liz, Eirik, and a few Mayan soldiers up through some little-used tunnels. They climbed until they emerged on a ledge that looked down over Popocatépetl.

Eirik began explaining the history of the city and how Malicious had come to live in Popocatépetl. "The southernmost limit of my father's realm is Toltec, a city a few days' journey north along the coastal route. Popocatépetl had existed as an underground temple for years before my ancestors established Toltec. Ancient peoples known as the Aztec worshipped in this temple. They were warlike and independent, and this limited the expansion of Asgard beyond Toltec. We had very little contact with these peoples but understood them to be learned in the ways of the dark arts. They had knowledge of plants and animals that could be made into potions to kill or control. The little mixing of our cultures that did occur happened in Toltec.

"When my sister was an adolescent, she visited Toltec and expressed an interest in learning about the healing properties of the plants and animals known to the peoples of the Middle and Southern Realms. My father was blind to the evil side of my sister, and he hoped Malicious would learn to be a great healer for our people.

"My sister met people from Popocatépetl in Toltec, and they invited her to visit their city. She asked permission from my father, who naively agreed when Malicious told him she hoped to end the estrangement of our cultures. Again, my father was blind to her plans. He announced that Malicious would travel as the ambassador of Asgard.

"Malicious spent several years in Popocatépetl and eventually made her home in the smoking mountain that sits above the River Fjorm. It was rumored during the early years that she traveled to the end of the southern tunnels, where she met the warlords who now supply her army."

"Yes," responded Xbalanque, "she did meet with the southern warlords. She also tried to enlist the Mayan people to her cause. However, my father rebuffed her. He refused to even meet with her emissaries. We have always preferred to remain independent of other cultures. Later, when we heard stories of her wickedness, we were pleased that we had ignored her false entreaties. Some say that Malicious considers herself to be the reincarnation of Tezcatlipoca, the supreme god of the Aztecs. Tezcatlipoca is also known as Smoking Mirror because ancient glyphs show the god with obsidian mirrors. Malicious is said to have obsidian mirrors and an obsidian sacrificial table in her castle. Images in the black glass look like shadows. Some say Malicious has the power to enter the mirrors and emerge as a shadow."

The group fell into silence, and Liz gazed down from the ledge. *For all the evilness, Popocatépetl looks beautiful,* she thought. Lava flowed from some deeper molten source and emerged from the center of the city and streamed north and south in a continuous ribbon of orange light. Ancient engineers had found a way to carefully control the amount of lava and restrict the liquid fire to a narrow band that coursed beside the River Fjorm. The same engineers had widened the portion of the River Fjorm that flowed under the volcano and had formed a huge harbor with dozens of black docks. The docks were built from lava that had been diverted into giant molds and then allowed to cool.

The volcano that sat upon this underground harbor was now mostly a hollow metallic shell with polished walls that sloped very gradually upward and inward and that rose at least a mile, towering over an immense city that sat upon an expansive plain that extended beyond the docks. Tiny pinpoints of light from the buildings sparkled below them in the darkness.

How can something so evil look so beautiful? thought Liz again. She felt as if she were looking down into a starry sky with an orange band of lava instead of a silver Milky Way.

The volcano had been excavated over many centuries and still continued to yield rich deposits of ore that were smelted into the metals used to forge the weapons for the soldiers. The mountain also yielded pockets of gemstones and was an especially rich source of rubies. The ores were smelted in furnaces located close to where the lava emerged. The metal ingots were cooled in the River Fjorm and then transported to forges located in some of the abandoned mineshafts. The finished weapons were stored in other mineshafts.

The numerous entrances to the mines, forges, and storage chambers were evident and looked like pockmarks at various heights on the metallic-looking walls, and there was a steady stream of rope-suspended platforms that served as elevators, moving the ore from the mines down to the smelters, the ingots up to forges, and the finished weapons down to the docks.

Above the ceiling of the volcanic cavern, a narrow cone-shaped shaft extended high up to the surface, where an almost imperceptible gray glow was the only evidence of the minimal and diffused sunlight that managed to penetrate the clouds that usually enveloped the cone. The sun moved into a position directly over the cone on only two occasions a year, and if at that time the volcano was not shrouded with clouds, a vertical beam of sunlight shone down to a sacred platform at the center of Popocatépetl. The appearance of the vertical sunbeam was considered very auspicious but had not been seen during the years that Malicious had lived in the crater. Many believed that she had purposely veiled the volcano with clouds to prevent the sun from reaching her fortress or the sunbeam from reaching the city.

Eirik pointed up to the central shaft and said, "I wonder how my sister accesses the crater. I only remember waking up in her castle. I cannot remember how I got there. I don't see any ropes or suspended platforms."

"There must be a connection with one of the mineshafts," suggested Xbalanque. "Either that, or perhaps she has learned to fly."

Liz had been studying the movements of the elevators and offered her own theory. "Eirik, Kate, and I escaped down the elevator that extends up from the south wall, just this side of the southwest corner. We were pretty close to the top of the cavern. The elevators that went up were almost always empty, and those that went down contained only uniforms and weapons. Likely the mineshafts above no longer yield good ore and are used only as storage chambers. We were kept in rooms specially built to watch and interrogate prisoners. Malicious came to these rooms every day to work her mischief on Eirik and Kate. There is probably a connection from that level to Malicious's castle in the crater, perhaps a carved stairwell." Liz looked at Eirik. "We need to carefully explore those rooms."

Then she turned to Xbalanque. "Can your men provide a diversion that will allow us to get back up the elevator?"

"Of course, that is why we are here. We will split our forces into three parties and attack the garrison on the eastern shore from the tunnels that emerge into the dock area. We will avoid the main tunnel that is dry, for I am suspicious that Malicious has cast a spell over this route. The enemy will have no way of knowing whether our strength is a few hundred or thousands and will have to relocate soldiers from the western shore. In the confusion, you should be able to make your way through the city and reach the mineshafts."

Chapter 55
Ian's Vision

The smoke burned hot on Ian's palate, and his chest screamed as he inhaled the single puff deep into his lungs. A moment later, the discomfort dissolved into a rather pleasant feeling, and for the first time in days, Ian felt relaxed. He wanted to take a second puff but remembered Zuni's injunction and placed the pipe on the floor of the hogan.

When he looked around, Ian was surprised to find that Shabear, Connor, and Zuni had left the hogan. He wondered where they had gone and why he had not heard them leave.

The fire burned bright, and for some time Ian enjoyed the flames dancing in the darkness. As he watched, the orange tendrils of fire slowly licked higher and higher until they were eventually level with his eyes. A dark void appeared below the flames and extended down to where the embers glowed. He felt compelled to pass his hands through this void and was surprised when he felt cold air swirling.

The flames continued to dance in front of his eyes, but the embers slowly faded until only four were left, and these were arranged according to the points of the compass and opposite the piles of colored powder that Zuni had placed.

The flames seemed to fade, and Ian's eyes were drawn to the ember burning on the west rim of the fire. As he studied the glow, he saw a sun setting on an ocean and a young boy running along the seashore. The boy was laughing. Ian realized he was seeing himself on a trip he had taken with his parents to Hawaii. The memory was good, but as he watched, the glow from the ember slowly waned until finally the vision disappeared.

His attention was next drawn to the ember burning at the north rim of the fire, and this one glowed brighter for the loss of the other. In the glow of this ember, Ian saw himself and Kate hiking into the valley. He watched as they enjoyed each other's company and took note of how happy they had been. Then a fog enveloped them, like the mist they had seen from the hot springs, and this vision also faded as the ember died.

The ember that burned at the south rim of the fire now glowed very bright. In this glow, Ian saw a woman who twirled slow circles in a beautiful white dress. The white dress and her blonde hair fanned out in symmetrical circles as she danced from one room to another, until she reached a shiny black table upon which she lay down. The woman looked up, and Ian realized she was Kate. A shadow slinked into the room and up to the table. As the shadow approached, Kate started to cry. The scene changed, and now Kate was on a rock slab at the top of a pyramid. She was tied to the slab, and her face, hands, and feet were painted blue. Her eyelids were droopy and her face expressionless. The shadow was now a woman in black who held her hands over Kate and spoke silent words. The woman looked up, and her red eyes bore into Ian. Suddenly, the woman was holding Kate's heart, which was still beating. The heart contracted rhythmically and spurted blood over Kate's lifeless face. When there was no further blood, the heart quivered for a few seconds and then stopped moving.

Ian couldn't look any longer and closed his eyes. When he opened them, the south ember was black and cold. The final ember at the east rim of the fire now burned with a brilliance that was difficult to look at. Nevertheless, Ian's eyes were drawn to the ember, and in the glow he saw a man groping in a black tunnel toward a red light. As the man drew closer, the red light split and became two red eyes that taunted the man. Ian recognized the man as himself. Suddenly he was on a cliff, facing the tall man with whom he had always fought in his nightmares. They fought like tigers and tore at each other with sword and knife. Four times, Ian gained the upper hand and struck his adversary what seemed to be a mortal blow, but neither blood nor wound appeared, and each time, the tall man renewed the fight.

Ian and his adversary continued to fight, but neither seemed able to gain an advantage. They fought back and forth along a high ridge overlooking a city that Ian did not recognize. They were still fighting when the ember died and the vision disappeared.

The flames disappeared with the last ember, and when Ian looked around, he saw that Zuni, Shabear, and Connor had returned. They were talking about how to make a healing poultice.

"Mixed with broom groundsel, the root of the showy aster makes a fine poultice, but it must be applied under a thick slab of river mud every hour," remarked Shabear.

"I use the pulp from fresh maize instead of mud, but agree with the proportions of showy aster and broom groundsel," replied Zuni.

"Where did you go?" asked Ian. "How long were you gone? Why are you interested in poultices? Was someone wounded? That smoke was very powerful. The flames separated from the embers. I saw things, and some of them were not pleasant."

"I imagine that is so," remarked Zuni. "We never left the hogan. Rather, it was you who journeyed to those places. Tell us where you went and what you saw."

Ian relayed his visions, and Zuni offered her interpretations. "Looking west, you saw yourself as a young boy. That was the past. Looking north, you saw yourself at the sacred hot springs. That was the present. Looking south and east, you saw possible future events. Neither future vision was pleasant, but the one to the east offered at least some hope. The tall man you fought was undoubtedly Lord Null, the commander of Malicious's army. You vanquished Lord Null four times in this vision, and even though he did not die, neither did you. This vision suggests that if you travel to the east, the outcome is not sure.

"The awful vision you saw in the south is worrisome and proves what I have long suspected. Malicious derives some of her power from the ancient rituals of human sacrifice that were practiced by the Aztec and Inca peoples who first settled the surface in the Middle and Southern Realms. She must mean to sacrifice Kate in an ancient ceremony. I cannot tell you when. Perhaps if you consult those who understand the celestial calendars, they might be able to tell you the most likely time for Malicious to practice this vile ritual.

"Until then, I will do what I can. I will perform the ceremony to restore the heart. I will do this every day until I hear either that your quest is successful or that Kate has died. Go in harmony."

Chapter 56
Jaguars on the Bridge

Liz and Eirik waited until they heard the sounds of Xbalanque's warriors attacking before they crept along the eastern bank of the River Fjorm toward the main bridge across to Popocatépetl. Several ships passed, and although the decks were filled with soldiers, none of them, including the officers, paid any notice to Liz and Eirik.

"Maybe we look like locals," suggested Eirik.

"Or traders," responded Liz, "but whatever we look like, I'm glad we haven't attracted any attention. Let's put our hoods up so they can't see our faces."

By the time they reached the bridge, the eastern shore was a sea of bodies running helter-skelter in response to the alarm raised when the Mayan warriors attacked. Streams of soldiers were running across the main bridge to support the garrison stationed on the eastern shore.

Liz looked across the bridge and noted that pandemonium had erupted on the western shore as well. Horns blasted, and officers shouted to muster soldiers to battle. The soldiers on the docks were mostly unarmed men who had recently disembarked from the ships and who were awaiting their weapons before continuing their journey north. Much confusion ensued when these unarmed men refused to cross the bridge and join the fight. Jaguars had been summoned and were sweeping the unwilling recruits across the bridge, weaponless or not. The jaguars summarily killed the soldiers who refused to cross and any others who otherwise straggled. Some of the soldiers were clearly terrified by the alternatives and chose to leap off the bridge; most of them disappeared beneath the water and never surfaced. Liz saw a few men swimming, but none reached shore before some hungry denizen of the deep pulled them under.

The bridge was well lit, and after awhile, the jaguars restored order such that the soldiers crossed in only one direction. Jaguars continued to patrol the western shore, and any soldier who thought of turning back decided otherwise when he saw how much the cats were enjoying their duties.

"Liz, we'll have to make a run for it and hope the cats will be otherwise preoccupied when we reach the other side," Eirik said, drawing his sword. "I'll go first."

"No, Eirik," Liz said as she grabbed his arm and held him back. "We must walk slowly over the bridge as if we have nothing to worry about. If we run, the soldiers and especially the jaguars will know we have something to hide. And we must not show or feel fear, for cats are drawn to the sight and smell of frightened prey."

Liz touched Eirik's hand softly. "Sheathe your sword and walk with me as if we were two traders on an errand to the city."

Some of the regular soldiers were marching in a disciplined fashion across the southernmost part of the bridge, and Liz led Eirik to a space between the edge of the bridge and the line of advancing soldiers. None of them seemed to notice Liz or Eirik.

The pair walked in single file, Liz ahead, and the way was clear except for an officer who was walking beside the soldiers and directly opposite Liz.

The wall of the bridge was chest-high, and there was a narrow ledge sufficient to permit a person to stand and walk along. In better times, Liz could envision young boys and girls fishing from this ledge. Today, though, the ledge served only as a convenient place to step out of the way of the officer.

Liz turned her head and whispered to Eirik to get on the ledge. "When he asks who we are, let me do the talking."

Surprisingly, the officer walked right by them as if he hadn't even seen them, and then Liz understood why they had gone undetected along the River Fjorm and even on the bridge. "Our clothes," she whispered to Eirik, "our clothes make us difficult to see, remember? We are blending into the surroundings." She silently thanked Queen Odontocetes for the wise gift of concealment.

They allowed several more officers and soldiers to similarly pass and soon found themselves coming upon the jaguar guards on the western shore. Liz's heart was pounding as they walked toward the nearest cat. She felt tiny beads of perspiration form in her armpits and drip down the inside of her arms and the sides of her chest. Her palms were cool and wet. She was anxious but felt better when she realized Eirik didn't look worried at all.

Eirik could tell that Liz was concerned. He took her shoulder and offered an encouraging squeeze and then gave her a warm smile and a cheeky wink.

Liz noted that Eirik's hand was warm and dry and without the telltale dampness of anxiety. His smile gave her strength, and her legs, which only a moment before had felt rubbery and had wanted to run, now relaxed. Her steps never faltered when she walked past the jaguar.

The big cat growled and turned as Liz passed, but she kept walking without looking back. There was only one more jaguar between them and the first buildings of the city, and Liz changed direction so as to put as much distance between them and this cat as she could.

She heard a growl and turned her head to see the cat sniffing the air in their direction. *The jaguar can smell my sweat,* she realized, which unleashed a new gush of perspiration. She felt a slight chill as the perspiration that had already soaked her tunic began to evaporate.

The big cat started to stalk her. Much to Liz's relief, the cat stopped abruptly only a few feet behind her and bounded back to the bridge. The jaguar would have been onto her had not an officer summoned all the jaguars to help with a minor mutiny on the bridge.

"That was close," said Liz.

"But we made it," replied Eirik.

Chapter 57
Change of Plans

Helga listened carefully as Ian related his vision and Shabear added her interpretations to those of Zuni.

"Ian's vision suggests that travel south is ill advised," Shabear concluded in agreement with Zuni.

"I agree," said Svein. "The tunnels south are thick with enemy soldiers. We have not heard any news from Toltec for at least a week, and I fear that dissidents have betrayed Oddur, the leader of the Toltec clan. We have long suspected Malicious of fermenting revolt in Toltec. The absence of any news is disquieting, and we must presume that Toltec is now under her control."

"So, farther travel south is neither advised nor likely possible," said Helga.

"Is there a route east?" asked Ian.

"Yes," replied Svein, "but not any easy one. There are two east-west tunnels between here and Popocatépetl, but only one is regularly used." Svein brought out a map that showed the connecting tunnels. "In the Northern Realm, both the coastal and the inland routes are fairly close to the surface. The inland route gradually goes deeper after the Green Cavern but still remains reasonably close to the surface. The coastal route also remains close to the surface. However, both tunnels that connect the routes between here and Popocatépetl drop down steeply and then rise just as acutely before they reach the inland route. The temperature in the deepest connecting tunnels is so hot that in places the air is stifling.

"The most traveled of the two connecting routes continues close to the surface until just north of Popocatépetl and then plunges deep below the level of the city before rising again to the River Fjorm."

"Show me the other route," asked Ian.

"The other route comes off the most traveled route but is dangerous and hardly ever traveled. The only people who venture in those tunnels do so to mine the exotic minerals at the lower depths. More people disappear on this route than make it through to the inland route. Often no trace of these people is ever found. I do not advise this way."

Helga looked around the room. "Do you all agree that we should take the more traveled route?" asked Helga.

They all nodded their assent.

"My people can lead you to the entrance of the tunnel," advised Svein. "The entrance is at the base of one of the stairwells to our cliff city, and you will find it easy to access the tunnel without encountering any of the soldiers on the plain."

Soon they arrived at the tunnel's entrance, where Svein's people gave them enough food for the journey, and Svein addressed them a final time. "My scouts regularly travel this tunnel to check for enemy soldiers that might try to surprise us, but no trace of the enemy has been found for at least a half-day journey. Thereafter, I do not know what you will find. The journey to Popocatépetl takes several weeks."

Just before they set out, Zuni arrived and asked to speak with the man with the heavy heart and the great warrior bear. She led Ian and Connor down a tunnel and into a small side cavern and asked them to sit with her.

"This room is a kiva, a ceremonial chamber used to perform the rituals of my people. A kiva is a sanctuary. The powerful spirits of my ancestors protect kivas, and nothing evil can penetrate these places, not even a bad dream. Anyone can come to a kiva, and whoever enters one will be safe from harm. Between here and Popocatépetl there are several rest stops with a kiva. You will know them when you see the sundog sign, a powerful symbol of my people."

Zuni took some red earth from a basket beside where she sat and made a line on the ground. She took some blue earth from another basket and made a parallel line above the red one.

"You made the same sign in the smaller circle in your hogan," said Ian.

"I am not surprised that you remember. Your vision is precociously clear for one so young. Now, I have spoken with my ancestors, and they agree with the path that you and the warrior bear must follow."

Ian wondered why Zuni mentioned only him and Connor and not the other members of the rescue squad. Before he had a chance to ask, Zuni went on.

"My ancestors asked me to tell you about the kivas and to offer you these gifts." Zuni turned to Ian. "For the man with the heavy heart, my ancestors offer this medicine bag with a healing stone and herbs."

Inside the bag Ian found a Green Crystal, a seashell, a bunch of dried leaves, and the roots of a plant.

"The Green Crystal will heal many wounds. Bind the crystal to the wound overnight. The divine leaves of immortality should be used when endurance is required. Crush a piece of the seashell and mix the powder with some leaves. Chew the leaves into a pulp and then place the mixture between your cheek and your teeth. Juice from the root will stop all bleeding but that directly from the heart."

Zuni turned next to Connor. "For the great warrior bear and descendant of Bear Old Man, my ancestors offer this compass stone. This stone lay between the south and east embers of the fire in my hogan and links the people Ian saw in those visions.

"The stone will lead you to these people. When you are close to Ian, the stone will glow green, the color of life. The stone will grow white for the innocence of Kate and red for the rubies that command Lord Null. Beware when the stone turns cold and black, for you will be close to Malicious. Wear the stone around your neck so that you will know when you are close to these people."

Zuni also had a gift for Shabear. She handed the gift to Connor. "Please give this kachina to your aunt. This is Aincekoko, the bear kachina. Kachina masks represent a god and are important in our rituals. This kachina is part of the mixed dance ritual that is performed in the spring. Each spring, the sleeping bear is awoken by thunder in the distant east. The bear is lonely after sleeping alone for so long in his den. He hears our people dancing and comes down from the mountain to join the dance."

Connor and Ian thanked Zuni for the gifts. Zuni stood up and led them out of the kiva and back toward Helga, Shabear, and Thorfinn, but she disappeared before they joined the group.

With the squad gathered, Helga led them, and as promised by Svein, they did not find any sign of the enemy during the first half-day they journeyed. They did, however, meet some traders from Popocatépetl, who advised that they had not seen any soldiers except around the entrance to the deeper tunnel system, where they had come upon a patrol that demanded a toll to use the tunnel.

"You were lucky," said Helga. "You came across a more civilized patrol that demanded only money and not your lives." Helga told them about the siege of Anasazi and wished them continued good fortune.

Thorfinn consulted the map provided by Svein. "The entrance to the deeper tunnel is many days away. The tunnel emerges in a cavern strewn with boulders, a perfect place for an ambush," advised Thorfinn. "I recommend we stop short of the cavern and send a scout ahead before we blunder into a possible trap."

"Agreed," replied Helga.

Closer to the deeper tunnel, they came upon some curious tracks that Helga could not identify.

"These are the tracks of a cloven-hoofed animal, about four or five feet long—and heavy," remarked Thorfinn.

"They look like pig tracks," said Ian. "Perhaps the enemy keeps pigs for food?"

The number of tracks increased as they closed in on the cavern. Besides the tracks of the hoofed animal, they also found the tracks of men, wolves, and large cats. When they were about a mile from the cavern, Helga sent Thorfinn ahead to scout the cavern.

He found the cavern floor covered in cloven-hoof tracks, some fresh, but saw no other sign of the enemy. Thorfinn explored east along the tunnel, and apart from more tracks, he found no further evidence of the enemy. He returned and reported to Helga.

Helga led them into the cavern, where she stopped to review the map. She posted Thorfinn as sentry, and while Shabear explored the deeper connecting tunnel, she conferred with Ian and Connor.

Shabear returned to report that enemy soldiers had used the deeper tunnel. "There are tracks everywhere, and their smell is strong," explained Shabear. "That confirms the information from the traders. Hopefully, the road east will still be free of the enemy. I'm glad we aren't going into the deeper tunnel. There was a strange smell that came from deep down, something awful that I've never smelled before."

"What's that noise?" asked Connor.

Just then, Thorfinn rushed back into the cavern. "Run, run!" he cried. "There are strange tusked animals coming, hundreds of them!"

Thorfinn jumped onto a boulder, and following his lead, Helga and Shabear also sought the high ground offered by the rock formations in the cavern. Connor and Ian ducked into the entrance to the deeper tunnel and climbed down a natural stairwell to a lower level.

Moments later, the huge animals stampeded into the cavern. They had grayish black woolly hair that swept up their sides and emerged as a mane of silver bristles that shimmered down their spine. They had foot-long tusks, and a continuous thick slaver drooled from their lower jaws. They where half the height but twice as heavy as a man, and as they rushed through the cavern, the walls shook, smaller rocks shifted on the floor, and a huge cloud of dust churned up.

Helga, Shabear, and Thorfinn held onto the boulders for dear life. For five solid minutes the herd barreled through the cavern while stalactites fell and portions of the wall collapsed.

After the thundering noise finally faded, the dust settled, and the air started to clear. Shabear looked around and saw several of the animals writhing, transfixed by stalactites that had fallen, and others skewered upon stalagmites.

"What were they?" inquired Helga.

"They must be boars," replied Thorfinn, "a kind of wild pig. They do not exist in the north, and I have only heard of these animals."

"Boars! Of course," said Helga. "Like those in old myths. The bristles on those boars shone just like those of Guillinbursti, the golden boar made for Freyr, and they charged faster than any man or horse. I hope we've seen the last of them."

As the air cleared further, Shabear surveyed the cavern for Ian and Connor. They were nowhere to be seen. "Where are Ian and Connor?" shouted Shabear.

"I saw them duck into the deep tunnel," Helga replied, and they both looked hopefully in that direction, but where there once had been an entrance, they now saw only a mountain of rubble.

"Let us hope they were deep enough to escape the cave-in," said Shabear.

Chapter 58
Inca Interlude

Liz and Eirik continued to walk casually through the plaza undetected by the soldiers and local merchants. Hundreds of pairs of eyes looked right at them but never saw them. Eirik was surprised, therefore, to notice that a young woman was following them.

They turned a corner, and Eirik pulled Liz into a stairwell and motioned for her to stay quiet, with a finger over his lips. After the young woman had passed, Eirik explained what he had observed to Liz.

"But no one else has seen us, Eirik," responded Liz. "Perhaps you are mistaken."

"I'm certain she saw us. When our eyes met, she quickly looked away."

"That might be a coincidence," said Liz.

"No, before she looked away, I saw interest in her eyes, and since then she has followed us precisely. Unless she just happens to be going exactly in the same direction we are, she is following us."

"Okay," said Liz, "let's presume for the moment that she is following us. She's gone now. Unless she turns up again, there is nothing else for us to do but carry on. With any luck, she won't find us again, and we can stop worrying about her. Let's go back the way we came to avoid her."

Eirik looked up and down the street but could not see the woman. As they walked, for several blocks Eirik periodically looked behind them, and he relaxed only when they reached the first of the stairwells that went up to the mineshafts.

They made their way along the cavern wall and passed dozens of stairwells until they finally reached the one they had descended during their escape. They were just about to start up when they heard someone walking toward them from a nearby street. Instinctively, Liz and Eirik both froze into the shadow of the stairwell. As they watched the street, they saw the same woman from earlier. She made no attempt to conceal herself and instead walked straight toward them.

The woman was tall with dark-brown eyes and long ebony-black hair that fell around her shoulders. She was attired in a simple beige tunic that ended just below her knees but that looked elegant courtesy of the excellent cut, which highlighted her shapely figure. Around her neck she wore a chain with a pendant that depicted a catlike creature with fierce-looking fangs and clawed feet. In one hand, the creature held a snake, and in the other a staff.

"Don't worry," she whispered as she approached, "I am a friend. You must come with me, or you will be captured." She motioned for them to follow her back into the street.

Liz and Eirik were reluctant to trust her and remained still.

"Hurry," she said, "the panthers will come any second, and your chameleon clothes will not afford any protection from their piercing eyes. As it is, your lingering scent alone might be enough to raise the alarm. Quick, you must trust me."

Liz grabbed Eirik's hand and pulled him into the street, and they followed the woman who thereafter never spoke, but who led them deep into the city through a maze of streets, sometimes passing the same place several times. Finally they came to a house where the woman advised they would be safe.

"We passed this house once before," observed Eirik.

"Twice, actually," replied the woman, "and we are in fact only several blocks from the stairwell, but I had to be sure we were not followed. All the walls have eyes. I do not trust anyone, especially those who live in this part of the city."

"Who are you?" asked Liz. "And how can you see us when no one else can?"

"My name is Viracocha, and my father taught me to see what others miss."

"How do we know we can trust you?" asked Eirik.

"When the alarm was sounded, I hurried to the docks, where I hoped to see some great army that had come to vanquish Malicious. I was heartened to see that the Mayan peoples had taken up arms against her, but I soon saw that they had not arrived in strength and realized the attack could only be a diversion for some other purpose. When I saw the jaguar smell the presence of something unseen, I closed my eyes and imagined you. When I opened my eyes, I could see you. I knew you were the reason for the diversion, and I followed you. If you are an enemy of Malicious, you are a friend of mine. As to why you should trust me, you are still alive, aren't you? Were I a spy for Malicious, you would be panther food by now."

"Why do you want to help us?" asked Liz.

"Because together we might help one another," replied Viracocha. "Many days ago, I saw you both escape with a third person down the stairwell. The panthers brought the third person back several days later."

"You saw Kate?" asked Liz. "Was she well?"

"She looked drugged," replied Viracocha.

"Malicious is adept with the use of the plant and animal potions," added Eirik.

"Tonight, I presume that you were going to climb back up the stairwell to rescue this person, but had you tried, by now you would be dead or imprisoned with her. Since your escape, the panthers have started to patrol the stairwells, and they are infinitely more efficient than the men who guarded you. Those men were killed in a public execution the morning after your escape. Their heads are now on display on the tzompantli in front of the temple by the docks."

"Thank you for warning us in time," replied Liz. "You mentioned that we might help one another. What are you trying to accomplish?"

"My father is also a prisoner, and I mean to rescue him or die trying."

"Why is your father a prisoner?" asked Eirik.

"My father is Manco Capac, ruler of Cusco and heir to the ancient throne of Tahuantinsuyu, the land of the Inca. The Inca have not been united for many years, and my father hoped to one day reunite the Inca peoples and to forge an empire in the Southern Realm as progressive and just as the Kingdom of Asgard in the north. Alas, his plans were thwarted by Malicious, who promised the other Inca leaders great wealth and access to the Green Crystal. My father alone resisted Malicious when she cajoled the other Inca leaders to join her greedy war. My father is still alive only because he is an important symbol to the southern peoples. They believe he has willingly joined Malicious in this war. Even so, time is running out, because once the southern armies have mustered in the north, I fear Malicious will find a way for my father to conveniently die … And what of you two? Why were you taken prisoner?"

Eirik explained that he was heir to the throne of Asgard and that he had been under Malicious's spell for several months. He continued, "Kate and Liz were kidnapped by Malicious so that she could twist an ancient prophecy to her foul purpose. According to the prophecy, Kate and I were to marry, and then I would be crowned king of Asgard. I expect that Malicious planned to conveniently kill us after the coronation, which would leave her the rightful heir to the throne."

"I see," said Viracocha. "With both my father and you under her control, Malicious hoped to legitimize her rule of both the Southern and the Northern Realms."

"But if her armies are successful, Malicious will not need any legitimacy," added Liz, "and your father's life and Kate's will no longer serve any purpose."

"This is true," said Viracocha. "I have heard that a great battle is imminent, at a place called the Green Cavern. All the soldiers are speaking about this battle. According to what I have heard, Malicious has over twenty times as many soldiers as your father."

"They will need more soldiers than that," boasted Eirik, with a bravado that spoke more for his youth than experience.

"We can only hope," responded Liz. "We can only hope."

"The autumnal equinox is only a few days away," said Viracocha. "This is a day of great significance in the Southern Realm. Like your people, we chose this time for special occasions such as marriages. Our ancestors also chose this time to attack their enemies, and prior to the battle they usually performed rituals that might please our gods. It is likely that Malicious has chosen the autumnal equinox as the day when she will attack your father's forces in the Green Cavern. Before she orders the attack, I believe Malicious will perform the ancient Inca war ritual, and we must rescue my father and Kate before this time."

"Yes," replied Eirik, "because if the army of Malicious is victorious, again, the lives of your father and Kate will serve her no purpose."

Liz, however read more into the words of Viracocha. "Tell me about this ritual," asked Liz. "Does it involve human sacrifice?"

"Yes," replied Viracocha. "My people have not practiced human sacrifice for over five centuries, but Malicious has revived this vile practice. I believe that my father, Kate, or both will be sacrificed in the Inca war ritual. We must save them before they can serve her vile plans."

"I explored the rooms off the mineshaft where Kate and I were held captive," said Liz, "and except for Eirik, I found no one else imprisoned. There might be rooms that I missed, but what if your father is being held in some other place?"

"That is possible," admitted Viracocha. "Although I do not know where my father or your sister might be imprisoned, I believe I know where Malicious is most likely to hold the Inca war ritual. She has a castle in the crater of the smoking mountain high above us. Within this castle is a temple built to be identical to the one in Cusco, the ancient capital of my peoples. The temple is so constructed that at dawn on the autumnal equinox, the light of the sun will shine upon the sacrificial altar. At that moment, Malicious will sacrifice a life to Inti, the sun god. If Kate is the victim, she will be dressed in white, and her face, hands, and feet will be painted blue. At the moment the sun moves over her heart, Malicious will thrust an obsidian knife into her chest and remove her heart, and while it is still beating, she will hold the organ in the sunlight. Afterward, she will kindle a fire in the chest cavity, and from the flames she will light torches. In the ancient days, the torches would be used to light the way to the enemy camp."

The details of the Inca war ritual as described by Viracocha had suddenly made Liz feel sweaty and nauseated. Eirik saw the color drain from her face and helped her to lie down before she passed out. A few minutes later, Liz felt well enough to sit up, and she apologized.

"There is no need to apologize," replied Viracocha. "The mental image of a loved one being sacrificed in this fashion is a powerful vision. Fear for your sister is a natural response. Were the vision of yourself, I doubt you would have fainted. I see selfless courage in your eyes. You will not faint when it counts."

Liz thanked Viracocha for her understanding words and encouragement. *I like this woman,* decided Liz, *a lot.* "So," Liz said, "if we do not find and rescue Kate and your father before sunrise on the equinox, they will be killed. Okay, then. We must find a way to reach the castle—today if possible." She spoke with a determination that impressed both Eirik and Viracocha.

Chapter 59
Deep Trouble

The collapse of the cavern wall was so sudden and complete that the confined air inside the tunnel was compressed, and Ian and Connor were catapulted farther down the tunnel. There was deafening noise one instant and eerie silence the next. When Ian landed, he rolled with his hands over his head and luckily came to rest without any serious injury.

By the time Ian looked around, Connor was already up and walking toward him. He was coughing as he emerged from a cloud of dust. "I'm a bit heavier than you, Ian. The blast didn't send me as far. Glad we didn't land on a stalagmite." Connor tested the sharp point of one with his paw. "Lucky, aren't we?"

"Are we?" questioned Ian. "Can we get back up to the cavern?"

When the dust settled, they realized that even if Helga and the others had survived, and if they dug toward one another, they could not hope to open the tunnel for days, if not weeks.

"Some of the rocks look too big for even a bear to move," remarked Connor. "Looks like our only way out is down."

Ian agreed, and remembering Zuni's parting conversation, somehow he wasn't surprised to find himself alone with Connor in the deeper tunnel.

They didn't have much time to collect their thoughts before Connor sniffed the air and turned to Ian. "An enemy patrol is on the way, probably to investigate the cave in."

They hid behind some of the rubble. A few minutes later they could hear the voices.

"Those boars are more trouble than they're worth. This is the third cave-in this week. Sure, they keep the upper tunnel free of travelers, but who has to clean up the mess they make? Us, that's who, and this one looks like the worst cave-in yet. I'll bet we can't clean this one out in a day, not without reinforcements at least. And who will be the one to ask for reinforcements? Me, of course! And do they ever reward the person who asks for reinforcements? No, they punish the poor sod. Those boars are going to be the death of me."

The soldier never stopped complaining as he walked right past where Ian and Connor crouched behind a boulder. They both considered the option of killing the soldiers, and both came to the same conclusion that the less the enemy knew of their presence, the better. They waited until the voices died away before they proceeded down the tunnel.

"Better to leave them alive," said Connor. "I can smell them, but they can only see or hear us. Had we killed them, our presence in this tunnel system would have been discovered, and they would have spared no effort to find us. Getting to Popocatépetl will take more stealth than strength."

Ian was glad Connor was with him. No one could ask for a better companion. Connor was honest to a fault, considerate of the feelings of others, and smart enough to keep out of trouble. If they did end up in harm's way, he was stronger than any ten men. He had a reputation for clumsiness, but Ian had not noted any of this on the trail. He concluded that like many men, Connor was clumsy in social situations, but on the playing field or in battle, he had the grace of a ballerina.

Without the map Svein had showed them, they couldn't be certain of their position, but Ian recollected that the trip to Popocatépetl was a one- to two-week journey, mostly going down and then up again. Connor remembered seeing at least three side tunnels, each leading to what looked to be a dead end.

"If the enemy has patrols here, they must occupy the tunnel as far as Popocatépetl," remarked Ian. "Keep that nose peeled, Connor. I expect we will come across a larger group fairly soon."

The pitch was steep and in many places required them to climb down and in some places even to crawl. More than once they were glad that Ian still had the rope in his pack.

The tunnels had not been reengineered by Bjorn's people, and there was no natural light, which meant they needed torches to navigate. The temperature increased as they descended, and they stopped at every stream to satisfy their thirst. Every place they stopped had enemy tracks.

Connor handed Ian a root from his pouch and suggested he chew on it.

"Tastes salty," said Ian.

"It is salty," replied Connor. "Keeping up with our water losses is important, but we also need salt."

Many times, Connor smelled men, and they hid while a patrol passed. Once, while they were stopped at a tiny subterranean pool, a patrol came upon them and rested in the area while Connor and Ian waited patiently out of sight. Like all soldiers, the men in the patrol mostly complained about the food.

"Why is it we only have corn? Boiled cornmeal when we wake up, dried cornmeal if we have time to eat during the day, and fried cornmeal in the evening. Always cornmeal."

"I wouldn't complain if I were you," said another. "I heard about someone who complained so much he disappeared, and the next day the men in his squad had meat. No one ate it, though."

"I don't believe that story. When someone disappears, they're gone for good. What I hear is that the ones who make too many mistakes are sent down the unexplored tunnels where Malicious keeps some of her special pets. No one goes down them tunnels and comes out alive."

"What kind of pets?" asked the other.

"How should I know? Why don't you go down and check? Come on, we need to get moving. Slowness is a mistake in this outfit."

After the soldiers had left, Connor sighed. "Guess we better avoid the side tunnels. What do you think Malicious has hidden down there?"

"Likely something that was there well before she came along," replied Ian, "and something that has never seen the light."

Even though they had to stop fairly frequently to allow soldiers to pass, they made excellent progress, and over the course of a day they penetrated deep into the tunnel system.

Crystalline minerals coursed beside them in multicolored veins, many of them new to Connor. Connor shined his torch upward and noticed a rusty ribbon of crystal that coursed along the edge where the wall merged with the ceiling. The crystal was about two inches deep and stretched in a wiggly fashion for several feet. He climbed up close enough to shine his torch directly behind the crystal and was rewarded with translucent layers of orange and yellow.

"Wow," remarked Connor. "Look at this, Ian."

"That's cave bacon. The crystal is called that because it looks like bacon," Ian said, "and that's kind of ironic."

"How so?" questioned Connor. "And what's bacon?"

"Bacon is the meat from a pig, and the boars that stampeded through the cavern and trapped us down here are a kind of pig."

"Oh! So they're good to eat, are they? Then I hope we run across a few more," Connor said, laughing.

In the same area, they walked by a huge stalagmite column that reached up in layers almost to the top of the cavern before the tip connected with a short, thin stalactite. The secondary stalactites that fell from the layers were much longer than usual and were bone white on one side and monarch butterfly–orange on the other. The long secondary stalactites gave the layers a trabeculated appearance and reminded Ian of the vertebrae of a huge humpback whale he had seen washed up on the British Columbia coastline as a boy.

Some of the layers in this stalagmite were rounded and in sections were connected by a smooth orange surface that flowed from one level to the next like a serious of glistening solid waterfalls. Black nodules of chert, a variety of silica containing microcrystalline quartz, poked from the eroding walls of brownish limestone around the cavern.

"This is a geological paradise," said Ian.

"If you mean the rocks are neat," replied Connor, "then I agree. Did you see those tubelike rocks hanging from the ceiling, the smooth, glistening ones with the golden brown color?"

"Yes, a little while ago I had to duck to miss some," replied Ian. "Those are called soda straws, and they aren't like ordinary calcite stalactites. They are made from a different chemical. If you taste the drop of liquid at the end of the tube, your tongue will sting a bit. The chemical is an acid."

"Acid?" queried Connor.

"Yes, something that burns when it touches."

In the same area they came across some stalactites that had fused and hung from the ceiling like brilliant white organ pipes or beige-colored flutes. The stalactites seemed like draperies that varied in length. Some were dappled with yellow hues. Most were opaque, but some were banded with translucent lines. The surfaces varied from rough grit to a mirrorlike finish. Some felt like coarse sandpaper, others like a pebbled surface, and a few like glass. Most were rough and dull, but some had surfaces as smooth and sharp as the finest blade.

Connor was happy to pass the time talking about the rocks, but Ian's attention to his questions seemed to wax and wane.

"I can see what attracted men to these dark depths," said Connor. "These crystals would fetch a good price in Asgard markets."

Ian didn't reply to this statement, and Connor realized the thoughts of his friend were as deep as the tunnels they plumbed. But whatever was on his mind did not slow Ian down. Rather, Connor noted, Ian had a progressively more determined look, and the more silent Ian was, the faster his pace.

Finally the tunnel leveled off and proceeded more south than east. "Perhaps we've reached the bottom," said Connor.

The walls and ceiling were wet with water and the floor mostly mud.

"Perhaps," replied Ian, "or maybe we're under the River Fjorm, or some other source of water."

Connor suggested they find a place to sleep for a few hours, but Ian was reluctant to stop. It was not that Connor was tired, for the endurance of a grizzly was legendary. But Connor knew that sleep, like food, was essential to maintain the alertness so necessary for survival, and he prevailed on Ian for them to rest until Ian agreed.

They found a dry place in a recess of the tunnel. "Others have slept here before," advised Connor, who detected the old scents of men, "but not recently. We best not both sleep at once. You sleep first while I keep watch."

Sleep came quickly to Ian and confirmed to Connor that his friend's reluctance to stop was an emotional matter that had no roots in common sense. Ian's soft snoring was a comfort to Connor. Connor did not feel especially tired, but his body was. His eyes soon drooped and then closed, and a few minutes later, his snoring was mingled with Ian's.

Connor dreamed that some birds were teasing him. They kept swooping down on him as he tried to pick globe huckleberries in the valley. The berries looked especially juicy, but each time he reached for them, the birds would dive-bomb so close that he instinctively put his paws up to protect his head. When he woke up, he was batting one of the pesky birds away.

Ian was still asleep, and Connor immediately felt guilty that he had not stayed awake, and he wondered how long they had slept. The top of his head felt funny, and Connor reached up and discovered that his fur was matted with something sticky, which on examination turned out to be blood—his blood.

At that moment something buzzed his head, and Connor understood both his dream and the blood. *Bats,* he concluded, *the kind that like blood.* Connor had seen many bats, but none like these. He was used to smaller, dark gray or brown bats. These bats were larger, with long sharp teeth and hairy legs. They were dark-colored except for the tips and the edges of their wings, which were white.

"Well, I guess I can afford a little blood." He looked over at Ian's head, which was fine, and wondered why they had preferred bear blood. *More to the point,* thought Connor, *why are there bats this deep? There must be a big cavern close by—and a source of water, perhaps even a shaft direct to the surface.*

Connor felt refreshed by the sleep and decided to look around before waking Ian. He didn't have far to go before he found the colony of bats. They had come from a small cavern with a pool. When Connor entered the cavern, most of the bats left their roosts and scattered into the tunnels. A few disappeared into a hole in the ceiling, and Connor wondered where it led, but the entrance was much too high to investigate.

There was a rotten smell in the air, and Connor couldn't decide whether the odor came from something living or dead. *Kind of like a stagnant pond,* he thought. Piles of bones were scattered about the cavern. *The piles are too neat,* thought Connor, *and clean but not gnawed, as if the meat was boiled off rather than chewed.*

Most of the bones were those of men, but a variety of other animals had met the same fate in this cavern. *What kind of animal does this?* he wondered.

A sound from the ceiling caught his attention, and he looked up in time to see bats scrambling out of the hole, flying into one another as if they couldn't move fast enough. Connor could smell their fear and was instantly on the alert.

He remained motionless for several minutes but did not hear or see anything. The rotten smell seemed stronger though, and Connor decided the smell had a slimy odor, like a fetid swamp. He left the cavern and returned quickly to Ian, who much to his relief was still sleeping soundly.

Chapter 60

Helga Carries On to Popocatépetl

Helga and the others knew they could not remove the rubble in a time frame practical to their circumstances. "The best we can hope is that they survived and that they are able to make their way to Popocatépetl through the deeper tunnel," said Helga.

"If the enemy soldiers can navigate the tunnel," said Shabear, "then so can Connor and Ian."

"Indeed. And our small band is now smaller, but our mission is no less important," said Helga as she led them into the tunnel.

The only tracks visible were those of the stampeding boars, and these were evident for many miles, until they came upon an enormous cavern directly connected to the surface.

"I have never seen these boars underground. They must prefer the surface," said Shabear. "Likely, the boars were herded on the surface, taken to this cavern, and then driven down the tunnels. They are not especially smart animals, but tusks wielded at the front of a charging boar are no less deadly for the stupidity of the animal."

No boar tracks were evident beyond the cavern; they saw only the tracks of men and occasionally great cats. Helga set a rapid pace, and for the rest of that day, they did not encounter any of the enemy and made good time.

None of them had ever traveled so far south of their native tunnels, and around every corner they discovered something new and wonderful, which helped distract the growing concern over how to accomplish their mission against odds that seemed to grow with each day's journey.

"Access points to the surface are more numerous in this part of Asgard than around Kwakiutl or the Castle of Light," remarked

Shabear. "In better times I would have explored the surface and looked for evidence of bear cousins."

"Yes," responded Helga, "in better times even we might have enjoyed sunshine on the surface."

"But that is forbidden for men and women," said Shabear. "If you were discovered, you might be forced to reveal the existence of the underground realms and jeopardize a thousand years of progress."

"True, to venture onto the surface during daytime is forbidden, but that has not stopped bold men and women from basking in the warm glow of the sun. I have witnessed many sunrises. Every day, the young Kwakiutl men and women who come of age climb up the vertical tunnels of a long-dormant volcano to the snow-covered crater at the top, and in this sacred spot they witness the miracle of the ascension of the sun in the east. As leader of the Kwakiutl, I have enjoyed this ritual many times. Before I die, I would like to climb again and in the same day also witness the disappearance of the sun in the west."

"Then I hope you shall," said Shabear. "As bears, we enjoy both the underground and surface realms, but each year we spend less time on the surface. Someday, when the final few surface bears disappear, killed by shameless surface men, we too might be forbidden to seek the special joy of the sun for fear of discovery. That will be a sad day for bear kind."

Chapter 61
Mac's Plan

King Bjorn and his army reached the region of the Green Cavern seven days before the autumnal equinox and within the next day were joined by the men from the Inuit and Haida clans. Companies of warriors from the Kwakiutl and Siksika clans had also arrived. Most of the warriors set up camps around Nakota, which was only a few hours' journey from the Green Cavern.

They established a command post in a cave that opened onto a ledge high on the northern wall of the Green Cavern. The ledge was accessed via a little-used passageway with a direct connection to Nakota. Since the cave did not open onto the floor of the cavern, they had not encountered any enemy soldiers. The unobstructed view over the cavern was perfect as a command post.

"Now that most of our force has gathered, let us hear from each clan leader and decide how we shall wage this battle. But first," said King Bjorn, "Magnus will describe the geography of the Green Cavern."

Magnus spread a map of the Green Cavern over a huge table in the command post. "Men have mined the Green Crystal for over five hundred years, and the Green Cavern now extends for miles in all directions. Originally, the mining proceeded in a circumferential fashion because crystal deposits were uniform in all directions. About a century ago the northern and southern limits of the crystal were reached, and since that time deposits have been mined only to the east and the west. As such, the cavern has a wider east-west axis than north-south. Areas now cleared of the mineral are used for crops. The green light allows as many as four crops every year."

"The first men who discovered the crystal were exploring an underground river of such size that they were able to row their longships downstream and right up to the site of the original mine. Since that time, the river has been damned to provide water to the cities in the Northern Realm. Only a tiny trickle remains of this once mighty river.

"The mine is located under a mountain range characterized by black hills, and the underground rock formations are considered to be some of the oldest in our realm. The caverns and tunnels in this region are very stable. There have not been any reports of earthquakes or volcanic activity in this region since the area was first explored."

"Where are the enemy deployed?" asked Ursus, who could not see more than a few patrols on the plain beneath the command post.

"Enemy soldiers occupy the southern part of the Green Cavern," replied Shasta. "The Green Cavern is so vast that they are only barely visible from our vantage point. They have not occupied the northern aspect, perhaps because they have chosen this as the preferred battleground."

"How large is the battle plain?" asked Runolfur.

"From the center of the Green Cavern, the excavated area extends for many miles in all directions," replied Magnus. "Malicious's army occupies the southern third of the cavern, but that still leaves an enormous field of battle. Until the enemy captured the Green Cavern, most of the ground was covered in orchards and farms. The enemy harvested the crops and then razed the land. Apart from enemy camps, the only other buildings left standing are those of the small mining community in the northern half of the cavern."

"There are only a few underground caverns of sufficient size to allow armies to maneuver," remarked King Bjorn. "Malicious could have sent her armies farther north without much opposition. She might even have reached the Castle of Light. Given the destruction that might have ensued, it is well she chose this location."

"Malicious chose this site to please the southern warlords who covet the Green Crystal," advised Magnus. "Even as we speak, their miners have started to excavate the crystal and transport the precious mineral south. When they first occupied the cavern, I wondered if the crystal might be the only objective, but the strength of her army is beyond that necessary to defend the cavern. It is clear that if she is successful here, she means to carry the attack north and to the Castle of Light."

"But now we are here," said King Bjorn, "and by the grace of Odin, this is as far as her soldiers will ever travel. Let us discuss how we will defeat her."

"Malicious has not occupied the mining community in the northern half of the cavern, and if we attack, the buildings can provide cover and ammunition for our catapults," suggested Runolfur. "We have built many catapults in preparation for this battle. Our scouts have not identified any enemy catapults. Malicious must believe that overwhelming numbers of soldiers are sufficient for victory."

"Five tunnels from the north converge on the Green Cavern," said Groa. "Enemy soldiers patrol the entrances but only in weak strength. These soldiers were not stationed to resist, but rather to raise the alarm. I suggest that each of the clans attack through one of these tunnels."

The leaders of the Inuit, Haida, Nakota, Kwakiutl, and Siksika clans agreed this was a reasonable strategy.

"When shall we attack?" asked Magnus.

"If we do not attack before, it is likely Malicious will attack on the autumnal equinox," said Ursus. "This day is considered favorable by the priests of the southern warlords."

"Then we should attack first and gain the momentum from the start," replied Magnus.

The war council dispersed to rally their warriors. Mac, Ursus, and King Bjorn remained, looking at the map of the Green Cavern. Ursus looked very sad.

"So many men and bears will die," said Ursus. "What a terrible shame."

Mac did not have any military experience and had not participated in the discussion. Instead, while the others had reviewed conventional strategic opportunities, he had considered whether there might be some geological help.

"Maybe there's a better way," said Mac. "As I recollect, the rose quartz map in King Bjorn's council chamber showed that the tunnels south are deeper after the Green Cavern. Is that true?"

"Yes," replied Ursus. "From the Castle of Light to the Green Cavern, the road gently falls, but thereafter the pitch is steeper."

"How many entrances converge on the Green Cavern from the south?" Mac asked.

"Only two."

"That suggests that Malicious's soldiers are likely congested for miles in two tunnels with a downhill pitch. Is that a reasonable assumption?" asked Mac.

"Yes, but these men are still available as continuous reinforcements for her army in the cavern," replied Ursus, "and according to our reports, she has thousands more still on their way. Her ships continue to dock at Cauldron Lake, the northern end of the River Fjorm, and unload soldiers, who are marching north."

"What if the Green Cavern filled with water?" asked Mac. "The water would drain down those two tunnels and drown the enemy."

"That's brilliant," said Ursus, who finally understood where Mac was going with his questions. "Of course, we can open up the dam and flood the cavern. The enemy will drown like cave rats."

"Ragnarök," said King Bjorn with a worried look.

"Who or what is Ragnarök?" asked Mac.

"Ragnarök is the day of reckoning when the gods decide they have had enough of men," said Magnus. "According to the ancient prophecy, a great flood will wash away the evilness, but the good will die with the bad, and only a few will survive."

Mac chose to ignore this gloomy prophecy. "How much water is behind the dam?" he asked. "Is there enough to do the job?"

"That I do not know," replied Ursus.

"And what will become of our warriors?" asked King Bjorn. "The water from the dam will also flood the five tunnels from Nakota south. Our own warriors will also drown."

"Not if we plan things correctly," said Mac. "If the royal engineers are as talented as I think they are, then only the evil will drown, and your good people will survive. Now, who can tell us whether we have enough water available, and if so, how to open the dam?"

Chapter 62

Redemption and Atonement

Sköll Wolf looked up from the northern plain in the Green Cavern where he had been assigned patrol duty and saw the cave high in the cavern wall where King Bjorn had established his command post.

Since rejoining the wolves at the Green Cavern, Sköll Wolf had suffered demotion and derision. He was dishonored to have been the lone wolf survivor from his entire pack, and as such, his fellow wolves had shunned him. He often wished that he had died with the other wolves. When Koda spared him, the grizzly had no idea that his merciful gesture would lead to such misery.

Sköll Wolf had resolved to either exonerate himself with a spectacular feat of valor in the upcoming battle or die in the attempt. When he spotted King Bjorn in the cave high on the northern wall of the Green Cavern, he saw an opportunity for redemption.

Sköll Wolf had grown up in the mountains on the surface above the Green Cavern, and he knew the subterranean tunnels and caverns well. He knew of a little-used and tiny passage to the same cave King Bjorn had chosen as his command post. The passage was only wide enough for a wolf or smaller animal to crawl through. Sköll Wolf decided that killing King Bjorn would be a feat more than worthy enough to redeem him in the eyes of his fellow wolves.

Sköll Wolf decided to attack while King Bjorn was asleep. He realized that killing the king while he slept might be considered cowardly, but his pride demanded that he survive to savor his redemption.

The night was well advanced before Sköll Wolf stole through the passageways and into the king's presence. His route bypassed the royal guards, and he arrived without raising any alarm. The bedchamber was suffused with starlight courtesy of some overhead shafts and sophisticated optical engineering. The moon was visible and full, and for a moment Sköll Wolf stood in the light and admired his shadow on the ground. A primeval instinct beckoned him to bay at the silver orb in the sky, but then he thought better of giving any advantage to the sleeping king. *I'll howl the cry of the kill once he's dead,* he decided. *The sound will carry well in the cavern, the other wolves will join my cry, and together we will sing of my victory.*

But Sköll Wolf was denied his victory. Out of the shadow beside the king's bed a knife flashed in the moonlight and found its mark in Sköll Wolf's chest. But before he gasped his last, Sköll Wolf tore at the throat of his attacker and locked his jaws in a death grip. Together Sköll Wolf and his assailant fell dead to the ground. The action had been so sudden and silent that King Bjorn never woke up.

The following morning, a royal attendant found Sköll Wolf and Jens dead and cold at the foot of the king's bed. What had happened was obvious, and Jens was lauded as a great hero.

In their final moment of life, neither Jens nor Sköll Wolf could have known how much each had helped the other. Sweet death released them from the sufferings of their guilt. Jens atoned for his sins of omission, and Sköll Wolf was redeemed for surviving alone while his pack was slaughtered.

Chapter 63
Quipu

"The panthers patrol the stairwells in pairs," said Viracocha as Liz and Eirik listened intently. "They walk up and down each stairwell and cross somewhere in the middle. As such, to reach the top without detection, we will need to hide in a mineshaft twice to allow a panther to pass.

"The main problem is not the timing or finding a place to conceal ourselves out of sight of the cats, but our scent. All cats have an especially keen sense of smell, which allows them to hunt in the dark, but these panthers were bred by Malicious in tunnels deep below Popocatépetl and in complete darkness for the first few years of their life. It is said that she released men and women in these tunnels for the panthers to stalk. Had one of these panthers been at the bridge, you would not have crossed. If a panther were given an article of my clothing to smell and told to find me, there would not be a safe place in all Popocatépetl."

"Okay," said Liz, "that means either we find a way to conceal our scent, or we need a diversion to distract the panthers."

"With a diversion, our scent would remain, and when the cats returned, they would quickly be on our trail," said Eirik.

"Something to conceal our scent then," said Liz, "and I know just the thing. Pepper will do nicely."

"Great," agreed Viracocha, who looked excited with this idea. "And I know where to obtain some of the strongest peppers in Popocatépetl."

Viracocha left the house with a promise to return shortly, and true to her word, she was soon back carrying several baskets filled with desiccated orange-red peppers. The basket also contained some fresh, recently picked peppers.

"My father and I have raised peppers since I was a little girl. Each autumn we made jellies and preserves that supplied our family all winter. We experimented with the various species and found that the hottest variety was a long, thin pepper that grew best in the full sun and in rich black soil. The pepper turns from green to orange and finally to bright red. To my people this pepper is known as breath of the volcano. Here in Popocatépetl, the pepper is known as lava tongue."

Liz watched while Viracocha cut the stalks off and then opened up the peppers. She removed the seeds and set them aside. Viracocha had chosen only peppers that had dried for an entire season, but even so, she culled out any that looked remotely fresh. She diced the chosen peppers and then pulverized them in a mortar until they were the consistency of a fine powder. She also ground the seeds in a similar fashion. Within an hour the basket of peppers was transformed into several cups of orange-red powder, which she separated into three piles and placed in tiny gourds, one for each of them. She coated their shoes with a paste she had prepared from the flesh of the ripe peppers.

"Rub the paste onto your hands and fingers, just in case you touch anything on the way up—but don't put your hands near your eyes!"

They completed the task, and Viracocha said, "Now we are ready to fool the panthers."

They waited by the stairwell to the prison cells until one of the two panthers had started back up. Once the panther was sufficiently far ahead, they crept up the stairs and sprinkled some pepper on every step and around the entrance to every mineshaft. When they reached a point just below where they anticipated the panthers would cross, they hid in a mineshaft and waited.

They heard the panther well before the animal walked past the mineshaft. The scent of the pepper was so strong that the panther started to sneeze well before reaching the areas powdered with pepper. They watched from their concealed locations while the cat instinctively searched out the strange scent only to be rewarded with more powder and uncontrolled sneezing. The sneezing became debilitating. Finally, the black beast stopped, sat on her haunches, and tried to lick the powder off her paws. This was a big mistake. Not only did the pepper burn her mouth, but some must have reached her eyes too, which started to water profusely. The panther started to whimper and then bolted down the stairwell, looking to separate herself from whatever had burned her eyes, nose, and mouth. However, her vision was sufficiently affected that in her haste to escape, the normally agile cat careened off the wall of the stairwell and tumbled down a flight of steps before she landed on her feet and continued to speed away.

The trio continued to place pepper up the stairwell and hid again while the other cat passed and was similarly incapacitated by the olfactory assault.

"Liz, your idea worked perfectly," congratulated Eirik.

"Yes. And ironic too," she responded. "We turned their sense of smell, perhaps their greatest asset, into their most profound weakness."

They carried on secure in the knowledge that with the panthers out of commission, they could take their time to conduct a careful search of the upper mineshafts.

The mineshaft where Kate, Liz, and Eirik had been imprisoned was empty, and they did not find any place to access the volcanic crater above. They searched every wall and ceiling carefully. Finding no success, they searched the mineshafts above, but these were similarly empty except for storerooms filled with uniforms and weapons and lacked any obvious way to access Malicious's castle. They returned to the rooms where Kate and Liz had been kept and brainstormed to find a solution.

"There must be a hidden door somewhere," said Eirik, "and the most likely place is on this level. I'm sure my sister would have preferred to come and go without being seen in the elevators or the stairwells, and she came to visit me every day for several months. We must have missed something."

They searched the entire mineshaft again, but to no avail. They had decided to climb back down and were almost back to the stairs when Eirik picked up a piece of string that was on the floor just outside one of the rooms.

"Wonder what this was used for," said Eirik as he showed the string to Liz and Viracocha.

"A quipu!" said Viracocha excitedly. "A message."

"Message?" asked Eirik.

"Yes, before my people learned a written language, we kept records with knots on strings. The size, position, and number of knots tell a story." Viracocha studied the string with great interest. "The message is from my father. He was imprisoned here for sixty days until yesterday, when he was transferred to a mineshaft four levels down. The timeline of the quipu extends for only two more days, until the first day of autumn. Since the string ends at that point, I expect that means my father did not expect to live beyond that date."

"How could he know where he was transferred?" asked Liz.

"I don't know, but the message is clear. Yesterday he made a journey of four knots south, which I presume means down. Perhaps he had been transferred there before and knew of Malicious's plans for him."

"Why down?" asked Eirik. "None of the mineshafts below had any evidence of habitation. They all looked like storage chambers. Wouldn't going up, closer to the crater, make more sense?"

"Perhaps, but that is not what the quipu suggests, and we've already searched all the shafts above. Whether it makes sense or not, we need to follow up on this."

They climbed down to the mineshaft four levels below, where a thorough search revealed nothing except stores of poorly made uniforms.

"What now?" asked Eirik.

"What if the message did mean south, as in the direction, rather than down?" asked Liz. "Eirik found the quipu beside the door to one of the prison cells. As I remember, there were only three more doors along that hall. Maybe there was a fourth door we missed?"

"Worth a check," said Eirik, and back up they climbed.

Unfortunately, the end of the mineshaft was only that. There was some rubble and even a few old tools seemingly left by miners, but no evidence of a door. They searched every crack for evidence of a hidden door but to no avail.

"Too bad," said Eirik, and he stamped a frustrated foot.

"Eirik, do that again," said Liz.

"Do what?"

"Stamp your foot. The ground sounded hollow, didn't it?"

"Yes," said Viracocha. "It did."

They all stamped a few times and confirmed the evidence of a chamber beneath them.

Viracocha ran back to one of the rooms and returned with a bucket of water, which she spilled over the floor. The water leaked away through cracks previously invisible in the dusty floor. A few moments later they found a crude handle that looked more like a rocky protrusion. Lifting the door out of the floor revealed stairs going down to a passageway.

"Thank goodness for your father's message," said Liz. "We never would have found this otherwise."

They climbed down, carefully closed the door, and proceeded to explore the passageway.

Chapter 64

Connor Smells Trouble

When Ian awakened, Connor explained the results of his reconnaissance.

"Sorry about the bats," said Ian. "Why don't you have a sleep while I scout around?"

Connor admitted that he had dozed off and slept almost as much as Ian.

"You are one honest bear," acknowledged Ian. "Most of my friends back home never would have admitted they'd fallen asleep."

As Ian mentioned home, he suddenly realized how estranged he felt from the surface world. His home and work seemed like a foreign land, so far away as to be unreal or a dream, like when you remember an exotic vacation or a posting that in retrospect was so different that you could hardly believe the place existed.

Connor showed Ian the cavern where the bats had roosted and the hole in the ceiling. "That smell is still here but fainter," said Connor.

"I don't smell anything out of the ordinary," replied Ian, "just the usual dampness and the smell of bat guano."

Now refreshed, they made good time, and had they not had to stop for several patrols, they would have done even better. Each patrol was another opportunity to pick up information from the soldiers, who seemed to talk nonstop.

"Couldn't you smell that filth?" asked one of the soldiers. "You know, back there in that cavern."

"Didn't smell a thing," replied another.

"Well, I did, and you'll notice I didn't drink any of the water in that pool either, but you others did, and I'll bet you get sick. Not all the streams are safe. Some have been poisoned by who knows what."

"You worry too much," replied the other. "There were no dead cave rats in that cavern, so the water must have been good."

"That's just it. There were no cave rats, dead or alive. Something lives in that cavern, something that smells putrid."

"Shut up, you men!" yelled an officer. "No more talk of things you can't see and don't exist."

After the patrol left, Connor agreed with the soldier with the keen smell. "The soldier could smell it too. To me it smelled rotten and slimy. He called it putrid. I wonder what it is."

"Don't know," said Ian, "and so long as whatever smells doesn't bother us, I don't much care, but just the same, we better be on our guard."

When they reached the cavern the soldiers had spoken about, the scent was thick enough for even Ian to smell. "Enough to make you sick to your stomach," said Ian. "Let's get out of here. I don't feel like drinking this water either."

They would not have lingered had Connor not seen some strange markings on the floor. "What do you think of these markings?" asked Connor. "Not really tracks. More like something was dragged or pulled along."

They followed a set of parallel lines about two feet across along the perimeter of the cavern until they disappeared into a hole big enough to admit a man.

"The scent is very strong here," said Connor. "I'll bet that whatever makes the smell lives in that hole." Connor leaned forward and put his nose by the entrance to the hole. "Wow, no doubt about it. The smell is coming from that hole."

They didn't stay to investigate further. The smell faded and was soon only an unpleasant memory.

The next cavern they came upon had two exits, both heading roughly south, and neither Connor nor Ian could visualize this intersection on Svein's map or recollect which one to take.

Connor sniffed the air in both tunnels and concluded that one smelled slightly more of men, and they took this direction.

"As long as we smell the enemy, we must be going in the right direction," said Ian. "Thank goodness for your nose. Do all bears smell so well?"

"Absolutely," replied Connor. "There is an old forest saying that attests to the keenness of our sense of smell. When a pine needle falls in the forest, the eagle sees it, the deer hears it, and the bear smells it."

Ian looked down and noticed some beetles and spiders nearby. Insects were common underground but less so with increasing depth. Well before the tunnel had leveled off at the lowest depth, Ian had noticed their absence and was surprised therefore to see them again now.

"How come all of a sudden the insects have returned?" he asked.

Connor shared the surprise but was more pleased than curious. "Some of the beetles are good to eat," he remarked, "but no self-respecting bear would eat a spider. Some of them are poisonous. I can usually tell by their markings, and none of these look dangerous, but we better not touch them all the same."

As they continued, the number of insects grew, and it was soon obvious that they were all going in the opposite direction of Ian and Connor.

"Must be escaping from something," concluded Connor. "Insects are just like mammals; they can sense danger and know enough to escape."

"What kind of danger?" asked Ian.

"No different here than on the surface," responded Connor. "Fire and flood are the worst enemies of living things. But I don't smell smoke, the air temperature doesn't feel warmer, and I don't recollect that we are close enough yet to the river to worry about a flood. I don't know what might be scaring them."

A little farther ahead, they entered a cavern where they found the insects swarming out of a hole in the wall almost identical to the hole they had seen before with the strange draglines leading up to it.

"Just like the bats," observed Connor. "They don't like whatever is in that hole. Let's get going. Curiosity killed the bear."

"Pardon me?" said Ian.

"Just another old grizzly saying," replied Connor. "It means sometimes it doesn't pay to be too curious. I think this is one of those times."

Ian laughed but didn't have the heart to tell Connor that on the surface the same saying referred to cats. They left the cavern but hadn't gone more than a few yards when they heard soldiers coming toward them.

"Quick, Connor, the cavern we just left had some cover," Ian whispered, and they ran back.

The cavern had only one good spot to hide. Ian hid behind a huge stalagmite and motioned to Connor to carry on down the tunnel, where the grizzly quickly found another safe place.

The soldiers did not want to remain in the cavern anymore than Ian and Connor had. "No sense stopping here," said the soldier in charge, "no good water available."

"Is that the only reason?" teased one of the others. "Or are you afraid?"

"I'm no more or less afraid than any man would be in these forsaken tunnels. There is something evil that lurks in the walls of these passages. I can feel it."

"Yes," replied a third soldier. "And sometimes you can smell it."

"So you are afraid," replied the second soldier.

"Yes, and fortunately, I'm in charge, and it might just be that my fear saves your skin as well as mine. Let's move on."

They did move on, but they stopped just short of the place Connor had chosen to hide, and much to his dismay, they decided on a rest stop to eat.

After fifteen minutes, Connor started to get nervous about Ian and weighed the advantages of killing the soldiers against the trouble of hiding their bodies. The patrol numbered only six soldiers, but he decided to wait in case one managed to escape and raise the alarm. *If only I could guarantee they would stay and fight,* thought the big bear.

Finally the patrol left, and none too soon, because by the time Connor reached the cavern, Ian was in dire need of his help.

Once the patrol had left the cavern, Ian expected Connor to emerge from the tunnel any moment. When he didn't, Ian scouted the tunnel and discovered the reason for Connor's delay. Ian was also impatient and considered attacking the patrol, but he rejected this option for the same reason as Connor.

Nothing for it but to wait, thought Ian, who sat on the floor of the cavern and practiced patience. He scanned the cavern and saw that the insects had stopped emerging from the hole in the wall. He also detected the return of the rotten smell, which seemed especially strong.

Suddenly, Ian felt something wet splash against the back of his neck. He put his hand up and wiped a thin blue liquid from his neck.

A moment later, Ian felt dizzy and then collapsed back onto the floor of the cavern. He was on his back and looking up as the most enormous snake he had ever seen slowly emerged from the hole in the wall.

Thin yellow longitudinal bands interrupted the back of a black head, which was the thickness of a husky man. The reptile was covered in a slime that reeked of the same rotten odor that Ian and Connor had detected.

There were no eyes in the triangular head of the snake, which appeared to navigate by smell and touch. A bright red tongue continuously searched the area ahead as the serpent slowly slithered toward Ian. Each time the mouth opened and the tongue lapped ahead, Ian could see a blue venom sac on the floor of the mouth, from which had emerged the spittle that had immobilized him. The snake's nostrils flared as the creature honed in on his helpless prey.

Ian wanted to stand but couldn't. His feet felt like lead weights, and a few seconds later, his legs were as stiff as a statue. His arms still worked, and he flailed them against the ground to try to pull away, but first one and then the other arm froze too. He tried to call out to Connor, but although his mind formed the words, his voice box wouldn't produce the sounds. The paralysis continued to ascend until his eyelids started to droop. The last thing he saw was the snake, with its jaws unhinged, starting to swallow his legs.

By the time Connor arrived, the snake had swallowed half of Ian, which fortunately for the great grizzly, prohibited use of the venom the serpent had used to immobilize Ian.

Connor's claws emerged in an instinctive reflex. He looked for eyes to blind but saw none and instead swiped his claws repeatedly across the head of the serpent, until the skull was visible under the flayed skin. For most animals, that would have ended the fight, but not so for this denizen of the subterranean deep. The snake was many times Connor's length, and in a flash, the serpent coiled its slimy body around the bear and started to squeeze.

Connor knew the ways of northern snakes but had never learned of the mighty constrictors that inhabited the Middle Realm, not that any knowledge might have improved his position. In a similar vein, the serpent had no experience with bears and could not have predicted Connor's exceptional strength.

Connor locked his jaws around the soft under-neck of the hideous python, whose taste was even viler than his smell. Connor squeezed his all until slowly but surely the coils loosened and then grew limp. Still he kept his jaws in a death grip and released them only once he had managed to completely sever the head with his claws.

Connor looked briefly at the dead serpent and wondered if, like the mighty Thor, he had killed a monster of the likes of Jormungand, the Midgard serpent of Norse legend. He had learned of Jormungand while studying with Eirik as a young cub. They had always been eager to learn about the battles with the giants and monsters that inhabited the nine different Norse worlds.

Connor quickly turned his attention to Ian, who had rolled out of the mouth when the snake went limp. Connor was devastated. Ian looked dead. His eyes were closed, and no matter how many times Connor pushed on his chest or turned him over, Ian never moved.

What a strange death, thought Connor, who could find no mortal wound on his friend. Ian did have a few fang wounds, mostly about the legs, but these were neither deep nor in any vital area.

Connor looked at the pendant Zuni had given him. Only a few minutes before the crystal had glowed brightly green in Ian's presence, but now the crystal looked dull. Still, a faint green glint remained, and Connor decided not to give up. He had heard of animals that looked dead and still recovered, and he refused to believe that Ian was gone.

In a manner taught to him by Shabear, Connor opened up the fang wounds and sucked out and then spat away as much of the bitter poison as he could. Into the wound he placed a mixture of ground root of showy aster and the leaves of the broom groundsel, ingredients that he carried in his medicine bundle. He placed the Green Crystal Zuni had given Ian over the largest of the fang marks and bound the wound with a piece of Ian's tunic. Finally, he offered a prayer to the God of All Creatures.

Ian, meanwhile, even though his eyelids were closed and he was unable to open them, was still acutely aware of his surroundings; he still had his senses of hearing, smell, and touch.

Before Connor had arrived, he could smell the disgusting breath of the creature, and he could feel the mouth of the snake as his body was slowly sucked and swallowed. Ian had steeled himself for what he presumed would be a suffocating death.

But then he heard Connor snarl, and a second later, he felt something wet splatter on his face. He could not know, but this was the blood of the serpent. Then he heard Connor's familiar battle roar, followed by the chomping of his mighty jaws as they locked into the flesh, sinew, and bone of the snake's throat.

Soon thereafter, Ian felt the snake's mouth and jaws relax, and had he been able to move, he might have wriggled free. As it was, Ian knew he was free only when his body landed on the ground with a thump.

When Connor cut open the fang marks on Ian's calf, the pain was significant, and he cried out in his mind, but no sound emerged from his lips. Thereafter, Ian felt sleepy, and as Connor chanted the prayer to the God of All Creatures, Ian drifted again into his recurring dream.

This time, however, the red eyes turned into snake eyes, and Ian found himself fighting with the Sword of Olaf against a red tongue that parried and thrust with the same deadly accuracy as the blade of Lord Null. Each time the serpent's mouth opened wide, Ian could see a woman inside, dressed in white and calling to him, and the blue venom sac turned into Kate's blue face. Ian fought the snake back and forth, but neither gained an advantage.

Some children came into his dream, and their laughter and play seemed to distract the serpent. Connor showed up to play the bear in the Siksika autumn thanksgiving ritual. His presence clearly infuriated the snake. The serpent turned away from Ian to attack the grizzly.

Ian chose this moment to swing his sword and severed the deadly tongue from the throat of the snake. The forked tongue wriggled on the ground and changed first into Lord Null and then into a woman dressed in black, both of whom the serpent ate before slithering away.

During the time Ian struggled in his nightmare, Connor explored farther along the tunnel and came upon a kiva. He knew at once by the blue and red bars, the sundog sign, that this was one of the havens described by Zuni, and he brought Ian to the sacred place. Connor sat with his friend, reapplied the poultices to the fang wounds, and changed the crystal Zuni had given Ian to another wound. He then waited and hoped.

Curiously, enemy patrols walked by numerous times, but none looked in, as if they had not noticed the entrance. Just as miraculously, Ian's recurring nightmares abated.

Chapter 65
Engineering Concerns

Ursus persuaded King Bjorn that releasing the water behind the dam would not usher in Ragnarök or the end the world, and the king accepted Mac's plan. The royal engineers made some calculations and concluded that the available water was enough to flood the tunnels and caverns at least as far down as the River Fjorm, and possibly even to Popocatépetl, and that the Green Cavern would be flooded to a depth of about a hundred feet, deep enough to drown the enemy, but not enough to fill the cavern.

"Releasing the water is not the concern," said Olafur, chief of the royal engineers. "Once we create a weakened area in the middle of the dam, the structure will collapse in due course. We can even predict the collapse to within an hour or so. However, it might take up to three days to complete the project."

"By then the battle will have joined," said Shasta.

"Yes," replied Olafur, "and even though our corps of engineers is already working hard on the project, weakening a dam in just the right manner such that it will collapse in a controlled fashion might not be possible in a faster time."

"Our warriors and bears can hold the enemy in the Green Cavern for many days," said Magnus with confidence. "You could take several weeks, and still we would have time."

"Yes," replied Olafur, "but the longer you battle, the more lives will be lost."

"This is true," responded Magnus, "but these lives would similarly be lost without the plan to flood the cavern and tunnels."

"I understand," replied Olafur, "but there are other, more serious problems for us to deal with."

"And these are?" asked Magnus.

"Nakota is downstream from the dam. We have started relocating the Nakota people behind the dam, but the community is large, and to evacuate everyone will take at least two days."

"So, two days is less than the three that you suggest is necessary to weaken the dam. This will not be a problem unless you weaken the dam sooner."

Olafur nodded in agreement but still had a concerned look on his face.

"Is there another problem?" inquired Magnus, a little impatiently.

"Yes, and the last problem is the most serious."

"And that problem is?" asked Magnus.

"Optimally, we would like to control the water and direct the flow into only one or two of the five tunnels so that our warriors can escape. We can accomplish this, but there will be only a short window of time for all our warriors to escape through the three tunnels that can be spared the flow."

"Why is that?" asked Magnus.

"Because," replied Olafur, "as the Green Cavern fills, some of the water will flow back into these three tunnels."

"How long will we have to escape into the tunnels?"

"Only about an hour."

"Is that enough time?"

"No. We have made calculations based on the width of the tunnels, an orderly retreat, and the rate at which we expect the water to rise in the cavern."

"And?" inquired Magnus.

"At best, perhaps a thousand of our warriors will survive."

"So what you are saying is that although the enemy will drown, so will most of our warriors."

"Yes," replied Olafur, "that is the sad reality."

King Bjorn sighed and said again, "Ragnarök."

"What about boats?" asked Mac.

"Boats?" asked Magnus.

"Yes, you were originally a seafaring people. I saw longships on the waters around the Castle of Light. Build boats, and when the cavern fills up, have your men get into the boats. Presuming the cavern does not fill completely and drains downstream in a reasonable period of time, the boats will slowly settle to the ground, and your men will be saved."

"How many boats would be necessary?" asked King Bjorn, who was impressed by yet another original suggestion from Mac.

Olafur did a quick calculation. "At least a hundred," he replied, "but a boat takes months to build, and we have only days."

"Simple rafts will do," suggested Mac.

King Bjorn and the leaders of the clans agreed to the plan. The engineers continued to work on the dam; warriors were sent to surface forests to cut enough tall spruce, fir, and pine to make the necessary rafts; and the armies of the five clans readied themselves for battle.

Chapter 66
So Close

The passageway they had discovered led to a circular stairwell that went both up and down. A platform interrupted the stairwell at every mineshaft.

"Looks like there is a hidden door at every level," said Eirik.

They continued to climb the stairs until they passed the last of the mineshaft platforms. Thereafter the stairwell continued without interruption toward the surface. They climbed for a long time and more than several thousand steps, until they reached a huge platform under what they presumed was Malicious's castle.

"I'm surprised at the lack of security," said Eirik.

"I'm not," replied Viracocha. "When you have the powers of Malicious, ordinary intruders are likely no more than a diversion, like the relationship between a cat and a mouse. Cats tolerate mice in their vicinity all the time."

Eirik didn't like the idea that he was as defenseless as a mouse, but he acknowledged that the analogy was a good one.

"Shush," said Liz, "I hear someone whistling."

They hid in the shadow under the stairwell that continued farther up and waited as the whistling grew louder. Eventually, they heard footsteps on the stairs above. The whistle was curiously different from the typical sound from pursed lips, and though intermittent, the whistle also had a kind of rhythm. As the sound drew closer, they realized that whoever made the whistle also had a game leg and dragged one foot.

They listened as the whistler limped down the stairs and past them. They did not dare come out from under the stairs, and they neither saw the person nor determined the cause of the curious whistle. The platform they had reached seemed to be a storage area and contained many baskets filled with vegetables and fruits, mostly dried, but some fresh.

They waited until the whistling sound had disappeared and then carried on up the stairs. In due course, they reached another landing. At this level, they found rooms secured with locks they could not open. *Could Kate be in one of these rooms?* thought Liz.

Viracocha must have read her thoughts. "I don't think my father or your sister will be in these rooms." She wiped a cobweb from one of the locks and said, "These rooms have not been opened for some time. I expect we will find my father and Kate somewhere in the castle on the surface."

"I wonder how many lower floors there are," said Eirik.

"Whether there are two, twelve, or twenty, the only way we will find out is to climb up," answered Liz, who led them back onto the stairs.

They climbed past several more storage floors, for a total of five, and finally came to a level where there were shuttered windows. But it was nighttime, and no light shone from behind the shutters.

The stairwell emptied into a central foyer with a hallway, with huge double doors that led outside and sweeping stairs that led up to the first of two additional floors, in what appeared to be a house within this larger structure. The house was deathly quiet, and for a moment each looked incredulously at the others, mostly in disbelief that they had come so far without detection.

On the second floor they found rooms that were locked and that might, they thought, be where Kate and Manco Capac were being held. They listened quietly at each door but could hear nothing.

The third floor contained more rooms that were locked and from which no sound could be heard and another wide stairwell up to a top level with a turret. The door to the turret was locked.

"The temple must be in the turret," said Viracocha, "and my father and Kate are likely in rooms on either this floor or the one below."

"If that is true, we have an even chance of picking the right rooms with our first try."

"What if we choose wrong," asked Eirik, "and open up the door to Malicious's bedchamber? We won't get a second chance."

"We have one more day before the autumnal equinox. We could find a place to hide until daylight and observe what happens," said Liz.

"If we split up and choose our places carefully, one of us will likely learn where they are being kept, and tomorrow night we can meet, free Kate and Manco Capac, and all escape together."

"Works for me," said Eirik.

"Yes, this is a good plan," concurred Viracocha.

Chapter 67
Battle of the Green Cavern

The morning of the second day before the equinox found King Bjorn and Magnus looking over the Green Cavern from the command post. They had been up for hours making last-minute decisions about the deployment of their forces. The warriors were chafing to engage the enemy. They awaited only the order to attack from their king.

"Magnus, I need some time alone," King Bjorn said.

Magnus left, and King Bjorn walked to the edge of the cave and looked out over the Green Cavern. The cavern was so vast that he could see the main enemy forces only by the dust they raised far to the south. He could see the buildings where the mining community had lived in the northern half of the cavern. The streets were deserted. The plain that was immediately south of the buildings and that would become the field of battle was mostly empty. There were a few enemy patrols visible, but the majority of the enemy forces were congested far to the south. From the amount of dust in the air, King Bjorn deduced that the enemy was deploying their forces in anticipation of the battle.

Alone with his thoughts, King Bjorn was well aware that a millennia of hard-won growth and the continuation of the five centuries of peace and prosperity depended on the outcome of the battle. The king sighed and spoke aloud to himself. "Is this the Plain of Vigrid foretold by my Nordic ancestors? Is this the plain where the last battle will be fought and lost? Will the flood that we unleash consume not only the wickedness nurtured by my foul daughter but also the good we have accomplished? Are we the last of the Viking race? Is this to be Ragnarök?"

King Bjorn knew that war was necessary, but he also realized that he could not predict the outcome. He had great confidence in his warriors. They had many advantages over the rabble they faced. They were stronger and better trained, they carried top-quality weaponry, and they believed passionately in their cause. One might think that a successful outcome could not be doubted. But the number of enemy soldiers was overwhelming. The latest reports from King Bjorn's scouts indicated that his warriors were outnumbered by more than twenty to one. *Sadly,* he thought, *might often triumphs over right.*

He kneeled and said a prayer to Odin. "Mighty Odin, greatest of gods, the peoples of Asgard are worthy of your support. A thousand years ago, Balder, our first king, refused to accept the Christian god and left Iceland with other like-minded men and women. They left so that they could continue to worship you and the other great gods. By your grace, we have forged a peace with many cultures. We found ways to merge our beliefs with theirs, and we have lived in harmony. Every day, we give thanks to you for your gift of vitality. Today, on behalf of all the people of Asgard, I give thanks to you for the millennia of prosperity you have granted us. If today should be our last, then let us each die with a sword in our hand and meet you in Valhalla. If today should not be our last, then tomorrow we will thank you anew for our continued prosperity."

With that, King Bjorn stood and asked a royal attendant to take a message to Magnus. He thought fondly of Jens, who had died to save him. "Yes," mused the king, "if all our warriors are as brave and devoted as Jens, we will acquit ourselves well on the field of battle." He turned to the attendant. "Tell Magnus to sound the battle horns. Today we will give the enemy a taste of Viking steel and bear claw, and by the by, we will learn if passion and skill can rout a larger force."

A few minutes later, the tunnels resounded with horn blasts, and the clan armies swarmed into the Green Cavern. The movement was so sudden and well orchestrated that the enemy guards and patrols were overwhelmed before any alarm could be raised.

The Inuit clan was the first to carry the battle into the cavern. They met only light resistance and soon crossed the plain and secured the buildings in the center of the mining community. The other armies achieved similar success, and in less than an hour, all the buildings were secure, the armies were positioned to repulse any attack, and the royal engineers had assembled the catapults and started the demolition of the stone buildings to provide missiles for the war machines.

Behind King Bjorn's army, the royal engineers arranged the tall, straight spruce, fir, and pine trunks into patterns that, once secured, would become rafts.

Now mindful of the presence of King Bjorn's army, the enemy soldiers to the south arrayed themselves in battle lines and advanced slowly toward the buildings. The ground shook with the clomping feet of tens of thousands of enemy soldiers. The dust churned up and hung over the oncoming hoard like a gray storm cloud, and the rhythmic drumming of the soldiers' feet sounded like rolls of thunder. For several hours the enemy marched, until finally the blurred mass became visible as individual soldiers. When they stopped, the silence was ominous, and every heart beat faster and louder as if to fill the still void.

As soon as the enemy soldiers were within catapult range, Magnus gave the order for the royal engineers to send volleys of stones into their ranks. A series of pulleys allowed them to send stones as large as a man deep into the lines, where the rocks burst into fragments and decimated the enemy.

Although the catapults wrought havoc in the enemy lines, some of the soldiers survived the aerial assault and renewed their advance. As soon as these soldiers were within range, warriors with bows unleashed a hail of arrows. The sound of the arrows hurtling through the sky heartened Magnus and his warriors. "Odin's wind!" they shouted with each volley.

Those soldiers who escaped both the catapult and the arrows found themselves victim to small companies of bears. Shasta ordered her bear commanders to roar at their loudest as they rushed upon the advancing enemy. Many of the enemy had never seen a bear, and most broke ranks and retreated back into catapult range before the grizzlies had a chance to engage them.

But the enemy regrouped and continued to advance even as the catapults continued to wreak havoc in their ranks. Once in action, the catapults never paused so long as there were stones to hurtle at the enemy. As the buildings were demolished to provide the stones, so did piles of rubble grow among the advancing enemy lines, as if a new city were being built in this more southern location.

"The battle goes well," said Ursus, who watched from the observation post with King Bjorn. "There is mayhem in the enemy ranks. They are running hither and yon without any direction, and all the while, the catapults are burying the rabble in rubble."

Mac was with Magnus on the field of battle. He had asked to help with the construction of the rafts and was positioned in the rear, close to where Magnus had established a command center.

"Mac," said Magnus, "can you see Shasta? She is positioning her bears for a surprise attack on the enemy. Fear will soon reign in their ranks."

Magnus pointed to where Shasta had positioned a dozen bears behind the Kwakiutl forces. "The Kwakiutl warriors have purposely fallen back to give the enemy a false sense of confidence. At a prearranged signal, the Kwakiutl will separate and allow the bears to charge. The enemy has no idea what is in store for them. I cannot imagine a more frightening sight than that of a dozen fearless bears running toward me."

Mac watched while the Kwakiutl fell back in the center and allowed the enemy to flow into the gap. From a position well behind the retreating warriors, Shasta was leading her bears. The bears picked up their pace, and once they reached their full stride, a horn sounded, and the Kwakiutl warriors separated to allow the bears to rush past.

By then, the bears were galloping so fast that many of them often had all four feet off the ground at the same time. The grizzlies ran with their snouts raised, as if they were sniffing the air.

"Why are their snouts up?" asked Mac.

"They're checking for the scent of fear. When a grizzly smells fear, and I expect they do, there is nothing that will stop them."

Mac agreed with Magnus that a dozen half-ton grizzlies running at full speed was an awesome sight, and apparently the enemy agreed as well because almost as soon as the bears were visible, the majority broke ranks and retreated.

They were much too late, however, for bears traveling full tilt into battle. The bears ran over the stragglers and hurled themselves into the fleeing line of the enemy, devastating hundreds of soldiers before Shasta called a halt and allowed Magnus's men to advance and reengage the enemy.

During the day, Shasta led her bears on sortie after sortie into the enemy lines, each with a similar effect.

"Shasta is giving the enemy something different to fear than the jaguars or cruel officers who have whipped them into battle," said King Bjorn. "Let us hope that our advantage continues."

But the enemy remained in disarray for only the first day, and on the morrow, they countered with wave upon wave of soldiers who marched without regard to the stones that burst around them. They all had wide eyes and seemed to focus only on the few feet in front of them. They walked over the slain bodies of other soldiers like a troop of zombies.

Magnus and Shasta had joined King Bjorn and Ursus at the command post for a morning conference. "They know no fear," said Magnus. "They must understand that they are doomed to die and do not care how their lives are lost. They march like the living dead."

"They look drugged," said Ursus. "Likely Malicious has concocted a potion to dispel their fear. Or perhaps she has had them drink *pulque,* which numbs the mind and is said by the priests of the Popocatépetl to confer sacred powers."

"Their toll is great, but there seems a never-ending supply of soldiers. I can't understand the strategy of their officers," said Magnus. "They send their soldiers to certain death and lose fifty for every one of ours. What kind of officer has so little regard for his soldiers?"

"Officers who are frightened more of Malicious than for the lives of their men," replied Shasta, who had yet to lose a single bear.

"Officers who are greedy for Green Crystal," added Ursus.

Notwithstanding their huge losses, battalion after battalion of soldiers emerged from the southern tunnels to replace their dead comrades, and the relentless flow of soldiers started to take a toll on King Bjorn's forces. By the afternoon of the second day, the forces of Asgard were starting to lose ground.

"Our men are tiring," reported Magnus, who had regularly sought counsel with the king and had just returned from the field of battle.

"Send companies of our reserves to relieve the clan armies and allow each soldier food and at least two hours rest," suggested King Bjorn.

"That will work tonight, but what of tomorrow when even the reserves too are tired?" asked Magnus. "The enemy engages us night and day. They have not stopped for even an hour. There are so many enemy dead that their bodies are slowing their advance, but this is only a cold comfort, since the advance continues relentlessly."

"Tomorrow is another day," replied King Bjorn. "Hope springs eternal that the royal engineers will collapse the dam sooner than predicted or that the resolve of the enemy will weaken and our warriors will continue to stand firm against the enemy onslaught."

By evening of the second day, only hours before midnight of the final day before the autumnal equinox, King Bjorn's men were all but spent. On the first day they had lost only one man for every fifty of the enemy; but throughout the second day, they had lost one for ten; and that evening their losses increased to one for five, and still the enemy marched inexorably upon them.

Back on the field of battle, Magnus was a fury; he was everywhere at once. He appeared here and there, shouting encouragement in one place, joining the fray in another, and gathering reinforcements to bolster a weakening line still somewhere else. He was covered in wounds.

Even the bears were weary, but now, while the warriors faltered, they were needed more than ever, and Shasta or Koda led one charge after another that routed the enemy and offered temporary respite to the exhausted clans.

King Bjorn had not slept and received hourly messages from Magnus and Shasta on the battlefield and from the royal engineers at the dam. None of the reports were encouraging. Although the ranks of his warriors were close to breaking, the dam was not. The royal engineers reported that a half day's work was still required. Ursus brought this news to King Bjorn.

"They will not be able to release the water until daybreak on the equinox at the earliest," Ursus reported.

"That may be too late," said King Bjorn. "How long can our warriors continue to fight without rest?"

On the battlefield, Magnus received discouraging news with every messenger. They had lost so many good men that he despaired for the future of Asgard. "Even if we win, will there be enough left to carry on?"

Suddenly, the enemy stopped fighting and regrouped. It was midnight and only hours before dawn on the equinox. Magnus was bleary-eyed with fatigue, but still savvy enough not to be lulled into any false sense of security by this unexplained lapse in battle. He sent messengers for his men to maintain their vigilance and ordered every second man to be sent back to eat, drink, and rest for a precious hour.

Shasta arrived with news that bear scouts had picked up the scent of something foul that was behind the enemy lines and moving toward them.

"What do you mean by foul?" asked Magnus. "What is it that you smell?"

"The smell is like death and decay," said Shasta. "No bear has ever smelled this smell before."

This news was reported to King Bjorn, who had been relieved to see the break in the battle and had hoped this meant the enemy was running out of reserves. *At the very least,* he thought, *for however long the respite lasts, our warriors can rest.*

The enemy did not resume the attack for several hours. For Magnus and Shasta, the blessed time passed very slowly. "The smell grows stronger, and I fear that the delay in the attack must have something to do with the stench," said Shasta.

"Yes," agreed Magnus, "but to me, the rest feels better than the smell seems bad. Whatever it is, I hope it takes its time."

As they spoke, the enemy lines parted, and new soldiers emerged, tall men with helmets and armor that glistened in the green light of the cavern. Their broadswords gleaming at their sides, they marched in the disciplined fashion of a real army. The men formed up in battalions and waited while companies of jaguars took positions at their sides.

The new soldiers positioned themselves just beyond the range of the catapults and shouted taunts at the warriors and bears. They continued to array themselves until it was clear that they outnumbered the remaining warriors in King Bjorn's army by at least ten to one. They stamped their feet in unison, which in the hollow cavern created a sound as deafening as thunder and which was meant to demoralize Magnus's men.

Suddenly there was silence, and the middle of the enemy line parted to allow a creature at least three times as tall as the soldiers to emerge and take a position at the vanguard. The creature stalked back and forth in front of the line, and the enemy soldiers cheered their new champion of terror and destruction

"What is it?" asked Magnus.

"I don't know," replied Shasta, "I have never seen such a creature, but that is the source of the smell; that is what smells like death and decay."

Mac joined them. "The rafts are ready. The royal engineers have done a remarkable job. They are sturdy and seaworthy. They will not tip or sink and can each hold several hundred warriors."

As he spoke, Mac could see that Magnus and Shasta seemed less interested in his report than in what was happening far to the south.

"What's happened?" inquired Mac.

"The enemy has positioned some foul creature to attack us, but the beast is nothing we can recognize," said Magnus.

"Perhaps I can help," said Mac as he removed his binoculars from his pack.

"What are those?" asked Shasta.

"The finest birding optics available," replied Mac. "With these, I can see the tiniest bird at the top of the tallest tree, and the bird looks as if it were only a few feet away. I'm sure we will be able to identify the creature you speak of."

Mac looked through his binoculars and adjusted the focus. "Ouch, what an ugly and vicious-looking creature," said Mac. "I've never seen anything like it. That thing is twice as tall as a bear. From the hip down, the beast is covered in greenish black scales coated in a slimy-looking film."

"The slime must be what smells," said Shasta.

"The creature has a long tail like a lizard. The upper body is pale pink and thickly cobbled like leather. The creature has a small birdlike head. If there are eyes, they must be very small. I see a hooked beak like a vulture and short front limbs with talons."

Magnus nodded, a look of recognition on his face. "What you describe is Hel."

"Hel?" asked Mac.

"The ancient ones knew of this creature. Malicious must have dredged this reptilian monster from the dark depths of the Middle Realm. Though known, Hel is a creature long thought dead. The ancient ones believed that Hel was the caretaker of death. Each of her possessions represented a calamity for our peoples. Her plate represented hunger, her knife famine, her bed sickness, and her bed-hangings misfortune."

Magnus looked dejected. "How can we defeat this hideous creature? I might as soon defeat Odin in hand-to-hand combat."

To Magnus, defeat seemed imminent. He looked out over his warriors and felt their weariness. Each warrior had already fought almost continuously for several days. All were wounded. Now they confronted Hel, a primordial monster, and a fresh and disciplined army that outnumbered them at least five to one.

Shasta was more optimistic. "The body of this monster will yield to our claws and blades the same as the rabble we have routed for the last three days. Clearly this is their last and best, and when we have defeated these soldiers, we shall have won."

"Well said, Shasta," responded Magnus, who straightened up and resumed a determined demeanor.

With that, Shasta ran forward and collected a company of bears to attack the lizard that was now slowly marching on their lines.

The jaguars and the fresh soldiers raced across the plain, and when the two armies met, the sound was riotous.

Again, Magnus was everywhere, and for a while it seemed as if they might break through the enemy lines and gain the upper hand, but several days of nonstop fighting now showed, and it was soon apparent that if Magnus did not call a retreat back into the tunnels, all his warriors would be lost. He sent a messenger to King Bjorn, who agreed with the need to retreat.

When the retreat sounded, Shasta was relieved. *The hellish creature barely bleeds,* she thought as she clawed again and again at the scaly underbelly of the lizard. The bears had not slowed the creature at all, and despite their dexterity, the grizzlies were no match for the crushing tail that swept them away, and their claws were little use against scales like steel.

King Bjorn's warriors never turned and ran. They answered the call to retreat with the same courage and discipline that had sustained them for almost three days on this grim battlefield.

As their ranks closed and they slowly made their way toward the tunnels, King Bjorn appeared with Ursus. "We wanted to be with you," said King Bjorn. "Even if victory has eluded us, honor has not, and I would like to fight beside my warriors and, if needed, die in the cause so many have suffered for."

"Well spoken, King Bjorn," said Magnus.

Although King Bjorn was late in years, he had been an excellent swordsman as a youth, and it was soon apparent that he had not lost his skill. Over the next hour, as the enemy slowly forced them back, King Bjorn fought side by side with each of the clan leaders. Together they showed the pluck and resolve of warriors who might die but whose spirit can never be defeated.

While King Bjorn was fighting with Grettir, a company of wolves attacked the Nakota. Hildolf, the commander of the wolves who had captured the Green Cavern, led the wolves. Hildolf was racing at Grettir, his mouth open in a slavering howl. Grettir's back was to the wolf; she was preoccupied with several enemy soldiers. King Bjorn was too far away to either call a warning or intervene with his sword. He grabbed a lance from a fallen warrior. "By the grace of Odin, allow this javelin to travel like Gungnir, the spear of the one-eyed god, and find its mortal mark." The spear sailed sure and stopped Hildolf dead in the air as he leapt toward the back of Grettir's neck.

Ursus joined Shasta, Koda, and the other bears, and they continued to shore up whichever lines weakened during the retreat.

As they were forced back onto the plain immediately in front of the tunnels, King Bjorn looked over at the rafts. He realized that the dam might break while they were retreating in the tunnels, in which case all the warriors would drown. *The plan was good, but our timing was off. Who can judge what is meant to be? At least we were prepared.*

He turned to Ursus, who was now fighting at his side, and thanked him for a lifetime of friendship. "This is not such a bad way to die, is it, my friend? I would rather die with a sword in my hand than drown in the tunnels. Let us stay here and fight to the last."

"Had we not fought this battle," Ursus said, "the enemy would have secured the dam, and there would have been no hope to defeat this horde of soldiers. This way, if the dam breaks, even if we die, there is still a chance for our people."

King Bjorn thought of Eirik and hoped his son would survive and somehow defeat his evil sister.

Ursus thought of Shabear and Connor and similarly hoped that their mission would succeed. Ursus also thought of Mac and the friendship that had grown between them and was saddened that he would not be able to say good-bye to him.

Just then, a strange sound stirred from the tunnels behind them, followed by a wind that buffeted them. Those closest to the tunnels actually had to lean into the wind to prevent being blown over. A moment later, Mac and a company of royal engineers emerged from one of tunnels, running with the wind.

"To the rafts!" they shouted. "Quickly, to the rafts! The water is coming!"

Chapter 68
Connor's Vigil

Connor knew the signs of death, and although Ian showed some, he did not show them all. So the grizzly still refused to give up and sat hopefully by his friend.

Ian's skin was cool but not cold, and the blood had not pooled in a dependent fashion; the parts of his body closest to the ground had not turned the ghastly blue that signals that the heart has stopped. Similarly, though Ian's pupils were wide and did not move with light, which was usually a reliable sign of death, the eyeballs had neither decompressed nor shriveled into the sticky gel that comes with putrefaction.

Until these signs appear, thought Connor, *I will not give up hope.* He looked at the crystal around his neck, which still had a faint glint of green. *And I won't give up unless the green disappears.*

Connor checked Ian's eyes several times a day, and each time, he expected the eyeball to look deflated, but the eyes continued to stare back blankly, neither definitely dead nor really alive. On the morning of the third day, Connor lifted Ian's eyelid with little hope, but this time he was startled to see the wide black pupil constrict ever so slightly to reveal a tiny rim of blue iris. He checked the crystal and saw that it glowed with a brighter green. Connor realized the spark of life had not vanished.

For Ian, his only respite over the three days had been sleep, which, courtesy of the power of the kiva, was peaceful and free of nightmares. However, his wakeful periods had been terrifying. While awake, he could hear Connor moving about, and whenever his eyelid was lifted, Ian could see the sad eyes of his friend. Knowing that he was alive but helpless was somehow worse than the wakeful visions of the burning red eyes. During those three days, Ian recollected stories he'd heard of men buried alive and realized that some of them must have been true. Clearly there were poisons in the world that mimicked death.

Like Connor, Ian had almost given up hope. He knew that his body was weak from lack of nutrition and stale from stillness. *How long can I survive?* he wondered. *Can I last longer than it takes for the poison to wear off?*

Death focuses a person's attention. Few are afforded the opportunity to reflect with a clear mind while in an indeterminate state between life and death. In this situation it was natural for Ian to think of his life, to try to sum up who he was and what he had accomplished. He realized that he had not accomplished much. True, he was bright and had achieved some academic and professional success, and he was strong and had served his country with distinction in the armed forces. But none of this seemed special. The only aspect of his life that did seem special was Kate and their hopes and dreams to raise a family. Ian had spent most of his adult life studying engineering and applying his skills, but he had never created anything unique. His time in the Canadian Armed Forces could not be called creative. In fact, as a soldier, he was more often a destroyer than a builder. The best that could be said about his military time was that he might have saved some lives. But this was not creative.

Life is a puzzle, thought Ian. *Surely I was meant to place a piece in the great puzzle of life. But so far I can't think of even a small piece that I've contributed.* He tried to think of what he might create if he somehow survived this ordeal, but nothing in his professional world seemed to offer much opportunity. He was an ordinary person and had never really aspired to do anything except his best.

Why then was I born? he wondered. *Why am I here?* Ian thought of his father, whom he had admired, loved, and emulated. *What did my father create?* His father had been a successful psychologist and had helped many people, but he had never discovered anything; he had never published an original idea. *He did create me,* admitted Ian. *Perhaps life is about creating new life.* Ian was reminded again that the only aspect of his life that he considered special was Kate, and he suddenly realized how important their plans to raise a family had been in their courtship. These plans had bound them together in a way that nothing else did. Until now he had never much thought about these plans. Now these plans seemed the most intuitively creative act he had ever considered. He and Kate shared a vision of something greater than either person alone. *That must be the piece of the puzzle that I was meant to place,* Ian concluded.

As he considered the idea that raising a family was *the* creative act of mankind, Ian thought of the concept of creation and found himself thinking of God. *Might it be,* he considered, *that we are here to add to the world that God created by raising a family and doing our best? Yes, that must be it. The answer to the why of life is as simple as that. The answer has to be simple, because that way everyone can add a piece to the great puzzle of life.* Ian thought of Shabear's earlier comment: "Children are the reason why." These thoughts strengthened Ian and filled him with love for Kate. He found himself praying that he and Kate might still live to raise that family.

Ian felt guilty that he should now think of God. *I only turned to God when I found myself facing death.* He was angry with himself for what he presumed was weakness and hypocrisy, but this anger faded quickly. Somehow he knew that God was not angry with him. God was merciful—he knew this—and mercy was the willingness of someone to enter into the chaos of another in the hope of easing their suffering. *I've certainly been suffering, and Lord knows, so has Kate.* He felt better for these thoughts and realized that the feeling was courtesy of a nascent faith that God existed. *I do have faith,* he acknowledged. For the first time, Ian understood: faith was the substance of things hoped for and the evidence of things not seen.

For the three days that Ian spent neither dead nor alive, struggling in his personal limbo, he slept for only a few hours at a time. Each time that he awoke, Ian thanked God, and the spiritual relief that he enjoyed increasingly fortified him. Although his physical strength was clearly ebbing, his emotional energy flowed strong, and in the absence of nightmares, he started to dream pleasant visions. Instead of snakes and sword fights, he dreamt of walking arm-in-arm with Kate in an alpine meadow; instead of shadows with fiery red eyes, he dreamt of orange sunrises with fluffy pink clouds. His faith in God grew with these dreams, as did his resolve to live and to rescue Kate. Even so, whether he lived or died was a decision he now gladly relinquished to God, and if death were to be his fate, then he wanted more than anything else for Kate to live. In this early and innocent relationship with God, he tried to bargain for her life. *Please, God, take me, but let Kate live.* If he had to die without rescuing Kate, then Ian wanted to believe that she would live.

On the third morning, when Connor lifted his eyelid, and Ian's eyes focused ever so slightly, Ian knew he would live, and a tiny tear also emerged from the corner of his eye.

Connor wiped the tear and shouted as if Ian were deaf, "Ian, you're alive! I can't believe it, but you are. Look, the crystal is getting brighter. Don't worry. Everything is going to be all right."

A few hours later, Ian coughed up some vile black phlegm, and thereafter he enjoyed taking a long and overdue deep breath. His breaths were shallow at first because his chest muscles were sore, but each breath was gloriously deeper, and when he finally achieved a full lungful of air, Ian decided the sensation was the greatest he had ever experienced, and he resolved never again to take breathing for granted.

With breathing came the power of speech, and Ian's first words were "thank you." Connor presumed the gratitude was meant for him, and he blushed with embarrassment, but he was only partially correct, for Ian knew that God had played a role, and it was with God as well as Connor that Ian wanted to share his appreciation for the gift of life.

Eating was glorious. After Ian finished some dried berries and nuts, Connor prepared a mixture of the leaves and seashell powder that Zuni had recommended for endurance. Ian chewed the leaves to a pulpy mash and then left the wad in his cheek. Within a few minutes he felt his lips tingle as if they were asleep, and he worried that this might be a sign of a relapse, but the tingling remained limited to his mouth, and rather than feeling sick or tired, Ian felt invigorated—so energized, in fact, that shortly thereafter, he suggested to Connor that they should resume their journey.

"Hold on, Ian. You've been lying like dead for three days. You might feel great now, but some of the serpent's poison might still be lingering. I think we should let you rest another day."

But Ian would hear nothing of delay. He felt impatient, not for his own safety, but for that of Kate. "No, Connor, we must press on. Kate needs me now more than ever. I can feel it."

Ian ran through the tunnels, driven by a sense of urgency he could not explain to Connor. When they came upon enemy patrols, stealth was no longer a concern, and Ian paused only long enough for the Sword of Olaf to scatter or slay the soldiers.

"We must be close to the inland route and the River Fjorm," said Connor. "By my recollection of Svein's map, the tunnel should start to climb soon, and when it does, we will be only a half-day from Popocatépetl."

True to this memory, the tunnel soon started to climb precipitously, and the steepness of the pitch slowed their pace considerably. For Connor, the climb was a minor irritation. His enormous hind legs were designed to run up mountainsides. Even so, Connor found it difficult to keep up with Ian, who seemed driven and pushed himself with a resolve greater than the bear had known in any man.

They reached a high point where the tunnel emerged high up on the wall of a huge cavern. Below, the River Fjorm coursed. The sides of the cavern sloped down and created a subterranean valley illuminated with the orange glow of the parallel lava flow that gave the River Fjorm its name. Enemy ships on the river seemed like toys pulling their way upstream. Ian and Connor could see enemy patrols along the trails and between them and the river.

"We'll have to fight our way down," said Ian, "but at the bottom, perhaps we can commandeer a boat and row downstream to Popocatépetl."

The enemy patrols might not be much of a problem, thought Connor, *but commandeering an enemy boat filled with hundreds of soldiers seems a bit more than a bear and a man can achieve.* When he looked over at Ian to question the boat idea, he saw a crazed look on his friend's face. Ian's eyes were wide, and they darted furtively up and down the valley. He was chewing the leaves in his mouth with an unnatural vigor.

As Connor watched, Ian put another plug of leaves in his cheek, and Connor wondered whether Ian had taken too much of the endurance herb.

"I'm feeling a bit tired," said Connor. "How about you, Ian? Why don't we rest here for a while and catch our breath. That was a long climb."

Ian gave Connor his medicine bag. "Take some of the leaves, and you won't need a rest," he said as he put yet another plug in his mouth.

Connor took the bag and placed it in his pouch. Ian didn't seem to notice. *Just as well,* thought Connor, who concluded that the herb was the likely explanation for Ian's irrational behavior.

Ian had just started down the slope when Connor heard a faint and far-off rumble. "Hold on, Ian. I hear something."

Ian perked his ears up but apparently heard nothing and continued down.

"No, wait, Ian. There is something coming from the north. Sounds like a waterfall."

"That's crazy," said Ian, who continued down the slope.

Connor felt the ground tremble under his hind paws. Suddenly, hundreds of cave rats emerged from every nook and cranny and started to scurry south. "Ian, the ground is moving. Something bad is happening."

By then the ground was shaking, and Ian stopped and looked around. Small stones had started to roll down the walls, followed by progressively bigger rocks.

Connor shouted to Ian to take cover behind a huge boulder, and together they watched as the cavern crumbled around them. The soldiers on the path below were crushed or swept screaming down to the cavern floor.

The noise Connor had originally heard was lost in the din created by the disintegrating walls of the cavern. But the cause of the first noise was soon apparent when water started to flood down the subterranean valley.

Cracks started to appear in the ground around them and the walls of the cavern above. Some of the cracks spouted scalding hot air.

"Time to seek higher ground," said Connor and they climbed higher up in the cavern.

Cracks continued to appear, and several times, Connor's long arms had to pull Ian across a widening split that otherwise would have separated them.

They reached a ledge, but without climbing equipment, they could go no higher. While the cavern walls were collapsing, the valley slowly filled with hissing steam as the water encroached upon and finally covered the lava.

"Nowhere to run and nowhere to hide," said Ian. "I can't believe we got this close to Popocatépetl only to be stopped by an earthquake."

More cracks appeared, and steam exploded from the depths and rained tiny droplets of boiling water that stung their faces and hands.

"What's it to be?" asked Ian. "Boiled alive up here, crushed in the moving ground below, or drown in the rising River Fjorm?"

A huge crack opened behind them, and they jumped aside just before a puff of yellow smoke burst out.

"Sulfur!" cried Connor. "Lava will be soon to follow. Quick, Ian, get out the protective buffalo hide that my grandfather gave you."

Ian didn't need to be asked a second time. He retrieved the medicine bundle from his pack, emptied the contents of the bundle back into his pack, and spread the hide out on the rumbling ground. The smoke gave way to molten rock only a second before they pulled the hide securely around and over them.

A huge crevasse opened up below, and they felt themselves sliding onto a wave of lava. The lava carried them slowly down toward the river. The waves undulated over the rocks and debris, and Ian felt as if they were surfing in slow motion. The thickness of the waves was conveyed through the buffalo hide, and Connor imagined they were sailing on a molten sea of honey. Both Connor and Ian were grateful that the spirit of the white buffalo protected them.

The hide was like a leather kiva, a protected place, immune from the natural disaster that was enveloping the valley. They could hear the cavern continue to collapse around them, and they could detect the faint whiff of sulfur, but the searing heat of flowing inferno never penetrated their haven. They were in a spiritual cocoon, insulated from the death and destruction that surrounded them.

Their descent slowed, and finally they stopped. They heard a popping and cracking noise, and then they felt themselves rising, as if they were floating upward. The sulfur smell disappeared, and they could feel something buffeting the sides of the hide, like gusts of wind. The sounds of cracking rock also disappeared and were replaced by a lapping noise.

A few minutes later, they felt themselves bump into something solid. Every few moments, something pushed them, and they heard a scraping noise.

"I hear voices," whispered Ian.

"And I smell men," said Connor.

They opened the buffalo hide to find themselves on the western shore of the River Fjorm. Popocatépetl was in front of them, and soldiers were streaming south, trampling one another in their attempt to enter the tunnels or board ships that could be rowed away. The bodies of enemy soldiers and jaguars were floating everywhere. The water was very warm, but safe to touch, and they waded to shore.

Chapter 69
Waiting Game

Eirik found a place on the second floor to observe the daytime activities in Malicious's crater-top castle. He had a clear view of both rooms on the second floor and the stairwell leading up to the third floor. Courtesy of the clothes from Queen Odontocetes, he blended into the shadows behind a woodpile in a stone storage area beside a fireplace and spent a safe day unobserved.

Throughout the day he saw only one person. Soon after dawn, a whistle awoke him. Eirik recognized the whistle instantly as that of the person who had limped down the stairs the previous night. Eirik watched while a man unlocked the door to one of the two rooms on the second floor and took in some food. The man was old and very thin; he had a withered leg and seemed breathless. The man came back out of the room a minute later and relocked the door. When he walked by, Eirik saw the cause of the whistle. The man had a large hole in the middle of his neck, just above the breastbone. Every time the man inhaled, the hole closed sufficiently to cause the whistle. His face was a mess of scar tissue. He looked as if his face had once been on fire. Only one nostril was open, and his lips had fused except for a tiny hole sufficient only for a straw. Eirik wondered what might have caused this accident. The fate of the tiny kitten came to mind, and he shuddered at the thought.

That morning, the old man opened both rooms on the east side of the second floor, and during the course of the day, he took three meals into each room. During the middle of the morning, he took fresh linens into each room. He closed and locked the doors each time he went in and out, and Eirik could not see or hear what went on in the rooms. *Kate and Macho Capac must be in those rooms,* he decided.

Eirik never saw his sister and doubted that she was in either of the two rooms the old man had entered. On the other hand, he did hear someone walking on the third floor in the turret room, and he presumed the steps were those of Malicious.

Viracocha found a place to hide on the first floor. Without the chameleon clothes that helped Eirik and Liz, she needed an exceptionally well-concealed spot and found one inside an empty tall wicker basket. She could see well through the gaps in the weave.

The first floor was a busy place. Several servants prepared food in the kitchen, which was delivered upstairs by the limping man with the scarred face. She was heartened when she saw that the evening meals contained papaya, which was a favorite of her father. The first two meals of the day were fairly sparse affairs compared to the evening meal, which, though still not lavish, was sumptuous by comparison.

Liz had found a hiding place outside the castle. An open window had allowed her to climb down to the floor of the crater, where she explored around the castle.

The castle was at the southern end of a crater that extended for a half-mile or so to the north and had an east-west diameter at least as long. Although the volcano was largely dormant, there was a lot of steam escaping from vents scattered around the crater.

The prevailing winds sometimes separated the clouds that surrounded the cone, and periodically Liz could see the moon, which was full, and also some stars. She saw the Big and Little Dippers and remembered the Indian legends her father had taught her about Great and Little Bear. She hoped her father was safe.

There was only the one entrance to the castle, but she doubted anyone ever used the door because apart from the castle, there were no other buildings in the crater. Unless someone was interested in studying dormant volcanoes, the landscape was bleak and uninviting.

Whenever the moon appeared, the landscape seemed to come alive with silver light, and shadows suddenly appeared behind lava sculptures that had been formed from past eruptions. The first time this happened, Liz jumped as if some strange creatures had suddenly come upon her.

While the moon shone, the exquisite colors of the landscape became visible, and she enjoyed the vivid greens and yellows from the minerals around the lips of craters and the shiny ground-glass appearance of obsidian deposits scattered on the surface.

She came upon a full-length plate of obsidian and saw her moonlit figure in the mirrorlike finish. She removed the scarf that covered her hair. Her image was blurred, but even so, she could see that her hair was tangled and that her skin had smudges of grime, *picked up who knows where,* she thought. Ordinarily Liz was fastidious about her appearance. She thought of Eirik as she looked at her unkempt appearance and wondered whether he found her attractive. She thought he might. He had certainly been attentive to her. She laughed to think of how he had seemed a bit jealous when Xbalanque had paid such attention to her.

If we escape from this hellhole, thought Liz, *I hope I meet someone as polite, good-looking, and courageous as Eirik. Too bad I'm not a princess.*

That made her think of her father, who had called her Princess for years until she reached grade school and she had asked him to stop. "We're not royalty, Dad, and I'm not a princess." She remembered how her dad had laughed. *Well, anyway,* she thought, *those days seem an eternity away,* and she walked away from the image and the thoughts.

While Liz walked about in the intermittent moonlight, mostly lost in her thoughts, she came upon two tall lumps of lava that stood like sentries to the east of the castle. Once, when the moon shone brightly, she thought she saw one of the lumps move. She froze and remained motionless while she studied the lumps. She waited until the moonlight had come and gone several times, and there had been no further change in the tall lumps, before she resumed her walk. *The shadows must have played tricks on my eyes,* she thought. *And I'm a bit edgy too,* she admitted, *and nervous fear makes you see things differently.*

Liz found a spot to the east of the castle that offered an excellent view of the rooms as well as the turret. The largest window of the turret looked east and would be perfect for the ritual, she thought. There were lots of great places that offered excellent concealment and still a good view of the castle, and Liz eventually found one that also offered a more-comfortable-than-not place to wait. She closed her eyes and was soon asleep.

She awoke with hot sun full in her face. When she opened her eyes, the brilliant sunshine momentarily blinded her. Her eyes closed in an automatic reflex, and against her closed eyelids she saw two orange-red orbs, which made her think of Malicious. She knew the orbs were only the image of the sun, but all the same, her heart raced. When she reopened her eyes, the sun was behind some clouds. She blinked away her sleep and let her eyes adjust. A brisk southerly wind was scattering a sparse cloud cover, and as the sun peeked in and out, cloud shadows raced across the surface of the crater. A dense cloud bank finally blew over, and when the sun disappeared, the metallic blue sheen of the rocks changed to a dismal gray. *Just like the sea,* she thought, *when the water turns from a brilliant blue to a chilly gray.*

Liz was hungry and drank some of the chocolate drink that Itzamna had given her. She felt immediately invigorated from the few drops she took.

Before she had fallen asleep, the curtains in the windows of the second- and first-story chambers had been drawn, but now they were open. There were no curtains in the turret window. She scanned the windows every few minutes but never saw anyone look out.

During that day, Liz developed a routine in which she checked the windows, then the front door, and then the surrounding area every five minutes or so. The plan was methodical but the results boring. No one came in or out of the castle, and no one ever appeared at the windows.

She had been daydreaming and had almost dozed off when she heard a flutter. She looked up just in time to see a raven land on the sill of the turret window and then hop into the room. She looked into the sky but didn't see anymore ravens and decided to try to creep closer to the castle, in the hope that she might hear something.

"I wouldn't do that if I were you," said a voice behind her.

Liz froze, and in the next second she felt woozy, as if she might pass out, but she steadied herself and turned to confront the voice. As she turned, she picked up a piece of lava, lifted the rock over her head, and stood poised, ready to throw, but she could not see anybody.

"Who are you?" whispered Liz, who looked all around and still saw nothing. "Where are you? Show yourself."

"Shush," said the voice, which now seemed to be coming from a tall lump of lava about twenty yards away. "If you don't keep quiet, that nasty woman in the turret will hear you, and then we'll all be in big trouble."

"And that rock won't help," said a second voice that came from a second tall lump a few yards away from the first.

Liz couldn't believe it; the voices really were coming from the two tall lumps of lava that had looked like sentries in the moonlight the night before, the same lumps that she thought might have moved.

"I saw you two last night," she whispered. "Who are you, or rather, what are you?"

"If you saw us last night, why didn't you say hello?"

"Well, I wasn't sure. Why didn't you say hello?"

"We were asleep," said one of the lumps.

"Just as well," said the other, "sound carries more at night, and Malicious might have woken up and heard you. Now, please sit back down. We've come to help. Queen Odontocetes sent us."

At the mention of Queen Odontocetes, Liz relaxed.

"We will move ever so little, and you should be able to see us. We are magnificent frigate birds, and I am much better-looking than my brother, and that way you should be able to tell us apart."

"Oh, please," said the second voice. "You know I'm better-looking and that I will find a mate long before you."

"Hush, I'm older than you by at least a few minutes, and it is unseemly for you to show any criticism of your older brother."

"Let the woman decide," said the second voice. "The female of any species would find me better-looking."

"Mother didn't find you better-looking," said the first.

"Or you either," said the second. "She never played favorites. But I'm sure she thought I was the most handsome."

"She did not. She thought I was."

"No, she didn't."

"Yes, she did.

"Didn't."

"Did."

"Didn't."

"Did."

"Didn't."

"Did."

"Didn't."

"Did."

"Stop, stop!" whispered Liz impatiently. "I thought the idea was to be quiet."

"Quite right, and we had better be extra special quiet now."

"Didn't," said the first bird.

"You always have to have the last word, don't you?"

"I do not."

"You do."
"Do not."
"Do."
"Do not."
"Do."
"Do not."
"Do."

"Please!" said Liz. "Can you two please grow up? This is a serious situation. Lives are at stake."

The two birds dropped their heads and looked sheepish, which was as difficult to accomplish for magnificent frigate birds as it was for bears.

Liz studied the two massive birds. She had seen many soaring high over the Florida and Caribbean coastlines, where against the sun, their sharply bent wings and stark-silhouetted shape had made them look like pterodactyls, but she had never seen one up close. They were at least five feet tall, and when one of them briefly opened his wings, she saw that the span was at least eight feet. Both birds were entirely glossy black except for a strip of pink skin that ran down the throat. The pink strip was the gular pouch, which would be inflated during mating season to attract females. Each bird's bill had a sharp and dangerous-looking hook.

"How long have you been here?" asked Liz.

"Three lonely days," replied the older bird.

"We arrived early," advised the younger bird. "We didn't really want to come. You see, it's the autumn social season, and we didn't want to miss out, so we thought that if we came early, we might be able to leave early too, but that hasn't been the case. My name is Magnificens, and this is my much older brother Fregata."

"Anyway, when we get back, I'm sure I'll find a beautiful mate with a gorgeous white throat patch, and Fregata will be left lonely for another season. It's his own fault, really. He's too haughty for the good-looking birds."

"Shush," said Liz. "You two have no idea how serious this is. Didn't Queen Odontocetes tell you?"

They settled down and explained what they had seen since their arrival. From the descriptions, Liz concluded that Kate and Manco Capac were in the second-floor rooms on the east side.

"They are both tied up, but they look well. We have been waiting for you to come and rescue them," said Magnificens.

"I expect they have too," said Fregata.

"Who?" questioned Magnificens, who opened his eyes wide and stared at his brother.

"The prisoners," said Fregata, who gave his brother a don't-be-so-stupid look.

"The prisoners what?" said Magnificens, impatiently.

"Oh, for heaven's sake, Magnificens, how can you be so obtuse? The prisoners have been waiting to be rescued," exclaimed Fregata with an exasperated sigh. Fregata leaned toward Liz and added, "You see, I'm not only better-looking but smarter. Mother knew that too."

"That isn't true, and you know it," responded Magnificens.

"Is too."

"Isn't."

"Is."

"Isn't."

"Is."

"Isn't."

"Is."

"Isn't."

"Is."

"Isn't."

Liz threw her hands in the air, rolled her eyes up, and walked away, hoping that without an audience, they would stop bickering.

Chapter 70

Stairwell to Hell

Popocatépetl was in pandemonium. Soldiers were scurrying in every direction, and their discarded weapons cluttered the ground. Connor watched while the captain of a boat tried to force soldiers to disembark. The soldiers mutinied, threw the captain overboard, and started rowing south. Other soldiers on other ships emulated this prudent course of action, and boat after boat disappeared from the docks.

Some of the soldiers were less concerned for their immediate welfare and were looting the stores and homes in Popocatépetl. The townspeople resisted, and fighting was evident in many streets.

"What a strange feeling," said Connor. "We're surrounded by the enemy but not threatened."

"We might not be, but Kate is, and she's here—I can feel it. We must find her right away," said Ian, who continued to feel a sense of urgency he could not put into words.

Connor had no reason to doubt Ian's word. The great bear looked around, but no place seemed like a good place to start. "Where might she be?" said Connor.

"I don't know, and if we don't find out soon, we might be too late. Minutes feel precious." The city was filled with hundreds of buildings, but none seemed a likely place for Kate to be imprisoned. "I don't think she's in the city," said Ian.

"What about the mineshafts?" offered Connor.

Ian looked up and saw that the cavern walls were honeycombed with mineshafts. He tried to count the stairwells and stopped when he reached twenty.

"That must be were she is, but which stairwell do we take? And which shaft do we follow?" asked Ian, whose voice cracked with desperation. "We just don't have time to search them all." Ian paused to think. "Which shaft, which shaft?" he repeated over and over as he scanned the walls for some clue. "Where would I make the entrance to my lair if I were Malicious?" he wondered aloud.

Men were pouring out of the mineshafts, and most of the stairwells were clogged with soldiers.

"We couldn't climb up those stairs even if we wanted to," said Connor. "They are filled with soldiers trying to get down."

"That's it," said Ian. "Look for stairwells without men. The men who are protecting Malicious will not be running away."

They identified three stairwells with little or no activity, all in the southwest corner of the cavern.

"We need to take one of those stairwells," said Ian, "but which one?"

Seconds seemed like minutes and minutes like hours as Ian puzzled over the decision. He knew that if he waited too long, Kate might die. He also knew that if he chose the wrong stairwell, the outcome would be the same.

"Which stairwell?" he cried out and grabbed a soldier running past. "Which stairwell leads to Malicious? Do you know?" he demanded.

The soldier babbled incoherently, and Ian set him free. Ian grabbed another soldier, this time an officer, but the man knew nothing of Malicious.

"Who can tell me?" shouted Ian. He looked up toward the ceiling and shouted again, as if imploring something in the air to answer.

And something did. Ian saw a solitary raven flying over the city. "Connor, watch that raven," said Ian.

They started running toward the southwest corner of the city and watched the raven enter the third mineshaft through the middle of the three inactive stairwells, at the top.

"That's the one!" cried Ian, who was sprinting through the streets and bowling over anyone who happened in their way.

When they reached the road that ran along the cavern wall, they saw a platoon of panthers in the distance, headed in the same direction. The great cats were walking in formation, seemingly oblivious to the soldiers pouring out of the stairwells and fleeing toward the docks.

Ian stopped short when he saw that two panthers guarded the stairwell, one on either side of the entrance. The great cats sat on their haunches; one calmly licked a paw, and the other played with his tail.

"We are definitely on the right track," remarked Connor. "The pendant Zuni gave me has started to glow red. That Lord Null fellow must be close by."

"Good," said Ian as he looked down the road. He saw that the panther platoon was still some distance away and not immediately available to reinforce the two cats in front of them. "Now or never," he said. He looked at Connor and motioned with his eyes for the great bear to attack the panther on the right.

But before they could attack, the two panthers simultaneously pricked up their ears as if they had heard something and immediately turned and ran up the stairwell.

Ian and Connor followed close on the heels of the cats, but just as Connor stepped onto the landing of the stairwell, he glanced back toward the panther platoon and saw that the great cats were now running in their direction. He turned to face them.

"Come on, Connor," Ian called down, "we can't waste any time."

"No, I'll stay here. Unless I'm mistaken, the other cats mean to follow us up the stairs, and I'd just as well fight them on the ground, with my back to the stairs. Keep going, Ian; Kate needs you. Don't look back and don't worry. I can handle a few cats, and I'll join you soon."

Connor knew about cats common to the northern mountains. He'd seen cougars and lynx many times. None had ever been known to attack a grizzly. Simply put, cats were no match for a bear. But these panthers were a different breed. They were bigger and faster and did not look as if they feared anything.

No worry, thought Connor, *in these close quarters, they can only attack one or maybe two at a time, and I have four sets of claws.*

The panthers were closing fast, and Connor released his claws one at a time and admired them for what they were: natural blades connected to massive arms and a body with the strength of ten men and, he was sure, more than a few cats. "Let them come," he growled.

The first panther lunged at his eyes, but Connor was prepared and parried the cat's outstretched claws with a swipe of his left paw and then brought his right paw up under the abdomen of the panther. The cat whimpered once and was dead when Connor threw him back to his comrades. When another cat met a similar fate, the panthers paused and circled about on the ground, now leery of Connor's claws.

Connor counted more than twenty cats and was pleased he had eaten well that morning. *No bear likes to fight on an empty stomach,* he thought.

Suddenly, the cats pricked up their ears, all at the same time, as if they had heard a call, and their calm stalking changed to frenzied pacing, and they started to snap at one another.

The panthers started to run at Connor and turn away at the last moment. Periodically a cat would turn too late and suffer a nasty slice courtesy of the claws on Connor's feet. They kept this up without pause, and Connor knew they were testing him. The panthers were hoping that he would tire of the attacks and let his guard down. Two panthers sat waiting, one on either side, for any mistake Connor might make.

Well, thought Connor, *who am I to disappoint these cats?* He feigned a stumble with the next lunge, and sure enough, the two panthers leapt at him at the same time, but Connor was ready. He blinded the first cat with a claw swipe to the eyes and pushed the panther out of the stairwell. He caught the other cat behind the ears with a blow that all but severed the head.

The remaining cats grew more frenzied and threw caution to the wind. One after another, they jumped forward, hoping to overwhelm Connor.

Connor learned that the blinding tactic was a good one and soon established a fighting rhythm that suited the situation. Blinded, the cats always brought their front paws to their eyes, and this exposed their soft neck and belly. At the start, Connor blinded each cat with a right forepaw sideswipe, followed this with a left forepaw uppercut, and then kicked the body away with whichever hind foot was convenient. The landing was soon slippery with panther blood. After every second or third cat, Connor changed the paw he used to blind so that they could not anticipate his rhythm. They never really had a chance.

But despite their collective lack of success, the panthers never gave up and continued to attack until only two remained. The final cats seemed reluctant to attack and instead circled slowly back and forth in front of the stairwell.

Connor had a few scratches but was neither tired nor even winded. He had spent a fair amount of time dealing with the panther platoon, and he desperately wanted to catch up with Ian, who he thought might need his help, but he didn't like to leave two panthers who might turn up at a less opportune time.

"Don't you cats have a death wish like your friends?" he taunted.

They didn't answer, and Connor had no idea whether they could understand him. He taunted them again, and still they circled.

Connor didn't want to leave the strategic advantage of the stairwell, so he backed up the stairs and hoped to draw the panthers in where they would fight, but they did not follow him. He climbed all the way up to the first mineshaft and looked down to see the panthers still circling the entrance. It bothered him to leave the cats, but his growing sense that Ian needed his help convinced him to leave, and Connor continued up the stairwell. He kept his ears and nose alert for the soft patter of panther paws or the smell of their panting breath.

Chapter 71
Water, Water, Everywhere

King Bjorn's warriors and bears raced to the rafts, which they reached just as the water started to empty into the cavern. The enemy did not understand at first and thought King Bjorn's army was finally giving up and running scared back to the tunnels.

The royal engineers had placed the rafts toward the sides of the cavern and clear of the tunnel entrances. The side locations did not obstruct movement of the warriors in and out of the cavern and also protected the rafts from the surge of water that eventually exploded into the Green Cavern like a tidal wave.

At first the water was merely a trickle, but the flow increased rapidly to a gush, and this turned into a thick horizontal column of water that shot out for half a mile and swept the advancing enemy back to the southernmost part of the Green Cavern.

The cavern filled rapidly, and the rafts rose higher and higher in the cavern, until much to everyone's relief, the water level reached a peak and stabilized.

Olafur, the chief engineer, who had maintained a relaxed manner throughout, explained that air in the cavern and lack of any outlet on the ceiling would limit the level the water could rise to about a hundred yards. "Once we reach the summit of the swell, the water level will remain steady until the majority of the water from the dam has dissipated. Thereafter, we will float in safety until the amount of water rushing into the cavern at the north end is less than the amount that drains into the southern tunnels. Then the water level will slowly fall."

"Well, Olafur, it was easy for you to stay relaxed," said Magnus. "But for those of us who don't understand science and math, the water seemed to be rising pretty fast, and the ceiling didn't seem that far away when we stopped going up."

The mood had lightened considerably compared to how they'd felt during the retreat on the battlefield. Warriors and bears congratulated one another on surviving and tried not to think of their brave comrades who had died in the cause.

Shasta and Magnus shared a raft and took turns telling battle stories while the rafts floated in lazy circles and moved slowly toward the south, carried by the same current that flooded inexorably south toward Popocatépetl.

While Shasta was describing her attempts to defeat Hel, the lizard-like bird monster, a huge pocket of air bubbled up to the surface with a popping sound. The released air smelled putrid.

"That smelled like a belch from Hel, the creature you were fighting," said Magnus. "The last I saw, you were underneath the foul creature."

"Yes, the creature was a formidable adversary. Slow and dumb, but very strong. The hide was like rock. My claws never once penetrated the thick scales. The only other animal I know with a hide so tough is a turtle."

"Hmm. I hope that creature isn't related to a turtle. Turtles can swim," said Magnus.

The idea that the creature might be swimming below them was disquieting, and for a few minutes, every set of eyes on the raft scanned the surface of the water for signs of the creature, but only the rafts were visible.

"The creature was too heavy to swim," said Shasta. "Those front paws were made to rip and tear, not to paddle."

In quick succession, five other bubbles belched forth with the smell of decay, each smaller than the last.

"I don't think any beast can hold its breath longer than that," offered Magnus.

"I agree," said Shasta. "Foul as it was, to my nose that last belch had the sweet smell of victory."

Magnus laughed.

Chapter 72
Null and Void

The panthers bounded up the stairs ten at a time and soon disappeared ahead of Ian, who although much slower, continued to push his body as fast as possible. When he reached the third mineshaft from the top, he paused and listened lest the panthers be waiting in the shadowed lee of the entrance, but he heard no sound.

He searched each room, but they were all empty, and when he reached the end of the shaft, a trap door in the floor was conveniently open and beckoned him.

Again he paused to listen for the sounds of an ambush, but he heard none and climbed down and then resumed running down the passage, toward where he knew Kate would be. The dread that hung over Ian was huge, but his love for Kate was strong.

He reached the stairwell and heard the sounds of soldiers below but silence above, and he correctly deduced that his rendezvous with Malicious would be at the top of the stairs. Candles lit the stairs, which Ian took two at a time as he hurried as fast as his legs would carry him.

His legs felt like rubber, and several times, even though he hated to, he had to stop and rest. His heart was pounding, as much from anxiousness as from exertion and perhaps, he realized, also from the effects of the leaves he had constantly chewed. The leaves had improved his strength, but the cost of this enhancement was edginess. Even so, he reached into his pouch for the medicine bag and was disappointed to find it gone.

Connor must still have it, he realized, and for a moment he was irritated with his friend, but the next second, he felt bad about the unkind thought. *No, I was crazy on that mountain, and the leaves had much to do with my insanity. But for Connor, I would have tried to slash my way onto a boat and never would have made it this far. No, Connor was right,* Ian acknowledged. *And I wish he were with me.*

When Ian reached the first of the lower storage floors, he paused to look around but found only baskets of vegetables. He was on his way to the next stairwell when he heard steps on the stairs above.

"You're too late; she's dead," said a voice from the stairs. "But don't worry—you can join her in death." The man laughed.

Ian recognized the voice as that of the tall person in his nightmare, the one Zuni had called Lord Null, and he realized that finally his nightmare had become reality. Now he would fight the man with the ruby-hilted sword for real.

Each of Lord Null's steps sounded like a shuffle, as if he were dragging his feet over the rock steps. The steps sounded lackadaisical, as if Lord Null was neither hesitating nor in a rush to reach Ian.

"Come on!" shouted Ian. "Don't dawdle. I've been waiting to meet you in person." Ian looked around as he waited, and for the first time he realized that the central stairwell was like a cliff. Suddenly he felt as if he were falling, as if the situation had conditioned this response, but he pushed the sensation away and called out again to Lord Null. "Kate is alive, or you would not be here. It is you who will die. Prepare yourself."

Lord Null climbed nonchalantly down and off the stairs, and for the first time Ian saw him in the flesh. He was at least a half-foot taller than Ian, and his height and longer arms were certainly an advantage in a sword fight, but he was thin, so thin that his ribs showed. *Still,* thought Ian, *it appears he has a sinewy strength about him.*

Lord Null drew his sword, clasped both hands below the hilt, and started to carve slow figure-of-eight motions through the air, always keeping the hilt and the rubies visible to Ian.

Ian found himself drawn to the rubies, and for an almost-fatal second, he was mesmerized and walked toward Lord Null without raising his sword.

Lord Null could not resist a snide laugh, which broke Ian's hypnotic concentration on the rubies. Ian jumped back just in time, as Lord Null's broadsword ripped through his leather tunic but missed his flesh. A moment later, the Sword of Olaf flashed bright in Ian's right hand while his dagger gleamed in his left, and once again, he was the seasoned warrior who had vanquished more than one hundred enemy soldiers in the ambush outside of Siksika.

"You are a dead man!" cried Ian as he launched a furious attack that drove Lord Null toward the stairwell.

Lord Null took a position on the other side of the stairwell, and over this tiny abyss they glared at each other.

"Fight me if you are a man," cried Ian, "and feel the steel of Olaf."

Lord Null backed away from the stairwell, and Ian followed him, lunging with his sword and slashing with his knife. Lord Null continued to back up until his back was against the wall of the room. Then with a haughty look, Lord Null began taunting Ian.

"Do you really think you are a swordsman?" asked Lord Null. With that the bald-headed fiend swept his sword back and forth, and in so doing, he forced Ian to the edge of the stairwell in as many seconds as Ian had taken in minutes to push Lord Null to the wall.

The display of power was awesome. Ian was tottering on the edge of the stairwell and only a hair's breadth away from falling. He started to sweat and felt his knees momentarily buckle.

Lord Null laughed mockingly, spread his legs for greater purchase, and with both hands, raised his sword above his head for the kill.

Just as the sword fell, Ian rolled under the swing and through Lord Null's legs. He thrust his dagger deep into Lord Null's groin and scrambled onto his feet. Lord Null never cried out, but he did stagger as he turned, and that was enough of an opportunity for Ian to swing the Sword of Olaf down in a mighty cut that opened up the fiend from shoulder to leg. The force of the blow was sufficient to send Lord Null over the edge and down the stairwell.

Ian lost no time. He raced up the stairs to the next level, where he found the locked rooms. He paused just long enough to convince himself the rooms were empty and then ran back toward the stairwell. Just as he was preparing to start up the stairs, he heard some steps and a voice above. He paused, not wanting to believe his ears.

"You're too late; she's dead," said the voice. "But don't worry—you can join her in death." And again, there was the laugh.

When Lord Null appeared, Ian was in denial. "No, I just killed you. You're not real. Go away." Ian had been witness to so many surreal images, nightmares, and wakeful visions that he was prepared to believe that Lord Null was a figment of his imagination. Sadly, he was wrong.

"My blade is real enough," said Lord Null as he drew the great broadsword with the rubies on the hilt. "Quite real. Come feel the steel for yourself," he taunted.

Ian was in a fury, and he foolishly exposed himself to a slash from Lord Null that cut open his thigh.

"That real enough for you?" sneered Lord Null.

"You are either some foul magic or a twin of the man who just found out how real my sword was," jibed Ian.

Ian and Lord Null fought back and forth without either giving or taking advantage. Ian's thigh wound was only a scratch, but it burned, and he wondered whether Lord Null's sword had been dipped in some foul poison.

Ian noticed that Lord Null preferred to slash from left to right and that for a fraction of a second, while the broadsword was at the acme of the swing, his arms were in front of his face. In that moment, Lord Null's eyes were covered.

This was the only advantage that Ian required. The next time Lord Null's arms were at the summit of his swing, the Sword of Olaf found its mark between the prominent ribs on the left side of his chest. Lord Null staggered with the blow. Blood gushed down Ian's sword, and as he withdrew the Sword of Olaf, Ian heard a rush of air as Lord Null's lungs emptied. He watched as the nightmarish fiend slumped to the ground by the stairwell.

Ian kicked the gurgling body into the stairwell and hurried up to the next level, where he was disappointed but not surprised to hear steps coming down and the now familiar litany of Lord Null.

"You're too late; she's dead."

Ian did not care whether it was magic or triplets that he fought. He only cared to identify the mortal weakness in this twice-killed specter.

"I've killed you twice, and the Sword of Olaf hungers for another taste of your black blood," cried Ian as he carried the fight to Lord Null.

They parried back and forth for minutes that passed quickly, but Ian knew that this might as well be taking forever for Kate, who was trapped somewhere and might die for this delay.

Lord Null played a defensive game, as if he knew that for Ian time was a greater enemy than his sword. With each passing minute, the rage that burned inside Ian grew larger until this powerful emotion exploded. "You cannot kill me. You lack both the strength and the courage!" cried Ian as he lunged forward.

The hilt of the Sword of Olaf locked with that of Lord Null, and in that instant, Ian thrust his dagger into the heart of his enemy and watched while Lord Null gasped his last and fell backward into the stairwell.

Ian was on the stairs in a flash, and at the next landing he did not pause to wait for a fourth fiend to appear but instead continued up and met Lord Null coming down.

Lord Null had not expected to meet Ian coming up, and he never had a chance to draw his broadsword in the cramped circular stairway. Ian left him choking on his own blood through two mortal knife wounds in his chest and throat and sprinted past him onto the main floor of the castle.

Ian could hear fighting upstairs and wondered which of King Bjorn's men could have reached the castle before him, but he was grateful for the sound of a potential ally.

Moonlight shone into the castle, and Ian realized it was nighttime. *How long has it been since I lost my sense of night and day?* he wondered.

Ian heard a scream from somewhere above and realized the cry was Kate's. He rushed onto the stairs, but halfway up, he heard the laugh.

"You're too late; she'll soon be dead," Lord Null taunted.

Ian's nemesis was standing on the castle's second-floor landing and in front of a door that led up to a third floor. Ian heard sounds of fighting and shouting coming from the third floor and realized that this was where he would find Kate.

"No," said Ian, "I'm early. You're the one who's late. Too late to save the other four who found out that the Sword of Olaf metes out a justice you cannot fight. You're too late to stop me, but you're not too late to die."

Ian climbed the stairs in a bound and squared off with Lord Null. "I don't know what kind of creature sired you five skinny hellhounds, but you are not human, and no man will mourn your passing. Prepare to meet your death." Ian attacked Lord Null with a vengeance honed on the bodies of the prior four.

Ian slashed and thrust, parried and cut, but could not find an advantage. This version of Lord Null looked the same but was stronger and more agile and cut Ian twice in the first few minutes of their swordplay.

Ian tried to maneuver Lord Null away from the stairwell that led up to the third floor, but the man stood his ground like an immovable stone. Try as he might, Ian could not get around him, and each time he heard a scream or something crash upstairs, his sense of urgency increased. Desperation reigned on the second-floor landing, and Ian felt stymied at his every turn.

A bloodcurdling scream came from the floor above. "Noooo!" responded an unfamiliar voice from the same room. A crashing sound and another scream followed. Ian could not be sure whether the voice was Kate's.

There was a clatter from downstairs, and Ian was relieved to see Connor bounding up the stairs. The pendant around his neck glowed red. His presence clearly affected Lord Null, who for the first time looked unnerved.

"Time for your departure," said Ian, who closed on Lord Null from the left as Connor did the same from the right. Just before Ian lunged at Lord Null, he glanced at Connor and then at the stairwell, and the great bear understood.

Ian drew Lord Null a step away from the stairs, which was all that was needed for Connor, who was up the stairs in a flash. With a mighty roar that shook the castle, Connor burst into the turret room.

For a minute, Lord Null and Ian fought like rabid dogs, and neither gained the upper hand. Even so, Ian felt relieved. Connor had related the defining dream he'd experienced on his vision quest. If Malicious could be defeated, Ian trusted that Connor was the bear to accomplish the task.

Connor had obviously made his presence known upstairs. The roof shook, and at times it sounded as if the walls might collapse. Ian wished Lord Null would let his guard down for just a moment so that he might gain the advantage, deal a mortal blow, and then support Connor upstairs.

Suddenly, there was stillness from upstairs, and in that instant, Lord Null seemed to lose his strength. *Either that,* thought Ian, *or somehow I've doubled mine.* Ian pushed his advantage, and much to his surprise, Lord Null turned tail and retreated down the stairs.

Ian ran upstairs. The stillness was ominous, and he was hesitant to open the door.

Chapter 73
Trapped Outside

Liz, Eirik, and Viracocha met as arranged just before midnight on the eve of the autumnal equinox and shared what they had learned.

Liz had hoped that they would be able to climb up to the windows, enter the rooms, untie Kate and Manco Capac, and escape before Malicious was the wiser. Unfortunately, the windows were covered at night with heavy wooden doors that were locked from the inside. They also tried to break into the rooms from inside, but the locks were secure, and they decided not to risk any noise that might wake Malicious.

"Surprise is still our ally," said Viracocha. "Malicious does not know we are here. There are three of us and only one of her. Unless there are soldiers in the castle that we have not seen, we should be able to rescue Kate and my father when the doors are opened in the morning, before Malicious has a chance to carry out the ritual."

"Malicious is not prone to overconfidence or poor planning," said Eirik. "We should not underestimate her powers, even alone. And we must remember never to make eye contact with her."

They slept in fits and starts that night, each trying to rest but each also too preoccupied with thinking of what might happen on the morrow.

An hour before dawn, the whistling servant opened the front doors of the castle and walked outside. Liz decided to slip outside and share their plans with the frigate bird brothers in case they might be able to help. Based on what she had witnessed the previous day, they seemed too hopeless to help, but still, she thought, Queen Odontocetes had sent them.

A wind was blowing, and even within the protected lee of the crater, Liz could feel a chill. The clouds had been thick all night; they seemed to cling to the cone like an obnoxious piece of gum on the sole of a shoe. A breeze came up, and courtesy of this wind, the clouds started to move, leaving the morning sky periodically visible. The light from the moon and the stars peeked in and out and created, if only fleetingly, an eerie landscape with flickering light and moving shadows.

Liz knew the frigate birds would be in the same spot, and it did not take her long to negotiate her way through the creepy grounds around the castle. The clouds parted as Liz came from behind a lava outcrop, and the moonlight gave her a clear view of the spot where she anticipated she would find the frigate birds.

She stopped short when she saw two large red circles reflecting the flitting moonlight. *Malicious,* she thought. But as she froze, terrified that surely the ghastly eyes had seen her, Liz heard the voices of the frigate birds.

"My mating pouch is much more handsome than yours. Wait until the next moonbeam shines and see for yourself. Mine has a rich velvety look that is most attractive."

"Your pouch is only a faded facsimile of mine, and mine is bigger than yours. Size counts, you know," said Fregata with a haughty air.

Much to Liz's relief, what she'd thought were red eyes were the inflated gular pouches of the frigate birds.

"Shush. You birds are incorrigible," said Liz as she approached. "Don't you ever stop arguing?"

They both looked down like little boys caught with their hand in a cookie jar. Liz explained the plans to the frigate birds, and they agreed to provide support as necessary.

The whistling servant returned from wherever he had walked and arrived at the castle door just before Liz. Much to Liz's dismay, he locked the door from the inside. After a quick survey of the windows on the main floor, Liz realized she was locked out of the castle. She went back to commiserate with the frigate birds.

Magnificens checked all the upper windows and returned to report that only the turret window was open. "We could fly you up to that window," suggested Magnificens.

"You might need to if I can't find another way in by dawn," replied Liz, crestfallen that she was trapped outside.

Chapter 74
Malicious Hears Bad News

When Liz did not return, Eirik and Viracocha worried that something had gone awry.

"There has been no alarm. Most likely she was locked out when the servant returned," surmised Eirik. "Let's open the doors."

This was a reasonable plan, but suddenly the second floor became a busy place. The door to the turret opened, and they heard someone walking down the circular stairs. The clicks of Malicious's metal-toed shoes were unmistakable.

"My sister," said Eirik, and he and Viracocha slipped behind a huge chest and watched.

As Malicious arrived on the second-story landing, a raven fluttered up from the ground floor and landed on her arm.

"Alfred, my pet, thank you for coming on this special day. What a sweet raven you are." She stroked the iridescent feathers on his nape. "Now, what news have you for Mother?" said Malicious, and she looked Alfred full in the eyes.

Eirik watched while his sister's eyes grew wide and pale pink with horror and then shrank to a burning crimson rage. Malicious threw her arms up and shrieked, and Alfred took that opportunity to fly into the turret room.

"No!" shrieked Malicious. "This cannot be so. My armies are in disarray and fleeing south? What happened to cause this?" she shouted to herself.

The next moment, Malicious was miraculously calm again. The transition from composed to shrieking and back to composed again in the space of a few seconds was disquieting to watch. Both Eirik and Viracocha realized her fuse was short and erratic.

Malicious turned and walked toward the rooms on the east side. While she walked, she talked to herself, just barely loud enough for Eirik or Viracocha to hear.

"No matter, the ritual will strengthen my power and give courage to my armies. Once I hold the hearts of the prophesied one's sister and the Inca king in my hand, and I thrust them still beating into the first sunlight of dawn, my powers will be invincible."

Malicious opened one of the chambers, went in, and locked the door behind her. Nothing happened for several minutes, during which time both Eirik and Viracocha fidgeted impatiently.

"Shall we rush her when she comes out or wait until she opens up the other door?" asked Viracocha.

Eirik wished Liz were with them. She seemed able to resist his sister's power. Without her, their chances would be lessened. *Even so,* he thought, *my sister cannot best me physically, and if I can avoid her eyes, I can defeat her.*

He turned to Viracocha. "No, we should go up to the turret room and wait until both your father and Kate are together in the room. Malicious will never expect an attack from within her own personal chamber."

Chapter 75
Outside Wanting In

Liz looked at the turret window and froze. On the sill, looking around at the ground, as if searching, was the raven. A moment later the raven took off and headed for a break in the cloud cover.

"That raven is mine," said Magnificens.

"Okay," said Fregata. "But make sure you don't fly in front of the window. And if that pale woman sees you, remember—don't look into her eyes."

With that Liz heard a whoosh, and the next moment, she saw the magnificent frigate bird take off and circle high in the sky and into the clouds. A few minutes later, he returned with Alfred struggling in his beak. Magnificens set Alfred down but held the raven's tail feathers firmly under his black foot to prevent him from escaping.

Alfred had a look that evolved from outrage to terror and finally settled into a practiced humility. His initial outrage at being treated so rudely on the doorstep of the princess quickly changed to terror when he realized the frigate birds might just decide to kill him, and that thought engendered humility as a survival posture.

"Cheeky raven," said Magnificens. "He pleaded with me to let him go. He says his name is Alfred and that he is Malicious's chief messenger raven. While in my beak he never shut up. He tried to tell me that he was related to some important ravens of days gone by. If you ask me, he's just a small black bird, and we should kill him."

Alfred squawked at these words. "No, please, I can help you. You'll see. I don't like Malicious. She treats me terribly. I can't count the number of times she has caused me to lose flight control and then laughed as she watched me careen off the walls of the crater. I'll do anything you ask. Please don't hurt me."

The frigate birds looked at Liz for guidance. "He seems harmless enough right now, but I suggest that we bind his beak shut and tie his legs to a large rock. Who knows? Perhaps before this day is over, he just might serve a useful purpose. I don't really trust him, but I don't doubt that he has been mistreated by Malicious and that he has a grudge to bear against her. If he has the chance to get even, he might prove a useful ally. The enemy of an enemy is a potential friend."

Chapter 76
Human Sacrifice

The turret room that Eirik and Viracocha entered was clearly a reservoir of evil. Two stone tables dominated the room. One was carved from black lava rock, and its surface was inlaid with a red crystal that sparkled like ruby. This table was proximal to a fireplace and was cluttered with baskets, gourds, and vials that contained seeds and powders. A carved jade mortar and pestle were surrounded by a variety of dried plants and dead animal parts. A light brown powder was visible in the mortar and on the surface of the pestle. A calendar stone was prominently displayed on a pedestal table.

The other table was immediately in front of the eastern-facing window and had been carved from a single block of obsidian. The glass-like surface reflected a shadowy moon and stars, and the silver light imparted an eerie feeling to the chamber.

A ladder led up to a tiny attic that offered an unobstructed view of the room, and Eirik and Viracocha chose this location to hide in wait for Malicious's return. This tiny alcove was strewn with treasures. Viracocha found gold masks and jade jaguars from her homeland and similar articles she identified as Mayan or Aztec. Eirik identified silver ornaments, glass beads, and an amber amulet, all possessions of his mother. He also found a leather bag filled with grizzly bear claws. "I don't want to know how she got these," he said. Eirik noticed the calendar stone on the pedestal. "What do you think that is for?" he asked Viracocha.

"The circular stone records the passing of time. Aztec and Mayan priests use the stone to decide on when to make a sacrifice, or to plant crops, or to wage war. They also use the stone for divination and prediction." Viracocha picked up a human skull inscribed with runes. "Can you decipher this?" she asked.

Eirik looked carefully at the skull. The runes were colored red. "I know about this skull. This is a charm. The runes invoke Odin to give protection against sickness of the mind. This charm was given to my father soon after Malicious was born. The woman who offered the charm was skilled in *seiður,* a traditional Norse magic, and called herself a clairvoyant. The woman had a vision on the day Malicious was born and made three predictions. She told my father that the pallor of Malicious's skin would be equaled only by the blackness of her heart. She also said that the sun would paradoxically be both a friend and a foe to Malicious."

"And the third prediction?" asked Viracocha.

"She told my father that there was not enough Green Crystal in the world to cure the evil that resided in Malicious's soul. My father didn't believe the woman and banished her from the Castle of Light."

"Too bad," said Viracocha. "I wonder what happened to the woman."

Eirik and Viracocha also found armor and weapons from the Southern Realm, presumably those of the southern warlords who had decided not to support Malicious.

"The sword of a vanquished warrior has great power," said Viracocha, and she selected one for herself.

Eirik found a sword that was from his father's personal armory. "This sword was meant to be mine," Eirik said indignantly. "I was to wear this ancient blade during my coronation. This blade belonged to King Balder and was forged from metals mined from Hekla, the Icelandic volcano. The sword disappeared at the time my mother died."

Eirik next found the crown worn by his mother on the day she married his father. "I loved my mother. I could talk with her about anything, and she was always there for me. I really miss her," said Eirik as he held the crown and relived old memories.

While he considered the crown and the memories, the look on his face changed from maudlin to sad to angry. For the first time, Eirik felt the full extent of Malicious's depravity. Suddenly he realized that his sister had certainly been responsible for his mother's death. The sadness was overwhelming, and he struggled to make some sense of all the emotions that welled up within. But anger soon predominated over pity, and but for Viracocha, he might have rushed downstairs to immediately confront Malicious.

"No, not yet, Eirik," Viracocha said when she saw his agitation building. "Wait your time. When both Kate and my father are in the same room, and hopefully when Liz arrives, we will strike together."

Eirik held the ancient Sword of Balder and waited. His breaths were slow and deep, and Viracocha saw the unmistakable flash of rage in his eyes. *The look might not be handsome,* thought Viracocha, *but under the circumstances, his demeanor is very practical.*

They heard steps on the staircase, and first Malicious and then the whistling servant entered, the former leading an obviously drugged Kate and the latter a sleepy Manco Capac. The servant set the Inca king in a chair while Malicious placed Kate on the top of the obsidian table.

"I will take care of my sister," whispered Eirik, and they would have seized this opportunity to carry out their plan had the two panthers not bounded into the room.

"Ah, there you are," said Malicious, who walked over and rubbed the cats fondly under the neck and down their sleek black abdomens. "These treats will soon be yours," she said, "but their hearts will be mine."

One of the cats looked up to the attic and sniffed, but only for a second as Eirik and Viracocha shrank into the shadows.

The panthers were a major complication, and they were losing precious time to indecision. By the time Eirik looked down again, Kate had been secured to the table, Manco Capac was tied to the chair, and the servant was leaving and closing the door behind him.

Malicious locked the door behind the departing servant, and the sound of whistling faded down the stairs. Malicious gave Manco Capac a drink of something, and he immediately looked more alert. Manco Capac looked noble and defiant. Kate remained sleeping on the obsidian alter. Her body had been painted blue according to the custom necessary for a sacrificial victim.

"You might snatch the life from our bodies, but our spirits will live on, and eventually you will succumb to the greater power of good," said Manco Capac. "Your spirit will never soar after death. Our death is a beginning, but your death will be an end, and mark my words, it will come soon."

"Well spoken, Manco Capac," scoffed Malicious. "I can see why so many of your people listened to you."

Malicious busied herself with some instruments on the lava-rock table and then looked over at Manco Capac. "Those of your people who resisted joining our cause have already started the new beginning that you speak of. I had everyone in Cusco killed. I had to make an example of your defiance."

Manco Capac slumped at this news. He had been abducted in the middle of the night and had no knowledge of the extent of the atrocities committed against his people. "Even Viracocha?" he asked, his voice breaking.

"Everyone was killed. No one escaped," she said, laughing.

Manco Capac tried to stifle his sobs but could not. Viracocha moved as if to rush down to him, but Eirik held her back. He held her hand with a tender firmness that said, "No, not yet," and he mouthed, "I'm sorry."

Malicious busied herself with some powders on the lava-rock table. There was lightness to her step, and she smiled happily. She had always enjoyed the prelude to killing. "Patience, Manco Capac," mocked Malicious. "I know you would like me to put you out of your misery, but the prophesied one's sister must be first. Too bad her sister is not here. I had hoped to make this a triple ceremony."

Manco Capac struggled to break free from his bonds but slumped back into the chair when he realized the bonds were too tight.

Eirik saw the faint glow of dawn through the window and knew that the sun might break over the crater any moment. Malicious moved immediately below the stairs to retrieve something from a basket. Viracocha touched Eirik on his arm. They both understood this had to be the moment.

Eirik and Viracocha leapt down from the attic rapidly and quietly, but their movement was enough to alert the panthers, who in one bound landed between the would-be rescuers and Malicious.

Malicious turned quickly, and before the panthers could attack, she motioned for them to stand down. "Eirik," she hissed, "so you survived. Very clever, little brother. And you decided to attend the ceremony after all. You seem to have recovered from your sleeping sickness. I'm so glad."

Manco Capac's eyes brightened with the sight of his daughter, and he pulled himself forward, straining to break his bonds with the strength that comes from a king and father who dearly loves his daughter and sees hope at last.

Malicious looked around the room and then back at Eirik. "Ah, you are thinking that this doesn't look like the setting for a wedding ceremony. Well, it's all a matter of perspective, or of faith for those who have a god. Do you believe in God, Eirik?" She looked him full in the eyes.

Eirik stumbled, and his sword drooped in his hand. The tip clanged on the floor.

"Eirik, don't look at her eyes!" shouted Viracocha. "Eirik, look at me," she implored.

Eirik broke eye contact with Malicious and looked at Viracocha. Both hands tightened around the handle of the sword, and in a flash he swung the sword up and around and sliced at the neck of the closest panther, but the agile cat was too quick for this maneuver.

Viracocha hurried toward her father, but the second panther blocked her way. Eirik and Viracocha scrambled to parry the sharp claws of the cats and soon found themselves backed into corners of the room. They were no match for the deadly cats. They were trapped at the mercy of Malicious.

But with a nod from Malicious, the panthers backed off and stood still. "Aren't my panthers perfect?" said Malicious. "They have you cornered like mice. I could let them play with you, but for now, I'd like you to watch as I perform the ancient Inca war ritual.

"Viracocha, dear. How nice of you to join us. We were just speaking of you. Not well of you, mind you—in fact, I thought you were dead. Proves the adage, doesn't it? If you want a job done, you need to do it yourself. All in good time, but first things first. You especially should enjoy this demonstration. I learned the ritual from the priest who betrayed your father to me. I found him in the Coricancha, the Temple of the Sun in Cusco. He spoke kindly of you. The first time I practiced the ritual, I used the priest. He didn't seem to appreciate the irony."

"You are a vile and evil person," exclaimed Viracocha, "and not fit to be a princess. You will never be a real Queen or reign over an enlightened people. No, Malicious, you might enslave and rule by terror, but you will never be noble."

"My, my, Viracocha. That seems an especially haughty position to take from one princess to another. And here I thought you might thank me for killing your father. You have no brother and upon his death will be queen, if only for a few minutes. It's not too late to see the light, or rather, should I say, embrace the darkness. Why don't you join me? I'm looking for someone to rule the Southern Realm for me. Tell you what—if you kill your father, I'll let you be queen."

"I'd rather die. I'll serve the gods of the overworld before I ever reign with a monster from the underworld."

A commotion erupted on the second floor below, and Eirik and Viracocha could hear the clang of swords. They were heartened to think that an enemy of Malicious, and therefore a friend, was fighting below.

Liz, thought Eirik, but this made little sense since she was not familiar with weapons, and the sounds below spoke for an excellent swordsperson. Who was the warrior who had come to their aid?

Dawn broke over the crater wall, and a beam of sunlight appeared below Kate's blue feet and started to creep up between her legs. A white crystal in the window focused the sun into a broad beam about the width of a hand. The sun reached the white dress that covered Kate to her ankles, and the bright light crept up the center of the dress and was soon at her knees. Malicious waved a vial in front of Kate's nose, and she immediately opened her eyes but at first was just barely awake. She looked confused.

Malicious had an obsidian knife in her right hand, and both her arms were outstretched above Kate's chest. She chanted something in a tongue unknown to anyone else in the room. Kate raised her head a bit and looked over at Viracocha. She smiled and asked innocently, "Do you know where Ian is?"

Malicious turned to the fireplace and threw some powder into the embers. A pungent smell suffused the room. Malicious continued to chant. The smell caused Kate to sneeze, and this seemed to wake her somewhat. She looked around and for the first time seemed to grasp what was going on.

Malicious picked a spine from the maguey cactus and pricked her own ear lobe. She raised the bloody needle into the sunlight. "Accept my blood first," she chanted. As the sunbeam reached Kate's abdomen, Malicious brought both her hands together around the knife and stood poised with the sacrificial instrument mere feet above Kate's chest. The cadence of her chant changed. The words grew louder and more staccato. Kate looked frightened and started to wriggle in an effort to escape her bonds.

The light continued to creep up toward Kate's chest, and Eirik realized that when the light reached the level of her heart, his sister meant to thrust the dagger into Kate's chest and remove her beating heart. "Nooooo!" shouted Eirik.

Kate screamed. Manco Capac struggled and managed to tip over his chair, which fell with a crash. But Malicious was oblivious to all these sounds. A sick smile emerged as she intoned the last few words of her chant.

Kate's eyes had been fixed on the obsidian knife, but after her initial scream of fear, she composed herself and looked over at Eirik and then Viracocha and smiled a thank-you for trying. Then she looked at Malicious and tried to fathom her evilness, but she couldn't. She resigned herself to death and prayed for Ian, Liz, and her father.

Malicious looked sadistically down at Kate and gloated with anticipation, but before she could thrust the knife down, the entire room shook with a thunder-like growl, and the door burst open.

The blast of Connor's entry was sufficient to stagger Malicious, and she dropped the obsidian knife on the floor. Malicious quickly retrieved the knife. The sun was now over Kate's heart, and Malicious raised the knife for the second time. Kate lost her composure and screamed again. Viracocha gasped. Malicious seethed.

For Connor, time slowed to a crawl. He had watched the obsidian knife slowly tumble toward the floor. He was aware of the panthers on either side of the room and Malicious in front of him. The panther guarding Viracocha to his left moved first and lunged at Connor. The great grizzly turned and positioned the claws of his left paw to sweep up and meet the soft exposed neck of the cat. As soon as he felt the claws rip through the throat, Connor continued to turn in a clockwise circle and brought his left paw up and around in an arc to meet the other panther, who, as the grizzly had anticipated, lunged at him a split second after the first. By then, his left paw had gained momentum, and the lunging panther was torn in two.

While the panthers were distracted, both Viracocha and Eirik rushed Malicious. Eirik knocked the knife from his sister's hand a second before Viracocha tackled her about the legs. Malicious fell, cursing, with both Viracocha and her brother on top of her. The obsidian knife shattered on the floor.

With a strength that neither Viracocha nor Eirik could have predicted, Malicious pushed them away and in a flash was standing over Kate. She drew a dagger from inside her robe. The sun was now on Kate's neck, and Malicious would have slit her throat, but again Connor's protective paw intervened.

The move was quick enough to protect Kate, but the blade sliced through Connor's right paw, and blood spurted around the room. Connor managed a backhanded uppercut with his left paw and cuffed Malicious to the floor.

When Malicious looked up, the sun had passed over Kate's head and disappeared out of sight above the window. Realizing that the crucial moment had been lost, Malicious moved quickly toward the window ledge and made a high-pitched sound. A moment later, two vultures appeared on the windowsill. They were huge, at least four or five feet tall with a wingspan of about eight feet. Their orange facial skin, white bill, red neck, and black feathers identified them as condors. Their ugly naked heads and piercing red eyes made them especially suited to be servants of Malicious. Eirik watched while his sister climbed between the two condors, who flew off with Malicious clinging to their shoulders.

Viracocha rushed to her father, Eirik to the window, and Connor to Kate's side. Connor released Kate's bonds just as Ian rushed into the room.

"Kate, my beloved Kate! Thank God." Ian ran into her arms and sobbed tears of joy onto her shoulder.

Chapter 77
Malicious's Escape

Liz felt helpless. When she heard a woman's scream, she knew the plaintive call was her sister's. She rushed over to where the frigate birds were standing and found them arguing as usual, albeit in whispered tones, this time about who was tallest.

"You are not taller, never have been, never will be. You wear your feathers fluffed up to give the appearance of tallness, when in fact you are not," whispered Magnificens.

"That is a bald-faced lie," retorted Fregata, who snickered with the comment. His use of the word "bald" had been purposeful. Magnificens's feathers on the crown of his head were showing an early tendency to thinning, and Fregata knew that his brother was very sensitive on this point.

By the time Liz reached the birds, she was in no mood to listen to further quarrelling. "You two are incorrigible," she interrupted. "Please be quiet and listen. Didn't you hear the scream? Did Queen Odontocetes send along two deaf and dumb dodos, or did she send two courageous magnificent frigate birds? It better be the latter."

The frigate bird brothers both shrank their heads into their bodies and looked to the side, obviously embarrassed.

"Which of you is going to fly me up to the window?"

Magnificens looked at Fregata, who looked at Magnificens, and then they both stepped forward at once. They were so eager that they collided and both fell over.

Liz sighed. "Good gracious! Conceited, deaf, and clumsy. This is altogether too much."

Magnificens was the first to stand back up, and Liz immediately jumped onto his back. Sadly, however, the big bird could not take off. Try as he might, he couldn't.

"I'm sorry. Perhaps my brother is stronger," admitted Magnificens in a surprising gesture of humility. However, this was not the case. Fregata too was unable to fly with Liz on his back.

By this time, Liz had heard another scream and then the sounds of fighting. The roar that resounded from the turret was unmistakably that of a bear, and this gave Liz some hope that her sister was not alone and at the mercy of Malicious.

"Okay, so neither of you can fly with me on your back. Well, maybe you need a bit of a run to gain momentum before you try to lift off."

"Good idea," the frigate birds said in unison, as only twins might.

Liz pointed out a clearing where the birds could run for at least thirty yards without any obstacle.

"I know this will work," said Magnificens, with a tone that seemed more designed to convince himself than full of real confidence. The frigate bird crouched so that Liz could put her hands around his shoulders. The big bird started to hop and then run. After a few yards he started to beat his wings up and down, but all to no avail. He could not fly with Liz on his shoulders.

"With your arms over my shoulders, I can't lift my wings high enough to take off," he explained. "Fregata can try, but unless his arms are much stronger than mine, I doubt he will fare better than I."

Fregata did try but also failed. Just as Liz slipped off Fregata's back, two condors swooped down to the window ledge of the turret. A second later, they flew away, with Malicious carried between them.

"That's how we should have done it!" exclaimed the frigate bird brothers, in almost choreographed unison.

Eirik appeared at the window. "Liz!" he cried out. "Kate is okay. Don't let Malicious escape!"

Liz looked at the frigate bird brothers. "This must be what Queen Odontocetes sent you for. Stop those condors."

Magnificens and Fregata were in the air before Liz had time to finish the sentence. As magnificent frigate birds, they had a wingspan one and a half times as wide as that of a condor, and within a few seconds and well before the condors reached the edge of the crater, they had caught up and forestalled the escape. They took special care never to make eye contact with Malicious and managed to force the condors to land.

Malicious was fuming. She screamed at the condors, stamped her feet, pulled her hair, and looked much more like a tantrum-prone toddler than anything remotely resembling a princess. The condors prudently flew off, lest Malicious direct her violent fit of temper at them.

While Magnificens and Fregata tut-tutted the fallen princess, Liz arrived. As soon as Malicious saw Liz, she regained control, as if her arrival might afford some opportunity for escape or revenge.

"Congratulations," smiled Malicious. "It isn't just anyone who can outsmart a sorceress with my powers. You should be very pleased. I submit to your greater power."

Liz was feeling rather pleased that Kate was safe and that the frigate birds had thwarted Malicious's escape. And though she didn't for a moment believe that she alone was responsible for the good fortune, she was prepared to accept some accolades. Whether it was the emotional relief of knowing that her sister was safe or the disarming nature of Malicious's humble-sounding words, Liz let down her guard. She made the mistake of looking Malicious directly in the eyes.

"No!" cried Fregata and Magnificens. "Don't look at her eyes!"

But it was too late. Liz staggered, and her arms went limp by her side. Fregata and Magnificens immediately flew between Malicious and Liz, spreading their black wings and preventing Malicious from working her spell any further on Liz.

Liz collapsed backward as soon as the eye contact was lost and would have smacked her head on the rocky ground had Eirik not arrived in the nick of time to catch her in his arms.

Magnificens and Fregata began beating Malicious with their wings. The princess had her hands over her head and was doing everything she could just to remain standing in the face of the furious flapping.

Liz opened her eyes and looked around as if she couldn't remember where she was. She looked up and saw Eirik. His eyes were full of concern and affection. Liz's smile reciprocated the fondness.

The smile embarrassed Eirik, who quickly helped Liz up to a standing position. They both turned to watch as the frigate bird brothers continued their frenzied flapping. Malicious had fallen to the ground and was cowering under the feathery onslaught.

Eirik drew his sword and advanced toward his sister. The frigate birds stopped flapping and backed away. Malicious looked up at her brother. Her face was covered in red marks, as if the wings had whipped her skin.

"You fiend," said Eirik. "I'm embarrassed to think we are of the same blood. There is only one way to deal with a daughter so foul that she would murder her mother." He raised his sword.

Malicious, for once, was silent. She never even tried to make eye contact with Eirik. She seemed resigned to death as well as to defeat. She even stretched her neck out a bit, as if to offer Eirik an easy target.

Eirik held the sword two-handed over her head. He paused with the blade poised like the Sword of Damocles. Malicious stiffened and steeled herself for the blow. Liz closed her eyes, not wanting to witness the execution. She wished she could close her ears as well.

However, instead of the rush of steel, the crunch and cut of the blade, and the thud of a fallen head, she heard Eirik sigh.

"No, I can't kill you. There has been enough violence and more than enough death. I will not stoop to this brutality. No, rather I will bind you and your eyes and take you back to Asgard. The Althing will judge you and decide your fate according to the laws of our land."

Liz could not have been prouder of Eirik. *He is quite the guy,* she thought.

They had bound Malicious's hands and were in the process of wrapping a cloth about her eyes when out of nowhere streaked a shiny black bird. Before anyone had a chance to react, Alfred pecked out Malicious's right eye and with a parting gesture scratched at her left eye with his foot, flying off with a beak-full of retribution.

Malicious screamed and clutched at her eyes. The frigate brother birds made as if to fly and capture Alfred, but Liz stopped them.

"No," Liz said. "It was as we thought. The raven was mistreated horribly by Malicious, and though vengeance is a petty act, the bird is no longer a threat without the power of Malicious."

With Malicious's eyes and therefore power seemingly controlled, Eirik and Liz returned to the turret to help with Kate and Manco Capac. They left Magnificens and Fregata to guard the presumed blind and defenseless Malicious.

As soon as Eirik and Liz were out of sight and hearing, Magnificens remarked casually that but for him, the outcome would have been different. "Malicious was totally overpowered by the flapping of my wings."

"The only things you know how to flap are you lips," replied Fregata. "If anyone deserves credit for subduing Malicious, it is I. My wings are much stronger."

"I don't think so. They are half the size of mine."

"They are not."

"They are."

"Are not."

"Are."

"Are not."

"Are."

While they bickered, Malicious managed to make eye contact with the condors and commanded their return. By the time the frigate bird brothers next checked on their prisoner, she had escaped and was nowhere to be seen. They scoured the skies, but to no avail.

Chapter 78

Anointed

By the time Helga, Shabear, and Thorfinn arrived at Popocatépetl, there were only a few southern soldiers still straggling in the streets. The deluge had retreated into deep cracks as quickly as it had arrived, and all that was left was wet ground and steam that hissed from the fissures.

They met up with Connor, Eirik, Liz, Kate, Ian, Viracocha, and Manco Capac at the sacred platform in the center of Popocatépetl. Connor was the first to see them as they approached. He ran to greet them and gave Shabear a literal bear hug. "We did it, Aunt Shabear, and everyone is safe."

Shabear saw that Connor's right paw was bound in a bandage. She looked concerned for her nephew.

"The wound is fine. Zuni gave Ian a root that stops bleeding. I made a paste just like you taught me, and the bleeding stopped as soon as the cream touched the wound. My paw feels great, but Malicious got away."

"No matter," replied Shabear. "Malicious has lost much of her power. Now is the time for healing for more than just your paw. We must be gracious in victory. Perhaps this will be a time of coming together when we can forge a lasting peace with the peoples of the Southern Realm."

As she spoke these words, Shabear looked up at the sacred platform and saw that the time of coming together had already started. Ian and Kate were standing with their hands locked in love. Manco Capac and Viracocha were also standing side by side, with the father's hand resting fondly on his daughter's shoulder. Shabear also noted with great interest that the last two people on the platform where also standing close together; Liz and Eirik were so close that they might have been touching. Shabear could see by the smile on Eirik's face that more than victory was on the young prince's mind.

Xbalanque and his retinue soon joined them as well. For the first time, royal representatives of the Northern, Middle, and Southern Realms stood together. Shabear thought it was fitting that this royal conjunction should occur on the sacred platform in the middle of their combined worlds.

As they socialized and spoke of better times to come, another conjunction occurred. It was noon on the day of the autumnal equinox, and there were no clouds to obscure the sun, which for the first time in years beamed down to the sacred platform. It happened that Liz and Eirik were standing directly beneath the cone, and the young pair found themselves basking in glorious sunlight. To Shabear and all those present, Liz and Eirik looked anointed. The sun passed in a second and left everyone wondering. Those around the sacred platform took this as an auspicious sign and applauded. Both Liz and Eirik blushed to be so selected, but their embarrassment was lost in the cheers of the populace of Popocatépetl, who had crowded around the platform to honor those who had liberated them from the tyranny of Malicious.

A messenger eagle arrived from King Bjorn with the jubilant news that Malicious's soldiers had been soundly routed at the Battle of the Green Cavern. The group at Popocatépetl sent similar joyous news back to the king.

Later the same day, they started their journey back to Asgard. The journey took many weeks, and during that time many stories were shared and friendships confirmed, but none were as important as, or more talked about, than the kindling romance between Liz and Eirik. Their mutual attraction was clear to everyone who saw them together, but depending on who cared to comment, the romance was either doomed or destined.

Kate knew her sister better than anyone in the world and could tell she was smitten. She saw no reason why Eirik and Liz should not marry.

Ian was overjoyed to be reunited with Kate and likely would have considered any romance fine so long as Liz was happy, and he could see that she was. Additionally, his brief contact with Eirik had suggested he was a worthy fellow.

Helga, however, advised caution. "Liz is neither of royal blood nor blonde. If Eirik is not destined to marry according to the prophecy, then tradition decrees that he marry a member of a royal family." Loyal Thorfinn concurred with this interpretation.

Manco Capac also considered the romance ill-fated. "Together they saved us. Perhaps it might even be said that together they saved the underground kingdoms. But together they cannot be. Eirik is of royal blood and must choose a royal bride."

Viracocha understood the importance of a royal pedigree. She herself had been betrothed to an Inca prince whom she did not love, but whom her parents had decided was the destined match. Even so, she refused to agree with her father about Liz and Eirik, and instead she remained curiously silent. She and Liz had become confidants and were often seen smiling and laughing together.

Xbalanque found Liz very attractive and for his part hoped the match might not come to fruition. When asked by Viracocha, he sighed and commented, "Young romance is always complicated, but tradition is tradition." Mayan traditions, however, did not specifically restrict a prince from marrying a nonroyal. In truth, Xbalanque had been lovestruck since the first moment he saw Liz. As such, he might be forgiven for such a selfish thought.

Shabear could feel the love that bound Liz and Eirik closer every day, and she knew the match was correct. For a bear, the bear path was always through the heart.

Connor was Eirik's best friend, and as such he was privy to the prince's intimate thoughts. Connor knew that although everyone could see that Liz and Eirik were attracted to each other, neither of the young lovers had expressed their interest in any way beyond looks or the bumbling body language of adolescent courtship. No words had been spoken or romantic vows implied. This was a delicate business, to be sure, and Connor was a patient listener for his friend Eirik.

Chapter 79

Prophecy, Tradition, and Love

"Connor, what am I to do? It is clear that I shall not follow the prophecy. Shall I follow my heart or the traditions of my family? Should I ask Liz to marry me, or should I choose a bride from one of the royal families?"

Eirik had sung this refrain, or a variation, repeatedly each day for the first few days of the journey back to Asgard. Each morning and then again in the afternoon, Eirik spent an hour or so with Liz, always properly chaperoned and in the company of others, and each day, he fell further and more hopelessly in love. Each evening, Eirik poured his heart out to Connor, who listened patiently to the day's new twist on love's anguish.

Throughout their adolescence, Connor and Eirik had been inseparable pals, but neither had ever become romantically involved with anyone. Most of the young men of Eirik's generation had already married, but everyone in Asgard knew that the prince would wed according to the prophecy, and as such, neither he nor any of the eligible young women had presumed to initiate a relationship. Bears hardly ever married until their fifth decade, so Connor had no experience either. However, even without any experience, Connor could tell that Eirik loved Liz deeply and that Liz was the right woman for him. Even so, he hesitated to encourage Eirik in this direction and chose merely to listen while his friend struggled to reconcile passion with tradition. Connor reckoned that choosing a mate was perhaps the most personal decision anyone would ever make and that not even a best friend should try to influence the outcome. Connor had spoken to Shabear, who had concurred with this approach.

However, on the third night after they had left Popocatépetl, Eirik pleaded with Connor for his advice. "Connor, help me with this decision. I've never known you to be so silent."

"Eirik, I've never known you to suffer from indecisiveness. I'm sorry you can't see the correct path more clearly, but I cannot help you with this important decision. However, if I were in your position, I would look for an answer in my dreams. The bear path is often revealed in a wakeful vision or a dream. Perhaps you should go on a vision quest."

"That's a great idea," said Eirik, who brightened up. "Queen Odontocetes gave me a crystal vial with some drops that might be helpful." Eirik remembered her exact words. "She told me, 'The water in this crystal vial was taken from the river that bathes the roots of the Tree of Life. A single drop of this water on your tongue will give you insight.'"

"So what are you waiting for?" replied Connor. "Try a drop."

Eirik retrieved the vial from his pack. The stopper was made of the same crystal and was easily removed with a slight turn. The top included a solid and slender glass dropper that was immersed in the liquid. Eirik put the open vial close to his nose but could not smell anything. He offered the vial to Connor for the same purpose.

A bear's smell is so acute that rather than put his nose to the vial, Connor chose to waft some of the scent toward his face by waving his paw over the top. Eirik could see at once that a smell was evident to his friend; Connor's facial expression changed immediately. He trembled slightly and then looked thoughtful.

"What did you smell?"

"I smelled truth."

"Truth? But truth isn't something with a smell."

"Well, all I can tell you is that I smelled, or rather felt, truth. I had a jumble of sensations all at once. I felt a presence that was something like the combination of my father's voice and my mother's touch. It was like a shudder in my soul."

Connor was not an especially philosophical bear, and his response was as much of a surprise to him as it was to Eirik. "I guess that means that if you take a drop, you will know the truth," Connor offered unassumingly.

Eirik raised the dropper to his mouth and dabbed a drop onto his tongue.

"Taste anything?" asked Connor.

"Not a thing. Tastes like warm water."

"Feel anything?"

"Nothing. And I don't feel anymore decisive either. Maybe the drops don't work with me. Perhaps you need to be a dolphin. Should I take more?"

"Didn't you say that Queen Odontocetes said that a single drop was enough?"

"Yes, she did."

"Then I wouldn't take more. No telling what might happen if you take too much. Maybe the drops take time to work. Why don't you get a good night's sleep? Perhaps you'll feel decisive in the morning."

Eirik heeded this advice, and soon thereafter, both he and Connor were asleep. Eirik, however, was awoken during the night.

"Eirik, wake up, dear." The voice was that of his mother.

"Ah, Mom, let me sleep a little longer. I did all my homework last night. I don't want to go to class this morning."

"Eirik, dear, please wake up."

"Oh, all right." Eirik opened his eyes and expected to see his mother sitting on the side of his bed. However, all he saw was a cavern with Connor sleeping beside him. Connor lay on his side and was obviously dreaming. His nostrils quivered, and his eyeballs rolled around in their sockets. His legs straightened, twitched, and then started to flail about. The grizzly mumbled something about cheeky squirrels and pinecones, and then he grunted, rolled over, and became still.

Eirik rubbed his eyes and stretched. *Must have been a dream,* he thought.

"No, dear. You aren't dreaming."

"Mom?" Eirik looked around and saw nothing. "Mom, are you there?"

"Yes, dear. I'm with you."

"But where? I can't see you. This must be a dream."

"No, Eirik. I am right here with you. You need to concentrate. Do you remember how I taught you to see the ancient petroglyphs when you were ten years old? The drawings were so old and faint that you couldn't see them. I told you to close your eyes and relax. I suggested that you let everything else go from your busy mind. When you opened your eyes, you could see them."

Eirik closed his eyes, let all his muscles go loose, cleared his mind, took a deep breath, looked in the direction of his mother's voice, and then exhaled as he opened his eyes. His mother was sitting beside him, much as she always had when she awoke him for school.

Her auburn hair tumbled in tight, full curls that just about reached her shoulders. She wore a white silk tunic that glistened; the silver glow reflected in the luster of her hair and created an aura. The tunic, which followed the curves of her body and fell gracefully to her ankles, was gathered at both shoulders by silver brooches carved with the Asgard coat of arms. Blue topaz stones ringed the periphery of each brooch. A thick ropelike necklace fashioned from braided silver hung close around her neck. She wore similar but thinner and more delicate bracelets around each wrist.

Eirik put his arms out to hug his mother, but his hands disappeared though her body. He frowned. "Then you're still dead."

"I will always be with you, Eirik."

Eirik brightened. "Are my grandparents with you? Have you seen Odin?"

"All your relatives are with you, Eirik. We are all here if you choose to see us. Balder is here. So is Kodiak. Even Eirik the Red, your namesake."

"And what of Odin and the other gods? Have you been to Valhalla?"

"The gods are not what you think, and Valhalla is different too."

Eirik felt confused and would have spoken, but his mother preempted him with an explanation that confused him even more.

"Odin and the gods were something we were encouraged to believe in, and we did. But each of us also believes in something more personal than the gods. When we die, we follow this personal belief. Like many parents, I always believed in the sanctity of children. I believed in you, and when I died, I returned to you. In a sense Valhalla is wherever you are. That is why I am with you."

Eirik did not grasp what his mother was saying. "So you decided not to go to Valhalla or to visit with Odin and the other gods, but you could if you wanted?"

His mother could see that Eirik was confused, so she tried another way to help him understand. "Eirik, have you ever wondered what happens to our bear friends when they die? Did you think they went to Valhalla?"

"They do if they're warrior bears and they die in battle."

"Do you think that the God of All Creatures lives in Valhalla with Odin?"

"Well, I don't know. I guess I always thought that the God of All Creatures and Odin were friends who lived in different places."

"The God of All Creatures is something the bears were encouraged to believe in, just as we were encouraged to believe in Odin. In this sense, they are the same. But every bear, like every person, has a personal belief. I believe that Bär, Connor's father, is with Connor."

Eirik still looked very perplexed, and his mother decided to refocus the conversation. "It is not necessary to understand this now. We will talk anon. Now, however, I sense there is something more important on your mind. A beautiful young woman, perhaps," she said with a playful smile.

Eirik blushed and smiled at the same time. His eyes lit up. "Oh, Mother, Liz is so wonderful, and I do love her. But she is neither blonde nor a princess."

"Oh, Eirik. You are just like your father. You can't see for looking."

"Pardon me?"

"She is delightful," replied his mother, "and she would be a remarkable friend, mother, and queen. Follow your heart, Eirik. Always follow your heart."

Connor rolled over on his back in that moment and immediately started to snore. Eirik looked over at his furry friend and smiled. And when he turned back to his mother, she was gone. He called out many times, but she was gone.

Chapter 80

Waiting for Good Eirik

Liz did have experience with courtship. At least, many suitors had courted her. They had all come up wanting. Now, however, she had found one she truly loved. That she loved Eirik was not in doubt. She kept daily counsel with Kate and Viracocha.

Kate assumed that Eirik and Liz would marry. "Just tell him," Kate kept saying. "He loves you. It was meant to be."

"No. This is his decision. I want him to choose me."

"Have it your way," replied Kate. "But be careful, and don't let your stubbornness ruin this relationship."

Viracocha also assumed the marriage would take place.

"Why are you so sure?" asked Liz.

"Until you admit the truth, I won't tell you," she replied.

"What truth?"

"All you need to do is tell him. He will choose you."

"Exactly. I want him to choose me over the prophecy."

Viracocha had a coy look. "Be careful, Liz. Most men are not especially perceptive about love. Eirik can't see straight, not just because he's in love, but also because he's a man. He's wrapped up in tradition, loyalty to his father, and all sorts of other male things. He might blow it. What if he doesn't ask?"

"Then we weren't meant to marry."

"Oh, come on. That's silly. If he doesn't ask before we arrive in Asgard, you must tell him."

Liz looked coy. "Tell him what?"

Viracocha looked exasperated. "Some might consider your position deceitful. You should be honest."

"I'm not a princess. He must choose."

"Like I said, be careful, Liz. Love is not something to be trifled with. Men have feelings too. Eirik might not know how much you care for him. Help him make the decision."

"I won't. I can't."

Once alone, Liz worried that her sister and Viracocha were right. *Be careful,* they had both admonished her. *Well, I am being careful,* she thought. *If Eirik really loves me, he will choose me, and he will tell me.*

Liz's position was not so much stubborn as it was romantic. She believed in an ideal and would not accept anything but true love. Liz's innate impatience, however, was a growing problem. *If only I could see the future, I would know whether to wait.* With this thought Liz realized that perhaps she could see the future. She had the crystal dolphin that Queen Odontocetes had given her. But she paused when she remembered the queen's caution.

"The dolphin is more than a memento," the queen had said. "When you look into the eyes of the dolphin, you will see further than you might otherwise. Be wary, though; you might not like what you see. Do not be intimidated by this glimpse beyond. If what you see disheartens you, focus instead on the heart of the dolphin."

On the same evening that Eirik took the drop of the elixir of insight, Liz looked into the crystal dolphin. She held the tiny sculpture in her right hand. The dolphin felt curiously warm. Although not superstitious, Liz instinctively held the dolphin over her heart, as if somehow this might elicit the favored vision. Then she cupped the sculpture in her hands and looked into the dolphin's eyes. For the first time she realized that the eyes were not made of the same golden crystal as the rest of the dolphin, but were clear and transparent like a flawless diamond. She wondered how she had not noticed this before. She could see through the eyes into the head of the dolphin, where a silver mist swirled. The mist turned into silver snowflakes that fell and left a clear view of a courtyard in a castle. She saw Eirik in the robes of a king, and beside him was a woman dressed in white. She was exactly the same height and shape as Liz, but her face was not visible. Eirik and the woman walked around in the courtyard, but her face never came into view.

Liz blinked, and the scene changed. Now she saw Eirik leaning over a cradle. Eirik picked up a baby and handed the child to a woman who sat in a rocking chair. She had the same figure as Liz. The woman breastfed the baby, but she never turned to allow Liz to see her face.

When Liz blinked again, the scene changed once more. This time she saw a slightly older Eirik with the same woman. They were at Connor's wedding. Eirik was the best man. The woman was standing to the side, again with her back to Liz.

Liz blinked and saw a final scene with a much older Eirik and the same woman. They were at a royal funeral that Liz presumed must be that of King Bjorn. Eirik was crying, and the woman was consoling him. The woman walked in the procession with Eirik, but again, her face was never visible. A younger man and woman were with them. The younger woman had a resemblance to Liz. *Could they be our children?* she wondered.

Liz put the crystal down and thought about what she had seen. She had seen the future, but she was not definitely in that future. *The woman could be anyone my size,* she thought. *Why couldn't I see the woman's face? What does it mean?*

Liz picked up the dolphin. She looked into the center of the dolphin, wherein lay a burgundy heart. The heart dissolved into a pink mist that cleared to reveal a happy scene. Liz saw herself walking with Eirik. She wore the crown of a queen. A young boy about eight years old, obviously their son, was walking hand-in-hand between them along a river. They came upon a group of cubs and children who were playing in what looked like a schoolyard. Connor arrived with his bride, and they too had a young cub. Their child ran to play with Connor's cub and the other children. A woman who Liz presumed was a teacher stood and watched over the children. Liz observed as Eirik and this future version of herself walked away with Connor and his bride. Everyone was very happy. Liz trembled with tender feelings for both Eirik and her future son. She sighed a romantic sigh and was just about to put the dolphin away when suddenly the scene darkened. The pink mist swirled back and coalesced into a solitary ruby-red eye that glared at Liz. The eye settled into the socket of the woman who watched over the children. The woman had a black patch over her other eye. A huge black panther slinked into the scene. Liz watched horrified as the woman snatched the young prince and rode off on the back of the panther.

"No!" she cried. "This can't be. Now I can't marry Eirik, even if he asks."

Chapter 81
The Proposal

The morning after Liz's vision, she met with Kate and Viracocha and explained what she had seen in the dolphin.

"When he asks for your hand, you must relate the vision," Viracocha insisted. "Forewarned is forearmed. Together you should be able to prevent Malicious from kidnapping your future son." Her advice reassured Liz.

"But what if Eirik doesn't want to risk losing his son?" asked Kate. "What if your first series of visions with the other woman was the correct future? Perhaps you are not meant to marry Eirik. After all, you only saw yourself when you looked into the heart of the dolphin."

"Both visions featured the same woman," said Viracocha.

"How do you know?" asked Liz.

"You never told us what color her hair was, did you?" said Viracocha with a smile.

"No, I didn't. That shouldn't make any difference," replied Liz, a little indignantly.

Before anyone could say more, Connor arrived to deliver a note to Liz. "Eirik asked that I await your reply," said Connor, who looked a little sheepish.

Liz blushed in anticipation and fidgeted with the note. Kate and Viracocha both looked impatient, as if they might open the note for her if she chose to dally any further. Liz opened and read the note.

> *Dear Liz,*
> *Please meet with me by the riverside where we ate dinner last night. I have something important to ask you.*
> *Fondly,*
> *Eirik*

"Please tell Eirik I will meet him in one hour."

Connor left with this response, and Kate and Liz immediately scrutinized the note and offered their interpretations.

"Of course he plans to propose. Didn't you see how embarrassed Connor was?" said Kate.

"Yes, and he signed the note 'fondly,'" added Viracocha.

"And he wants to *ask* me something," Liz said, smiling. "Well, I want to look my part. We have an hour to turn me into a princess." And they did.

When Liz met with Eirik, she wore a gown Viracocha had designed. The dress was made from the best Inca silk. Somehow Viracocha had known that the gown would be necessary, and in the few hours they had spent at Popocatépetl before beginning their journey back to the Castle of Light, she had arranged for a renowned seamstress to sew the garment. The gown was simple, modest, and beautiful, and it was a perfect fit. Liz wore no jewelry, and her hair was gathered up on her head in a most flattering fashion.

Kate and Viracocha walked with Liz to the riverside and then remained to chat for a few minutes before they left the young couple alone. The minutes seemed like hours to Eirik, who seemed barely able to keep himself still and to engage in the polite badinage necessary for the situation. Kate and Viracocha had not been out of sight for a moment when he dropped on one knee and proclaimed his love.

"Liz, I love you more than anything. I would rather marry you than be King of Asgard. I would rather spend my days as your husband and the father of our children than rule any kingdom. I don't care about the prophecy. I only care about you." After he blurted out the sweet words of love, he smiled hopefully and reached out his right arm to symbolically offer his hand in marriage.

Liz smiled, and a tear appeared in the corner of both eyes. She knelt beside him, accepted his right hand, and placed the palm over her heart. "Eirik, I love you and always will. Thank you for choosing me, but before I accept your proposal, you must first hear of two visions I had, another prophecy of sorts. If this prophecy does not change your mind, then I will gladly marry you."

Liz explained her visions in the dolphin, but Eirik was not dissuaded by them. Rather, he believed that the visions were the key to prevention of any calamity.

"Liz, this just proves we were meant to marry. The second vision was meant to protect us. Now that we know what Malicious is planning, we can stop her. And your first vision showed us together with our son when he was older than he was in the second vision."

"Oh, Eirik. I love you so much."

They hugged tenderly, and then their lips met for the first time.

"And you don't mind that I'm not a princess?" asked Liz demurely.

"You are my princess."

"And you're sure that the prophecy isn't important?" she asked.

"Prophecies are like dreams. Some come true, and others don't. I've dreamt of you, and that is what counts."

While Eirik gathered her into another romantic embrace, Liz reached behind her head and undid the clip in her hair. For the last three months, Liz had mostly kept her hair gathered at the back or under a scarf. She had rarely let her hair down and had never done so in the presence of Eirik. Her auburn hair was soft and full as it fell over her shoulders. She finished the kiss and then stepped back into the light from one of the overhead shafts built by the royal engineers. Liz purposely tossed her hair and allowed the light to catch the locks as they swirled about her head. At least three inches of blonde color was visible in the roots, and the difference was not lost on Eirik. "Dreams really are like prophecies," Liz said with a smile as she kissed her prince again.

Epilogue

Kate and Ian decided to return to the surface for the intervening months before the spring equinox, when the royal wedding and coronation would take place. Kate, for one, could not get back to the surface fast enough. She was troubled by moments of anxiety and nightmares. The shadow still seemed part of her life. Zuni heard of her troubles and sent along a message that helped ease her thoughts: "Always walk into the sunshine, and the shadows will fall behind you." Kate embraced this advice, and when she arrived back on the surface, everything sparkled, looked more vivid, and had a clarity that she had heretofore never appreciated. For his part, Ian realized that although he had set out in search of Kate, he had also found himself and something perhaps even more precious: faith.

Liz, of course, stayed in Asgard. Mac chose to stay as well. He had much to learn from Ursus and no desire to return to the surface. Kate and Ian took back a story of woe whereby Liz and Mac had drowned off the Queen Charlotte Islands just west of British Columbia.

Manco Capac returned to his people in Cusco, who were grateful for the return of a just king after suffering the dark times under Malicious. He was proclaimed Sapa Inca, ruler of Tahuantinsuyu, the entire Inca Empire. After Manco Capac culled out the remnants of the southern warlords who had supported Malicious and brought justice and order back to the Southern Realm, he abdicated in favor of his daughter Viracocha. As *qoya,* or Inca queen, Viracocha chose not to marry the Inca prince to whom she had been betrothed. Instead she hoped to marry for love, just like her friend Liz. She and her father were delighted to accept the invitation to the royal wedding and coronation.

Xbalanque returned to Copan. His father had decided that the time was right to open their society and integrate the Mayan peoples of the

Middle Realm with those of the Southern and Northern Realms. The following spring, Itzamna abdicated in favor of Xbalanque. They were also delighted to accept the invitation to attend the royal wedding and coronation.

All the clan leaders attended. Helga and Thorfinn attended from Kwakiutl. Sigurd attended from Inuit, Groa from Haida, Grettir from Nakota, Runolfur from Siksika, Svein and Zuni from Anasazi, and Oddur from Toltec. Magnus, Koda, and Shasta represented the valiant warriors who had fought and won the Battle of the Green Cavern.

Zuni turned out to be the woman who had prophesied Malicious's evilness after her birth and who had been banned from the Castle of Light by King Bjorn. Zuni became a spiritual advisor to Eirik and Liz and served the royal family for many years.

The pristine waters that had flooded the Green Cavern and caused the deluge of Popocatépetl swept away the murky waters that had threatened Miocena. The thaw in the Northern Realm came early the next spring and was much heavier than usual. The subterranean rivers were so clear and deep that it was possible for Queen Odontocetes to accept the invitation to attend the royal wedding and coronation. She attended with a retinue of dolphins, seals, and river otters. Queen Odontocetes chose the occasion to share the location of Ceiba, the Tree of Life, with Itzamna, who wept with joy.

The wedding and coronation were held at the base of Franang Falls, where the dolphins, seals, and otters sang sweet love songs in honor of the royal couple. Before the ceremony, King Bjorn announced that his last act as king of Asgard would be to commission the royal engineers to mine the new vein of Green Crystal that had been discovered by Helga and the rescue squad. The lake and the cavern where crystal had been discovered were named in honor of Gudrid and Stefan. The new deposits of Green Crystal proved vast and were shared with the peoples of the Middle and Southern Realms. All present believed that the wedding would usher in a new millennium of prosperity.

Connor was the best man and Kate the maid of honor. At the moment Eirik and Liz were pronounced married, a rainbow appeared and was likened by King Bjorn to Bifrost, the rainbow bridge that connected the land of the gods and the land of the mortals.

Afterward, Shabear and Zuni spoke prayers for the new couple, and then Mac concluded the ceremony with a passage from the Bible. When he came to "God," Mac substituted "God of All Creatures."

"Congratulations, Mac. You've come a long way to be here," said Ursus, who smiled and gave his friend a brotherly bear hug.

Index of Proper Names

Alfred: Malicious's messenger raven
Balder: Viking who settled Asgard; first king of Asgard; in Norse mythology the son of Odin and Frigg; a beautiful, wise, and gentle god; the god of light
Bär: son of Ursus; German word for bear
Bjorn: king of Asgard; Swedish word for bear
Connor: grandson of Ursus
Eirik: prince of Asgard; descendent of Eirik the Red
Freki Wolf: wolf who captures Liz; in Norse mythology one of the two wolves who accompany Odin
Fregata: magnificent frigate bird; twin of Magnificens
Freyja: queen of Asgard; in Norse mythology a goddess of fertility
Frigg: wife of Odin
Geri Wolf: messenger wolf; in Norse mythology one of the two wolves who accompany Odin
Grettir: clan leader of Nakota
Groa: clan leader of Haida
Gudrid: Kwakiutl warrior; twin of Thorfinn
Helga: clan leader of Kwakiutl; commander of the rescue squad
Hildolf Wolf: commander of the wolf army that captures Nakota and the Green Cavern
Hrolf: Balder's cousin and second in command on the voyage to Vinland; eaten by the Kraken
Ian: Kate's husband; geologist
Itzamna: king of Copan
Jens: boot boy in royal household; later King Bjorn's personal attendant
Kate: Liz's sister; Mac's daughter; wildlife management specialist

Koda: leader of bear squad; battalion commander at battle of the Green Cavern
Kodiak: grizzly who with King Olaf brought peace to the underground realm
Lars: common soldier
Liz: Kate's sister; Mac's daughter; PhD student in archaeology
Lord Null: Ian's nemesis
Mac: Kate and Liz's father; professor of geology
Magnificens: magnificent frigate bird; twin of Fregata
Magnus: commander of the Asgard Army
Malicious: princess of Asgard
Manco Capac: king of Cusco
Oddur: clan leader of Toltec
Odin: in Norse mythology the god of wisdom, war, art, culture, and the dead and the supreme deity and creator of the cosmos and humans
Odontocetes: queen of Miocena
Olaf: king of Asgard who with Kodiak brought peace to the underground realm
Olafur: chief of the royal engineers
Rognvald: Kwakiutl warrior who speaks for Helga at war council
Runolfur: clan leader of Siksika
Shabear: sister of Ursus
Shasta: Kermode bear; commander of the bears
Sigurd: clan leader of Inuit
Sköll Wolf: pack commander; in Norse mythology the wolf who pursues the sun
Stefan: Kwakiutl warrior
Svein: clan leader of Anasazi
Thorfinn: Kwakiutl warrior; twin of Gudrid
Ursavus: grizzly whom Balder meets; *Ursavus elemensis* was the first true bear (twenty million years ago)
Ursus: chief counsel for King Bjorn; father of Bär; grandfather of Connor; brother of Shabear
Viracocha: princess of Cusco
Xbalanque: prince of Copan
Zuni: spiritual leader of Anasazi

Glossary

Aincekoko: Navajo; the bear kachina; part of the mixed dance ritual performed in the spring.

Alluvial: Sediment deposited by flowing water, as in a riverbed, flood plain, or delta.

Alpha: individual in a community with the highest rank.

Alpine forget-me-not: *Myosotis alpestris*; common in moist subalpine and alpine meadows; azure flowers with a yellow eye.

Althing: The parliament of Iceland; the oldest assembly in Europe; first convened in 930.

Amber: A hard translucent yellow, orange, or brownish-yellow fossil resin.

Anasazi: Pueblo; a Native American culture that flourished in southern Colorado, Utah, northern New Mexico, and Arizona from about AD 100, and whose descendants are considered to include the present-day Pueblo peoples.

Aquifer: An underground bed or layer of earth, gravel, or porous stone that yields water.

Arctic char: A char (*Salvelinus alpinus*) native to the fresh waters of Alaska and northern Canada.

Argillite: A metamorphic rock, intermediate between shale and slate.

Argus: Greek mythology; a giant with one hundred eyes who was made guardian of Io and was later slain by Hermes.

Army cutworm moths: *Euxoa auxiliaries.*

Arnica: Any of various perennial herbs of the genus *Arnica* in the composite family, having opposite, simple leaves and mostly radiate heads of yellow flowers.

Ascender: A mountaineering device used to assist with climbing up a rope.

Asgard: Norse; heavenly residence of the gods and slain heroes of war.

Aster: Any of various plants of the genus *Aster* in the composite family, having radiate flower heads with white, pink, or violet rays and a usually yellow disk.

Aurora borealis: An aurora that occurs in northern regions of the earth. Also called *northern lights.*

Bald eagle: A North American eagle (*Haliaeetus leucocephalus*) characterized by a brownish-black body and a white head and tail in the adult.

Balder: Norse; the most beautiful of all the gods; the son of Odin and Frigga.

Bär: German word for bear.

Bear Old Man: Pueblo; in Pueblo mythology, Bear Old Man leads the first people from the Lake of Emergence.

Bear transformation mask: Kwakiutl; ceremonial mask carved in the likeness of a grizzly bear that opened to reveal the person and to give the illusion of transformation from a bear to a person.

Bearberry: Any of certain mat-forming shrubs of the genus *Arctostaphylos,* especially *A. uva-ursi,* native to North America with small leathery leaves, white or pinkish urn-shaped flowers, and red berrylike fruits. Also called *kinnikinnick.*

Beitiáss: Norse; wooden pole used as a tacking spar on Viking longships.

Berserker: Norse; one of a band of ancient Norse warriors legendary for their savagery and reckless frenzy in battle.

Bjarni Herjolfsson: Norse; first European credited with discovery of North America.

Boreal toad: An amphibian two to five inches long that lives in small ponds, marshes, and streams; *Bufo boreas boreas.*

Brattahild: Norse; original Greenland settlement of Eirik the Red.

Broom groundsel: A herbaceous perennial of the sunflower family.

Burgess shale: A rock formation in the western Canadian Rockies that contains a wealth of fossilized invertebrates of the early Cambrian period.

Buri: Norse; forefather of the gods; his son Börr was the father of Odin.

Butte: A hill that rises abruptly from the surrounding area and has sloping sides and a flat top.

Calcite: A common crystalline form of natural calcium carbonate, $CaCO_3$, that is the basic constituent of limestone, marble, and chalk; also called *calcspar.*

Calcium carbonate: A colorless or white crystalline compound ($CaCO_3$) that occurs naturally as chalk, limestone, and marble.

California condor: A very large vulture (*Gymnogyps californianus*), related to the condor of South America, found in the southern California mountains and nearly extinct.

Carnelian: A pale to deep red or reddish-brown variety of clear chalcedony.

Cave bacon: Cave bacon is formed when the water drops flow down a sloped ceiling and calcite builds up in a thin line before dropping to the floor.

Ceiba: Mayan; Tree of Life.

Cenote: Mayan; a water-filled limestone sinkhole of the Yucatán.

Cere: A fleshy or waxlike membrane at the base of a bird's upper beak through which the nostrils open.

Chert: A siliceous rock of chalcedonic or opaline silica occurring in limestone.

Chichén Itzá: Mayan; ancient Mayan city built in the sixth century.

Chlorophyll: Any of a group of green pigments that are found in the chloroplasts of plants.

Cinquefoil: A plant of the genus *Potentilla* in the rose family, native to temperate and cold regions, with yellow flowers.

Codices: Mayan; books written in Maya.

Common fireweed: A North American wildflower of the primrose family with four pink or red petals; *Epilobium angustifolium.*

Common yarrow: Any of several plants of the genus *Achillea* of the composite family, having finely dissected foliage and flat corymbs of usually white flower heads.

Copán: Mayan; ruined Mayan city of western Honduras that flourished from ca. 300 BC to AD 900.

Coricancha: Inca; the "golden enclosure" or the Temple of the Sun in Cusco; considered the spiritual center of the Inca Empire.

Coruscate: To vibrate, glitter, sparkle, or gleam; to give forth intermittent or vibratory flashes of light; to shine with a quivering light.

Coxswain: A person who usually steers a ship's boat and has charge of the crew.

Cusco: Inca; city of southern Peru in the Andes east-southeast of Lima; founded according to legend by Manco Capac around the twelfth century; became the center of the vast Inca Empire and was rebuilt by the Spanish after its plunder by Francisco Pizarro in 1533.

Dawn star: Venus, morning star.

Deer mouse: A North American mouse (*Peromyscus maniculatus*) that has white feet and underbelly and a long, bicolored tail.

Dira Cocha: Inca; staff god; creator god; fanged deity with feline face and clawed feet; earliest record is a 4,000-year-old Peruvian gourd.

Dodo: A large, clumsy, flightless bird (*Raphus cucullatus*), formerly of the island of Mauritius in the Indian Ocean; extinct since the late seventeenth century.

Eider: Any of several large sea ducks, especially of the genus *Somateria,* of northern regions that have soft, commercially valuable down and predominantly black and white plumage in the male.

Einherjar: Norse; the slain soldiers who were brought to Valhalla; they fought during the day and feasted during the night.

Eirik the Red: Norse; Viking who discovered and settled Greenland; father of Leif, Thorvald, and Thorsten; in the book, also the father of Balder.

Eiriksfjord: Norse; fjord in Greenland where Eirik the Red settled Brattahild.

Elbow adze: An axe-like tool with a curved blade at right angles to the handle, used for shaping wood.

Equinox: Either of the two times during a year when the sun crosses the celestial equator and when the length of day and night are approximately equal; the spring equinox or the autumnal equinox.

Faering: Norse; a four-oared boat styled like a longship.

Feldspar: Any of a group of abundant rock-forming minerals occurring principally in igneous, plutonic, and some metamorphic rocks and consisting of silicates of aluminum with potassium, sodium, calcium, and rarely, barium; about 60 percent of the earth's outer crust is composed of feldspar.

Fenrir: Also Fenris; an enormous wolf; the son of Loki and the giantess Angrboda; Fenrir bit off the hand of Tyr.

Figure-of-eight descending tool: mountaineering device shaped like a figure eight and used to control the rope during a descent.

Fjorm: Norse mythology; one of the Elivagar's streams that floated out of the well Hvergelmir.

Flokkr: Norse; poem to commemorate an individual.

Fourscore: Four times twenty; eighty.
Franang's Falls: Norse; a waterfall in Midgard.
Freki: Norse; one of two wolves who accompanied Odin.
Freyja: Norse; also Freya; goddess of women.
Freyr: Norse; also Frey; god of fertility.
Frigg: Norse; also Frigga; most important goddess of Asgard; one of the three wives of Odin; mother of Balder.
Fumarole: A hole in a volcanic area from which hot smoke and gases escape.
Geri: Norse; one of the two wolves who accompanied Odin.
Giallar-horn: Norse; Heimdall's horn that could be heard throughout the nine Norse worlds.
Gimli: Norse; the hall that, after Ragnarök, will be populated by the surviving gods; a Canadian community in the province of Manitoba that experienced a substantial migration of Icelandic people in the late nineteenth and early twentieth centuries.
Glacial bear: A black bear with blue-gray fur found in southeastern Alaska and northwestern British Columbia.
Globe huckleberry: A deciduous huckleberry with blue-purple berries favored by grizzly bears; *Vaccinium globulare.*
Golden eagle: A large eagle (*Aquila chrysaetos*) of mountainous areas of the Northern Hemisphere, having dark plumage with brownish-yellow feathers on the back of the head and neck.
Great auk: A large flightless sea bird (*Pinguinus impennis*) formerly common on northern Atlantic coasts but extinct since the middle of the nineteenth century.
Great Bear: The constellation otherwise known as the Big Dipper.
Great horned owl: A large North American owl (*Bubo virginianus*) with prominent ear tufts and brownish plumage with a white throat.
Gripping beast: Norse; Viking art style in which an animal grips to the edge of an ornamentation border, to neighboring animals, or to its own body.
Grizzly bear: *Ursus arctos*; brown bear of northwest North America.
Grizzly sow: Female grizzly.
Guillinbursti: Norse; huge boar made by the dwarfs Brock and Sindri.
Gular pouch: A pouch in the neck region that can be used to hold food; in frigate birds the pouch is inflated as part of a courtship display.
Gungnir: Norse; Odin's spear that was always accurate.

Gypsum: A widespread colorless, white, or yellowish mineral; $CaSO_4 \cdot 2H_2O$.
Hafvilla: Norse; word for lost at sea.
Haida: A Native American people who inhabit the Queen Charlotte Islands of British Columbia, Canada, and the Prince of Wales Island in Alaska.
Haida Gwaii: An island off the coast of the Canadian province of British Columbia, renowned for enormous red cedar trees.
Halocline: A vertical gradient in ocean salinity.
Hamrammr: Norse; shape-shifter.
Hecate Strait: A water passage between Haida Gwaii and the British Columbia mainland, renowned for bad weather and treacherous passage.
Heimdall: Norse; god born simultaneously from nine giantess mothers; guarded Bifrost, the rainbow bridge; his horn could be heard throughout the nine worlds.
Hekla: Volcano, 4,892 feet high, in southwest Iceland.
Hel: Norse; realm of the dead in Niflheim.
Helluland: Norse; Rock Slab Land; the region discovered by Thorvald, second son of Eirik the Red, and thought to correspond to present-day Baffin Island.
Hildolf Wolf: Norse mythology; battle wolf.
Hnefatafl: Norse; Viking board game thought to be similar to chess.
Huginn: Norse; one of Odin's ravens.
Humpback whale: A baleen whale (*Megaptera novaeangliae*) that has a rounded back and long knobby flippers.
Hymir: Norse; elderly giant who owned an extremely large cauldron.
Inca: Inca; Quechuan peoples of highland Peru who established an empire from northern Ecuador to central Chile before the Spanish conquest.
Indian paintbrush: Any of various partly parasitic plants of the genus *Castilleja*; the plants have spikes of flowers surrounded by showy, brightly colored bracts.
Inti: Inca; sun god.
Inuit: Inuit; a member of a group of peoples who inhabit the Arctic from northern Alaska eastward to Greenland, particularly those of Canada.
Itzamna: Mayan; creator god, patron of culture and learning.

Iving River: Norse; also Ifing; the river that separates Asgard from the land of the giants; the river never freezes; in the book, the river courses from Popocatépetl through the Middle Realm toward the Maya and Miocena.

Ix Chel: Mayan; goddess of healing and childbirth; rainbow goddess.

Jasper: An opaque cryptocrystalline variety of quartz that may be red, yellow, or brown.

Jelling: Norse; a Viking art style popular between about AD 875 and 975; characteristics of the Jelling style include an animal head with a round eye, an open mouth, a rolled-up nose tendril, and a neck tendril, as well as a ribbon-shaped body laid out in an S-shaped loop.

Jormungand: Norse; the Midgard serpent; one of the three children of the god Loki and his wife, the giantess Angrboda.

K'ul Ahau: Designation of supreme or sacred head of state during Classic period of Mayan history.

Kachina: Navajo; a doll carved to represent any of numerous deified ancestral spirits of the Pueblo peoples; usually presented as a gift to a child.

Karabiners, chocks, cams: Mountaineering equipment.

Kermode: Spirit bear of Princess Royal Island; off the west coast of British Columbia.

Kiva: Pueblo; an underground or partly underground chamber in a Pueblo village; used for ceremonies or councils.

Knörrs: Norse; wide-bottomed boat; oceangoing cargo ships.

Kraken: A mythical squid, likely *Mesonychoteuthis hamiltoni*; eyes as big as dinner plates and razor-sharp hooks on its tentacles; not the same as a giant squid, which is smaller and more common; dives to 2,000 meters; principle nutritional source for sperm whales.

Kwakiutl: Kwakiutl; Native American people who inhabit parts of coastal British Columbia and northern Vancouver Island.

Lake of Emergence: Pueblo; the first people are led from the Lake of Emergence by Bear Old Man.

Langskip: Norse; Viking longship.

Lapis lazuli: An opaque to translucent blue, violet-blue, or greenish-blue semiprecious gemstone composed mainly of lazurite and calcite.

Least chipmunk: The smallest of all chipmunks (*Eutamias minimus*); has black and white stripes that run down the middle and sides of the back and white stripes that run from the nose to the ear above and below the eye.

Leif Eiriksson: Norse; son of Eirik the Red; credited as the first European to land and establish a settlement in North America.

Little Bear: The constellation otherwise known as the Little Dipper.

Logograph: Maya; word pictures used in syllabic writing.

Longhouse: Norse; communal home built by the Vikings.

Lyngvi: Norse; an island on Lake Amsvartnir where the wolf Fenrir was bound.

Magnificent frigate bird: *Fregata magnificens*; longest wings relative to weight of any bird; soars over Mexican and Caribbean coasts.

Manco Capac: Inca; the first Inca emperor who emerged from caves in the earth.

Markland: Norse; Forest Land; the region discovered by Thorstein, third son of Eirik the Red, and believed to correspond to current-day Labrador.

Maya: Mayan; people who lived in southern Mexico, Guatemala, Belize, and Honduras; the classical age extended from AD 300 to 900.

Mead: Norse; alcoholic beverage made from fermented honey and water.

Middle Realm: Roughly corresponds to Mesoamerica or ancient Anahuac, the Land Between the Waters.

Midgard serpent: Norse; see Jormungand.

Miocena: A geological period that extended from 23 million to 5 million years ago.

Mjollnir: Norse; hammer that belonged to Thor; forged by the dwarfs Brock and Sindri.

Monarch butterfly: A large butterfly (*Danaus plexippus*) with light orange-brown wings, black veins, and white-spotted black borders, noted for its long-distance migrations and its brightly striped caterpillars that feed on the milkweed plant.

Morning star: Venus, dawn star.

Moskoestrom: Norse; whirlpool.

Mount Assinaboine: A mountain, 11,870 feet high, in the Canadian Rocky Mountains on the Alberta–British Columbia border near Banff.

Mountain blue bird: *Sialia currucoides*; found in open mountainous areas with scattered trees; generally blue with a trace of rufous on throat and breast.

Muninn: Norse; one of Odin's ravens; known for his memory.
Nakota: Sioux; branch of the Sioux people composed of the Yankton and Yanktonai.
Narwhal: An Arctic whale (*Monodon monoceros*) that has a spotted pelt; the male has a long spirally twisted ivory tusk that projects from the left side of his head.
Niflheim: Norse; land of darkness; contains the region of Hel.
Nitrogen narcosis: A condition of confusion or stupor that results from increased levels of dissolved nitrogen in the blood, such as occurs in deep-sea divers who breathe air under high pressure.
Njord: Norse; god of the sea; father of Frey and Freya.
Norn: Norse; any of the three goddesses of fate.
Northern Realm: Roughly corresponding to North America.
Null: Amounting to nothing; absent or nonexistent.
Obsidian: A usually black or banded hard volcanic glass that displays shiny, curved surfaces when fractured and is formed by rapid cooling of lava.
Odin: Norse; god of wisdom, war, art, culture, and the dead; supreme deity and creator of the cosmos and humans.
Odin's wind: Norse; the sound of arrows whistling in the sky.
Odontocetes: Toothed whales; includes dolphins, porpoises, and larger whales such as the sperm whale.
Osprey: A fish-eating hawk (*Pandion haliaetus*) with plumage that is dark on the back and white below.
Palenque: Mayan; ancient city of southern Mexico.
Parabola: Apollonius wrote about and named the ellipse, parabola, and hyperbola in 200 BC.
Penannular ring brooch: Norse; used to fasten cloaks at the shoulder; the length of the pin, ring decoration, and preciousness of the metal announced the standing and wealth of a man.
Plain of Vigrid: Norse; the plain in Asgard on which Ragnarök will take place.
Popocatépetl: A volcano within view of Mexico City that last erupted in December 2000.
Pterodactyl: Any of various small, mostly tailless, extinct flying reptiles of the order Pterosauria; existed during the Jurassic and Cretaceous periods.

Puffin: Any of several sea birds of the genera *Fratercula* and *Lunda* of northern regions; characteristically have black and white plumage and a vertically flattened, triangular bill that is brightly colored during breeding season.

Pulque: Aztec; fermented milk of the agave cactus; the drink was thought to confer sacred power.

Qoya: Inca; queen of the Inca; primary wife of the Sapa Inca.

Quetzal: A Central American bird (*Pharomachrus mocino*) with brilliant bronze-green and red plumage and, in the male, long flowing tail feathers.

Quipu: Inca; a record-keeping device based on a decimal numeration system that consisted of a series of variously colored strings attached to a base rope and knotted so as to encode information; used especially for accounting purposes.

Ragnarök: Norse; the final battle during which the gods will succumb to the forces of evil.

Raven: A large bird (*Corvus corax*) with black plumage and a croaking cry.

Reykjavík: Capital of Iceland.

Rhpisunt: Haida; bear-mother-goddess of the Haida.

Runes: Norse; characters in the ancient Norse alphabet.

Sapa: Inca; king of the Inca; believed to be a direct descendent of the first king, Manco Capac, as well as the earthly manifestation of the sun (inti).

Seiđur: Norse; a special kind of magic possessed by Odin; most often practiced by women and used for divination; could also be used to bestow good or bad fortune, communicate with the unseen, or manipulate the weather.

Selenite: Gypsum in the form of colorless clear crystals.

Siksika: Blackfoot; the aboriginal word for the Blackfoot Nation.

Silica: A white or colorless crystalline compound (SiO_2) that occurs abundantly as quartz, sand, flint, and agate.

Silverberry: A northeast North American shrub (*Elaeagnus ommutate*) that has silvery flowers, leaves, and berries.

Skald: Norse; a medieval Scandinavian poet, especially one who wrote in the Viking age.

Sköll: Norse; the wolf who pursued the sun; just before Ragnarök, Sköll will catch and eat the sun.

Skraelings: Norse; name for the aboriginal peoples of North America encountered by the early Viking explorers.

Sleipnir: Norse; Odin's eight-legged horse.

Snowshoe hare: A medium-sized hare (*Lepus americanus*) of northern North America, with large, heavily furred feet and fur that is white in winter and brown in summer.

Sockeye, chinook, coho salmon: The various species of salmon common to the rivers of British Columbia and Alaska.

Soda straws: Straws represent the earliest growth of stalactites; hollow, elongate, and generally translucent tubes of calcite equal in diameter to the water drops conducted along their length.

Solstice: Either of two times of the year when the sun is at its greatest distance from the celestial equator; the summer solstice in the Northern Hemisphere occurs about June 21 when the sun is in the zenith over the tropic of Cancer; the winter solstice occurs about December 21 when the sun is over the tropic of Capricorn; in the Northern Hemisphere the summer solstice is the longest day of the year, and the winter solstice is the shortest.

Southern Realm: Roughly corresponds to South America.

Spelunker: A person who explores caves chiefly as a hobby; a caver.

Stalactite: An icicle-shaped mineral deposit, usually calcite or aragonite, that hangs from the roof of a cavern, formed from the dripping of mineral-rich water.

Stalagmite: A conical mineral deposit, usually calcite or aragonite, built up on the floor of a cavern, formed from the dripping of mineral-rich water.

Steatite: A soft metamorphic rock composed mostly of the mineral talc; also called *soapstone.*

Stelae: Mayan; an upright stone or slab with an inscribed or sculptured surface; used as a monument or as a commemorative tablet in the face of a building.

Sundog sign: A parhelion or sundog is an atmospheric phenomenon that creates a halo around the sun.

Sword of Damocles: From Greek mythology, an allusion to a sense of impending doom in a precarious situation that could change quickly.

Tahuantinsuyu: Inca; name of the empire of the Inca; "the four united quarters."

Tephra: Solid matter that is ejected into the air by an erupting volcano.

Tezcatlipoca: Aztec; supreme god; the "smoking mirror"; patron of sorcerers; master of human destinies.

Thingvellir: The location of the Icelandic Althing.

Thjodhild: Norse; wife of Eirik the Red.

Thor: Norse; son of Odin and Fjorgyn; associated with thunder, the sky, fertility, and the law.

Thorstein Eiriksson: Norse; third son of Eirik the Red.

Thorvald Eiriksson: Norse; second son of Eirik the Red.

Three-toed woodpecker: Either of two woodpeckers (*Picoides arcticus* or *P. tridactylus*) of northern North America that lack the inner hind toe on each foot.

Tikal: Mayan; ancient city of northern Guatemala.

Toltec: Toltec; a member of a Nahuatl-speaking people of central and southern Mexico whose empire flourished from the tenth century until it collapsed under invasion by the Aztecs in the twelfth century.

Tree of Life: A concept of interconnectedness of individuals or living creatures, especially with a God, found in numerous mythologies and religions.

Trefoil-shaped: Norse; ornament form that has the appearance of a trifoliate leaf.

Trilobite: Any of numerous extinct marine arthropods of the class Trilobita; fossils depict a segmented body divided by grooves into three vertical lobes; Paleozoic era.

Tsetsehka: Kwakiutl; winter ceremony; prayer for the return of the grizzly in the spring.

Turtle: Maya; in Mayan mythology a metaphor for the earth floating upon the sea; any of various aquatic or terrestrial reptiles of the order Testudines (or Chelonia) that have horny toothless jaws and a bony or leathery shell into which the head, limbs, and tail can be withdrawn.

Tyr: Norse; god of war.

Tzompantli: Toltec; a low platform near the main pyramid with racks that displayed the severed heads of sacrificed human beings.

Ursavus: *Ursavus elemensis* was the first true bear; twenty million years ago.

Ursus: Genus of the bear family.

Uxmal: Mayan; ancient city of Yucatán in southeast Mexico; flourished from AD 600 to 900.

Valhalla: Norse; hall in which Odin received the souls of slain heroes.

Valkyries: Norse; warrior maidens of Odin; they presided over battles, chose those who were to die, and brought the souls of the dead heroes back to Valhalla.

Vampire bats: Any of various tropical American bats of the family Desmodontidae that bite mammals and birds to feed on their blood and that often carry diseases such as rabies.

Viking: Norse; Scandinavian seafaring peoples who explored, traded, and raided in the North Atlantic region from AD 780 to 1070.

Vinland: Norse; "wine land"; region discovered by Leif Eiriksson, second son of Eirik the Red.

Viracocha: Inca; Con Tici Viracocha Pachacuti was the creator god; the Maker; the Dweller in the Void; the Teacher of the World.

Wadmal: A wool cloth made from the long hairs of Icelandic sheep.

Wedge-tailed sabrewing hummingbird: *Campylopterus curvipennis*; native to the Yucatan peninsula; greenish with violet forehead and white below; long wedge-shaped black tail.

Western spring beauty: A wildflower of the Purslane family with five delicate white petals; *Claytonia lanceolata;* the starchy corms are dug and eaten by grizzly bears before the plant flowers.

Woad: An annual Old World plant (*Isatis tinctoria*) in the mustard family; formerly cultivated for its leaves that yield a blue dye.

Xbalanque: Mayan; with Hunahpu, one of the Hero Twins who defeated the rulers of the underworld in an athletic contest and then rose victorious to the sky, where they were deified as the sun and the moon.

Yellow lady's slipper: *Cypripedium calceolus*; an orchid that grows in crowded clumps in moist forests and mossy bogs.

Yggdrasil: Norse; the World Tree; the ash tree that linked the nine worlds.

Zuni: Pueblo; people located in western New Mexico.

Bibliography

Beck, M. L. 2000. *Heroes & Heroines in Tlingit-Haida Legend.* Portland: Alaska Northwest Books.

Beyers, Coralie, ed. 1980. *Man Meets Grizzly.* Boston: Houghton Mifflin.

Bierhorst, John. 1985. *The Mythology of North America.* New York: William Morrow.

Bourne, J. K., Jr. 2003. "Ol Doinyo Lengai." *National Geographic,* January: 24–49.

Bringhurst, Robert. 1999. *A Story as Sharp as a Knife.* Vancouver: Douglas & McIntyre.

Clendinnen, Inga. 1991. *Aztecs: An Interpretation.* Cambridge: Cambridge University Press.

Craighead, F. C. 1982. *Track of the Grizzly.* San Francisco: Sierra Club Books.

Crossley-Holland, Kevin. 1980. *The Norse Myths.* New York: Pantheon Books.

Cuevas, Lou. 2000. *Anasazi Legends.* Happy Camp, CA: Nature Camp Publishers.

Davis, Wade. 1996. *One River.* New York: Touchstone.

———. 1997. *The Serpent and the Rainbow.* New York: Touchstone.

———. 1998. *Shadows in the Sun.* New York: Broadway Books.

Erdman, David V., ed. 1988. *The Complete Poetry and Prose of Wm Blake.* New York: Doubleday.

Erdoes, R., and A. Ortiz. 1984. *American Indian Myths and Legends.* Toronto: Random House.

Ferguson, Diana. 2000. *Tales of the Plumed Serpent.* London: Collins and Brown Limited.

Fitzhugh, W. W., and E. I. Ward, eds. 2000. *Vikings—The North Atlantic Saga.* Washington, DC: Smithsonian Press.

Gilbert, A. G., and M. M. Cotterell. 1999. *The Mayan Prophecies.* Boston: Element.

Graham-Campbell, James. 2001. *The Viking World.* London: Francis Lincoln Limited.

Grambo, R. L., and D. J. Cox. 2000. *Bear—A Celebration of Power and Beauty.* Verve edition. San Francisco: Sierra Club Books.

Grant, John. 2002. *An Introduction to Viking Mythology.* London: Quantum Publishing.

Herrero, Stephen. 1985. *Bear Attacks.* Piscataway, NJ: Winchester Press.

Hebrews 11. Holy Bible.

Krupp, E. C. 1997. *Skywatchers, Shamans & Kings.* New York: Wiley & Sons.

Malmstrom, V. H. 1997. *Cycles of the Sun, Mysteries of the Moon.* Austin: University of Texas Press.

McLaughlin, M. L. *Myths and Legends of the Sioux.* New York: New Millennium Library.

Miller, Thomas. 2000. "Inside Chiquibul." *National Geographic,* April: 54–71.

Murray, J. A., ed. 1992. *The Great Bear.* Seattle: Alaska Northwest Books.

Rockwell, David. 1991. *Giving Voice to Bear.* Toronto: Key Porter Books.

Rostworowski de Diez Canseco, Maria. 1999. *History of the Inca Realm.* Cambridge: Cambridge University Press.

Russell, Andy. 1987. Introduction. *Great Bear Adventures.* Toronto: Key Porter Books.

Russell, Andy. 1967. *Grizzly Country.* Vancouver: Douglas & McIntyre.

Russell, Charles. 1994. *Spirit Bear.* Toronto: Key Porter Books.

Russell, Charles, and Maureen Enns. 2002. *Grizzly Heart.* Toronto: Random House.

Sabloff, Jeremy A. 1990. *The New Archaeology and the Ancient Maya.* Scientific American Library. New York: W. H. Freeman and Company.

Schele, Linda, and David Freidel. 1990. *A Forest of Kings.* New York: William Morrow.

Smiley, Jane. 2000. Introduction. *The Sagas of Icelanders.* New York: Penguin Books.

Taube, Karl. 1993. *Aztec and Maya Myths.* Austin: University of Texas Press.

Taylor, M. R. 2000. *Caves.* Washington, DC: National Geographic Society.

Urton, Gary. 1999. *Inca Myths.* Austin: University of Texas Press.

Wissler, Clark, and D. C. Duvall, trans. 1995. *Mythology of the Blackfoot Indians.* Lincoln: University of Nebraska Press.

INDEX

C

D

H

I

J

K

L

M

N

O

P

Q

R

S

T

U

X

Y

Z